I0761518

HOLLOW

CAROLINE PECKHAM

SUSANNE VALENTI

FANTASY ROMANCE SERIES
BY CAROLINE PECKHAM & SUSANNE VALENTI

Ruthless Boys of the Zodiac

Dark Fae
Savage Fae
Vicious Fae
Broken Fae
Warrior Fae

Zodiac Academy

Origins (Novella)
The Awakening
Ruthless Fae
The Reckoning
Shadow Princess
Cursed Fates
The Big A.S.S. Party (Novella)
Fated Throne
Heartless Sky
Sorrow and Starlight
Beyond The Veil (Novella)
Restless Stars
The Awakening: As Told by The Boys (Alternate POV)
Live and Let Lionel (Alternate POV)

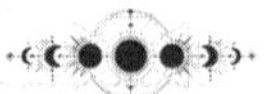

Darkmore Penitentiary

Caged Wolf
Alpha Wolf
Feral Wolf
Wild Wolf

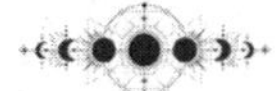

Sins of the Zodiac
Never Keep
Echo Fort

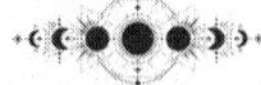

Crown of Hearts and Chaos
Hollow

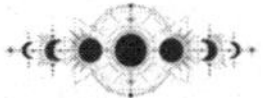

A Game of Malice and Greed
A Kingdom of Gods and Ruin
A Game of Malice and Greed

Age of Vampires
Eternal Reign
Immortal Prince
Infernal Creatures
Wrathful Mortals
Forsaken Relic
Ravaged Souls
Devious Gods

First published in the UK in 2025 by King's Hollow LLP
This edition first published in US in 2025 by King's Hollow LLP
20 Eversley Road, Bexhill-On-Sea, East Sussex, UK, TN40 1HE
Distributed by Simon & Schuster

www.kingshollow.co.uk

Interior formatting & design by Wild Elegance Formatting
Map design by Fred Kroner
Dust cover jacket art by Stella Colorado
End paper art by @palinlineart
Cover design by Caroline Peckham
Stock photos from DepositPhotos

ISBN: 978-1-916926-58-5

5 7 9 10 8 6 4

This book is typeset in Times New Roman & Bodoni 72 Smallcaps
Printed and bound in US

This is a warning to any who choose to turn this page. Beyond this point you will be subject to heartache, anguish, rage and romance of the utterly ruinous variety. There will be a morally-grey man whose dark gaze pins you in place and whose actions are totally unacceptable in any situation – unless of course he happens to be Fae. Which luckily, he is. So all bets are off. But if you don't like them closer to seven foot than six, rough around the edges, dark of hair, battling inner demons and smouldering from the corners of every room they occupy, then this probably isn't the book for you. Then again…a little smouldering never hurt anybody… It's probably the corrupted soul and dark intentions that will put you off – unless he happens to be devastatingly attractive of course… Which he is. In which case I suppose you're as doomed as the rest of us. So turn the page, my sweet. We all knew this was inevitable anyway – but don't say I didn't warn you…

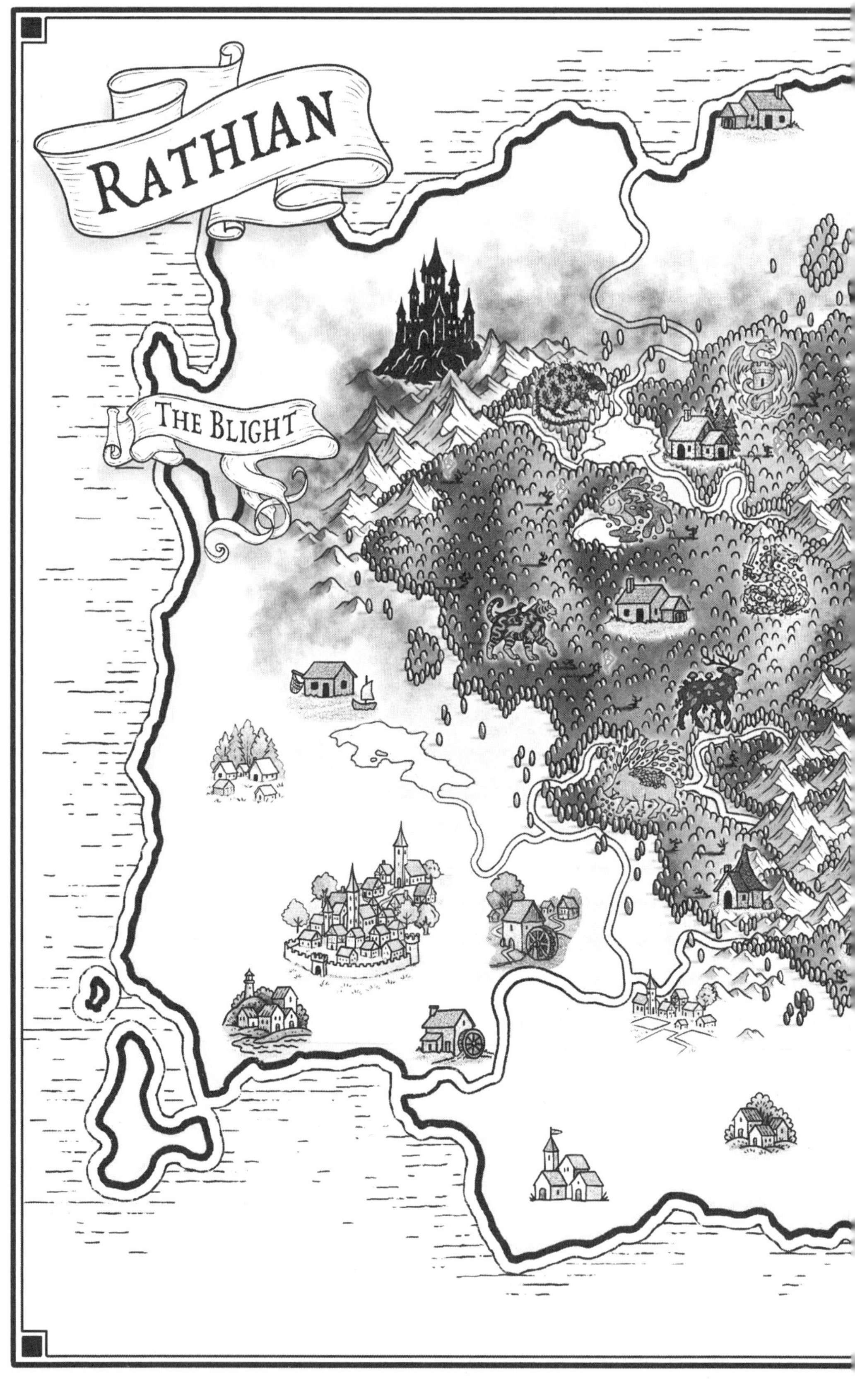
RATHIAN
THE BLIGHT

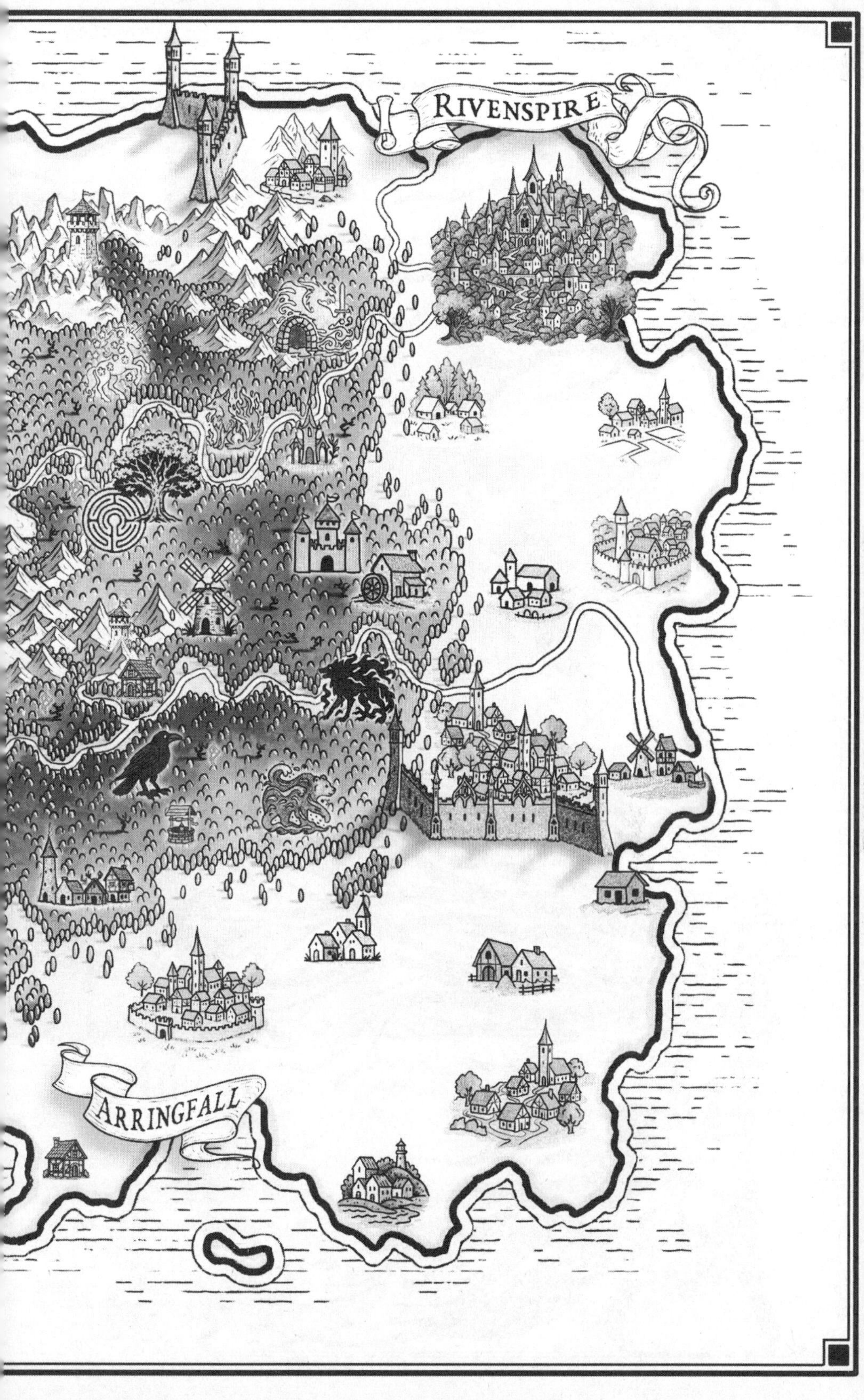
RIVENSPIRE
ARRINGFALL

FERRIS

CHAPTER ONE

My nights were filled with haunting music, spun from a tongue I'd once known to whisper jokes and pass gossip from ear to ear. The words struck chords in my heart which stung when I woke and ached throughout the days until finally I succumbed to slumber and her songs found me again.

I dreamed of trees so tall they blotted out the sun, their bark a rough and anciently marred map to the one and only want I held dear. Sometimes I found myself running between those wicked trunks, calling out to a girl who ran ahead of me, her song just out of sight, always coming from beyond the next bough, next branch, next bramble.

Of course, I'd never truly set foot in the cursed forest. The path was barred to all; the trees and the magic tangled through them made a wall of the forest's border which was utterly impenetrable - unless the trees chose to admit you. And they only ever moved at night. But I knew better than to risk approaching them in the dark.

The lyrics which knotted with my dreams turned to screams when the sun went down and the wicked nature of the forest was unleashed to its fullest. I'd considered risking it; I'd planned to sit at the edge of the forest while the sun set and allow the trees to claim me, but I'd found reason in the one thing I truly trusted. The written word never turned me wrong. And if there was one thing all of the tomes and scrolls I'd scoured agreed upon it was that facing the trees at night was nothing less than a death sentence. The blood smearing those cursed branches on the nights the forest found prey was proof enough of that. And I was no good to anyone if I was dead.

The song I cherished and loathed wrapped itself around me in my fitful dreams, her words both a caress and a warning.

"Come to the trees where their faces grow pale,
Lean close to hear secrets of terror and scale,
My worth was well measured, my journey awaits.
You'll only come find me when we un-bar our gates."

It was painted in the whispered words of a child, its lyrics like a river which changed course and spun secrets, never the same yet always pulling me in one, unchanging direction. And I was done resisting the draw of the current. It was time I dove in and let it carry me away.

Music of another kind carried across the town, the jolly tune at odds with the knotted dread in my gut and drawing my thoughts back to the present. It was finally here. The day of the Great Hunt. It had been fifty long years since the last of its name and for eight of those, I'd been bracing for the impact of its arrival.

I swallowed. A shaky breath skipped down my throat, and I fought the urge to forget everything I'd been planning and simply accept the fate which had been dealt to our family all those years ago.

This path had been laid out for me for far too long to allow doubts to turn me from it now.

"Are you ready?" The firm banging of my mother's fist against the weathered wood of my bedroom door jarred me out of the daydream which had seen me standing before my window, peering out at the not-so-distant treeline. "The drums are already sounding and the Bradeys will be wondering where you are," Mother hissed, pulling my inner turmoil from fear into disdain. I couldn't give a withered fig what the Bradeys thought of me one way or the other.

The panicked screams of my past faded, the frantic scouring of the village, the despair, the horror, the grief; all of it slipped back behind that mask my family wore, never to be spoken of, never to be acknowledged.

I glanced at the small pack I needed to bring with me, a lie silently forming on my lips, the rehearsal giving me something to focus on as the door was predictably pushed open.

Mother bustled into the room, her brown hair perfectly coiled, her deep blue dress recently re-fitted and trimmed to appear almost new. She stalled on the threshold to my room, looking me up and down while working to choke down the words I knew were expanding in her chest. She managed to contain them for an impressive six seconds before they inevitably burst free.

"You chose the green?" she asked, though what she really wanted was to ask me why I'd ignored the pale pink satin she'd laid out.

"I'll wear that one later," I told her, barely even flicking a glance at the new dress and wishing she hadn't wasted so much money on it. "It rained for half of the week, and the Hunt is launching right outside the town hall where the mud is practically a swamp. The green is more practical."

Mother pursed her lips, the sense of my words colliding with her desire to impress the Bradeys. I knew she expected the marriage proposal to come at the feast tonight. I knew she wanted that life for me, the comfort, the security. And truly, Axel Bradey wasn't the worst option in this forsaken corner of the human lands, but I had no intention to wed anyone. Not yet. Not until I'd followed through on the promise I'd made to Rissa.

So yes, the gown I'd selected was plain compared to what most of the women in attendance would have chosen, the mossy green colour of it like a reflection of the forest which awaited us at the edge of town. Though truthfully, it wasn't the edge any longer – the forest had devoured eight homes and the inn this last month, and we all knew we didn't have long before we would have to abandon Arringfall altogether. Our town was one of the last still standing between here and the cities which lined the coast where the last hope for humanity lay. Beyond the cliffs at the southern border of Rathian, there was nothing but sea. If the trees ever made it that far, we would be faced with a choice between them and the waves and both, were certain death.

The skirt was long but not voluminous, the fabric thick but not too heavy. I'd always favoured it for that fact. It was practical, easier to move in, run in if needed. And it *was* needed all too often with the forest creeping ever closer to our border and the Hollows haunting us in the space between breaths.

"At least let me fix your hair," Mother begged, and I conceded, sitting on the edge of my small bed and closing my eyes while she worked my warm brown hair into a braid.

I breathed in the scent of our home as she worked, the hint of lavender from the sprigs of the plant Mother hung in every window to ward against foul spirits, and the underlying warmth of pine from the beams which held the whole place together. It wasn't a grand home, but it held the memories of all I cherished in this world within its walls.

"There are whispers that the Fae have selected twenty-five of their greatest warriors to enter the Hunt this time," she said, drawing my focus away from the ache of this place. "Perhaps this will be the final hunt. Perhaps all isn't lost…"

She didn't need to say more than that. The cursed forest – or the Taking Trees as we called them - had spread further in the last few years than ever before and all the realms surrounding it were suffering, pushed to the edges of the land, resources running thin, their people plagued with hardships which layered upon one another until the weight of them had become suffocating.

I didn't know whether to be pleased about the Fae investing so much into the Hunt or not. Their kind had turned their backs on us a long time ago – hundreds of years before I was born. They'd built their walls of dark stone and kept their borders well-guarded, leaving the humans to suffer the wrath of both the forest and then the Hollows without aid. Resentment for their kind had bred into hatred once the sacrifices had started. The cursed forest placed many burdens upon us but none so cruel as the Offerings it demanded. The Fae had been quick to decide that the humans would be the ones forced to pay the price each year when the blood moon rose in its fatal demand. A price which my family had been selected to endure.

My breaths grew thin and faltered as the weight of that truth pressed down on me. It didn't matter how many years passed. It still felt like yesterday.

I'd seen a few of their kind, the ones who deigned to travel to our lands and trade with the lowly humans. My people were too desperate to turn them away and too weak to refuse them regardless. But I was never sure what exactly the Fae got out of the trades they made with us. The ethereally beautiful males and females I'd caught glimpses of had seemed better nourished than our kind and clearly far wealthier too. I'd often wondered why they travelled our lands, suspecting their deeds were motivated by far darker desires than they pretended. The Offerings proved they were capable of anything after all but despite their part in those atrocities, I'd never seen a single human stand against one of them.

The reality was, we needed all the help we could get out here, and the fact that they were able to dispatch Hollows in our land waylaid any questions the humans might have demanded of them. We weren't strong enough to stand against Hollows regardless of our hatred of the Fae, so we scowled and muttered curses at their backs but did nothing to stop them passing through our realm whenever they deigned to.

Still, there was no explanation as to why they never came in force or why those who did travel through our realm never stayed in one place for more than a night. They never spoke of their own lands or offered much communication at all. They wanted stories in payment for their wares more often than not, and there weren't many willing to deny them what they sought in favour of pride. Though I'd have spat in their faces should any ever dare to ask for a tale from my lips.

Despite my hatred of their kind, I couldn't deny I'd wondered why they didn't make a real stand against the Hollows, why they hid behind their walls. If they were able to fight the monstrous beasts the Necromancer had risen to plague our lands, then why not do so? Why leave us all to suffer their wrath?

Just ten days' travel from here to the east of our town lay the border with the Fae. I'd never seen the wall which marked the division between our lands myself but I'd seen sketches, heard tales. And they all matched. The Fae lands were closed to humans. Just as the forest was closed too – unless it claimed you for its own.

My stomach knotted as I considered that, the nearness of those damned trees making me uneasy as they always did.

When I'd been a child, the forest had been a full week's travel north of here. Our town had seemed safe from its grasp. But every year, its boundary spread, the trees inching outward, stealing land from the three realms. So far as I knew, no one had ever been able to slow the forest's advance, let alone stop it. And so every living creature in Rathian was losing the battle to save themselves from its clutches, just as we were losing places to run to.

We were surrounded. The Taking Trees to the north, the Hollows and their Necromancer king to the west, the Fae and their wall to the east and nothing but the open ocean and a promise of oblivion to the south.

"There," Mother announced, turning me so that I could appreciate her handiwork in the mirror on my dressing table.

My brown hair was braided in a style I could never replicate alone, the strands knotted and intricate, drawn together while still framing my heart-shaped face. I studied the warmth of my skin, the dusting of freckles which coated my cheekbones and touched my nose. As always, my eyes stood out the most, their sapphire colour flashing to a deep violet in the light. Rissa used to say they changed with my moods, sometimes as bright as a summer's day when I laughed, others as dark as an oncoming storm when I frowned. I wasn't certain that was true, but I had always appreciated their otherworldly allure. It was the one thing about myself which seemed to agree with my heart – they didn't fit. Didn't belong. Perhaps my eyes were the one thing about me which betrayed my intentions because they spoke of something outside of this place, they spoke of something…other.

I stood, smiling at my mother and hoping she couldn't read what I was planning in the tempest of my expression. I felt as though my long-held secret was suddenly becoming so obvious, like perhaps she'd suddenly see it there in my face, plain as day, and realise what I planned to do.

"Ferris…" she said slowly, rising too and taking my hand in her own. "I wanted to-"

"The day is wasting," Father called jovially from downstairs.

He had always been a jolly kind of man, the type to gather friends as easily as plucking weeds, the kind to have compliments scattered in his wake. But I could see through his smiles. For eight long years, they'd failed to touch his eyes. No matter the fact that we didn't speak of it, no matter how hard we all worked to pretend.

"Mother?" I urged, squeezing her fingers as she made to withdraw them.

She squeezed mine in return, then smiled. "I only wanted to say…be happy. If Axel Bradey isn't what it will take to make your heart shine, then you don't have to accept him. You don't have to do anything which would demand something you can't offer."

"I know," I told her, my secret burning through the pit of my stomach.

It would break her. Father too. I knew it with a certainty that had stopped me from sleeping properly for weeks. It was the one thing which made me doubt what I had to do, the one thing which made me question this choice.

But it really wasn't a choice at all. Even on that night, eight years ago, I'd known it would come to this. I'd been a girl then, only fourteen, yet overnight, the innocence of childhood had been ripped from me.

I'd have done it then if it had been possible. I wished with all my heart that I could have tried – I'd even attempted it before. But this was my only true chance to keep the oath I'd made to Rissa back then and I couldn't turn from it. Even though I understood how high the price of it would be.

"I love you," I said, my voice cracking on the last word, and Mother blinked at me as if she understood the finality of that declaration. But then the evidence of my betrayal cleared from her eyes and she breathed a laugh, drawing me close in her arms and kissing the top of my head the way she'd done ever since I was a babe in her arms.

"I love you more," she told me, squeezing me tightly and making me hate myself for what I had to do.

We parted on an awkward laugh at our emotional moment, and I waited as she headed from the room, stooping to grab my pack once I was confident she wasn't watching. The weight of it felt like evidence, the bulk too.

I grabbed my grey cloak and swung it around my shoulders, concealing the bag and tugging my hood up for good measure. The day was bright but a chill still clung to the air, so I wouldn't be alone in dressing for the harsher edges of the weather.

Father made a show of fussing over our lateness and bustling us out the door. His hair had greyed in the last few years, his eyes and brow lined more heavily too, like his body was tired of the weight he fought to carry, the burdens he bore painting themselves onto his flesh in defiance of the smiles he tried to hide them behind.

He offered an arm each to Mother and me, and I took it, enjoying the warmth of his body beside mine, the rough wool of his brown coat a familiar, steadying point for my slick palms.

Our village was large – practically a city now by the old standards, if my parents were to be believed. But the flint houses and thatched roofs looked as tired as the people who dwelled within them.

Wooden doors were branded with scars, symbols to ward off evil scratched or burned into them, sometimes painted in blood. So far as I knew, nothing truly helped. But without our superstitions, I supposed we would all have succumbed to hopelessness long ago.

I glanced over my shoulder as I thought on that, the cobbled street empty behind me, a dozen houses just like our own gazing after us.

A shiver ran down my spine as if I were being watched.

I slipped my fingers into the pocket of my cloak and turned over the wooden relic there three times before releasing my hold on Father and crouching to scrawl an X into the dirt with my fingers.

Superstition or not, I took no chances in this lawless world.

My parents paused so I could catch up to them, the three of us moving towards the northern edge of the town where the music rang out loudly and the excited chatter of the crowd could be heard too. It wasn't often the people raised their voices in jubilation like this, and I wasn't certain if my spirits were lifted by the sound or if it only stoked my nerves.

This had to work.

The forest wouldn't give us another fifty years. In that time, it would consume everything. Our town alone likely had less than a handful of months left. We'd all been preparing our possessions for weeks, packing up our lives in preparation to relocate south. Many of the people living here had already fled the forest before, some had done so five or six times, others had simply passed right through our village and kept going to the southern border where most of our population now resided in the towns along the shore, awaiting the inevitable at the end of the world.

No.

I stopped that thought in its tracks.

Not inevitable. If I believed that, then I would have run too. I wouldn't be here, grasping onto my secrets like they were sand in my fist, the grains spilling away like the seconds they marked, my truth so close to revealing itself.

We stepped into the square where the town hall stood proudly, and I couldn't stifle the breath which sawed into my lungs in a sharp gasp.

The forest had moved again. I'd been here only two nights prior. Beyond this square there had been four rows of houses, a tailor, a blacksmith's forge, a stable…

"When?" I breathed, my eyes on the colossal trees which loomed like glowering statues just a handful of steps away from us. Their trunks were thicker than carriages, so tall they appeared to brush the clouds with their spindly branches. The space between them was thick with bracken and brambles, thorns knotting together to create a wall which I knew to be impenetrable.

No one could enter that forest at any time other than during the Hunt. Not by their own choice anyway. And legend had it that any taken in the night fell prey to the most monstrous of beasts within its wild walls.

My thumb rolled over the faded scar on my forefinger, the most prominent of those left to me by the same thorns which now tangled together so close to our home.

The music didn't change in pitch but there was something about it which sounded less jovial and more hurried now that I was closer to it. Like those who were playing wanted an end to this celebration so that they might run from it.

The smiles on the faces around us were tight at their edges, whispers passing between the crowd which all carried the same message.

"We'll be on the road by nightfall," Father said gruffly, and I knew he was speaking for the entire town.

It was madness to linger once the forest crept this close. I'd watched countless others make the pilgrimage away from their homes throughout my lifetime and had always known our time would come too. But it had never seemed so real as it did now.

I swallowed thickly, thinking of the familiarity of my bedroom, the whorl on the edge of the table that I'd skimmed my fingers over at every meal, the stains of my childhood in each corner and crevice. Within days, it would be gone, seized by the forest and lost like so much of our land. This Hunt really might be the last.

"Ah, Ferris, you look dazzling this morning," a voice crooned, and I turned to find Axel Bradey approaching with his parents. I gave him a smile, assessing the mud splatters on his pants and boots, the sheen of perspiration on his brow and the windswept look of his golden hair.

"As do you," I said, the corner of my lips lifting a touch while he did very little to disguise his recent arrival.

His father frowned at him then turned to exchange pleasantries with my parents, the three of them moving aside to give us a chance to speak alone.

"The miscreants have been abandoned to one another again then?" Axel said conspiratorially, and I offered him a slight smile. We'd both quickly realised that the pairing our parents were so keen on was something of a practical one too. Neither of us were perfect, our reputations those of recklessness and defiance - which I supposed might have meant we were a good fit in theory. Axel was nice enough, handsome enough, kind enough… But I had no intention to tie my life to his and turn my back on everything I'd waited so long for.

"Was anyone lost in the Creeping?" I asked, glancing at our parents to check that they weren't listening. Clearly no one here planned on discussing the shocking advance of the forest, but I couldn't get it out of my head.

Axel glanced at the trees, hatred darkening his brown eyes before he nodded once. "The Penleys were in their house. The Truewards too, and possibly several more families besides. There's disagreement over whether some of them left already or not. And there were nine horses in the stables," he added.

My skin prickled at his words, my eyes roaming the impenetrable wall of vegetation, my ears straining to hear over the musicians. The shadows between the trees loomed with a darkness so thick that I had to wonder if even sunlight could penetrate the dense canopy of the trees.

"What about the carriages?" I asked, trying to keep my voice steady.

Axel's silence was answer enough. Every carriage in the stables had been lost too. Without them, the people would have an even harder time escaping to the next town. The carriages were essential to transporting goods, but more than that, they were the only form of shelter that would be offered on the long road – the only place which might offer a chance of survival if the Hollows came.

How could this have happened? The forest never moved so far in such a short space of time. At this rate, the entire town could be consumed within days. The trees might even reach the coast within months, and then there would be nowhere left to run to. Beyond the cliffs which lined the southern border of Rathian, the ocean extended on to the edge of the world. We were staring at the end of our people, this Hunt the last hope any of us had for survival.

"Listen, Ferris…" Axel took hold of my arm, drawing me closer, leaning down to say something with urgency in his expression, but before the words could leave his lips, the music fell quiet and Chancellor Haydon called out for our attention.

"Don't do it," Axel breathed, his fingers locking tightly around my wrist, and I startled.

He couldn't know. Surely he couldn't have figured it out.

I shook my head at him, not trusting any words I might speak.

"I see you, Ferris," he hissed, closing in on me as I tried to pull away, his voice low and his words intended for me alone. "I've always seen you. All those ancient tomes, the scrolls, the relics. Not to mention the way you run laps around Old Mitchel's field when you think no one will see you. You move as if you're running for your life."

"I don't know what you mean," I muttered, the weight of the pack which was concealed beneath my cloak seeming to weigh me down more heavily as my cheeks stained in clear admission of my guilt.

I tried to tug my arm free of his hold and a few people glanced at us as he pressed closer.

"The trees only take," he said in a low, warning tone. "They don't barter or bargain, they don't offer or gift. The boon could be a lie, a trap, a trick. You know they'll never-"

"I don't know," I snapped, jerking my arm from his grip. "And neither do you."

Mother was looking to us, reaching out an arm, and I hurried closer to my parents, moving with the crowd towards the small stage which had been erected as close to the forest as anyone in their right mind would dare to go.

Axel's gaze bored a hole into the back of my skull, but I ignored it resolutely, refusing to acknowledge it, my decision made long ago and his words nothing to all the warnings and discouragement I'd offered myself.

My fingers twisted into the straps of the small pack I'd brought with me, its contents seeming to heat against my skin as if daring those around us to look at it more closely. But none did. No one was interested in me today. All hope was pinned on the collection of people who were moving up onto that stage.

"Today is a day unlike most others!" Chancellor Haydon called out, his voice silencing the murmurs of the crowd, his jowls wobbling with each word. He had led the people of our town for years unopposed. In part, I suspected, because no one else wanted the burden of his job – who would wish to lead a people doomed in every direction anyway? But it was also because he was in fact a good man by all accounts.

He truly cared. He did whatever he could to help us survive here. He even offered out aid to all who fled the horrors beyond our small sanctuary. He made sure we grew enough crops and guarded them sufficiently to survive each winter on the harvest they brought. Honestly, I believed he was the reason we were still here to bear witness to this moment at all.

"The Great Hunt is the one opportunity the forest gives us to break this curse upon our lands and the lands of our neighbours," Chancellor Haydon went on.

Mutters broke out at the mention of the neighbours who had so wilfully abandoned us to our plight. Yes, they were all struggling to survive the forest and the Hollows, but our histories told of the way they'd shunned us when the outlook darkened. Humans had been willing to work with the Fae to face what was coming, but they'd chosen to abandon us to our fate. Hell, we would have worked with the Hags if there had been any way to secure such an alliance. But the wandering nomads who were blessed with the gift of foresight and use of old magic didn't even hold loyalty to one another, let alone make deals with outsiders who didn't bolster their own fortune.

"This day is one of hope," Chancellor Haydon continued earnestly, and the brightness in his eyes said he really did believe that. "It is our chance to finally reclaim the land we have lost – to break the curses, unite the spirits and defy the fate which has been creeping closer like a tightening noose for so many years."

Silence followed his words as the people acknowledged the truth of them. Arringfall was dying. We all knew it, we all felt it on the breath of the wind, we could see it in the decay of the land and decline of the homes we'd once treasured. Our world was running out of time even without the forest devouring it bite by bite. And the Hollows only made the clock tick faster.

I glanced over my shoulder, the feeling of eyes on my skin intensifying, making me wonder if some beast might be considering me for a meal. But nothing lurked between the rough stone of the buildings and it was impossible to see into the shadows of the forest.

"And so, without further preamble, I present to you our brave and ferocious band of Champions. As you know, each of them has been tirelessly preparing for this very day, gathering their strength and voracity in the pursuit of redemption for us all! They will risk everything for the slim hope of our survival, entering the Great Hunt and seeking out the lost spirits in hopes of finally freeing our land from the grasp of these forsaken trees!"

A cheer went up from the crowd, the noise an explosion which made me startle, my heart thundering in anticipation.

The sun was almost at its apex overhead, the hour drawing closer at last. I hadn't been born before the last Hunt took place but I knew how it went. At midday, the trees would part to allow entry for the Champions, their twisted branches at last allowing admission to the daunting labyrinth within.

There weren't any tales of what awaited those who entered because none had ever emerged victorious. There was no way of knowing what happened among those trees but the screams had been heard. Battle-hardened warriors crying out in terror, human and Fae alike finding nothing but death between those boughs.

I'd read every chronical of every Hunt I could find, screams and cries noted, sightings of spirits between and above the trees which had been glimpsed on rare occasions. There had been little I could call real fact, not much of substance, but I'd devoured every scrap of insight regardless, compared notes and complied lists of whatever information I could glean.

But I knew in my soul that there was more to the forest than simply death. When it took people in the night, we heard them singing long after they were gone, their voices travelling beneath the light of the moon, calling out to the loved ones they'd left behind.

The Offerings the trees demanded were more proof of some greater purpose. The children it stole in sacrifice couldn't just be more fodder to the savagery of the spirits which roamed the forest. So I believed with all my heart that there was more than bloodshed within those woods, but that didn't lessen the terror I felt as the minutes ticked on.

Chancellor Haydon was making a show of announcing the Champions who were ready to enter the forest, speaking loudly of their prowess and the preparations they'd made in anticipation of this day. There were twenty-five of them, and I knew them all by sight, if not to speak with. They'd spent the last few years like gods among mortals, the hopes of every person in our realm depending on them. They had every meal paid for at every tavern they visited, bedded half the people in the village too – even married couples allowing for a night of carnal worship at the altar of the people they believed destined to save us.

I didn't see heroes when I looked at the warriors who preened beneath the attention of the crowd. I didn't see hope. There had been Hunts before this one, and the Fae sent their warriors to compete in them too. It didn't matter how impressive they seemed here and now. It mattered what they found within those trees and whether they were able to fulfil the task the forest had set. And I wasn't convinced they could. Why now, when none had ever succeeded before? Endless generations had attempted the Hunt and none had ever completed it.

I feared we were all doomed either way. But that didn't stop my heart from rioting as the sun shifted to its zenith and the trees began to groan before us. The point of no return was fast approaching.

The Great Hunt was about to begin.

FERRIS

CHAPTER TWO

The music fell quiet and the crowd hushed, all of us enraptured by the movement of the trees before us. We all knew they could move. We'd awoken countless times to find their positions changed, their borders having stolen more of our land, of our people, but no one had ever witnessed their movement and lived that I knew of.

To watch the forest wander was to be consumed by it.

A weight formed in my chest as boughs creaked and leaves rustled, a swathe of hanging white moss moving across the thick trunks like a curtain being pulled wide. I couldn't see much of what was taking place as the crowd surged around me, every pair of eyes peeled wide to gain a better look at the spectacle before us, a sea of heads bobbing and necks craning ahead of me and blocking all too much from view.

The Champions filed from the stage, their footsteps loud as they descended the wooden steps, and my attention snapped to them, the line of humans approaching their fate while unknowingly beckoning me to seize mine.

I gave my mother and father a lingering look, my throat thickening with the goodbye I couldn't utter before I slipped away, using the distraction of the forest's movement to my advantage. Pain splintered through my heart as I hurried from them, that final glimpse of their faces searing itself into my mind as I captured it like a butterfly in a jar, wanting to keep it to cherish in the dark that awaited me.

"This day will go down in the histories," Chancellor Haydon called, his voice perhaps less steady than it had been. I supposed he knew as well as all of us did that if no one won the Great Hunt this time, then history would only tell of our demise – not that anyone would be left to lament it. We were out of chances to complete this challenge and everyone here knew it.

The trees were still shifting beyond the crowd, but I couldn't see more than the rustling of their upper branches from within the density of the nervous bodies. Birds took flight and a piercing trill hummed through the air, the sound so beautiful in its other-worldly nature that it drew a tear to my eye. The spirits were calling to us from within the cursed forest and I could almost believe there was something more than death awaiting us at the sound of that cry.

"These fine Champions are tasked to save us all from ruin, to lift us out of hopelessness and return the land that was stolen to our people. When the spirits are aligned once more, the forest will quiet, the trees will be tamed and they will return to the heart of this land where they belong. Think not of the fate that awaits us if we fail but of the hope success can offer. This curse *will* be broken!" Haydon exclaimed.

A cheer followed his proclamation, a raucous frenzy to the sound which betrayed the panic we all felt. My lips stayed closed against their cries, my pulse pounding in my ears and perspiration gilding my spine. I was no Champion, no hero. Hell, I wasn't even a fighter by any means of the word. I was a woman who had been sheltered with a desperate protectiveness for almost all of my life, the burden of loss clinging to me like a second skin. I hadn't trained for years like the Champions before us or honed my body into a weapon worthy of the challenge ahead. But my steps stayed steady all the same, my focus fixed on what I needed to do, what I had needed to do for so long that it felt as though my entire life had been consumed by it.

"I'm coming, Rissa," I breathed to no one but myself.

I finally made it to the edge of the crowd, finding a gap between the town hall and the edge of the platform the Champions had been crowded upon moments before.

All of them stood facing the forest several feet from the onlooking spectators, and I couldn't help the way my feet faltered as I beheld what they were staring at.

The ground sloped downward towards the trees, their looming trunks blocking the view to both the left and right of my vantage point, and only one space between them lay open.

My lips parted as I stared at the writhing movement at the edge of the forest, the trees creeping aside on tangled roots, vines twisting through the hanging boughs like knotted twine cracking open a door.

Everything within the forest looked utterly ancient, the massive trees stained with a bright and eerie green moss. The bark that was visible was chipped and scarred as if having survived a thousand storms. And yet, none of those trees had been here yesterday. It was impossible in the way all magic was impossible, but water sprites and bargaining Hags were nothing in comparison to this. The magic here was ancient, sentient and hauntingly intimidating. Something in my bones told of a wrongness to that place without me needing to take a step closer to see more. Whatever had caused the forest's curse had done its job well.

A dull cry echoed out from within the dense canopy of the trees, its source lost to the deep darkness of the woodland.

I sucked in a sharp breath as I spotted a face protruding from the bark of a tree to the right of the opening. Moss and lichen had claimed most of the man's flesh, but his blue eyes were open wide and staring out at us, filled with pain. I stared at the poor soul in horror. His body was almost indistinguishable from the trunk of the tree which had consumed him, only the rough outline of his shoulders and arms discernible at all while everything beneath his chest had vanished into the tree. His lips parted on another groan, and I couldn't help but wonder what madness had made me believe I could face this. How was he still alive? How long had he been there?

I'd heard whispers that the victims of the forest were destined to become a part of it, but never had I imagined a fate so twisted as this.

A chill ran through my veins and coated them in ice, my boot slipping in the mud as I found myself questioning the choice I'd made so long ago. Surely no one could survive the clutches of that place for long. Certainly not for years.

But the songs I'd heard hadn't been lies. I knew that in my soul. And I'd made her a promise.

I took a deep breath, trying to quiet the panicking drum of my heartbeats, but my terror only increased as a crooning voice called out from the depths of the forest.

"Don't walk into the woods, my dear,
For worse than darkness lingers here,
The spirits sleep between the trees,
Their voices lost to sultry breeze.
A long time I have mourned my loss,
Your children gained but mine forgot.
Your Offerings soothe my pain,
And stealing them is not in vain.
For here within the woods that wander,
We wait for those who chance did squander.
The time shall come for truth to rise,
And justice return to the skies.
My power waits for one to claim,

But no two spirits are the same.
One blesses with a force of grace,
Another curses in its place.
The weak may rise by claiming one,
The strong might find they can claim none.
But one fate strikes all who wander,
The spirits pull all souls asunder.
To halt the progress of the trees,
You must unite them all with ease.
Return the world to what it was,
Before greed corrupted my cause.
In forty days, your time is done,
Their amulets must all be strung.
For if you fail to find them all,
The price you pay will be your soul.
But should you happen to succeed,
A boon you'll win for such a deed.
A prize worth more than any other,
A gift for which you will not suffer.
The one who finds most of my kin,
Shall be the one to truly win.
And beneath the light of sultry moon,
I'll grant my favour with your boon.
Be warned, though, if this curse endures,
The final price to pay is yours."

I looked between the Champions who had all fallen stock-still to listen to the words the forest whispered. A few of them exchanged glances, and one even took a step back, but my gaze lingered on Colton Evast.

I knew him just like all the others, his prowess and strength having been boasted of throughout our realm for years in anticipation of this day. He was taller than the rest, broader too, and I couldn't deny that there was good reason for so many of my peers to swoon over him. I'd always found him to be boorish and arrogant beyond the point of me allowing myself to admit to the somewhat obvious attractiveness of his features, but in that moment, I couldn't deny it. More than any of the others, he looked the part of the hero destined to save us all from this fate. I could practically hear the other unwed women swooning throughout the crowd even though we all stood staring into the face of our demise.

He pushed his fingers into the strands of dark hair which had spilled into his even darker eyes and glared at the forest like it was little more than a bug standing between him and his destiny. My stomach knotted as I watched him, a spike of adrenaline coursing through my limbs as he broke from the line and began to stride towards the opening in the forest as though it were the most natural thing in the world. It was impossible not to admire his courage.

Cries went up, cheers and wails alike, women calling out for him to be careful, men begging him to save us all. The other Champions may as well have not been there, though they had all started walking too, descending the hill in a long line, their armour glinting in the bright sunlight, weapons hanging heavily around their bodies.

Then that haunting voice called out from between the trees once more, halting them where they stood.

"Beware the woods when darkness falls – protect yourself within four walls.
Unite the spirits wild and good - but you cannot earn them shedding blood.
Forty days to do it all – earn your boon or you shall fall."

The forest's warnings had been recorded at every Great Hunt since they began, and they never changed. It was the one thing about the cursed trees that every person in this crowd knew well. The rules of the Hunt. Don't be caught out at night. Don't kill another Champion for their amulets or the spirits they hold won't bond to you. Complete the Hunt in forty days or you're all fucked.

As the voice fell silent once more, the Champions started walking again, led by Colton who continued forward with a certainty to his gait which I couldn't help but envy.

My muscles coiled in anticipation. The timing had to be right. I couldn't screw this up.

I took a single step before a hand caught mine, jarring me to a halt, and I flinched as though captured doing something I shouldn't.

"Axel?" I questioned with a frown, glancing between him and the Champions who were now halfway to the forest.

"Don't do this, Ferris," he said in a low voice. "I understand why you feel you need to, but Rissa wouldn't want-"

"Don't speak about her like you know her," I hissed, trying to yank my hand from his, but he only tightened his hold.

"You know I can't let you-"

I punched him square in the nose, pain splintering through my fist at the contact with his hard face and a curse escaping me as I tried to yank my arm free, but he still held on. I wasn't a fighter and my strike hadn't so much as bloodied his nose, much less freed me from his grasp.

"What the fuck, Ferris?" he growled, tugging on my arm, hauling me away from the Champions who were just approaching the edge of the trees.

My time was running out. Panic flared through me. He was going to cost me my only chance.

"Axel, let go of me," I snarled, shoving his chest and trying in vain to wrench my arm away but he held me tighter.

"I know I'm not the fate you wanted, but I'm more than just the man they think me to be," he ground out, snatching my other wrist as

I tried to strike him again. "I *will* protect you, Ferris. Even if it has to be from yourself. I-"

The ground bucked beneath us and we stumbled back, my side slamming into the wall of the town hall as something beneath the dirt almost knocked me from my feet.

Screams came from the crowd, my mother's voice rising above them all, calling my name with a note of pure terror.

Pain splintered through me at that sound, my choice haunting me even though I knew I couldn't un-make it.

Axel cursed, his grip on me slackening as the ground bucked beneath our feet once more, almost knocking us over.

I spun to try and see what was happening, adrenaline coursing through my veins as if we were under attack. I caught a glimpse of green before something coiled around my ankle and yanked so hard that I was flung onto my back.

Axel fell with me, his hold on me unyielding as I was dragged across the ground at an alarming pace, a scream spilling from my lips, my cloak and pack snagging and tearing while they cushioned me from below. Mud and dirt billowed up in a great cloud, coating us in a layer of dirt and concealing us within it.

I screamed louder as I was hoisted downhill, my throat ripping raw at the sound, and all the world screamed with me, my mother's voice the loudest of them all.

I thrashed against the hold on my ankle, my arm colliding with the body of someone else who was being dragged across the dirt too, but nothing I did came close to freeing me from the vice-like grip on my leg.

I tipped my head back to the sky, clouds whipping past overhead at a furious speed, the sun blazing so brightly that it burned my retinas and then, so suddenly that it was akin to thrusting my head beneath water, darkness snatched me.

The forest closed in around me. The people closest to me were screaming differently now, their voices filled with anguish in place of fear.

Something wet splattered across my face. Axel's grip on my wrist grew bruising as he cried out in pain.

The thing around my ankle stopped dragging me along and I cursed wildly, fighting my way to my feet through the torn fabric of my dress, my ruined cloak falling off of me as I made it upright at last.

Horror tore chunks out of me and I stumbled back, shaking my head at the sight before me.

Axel lay unmoving on the ground, his glassy expression taking my attention captive for endless seconds before I could process the unnatural twist to his neck.

"No," I breathed, backing away, shaking my head. He shouldn't have been here. This wasn't how it was supposed to happen. I was… he was…

I whirled around, the deep green of the trees pressing in on me from every direction, my scream rebounding off of them as I stumbled towards the one, shrinking patch of sunlight with desperate need, panic bleeding into every piece of my soul.

I reached for that scrap of light where the towns folk watched on, breaking into a run, my pack falling from my back, my boot slipping off my foot along with the tangled green vine which had hauled me into these cursed trees.

With every sprinted step, the space between the trees shrank, the trunks closing together like an ancient gateway, vines tangling between them to block out every speck of the world beyond until only one tiny path of light remained, my mother's frantic face framed within it, devastation crumpling her features as her eyes met mine and the forest slammed closed between us.

Before I could hurl myself against the trees, strong arms banded around my body, a hand slapping down over my mouth to stifle the endless scream which had broken from my lips.

Blood dripped into my eyes as Colton Evast held me tighter, his words a rough growl against the shell of my ear, his arms a bind I couldn't free myself from even as tears burned pathways down my cheeks and I shook my head in denial of what had just happened.

"It's too late to turn back now, Ferris Creed," he said roughly. "Welcome to the Great Hunt."

FERRIS

CHAPTER THREE

I ripped free of Colton's grasp, whirling on him and barely managing to choke back more screams as I took in the carnage that surrounded us.

Blood stained the trees, limbs torn from corpses which were hung like twisted decorations from bough to branch.

Bile pooled in my mouth as I took in the bloody lumps of flesh which had been Champions and townsfolk alike. They were barely recognisable, the faces I could see twisted in agony. There were only ten of us left breathing, and at least double that number had perished already, dead before the trees had even sealed us inside the forest.

Axel stared lifelessly at the thick canopy of leaves above us and guilt tangled in my chest as I took in the sight of his broken body. He'd only been dragged into these cursed woods because he'd been trying to stop me from entering them. But it seemed the trees themselves had wanted me here regardless of his attempts to save me from this fate.

"They…the trees…a vine…" My words were a tangled knot in my throat, my heart racing so powerfully that the sound of it practically drowned out Colton's attempt at calming words.

I looked down at my ankle, my gaze locking on the vine which had coiled around it and hauled me into the cursed forest. It had broken in my struggle, just a short length of it left, like a macabre manacle to remind me of what it had done. I dropped down to one knee, tearing the vine from my ankle with ease which defied the truth of what it had done to me just moments before.

My boot was gone, lost in the struggle with the vine, half the contents of my pack along with it, thanks to the great rip I found down its middle.

"It seems these woods have a want for you, Ferris," Colton mused, looking down at me from his great height, his bulk seeming to have grown within the shadows of the trees.

"Is that what you call this?" I demanded, splaying my arm at the nightmare which surrounded us. "The wants of the woods?"

His brow lowered, his head shaking slowly. "I don't have a name for this. But the trees snatched you into their grasp."

"They snatched them too," I pointed out, not looking as I indicated the broken bodies of the townsfolk who had joined me in this fate.

"But none of them still draw breath. You're the only person still living who wasn't destined to be here," he said.

I glanced at the other survivors, understanding dawning as I realised he meant that I was the only non-Champion to still be breathing.

Panic threatened to consume me whole, every terrible tale I'd ever heard of this place echoing through my skull at full volume, mocking me for my stupidity in coming here. And maybe I was a fool to have made this choice. Maybe I'd doomed myself by coming. All of my preparations had been so swiftly proven lacking. I was in over my head here, and I knew it now more than ever.

A sob threatened, tears clawing like ragged fingernails at the corners of my eyes, but I fought them back. Descending into despair would do me no good. I'd made this choice a long time ago, and I wasn't going to lament it now that I'd finally followed through on my plans. I would have entered even if the forest hadn't made it impossible for me not to.

I stood, raising my chin as I looked into Colton's dark eyes and swallowed down my terror.

I was tall enough to look most men in the eye at five foot ten, but Colton still scraped a few inches over me. It didn't matter. He found what he was clearly hunting for in my defiant gaze and nodded gruffly.

"You'll be needing a new boot," he said, turning to survey the dead and trudging towards a corpse which had been ripped in two. I knew her. Only by name, but it felt wrong to steal from the Champion while her body was still warm.

"Wait," I said, catching up to Colton as he bent to retrieve her boots from her oddly-splayed legs.

He turned to arch a brow at me, the dappled light from the forest catching on the strength of his features, and for a moment, I only held his gaze before forcing myself to speak again. I'd meant to stop him, to tell him to leave her body in peace, but I could already feel the cold of the forest floor leaching warmth from my foot, mud slick between my toes through my sodden sock, a stone digging into my heel. Those boots were no help to her anymore, but I wouldn't last long out here without them.

"I'll do it," I said firmly, and Colton shrugged, pushing to his feet and striding over to the other Champions who had survived the entry to the forest.

I fought the urge to gag as I lowered myself in his place and began unlacing the boots from Evain's feet. She'd been a stoic kind of character, lacking in the bluster and bravado so many of the other Champions claimed, but in a way that demanded a quiet kind of respect. I'd believed in her before this. I'd believed in all of them, though that hadn't lessened my need to come here myself. Their goal wasn't aligned with my own after all. Yes, I needed the curse to end, but most of all, I craved the boon the forest promised the victor of this twisted game.

I retrieved the boot and was pleased to find it fit well enough – though it would have been smaller ideally. It was well made, both water-tight and thickly lined, the sole strong and broken in. Far better quality than my own boots, in all truth. I tried not to look at the blood which speckled them as I made the decision to take the pair, not wanting the mismatched soles to slow me down.

I muttered a word of thanks to her, then turned away to hunt the ground for a pair of stones to place over her closed eyes.

The Champions were talking in low voices, and I could feel their gazes on me too. I knew what they were discussing. They thought I'd slow them down. I hadn't prepared for this the way they had. I wasn't strong or trained for battle. I was lean and bookish, known to settle in any quiet corner I could find with a book in hand rather than a mug of ale or a group of friends. But they didn't know what it was I'd been reading in those books. They didn't know that I was ready for this in ways that they weren't. I was fast and agile, cunning and clever, and most of all, I was more determined than any of them to see this thing through to its end.

I let them whisper about me while I hunted down stones for the dead, scrawling an X on one and an O on a second using mud I scooped from the forest floor before placing them over their eyes. Then I plucked flowers from wherever I could find them, white weeds which clung to the roots of the trees and little bluebells which sprouted in the spaces between them. I tangled them between the fingers of the dead and made certain they each clasped some form of weapon beneath them.

Flowers so that no one would scent their sins on them while they crossed into the afterworld. Weapons so that they might fight their way past anything which couldn't be fooled. An X and an O to mark a beginning and an end, and the placement to stop all ill spirits from watching them. These acts were superstitions that I had often denied believing in, but it seemed only right to offer them to these people who had died for a curse they'd never been given a chance at breaking.

I stood when it was done and the Champions turned to face me, a mixture of judgement, contempt and pity in their expressions.

"We need to find shelter before night closes in," Devlan said, his words for everyone but his eyes on me. He was a brute of a man, the oldest of the remaining group, his skin lined and hair silvered, though he was arguably the most muscular among the Champions too. He'd watched his mother enter the forest fifty years ago and had still spent his life training to do the same even after she'd never returned. "We can't waste time on moving slow."

"Then perhaps you shouldn't be wasting time on standing still either?" I suggested, squaring my shoulders against his clearly disparaging judgement.

Helga snorted in amusement, her green eyes glimmering in a way that made me warm to her. At least she wasn't eyeing me in a way that suggested she planned on ditching me like a few of the others were.

I knew them all, though I doubted many knew my name. I'd been surprised when Colton had spoken it with such familiarity, but then he had grown up in my village and he was only a few years older than me. Perhaps it wasn't such a shock that he knew the names of the people who had surrounded him while he trained for this day - even if we hadn't been consequential enough for him to converse with much while doing so.

Emmy and Tyson were from my village too, and I knew a little of their character – Tyson was hot-headed and often responsible for brawls at the inn. He was broad and fairly good looking, though clearly he believed himself to be nothing short of godly. Emmy with her mane of dark hair was the only Champion who seemed likely to have an even bigger ego than he did, and I was certain *she* didn't know my name. Common villagers like me were definitely beneath her notice, and I'd always been confident that we were all better off for it.

I turned from them as they prepared to move on, taking my torn bag from my back and hurriedly checking the contents, a knot loosening in my chest as I found the two books I'd brought with me still securely wrapped in their waterproof bindings at its base.

A few more of my supplies still sat beside them; some bandages and a healing poultice I'd traded for in town last summer, a couple of apples and a wrapped heel of cheese. Thankfully, my slingshot was still lodged in my pocket, though I knew the meagre weapon was laughable in comparison to the blades the Champions carried. But I was a good shot and it was the best I had. The rest of the food I'd brought had gone, along with the spare clothes I'd brought with me, and I tried not to wilt in disappointment.

I hesitantly took Evain's pack from her, guilt stirring in my gut as I did so. But she had no use of it where she was now, and my torn bag was only going to cause me more trouble than good. I emptied her belongings onto the ground and sorted through them, claiming her supplies of food, bandages, a small knife and her water canteen before packing it all away with what remained of my things.

I looked around, hunting the undergrowth for any more of my belongings, to no avail. Likely they'd been lost while I was dragged into this cursed place and lay beyond the boundary of the forest. I swallowed back my disappointment and snatched my tattered cloak before shouldering the pack at last.

I sought out Colton who stood observing me critically, his attention lingering on my new boots before he shrugged and turned towards the heart of the forest.

"She'll keep up or she'll perish. We've already wasted enough time," he said, striding away, and like a flock of geese following a food bucket, the rest of them turned to hurry after him.

I glanced around at the trees, the webs of green and white moss hanging between them already disorienting me, and I hadn't even taken a step out of the clearing yet.

I stole a final look at Axel, muttering an apology for ever getting him mixed up with me before painting a cross against the closest tree and striding after the gaggle of Champions.

We'd see who was cut out for this place before long. I was hoping that my studies had prepared me in ways their training hadn't. I wasn't here for glory after all. I was seeking something far more important.

Redemption.

FERRIS

CHAPTER FOUR

The trees here weren't like any trees I'd ever known beyond the limits of the forest. They watched us. They whispered too, their boughs creaking as they leaned close to one another, their trunks splitting into grins, sharp with hidden thorns.

There were animals here as well. Not that I'd laid eyes on a single one, but a chorus of chittering and twisted birdsong filled the space between the leaves. There was a mocking tone to it, like the things that watched us were sniggering and bickering, placing bets on which of us might survive this hellish place. I doubted any were weighing me with much promise. But that was just fine by me. I was used to being underestimated.

I shifted the pack on my back. It was bulkier than the one I'd brought with me and I'd packed it in a hurry, clearly having done a poor job of it. The largest of the two books I carried with me didn't sit right inside this new vessel. Sharp corners dug into my spine, the metal which tipped them proving itself to be a vicious travelling companion. Not that I'd voice a complaint on it or even think of leaving it behind, but I would attempt to reposition it whenever we took a moment to rest.

The Champions stalked through the trees around me, hacking aside swathes of trailing green and white moss with their swords to clear a path, carving a trail into existence where there hadn't been one before.

Everything beneath the trees felt alien, familiar and yet utterly unknown at once. I recognised the little white flowers which had grown in our back yard, but these were larger, their petals shimmering and moving in a breeze I couldn't feel. This place was alive in a way that defied the common laws of nature, magic imbuing it. Every intake of breath was laced with an undercurrent of power, every exhale a disturbance to the serene habitat we were invading.

My eyes shifted to the right of our route where a narrow passage between the undergrowth beckoned. My steps faltered, my mouth watering as I noted a delicious scent coiling around me. Something awaited me at the end of that trail. Something I wanted to find.

"This way," I called as I turned towards the path, but another of the Champions beat me to it.

Tyson shouldered me aside, my feet stumbling over one another at the collision with his bulk before he strode down the narrow opening which had beckoned me so enticingly.

I made to follow him but Emmy knocked me aside next, a mocking smile on her lips as she took the lead. "Champions first, runt. Stay in your lane at the back of the group and maybe start thinking about what you're going to rustle us up for dinner – you're going to need to earn your keep after all."

"My cooking skills are about as refined as your manners, I'm afraid. So you'll have to make your own meals," I called after her.

"Is that so?" she sneered over her shoulder. "Then perhaps you'll have to find your own way through the-" Her words cut off with a shriek of alarm, and she fell to the forest floor with a heavy smack.

I stared at her in surprise, her dark eyes widening in fear as she reached for me with a desperation which made me lurch forward despite her disagreeable personality.

She screamed as she was yanked backwards, Tyson's cries coming from within the foliage ahead, and my fingertips grazed hers as I made a grab for her hand.

My fist closed on nothing, and I threw myself forward again, my knees striking the mud, my free hand flying out to brace myself as I landed in front of her and managed to grab her fingers.

"Don't let go," she begged, her brown eyes locking with mine, pure terror sparking in their depths.

The other Champions were yelling around me, boots hitting the ground as they ran for us, but Emmy's hand was slipping from my grip, my own body being dragged a few inches through the mud as whatever had hold of her tugged harder.

"I've got you," I swore, digging the toes of my boots into the mud, heaving on her hand with all my strength.

The leaves of the surrounding trees closed in around us, rustling and whispering, hiding her legs from view, making it impossible for me to tell what was trying to drag her from my grasp.

Something yanked on her so hard I almost lost my hold and I was forced down onto my front, my pulse spiking. I was dragged through the mud, the bracken lining the edge of the trail scratching at my exposed skin with thorny fingers.

"Help us!" I yelled, her fingers slipping in mine again, my hold on her fracturing piece by piece.

"In the trees!" Colton yelled from somewhere behind me, and despite all of my instincts screaming at me not to look, I arced my neck and peered up into the branches which loomed overhead.

A flash of something dark sped between the outstretched boughs, shadows trailing through the leaves in coiling whisps of darkness.

My lips parted on words which never formed, the movement above me so fast that it appeared as little more than a flash of deeper darkness speeding above our heads.

Emmy screamed, her free hand clamping down on my arm,

fingernails tearing into my skin as she was hauled backwards again and I was dragged along after her.

Tyson's screams were echoing between the trees, raw agony colouring them, and my eyes met with Emmy's as she was yanked back once more, our hands almost parting from the force of the pull.

"Hold on," I commanded ferociously, the panic in her face haunting me. "They're coming. Just hold on."

Boots pounded the forest floor around me, the other Champions finally reaching us, swords swinging above our prone bodies as they hacked at the bracken so they could reach for Emmy too.

Colton dropped down over me, straddling my back with his knees pressing into the mud on either side of me, then he reached over my head and grasped Emmy's wrist.

Relief spilled through her eyes as he tightened his hold and hauled on her arm and I pulled too, both of us fighting to release her from whatever foul creation was holding onto her.

Tyson's screams of agony cut off sharply and a blast of strong wind crashed into my face, sending dust and debris flying all around us and forcing me to close my eyes.

The scent which had seemed so delicious just moments before turned pungent in its sweetness, the weight of it heavy on the back of my tongue, a sickening rot to it which I hadn't noticed at first.

Emmy clawed at my fingers, and I hauled her backwards with Colton's help, relief finding me as we managed to shift several inches. But it was short lived.

A shrieking cry went up like the curse of a raven, but filled with vitriol and fury that made the sound cut me to my core.

Emmy was ripped backwards with such force that I was dragged several feet after her, Colton still straddling my spine as he was hauled forward too, before we lost our hold on her entirely.

With a harrowing scream, Emmy was consumed by the bracken that lined the trail, her terrified gaze spearing me to my core as I shouted her name, my hands still outstretched for her as if I might catch her yet.

Shock jarred my bones, my lips trembling over ragged breaths as I stared at the place where she had been. I only moved when Colton stood and dragged me upright with him.

"We have to go!" he barked, whirling me around and shoving me towards the path the Champions had been carving through the trees.

"But Emmy-" I protested as her screams raced through the forest, painting it with terror.

Another flash of darkness tore through the canopy above us, and I spied a flicker of ebony wings trailing shadows in their wake.

"The Raven!" Gunther called, recognising the spirit while my brain worked to process the horror that had befallen us.

Gunther took off in pursuit of the mass of darkness in the trees above, and Colton gave me a shove to make me run too.

I looked back over my shoulder, my lips parting on a protest just as Emmy's screams cut off with a sickening gurgle which could only have signalled her demise.

The eight remaining Champions were aiming bows and spears towards the treetops, loosing arrows after the rush of darkness which kept swooping between the canopy overhead.

I broke into a run as they raced into the depths of the trees in their pursuit, no further mention of Tyson and Emmy's fate passing between us.

Horror clung to my bones like a second skin but I fought it away, reaching into the pocket of my cloak and claiming the slingshot I kept there.

The wooden shaft was carved with tiny effigies of the spirits of the forest, my own little reminder as to what lived between these trees.

The Raven.
The Rat.

The Wolf.
The Tiger.
The Stag.
The Unicorn.
The Phoenix.
The Bear.
The Boar.
The Serpent.
The Carp.
The Fox.
The Dragon.

Thirteen spirits. Thirteen Amulets to claim when taming them. One curse to break once they were all united. A boon to the one who did the most to return harmony to the wayward wants of the forest.

A fatal stillness crept through me as we broke into a sprint in pursuit of the Raven. This was why I was here. It was the reason I'd braved these damned woods and laid my life on the line to enter them. I needed to seize the Raven and many more besides. I *needed* the boon of the forest.

I snatched a stone from the collection in my pocket, testing its weight in my fingers and painting an invisible X over the smoothness of its shell before loading it into my slingshot.

With my eyes on the branches overhead, my boots kept snagging in the roots and brambles that littered the forest floor, but through some miracle, I managed to remain upright.

Gunther released a battle cry and hurled his spear at the roiling darkness overhead, but it sailed through nothing except shadow as the Raven disappeared into the canopy.

The spirit cawed mockingly, the sound reverberating through the trees, making the leaves quiver and rattle like an applauding audience.

I aimed a shot which disappeared pointlessly into the canopy, then fired off another and another. Each stone struck a little closer to our quarry, but the Raven moved so quickly that I could barely take aim before it had gone again.

We burst into a clearing where an old stone well with a thatched roof stood innocently at its centre. The thatch was ripe with mould, clumps of it having fallen to the ground beside the mossy stone of the well's base, and the bucket lay broken beside it.

My focus lingered on the strangeness of finding such a thing in these woods for a moment too long, and Colton yelled a warning at me as a flood of darkness swept out of the trees at my back.

I twisted around, loosing the stone from my slingshot, but my aim went wide and the stone sailed into the trees a breath before a massive weight collided with me and sent me flying back towards the well.

The thatched roof crumbled to nothing as I struck it, clumps of sodden thatch falling into the murky water below as the beam which had supported them split in two.

I shrieked in alarm as I fell backwards, my arms splaying and striking the stone just in time to stop me from tumbling straight down into the well itself.

The Raven's feathers brushed my cheeks, soft as spider's silk and threaded with a darkness so complete that it was as if the world itself fell away to nothing.

The weight of the enormous bird almost dislodged my grip on the mossy stones, and I slipped several inches into the mouth of the well, the weight of my pack urging me downwards while I hooked my knees over the stone and fought to hold on with all my might.

As fast as the Raven had appeared, it was gone, and I cried out in alarm as a volley of arrows and two spears all hissed through the air inches above my face in pursuit of it. The Champions clearly valued the prize of the spirit far more highly than my life.

The cries of the group rushed around me, their footfalls thundering by, and I caught a glimpse of Helga's back as they charged past, consumed by the hunt and unwilling to waste a moment on helping me.

"Oh, fuck you!" I shouted after them as they sprinted into the trees.

I cursed as my grip on the slick stones slipped, my fingernails tearing on the roughness of them before I managed to halt my fall once more.

My dress had ripped along the side of my leg, the cold stone pressing to my calf as I lay there like a damned fool, the dank well whispering my name in welcome from below.

With a grunt of exertion and a determined snarl, I threw my weight to the side, my arm flying out in a desperate grab which seemed all too likely to fail but somehow, miraculously, I managed to seize the wooden beam which had once held up the well's roof.

I wrenched myself free of the well, tumbling to my hands and knees in the dirt, panting wildly through my relief.

My slingshot lay in the mud before me, and I crawled a few paces to snatch it into my grip, needing the security of being armed in this maze of hellish design.

I scrambled to my feet, adjusting the strap of my pack and looking towards the far side of the clearing where the Champions had all disappeared into the trees once more without me.

I cursed at the bastards before breaking into a run to pursue them. They were my best bet at the moment, and though I wasn't particularly fond of their company, I had decided that remaining with them was the better option than going it alone.

I managed three steps before a rush of darkness burst from the trees, and I barely managed to skid to a halt before colliding with it.

The Raven landed ahead of me, its talons made of shadow given form, coils of darkness rising around the sharpened silver tips. This was no normal creature, its size alone rivalling mine, its head barely a foot lower than my own as it studied me with eyes the colour of a wandering storm.

Its feathers were slick with darkness, an oil spill over cobwebs, and as it outstretched its wings, I found tethers of night pooling between them. There was nothing normal about this bird. Its entire being was crafted with magic so ancient it made me feel utterly insignificant in its presence, like a flea before a god.

The Raven's beak was gleaming gold, embossed with twisting patterns which ached for the brush of my fingertips across their ridges. I had no desire to lose my arm to the sharpness of its beak, so I made no move to attempt that, but I couldn't deny that I was enraptured by the ethereal, other-worldly beauty of this spirit.

My fingers trembled where they still gripped my slingshot, but I raised it all the same, loading my last stone into the hold and drawing the rubber taut as I prepared my shot.

The Raven released a tremendous caw, the sound piercing my chest and making my heart tremble to the chord it struck.

There was a haunting beauty to that cry, a pain so ancient that it brought a prickle of tears to my eyes.

The stone burst from my slingshot but the Raven was already gone. I could only watch as it sped into the trees, the darkness swallowing it as its shadows coiled into all the empty places between the branches and claimed them for its own.

It was lost.

I stood staring after it with my breaths coming in laboured pants, my hope dropping to the pit of my stomach just as surely as every stone I'd launched after my prey had dropped to the forest floor.

I'd been such a fool to believe the spirits of the cursed forest would be a challenge that a lowly human like me could rise to.

The Raven had been toying with us, and not a single one of our group had come close to securing its amulet.

The Champions returned with heavy steps and grumbled curses, though none seemed to know what had become of Devlan. Already our number had fallen to eight.

"It's getting dark," Colton said, his tone gruff and filled with the disappointment consuming us all. "We need to find shelter before night falls."

I nodded along with the others. He was right of course. The forest hadn't warned us about the night for mere theatrics. None of us wanted to risk so much as a moment between these trees once the moon had risen and darkness cloaked this cursed place.

So, with a heaviness in my chest which I couldn't loosen, we trudged on into the trees, hunting for a place to take shelter while the Raven's cry still echoed in my ears.

FERRIS

CHAPTER FIVE

As night drew in, the shadows beneath the trees deepened to the point where we could hardly see the forest floor beyond our feet. My boots thumped against the tangles of roots which lined our path, threatening to trip me at every step. Dead leaves kicked up around us like swarms of rustling butterflies only interested in roosting in the underbrush.

A silence had fallen between the Champions that was marked with tension.

We'd all heard the forest warn against being outside at night. We were in desperate need of shelter and almost out of time to claim it.

Gunther, Helga and Damon walked closest, their powerful bodies surrounding me as if they were my own personal guards. But I knew better. They'd left me easily enough when the Raven had shown itself. If anything, I was serving as a conveniently expendable snack for anything that might come after us, a weak link to sacrifice should something swoop out of the darkness.

I bristled at the thought. I may not have been trained for battle or well-versed in the use of blades and bows, but I was the farthest thing from weak. I'd survived more than they knew, fighting for this life of mine and braving each day with the full weight of my need for redemption weighing me down at every moment.

My pockets were heavy with stones I'd gathered while walking the forgotten trails through the forest, my slingshot ready in my pocket should I need it. I had no sword to swing but I wasn't unarmed, and a stone to the skull could be just as effective as any blade, given enough force and good aim. And one thing I had was impeccable aim.

Devlan hadn't returned and we'd found no sign of him among the trees. I didn't know whether to think of him as dead or not. I supposed it didn't matter much at the moment regardless.

"We've got fifteen minutes at best before night falls, and then we all die out here," Esther called as if any of us might be unaware of the fact. She was a mean-looking woman with pinched features and hard muscles lining her compact frame. She clearly held no interest in me, and the feeling was mutual, so I'd had little to do with her aside from listening to the numerous complaints she liked to voice.

"Let's move faster then," Colton decided, swinging his sword at a swathe of vines and trailing moss to reveal a new path.

The group broke into a jog, making my chances of tripping on this ragged terrain even likelier.

We'd come across a few rotten barns and a collapsed farmhouse but nothing we could use for real shelter overnight. The forest had stolen so much of our lands that I'd assumed finding those lost houses would be easy, but either they'd been consumed by the trees or we weren't looking in the right places.

In my pack I had a map which had plotted the lost human lands and all of the buildings I'd known to have been swallowed by the trees in the last century, but I hadn't even bothered to get it out. This place was a maze and we'd gotten more than lost in it during our encounter with the Raven.

I hoped to come across some kind of landmark which I might be able to use to define our location, but so far, there had been nothing but trees and trees and trees.

The Champions ran faster, my breaths coming heavily in their stead. I'd taken care to spend time running while preparing to enter this doomed place, building up my stamina as best I could while keeping my intentions secret, but I was nowhere near as fit as them and it was beginning to show.

Damon had already left me behind, Helga and Gunther powering on without me too. I could barely make out Colton's silhouette at the front of the group, the sound of him hacking through the forest more of a clue to his location than anything I could see.

The others passed me too, and I shoved my slingshot into my belt before hoisting my pack higher on my back and forcing my legs to move faster.

If I was left behind out here, then I'd be facing the threat of the dark alone. And though I had no real belief that any of us would survive the forest once night fell, I preferred the idea of standing among the Champions when it happened than meeting it alone.

I hurried on but a root snagged the toe of my boot and I tripped, my arms wheeling wildly, my palm colliding with the thick trunk of a tree.

I almost smacked my face into the rough bark, but by some miracle, I managed to twist my head aside in time.

Ragged pants escaped me and I blinked into the trees to the right of our path, something pale looking back at me within them.

"Wait!" I called, though the Champions ignored me, running on without so much as a glance back in my direction. Assholes.

I shoved away from the tree and pushed through the undergrowth, a chaotic laugh spilling from my lips as I found an old tavern beyond it. The walls were thick with foliage, vines climbing them to gather on the roof, encasing it in lines of tangled green, but the door stood firm, the roof intact. A sign hung lopsidedly above the entrance, an image of an archer taking aim at a deer mildewing above thick letters which named it 'The Hunting Man.'

"I found shelter!" I yelled, though I was tempted to let them all run on into the night and face the threat of the dark for having left me behind so callously. I understood it though. Out here, it was every person for themselves when it came down to it. The strongest couldn't risk their lives for the weak – the aim was and could only be to claim the amulets and break the curse.

I stumbled towards the tavern door with a smile breaking like dawn across my lips. The handle resisted my turn at first and then gave, the door creaking open just as the thunder of footfalls announced the return of the other Champions at my back.

Colton pushed through the group and joined me at the door, his grin a wicked, conspiratorial thing as he shoved his weight against the wood and forced it wide.

Darkness had almost enveloped the forest entirely, and as we all spilled into the safety of the tavern, howls and wild whispering erupted from the trees.

The sound enveloped me in terror, but Helga threw the door shut on it with a savage thrust and with mere seconds to spare, we were awarded the prize of safety.

I woke with a jolt, my pulse thundering and fingers curling around my slingshot before I could even determine what had roused me from my sleep.

For a moment, I'd thought I'd heard singing, but as I focused on my surroundings, I realised it wasn't the haunting lullaby I'd come to fear with the rise of the moon.

A series of ragged grunts were coming from somewhere beyond the door and I frowned, certain that hadn't been what had woken me but unable to detect anything else.

We'd made camp in the largest room, which had once been a bar, the tables and chairs now shoved against the walls, many of them broken so we could use them for firewood. Our bedrolls were made up on the floor next to the wide stone fireplace, our group huddling close to make use of the heat from the flames.

Thick beams crisscrossed the ceiling overhead, old paintings of hunters hiding behind trees or aiming bows at various prey decorating the wood-panelled walls, forgotten by the people who had fled. I could almost imagine the way this place had once been, with the sconces lit and the old piano which was mouldering in the corner playing a jovial tune while people danced between the tables and fought to get service at the bar. There was an echo of the noise they'd have made in the heaviness of the silence here, like that moment in time was just out of reach rather than lost to the depths of the forest.

We were haunted here by the people whose homes had been stolen by these trees, and I couldn't help but feel like their eyes were on me, their expectations a burden I hadn't intended to take on. This curse had come for all of us, and my pain wasn't the only wound which demanded to be healed.

The fire had burned down to smouldering embers, Esther dozing against the wall, her head lolling onto her chest where she sat beside the kindling and failed miserably at her turn on watch.

I pursed my lips, the grunts coming again and prickling at my subconscious. There was something about the noise which tugged at my memory, conjuring up the descriptions I'd studied of the thirteen spirits. I rubbed the sleep from my eyes, a thought coming to me which had the last vestiges of fatigue slipping away: the Boar.

I glanced around at the sleeping Champions. It was hard to make out much more than the lumpy shapes of their bedrolls in the gloom, but I didn't find any other eyes peering back at me.

If it was the Boar, then I might have a chance at claiming it for my own without them ever realising it. For now, they were content for the group of us to travel together, the need for safety in numbers outweighing their individual desires to win the most amulets and earn the forest's boon for themselves. But I knew that wouldn't last. They all wanted the prize I'd come here for, and there was no way I could allow any to seize it but me.

I pushed aside the thin blanket I'd been shivering beneath and slowly stood.

The grunts came again, louder, definitely a large pig. My smile bloomed wickedly. If the spirit was inside this building, then perhaps it too had to shelter from the forest at night. Perhaps it would have nowhere to go and I really would be able to take it for myself without the others knowing a thing about it.

I crept from the room, my eyes seeking shapes in the shadows beyond the dim light of the fire and struggling to find any. We'd blocked off the windows in the room we'd chosen to sleep in using the bigger pieces of furniture we could find. We'd had nothing left over to do the same in the rest of the building, so we had to hope the door would be enough to keep us safe.

Silvery moonlight illuminated the old bar area up ahead of me, and I padded closer to it, the grunts getting louder, more frenzied. My gaze caught on a portrait of a woman in a voluminous blue gown whose violet eyes seemed to track me as I passed it by. I frowned at her, unable to see much of her face in the dim light aside from those eyes which were eerily similar to my own.

A grunt drew my attention from her, and I frowned at myself for allowing the distraction. This forest was full of tricks and I refused to fall prey to any of them.

I readied a stone in my slingshot, my pulse pounding to a crescendo as I closed in on my prey.

The Boar was rumoured to have a hide of that was near impossible to pierce, its cloven hooves sharp as knives and its tusks deadlier than any human-made spear. It would take a direct strike between its eyes to down him. Nothing less would suffice. I needed to get into position without it detecting me so that I could-

I fell still as I rounded the corner into the small bar at the rear of the building, my lips parting and fingers almost slipping on my drawn stone.

The grunting wasn't coming from the Boar.

In the centre of the room, their eyes thankfully pointed towards the bar on my right, Gunther had Helga bent over a table and was ploughing his cock into her with rapid, jagged thrusts. His shirt was crumpled on the floor, but his trousers were hanging loose beneath his ass, sweat rolling down his bare skin as he pounded away, grunting with effort and stealing all hope of the Boar from me at once.

"Harder, for fuck's sake," Helga hissed, gripping the table she was bent over and driving her ass back against him.

I swallowed a lump in my throat, standing there for far longer than I should have as I scrambled to recover from the shock of my discovery.

"You fucking love my cock," Gunther panted, thrusting harder, grunting louder.

"I would if I could feel it," Helga growled, and Gunther cursed her, slamming his dick into her more firmly and making the table legs scrape against the floor.

The shriek of wood on stone snapped me out of my shock and I whirled away from them, slipping back into the darkness of the corridor and colliding with a hard body before I even realised someone else was there

"See something you like, Ferris?" Colton asked me in a low, amused tone.

Gunther was grunting so loudly now that I doubted he or Helga could hear anything other than his piggish sounds of pleasure, but I still cringed at the thought of being discovered here.

"I thought he was the Boar," I blurted, knowing Colton couldn't see the heat of my cheeks in the darkness, my embarrassment shielded in bravado.

Colton breathed a laugh, his hand finding my waist as he leaned down to speak into my ear.

"I imagine Helga would gain greater pleasure from the encounter if he was."

I snorted in amusement, and the grunts in the bar became a drawn-out wail of pleasure that belonged solely to Gunther.

"Are you fucking kidding me?" Helga growled while Gunther panted, and Colton tugged me back towards the room with the fire.

"Best we don't let them find out that you were watching. If I'd known you were into voyeurism though, Ferris, I'd have gladly put on a show for you myself."

"I'm not," I hissed, slipping through the door and finding the fire blazing again. Esther was still asleep against the wall, so I had to assume that Colton had built it back up.

I headed for my pathetic excuse for a bed, intending to sleep away my disappointment and embarrassment, but Colton hounded me.

"What?" I asked, stalling short of returning to my thin blanket. "Are you planning on following me into my bed?"

"Is that an offer?" he countered.

"No," I replied firmly, though my skin prickled a little at the insinuation. Colton was...well, *Colton*. He was the man every woman in town had claimed to want for a husband should he return from the forest and who had certainly done the rounds of testing their marital beds, even if he never lingered in any of them for long. He was precisely what all the books described a Champion to be; tall, strong, handsome and irritatingly deserving of the admiration he drew for his battle prowess. I may not have been one of the simpering fools who had followed him about town in hopes to gain his attention for a night or three, but I wasn't blind.

"Pity." Colton looked me up and down, the edge of his lips tugging towards a smirk, as if he'd known precisely where my thoughts had just wandered to, but I wasn't going to be distracted by his obvious flirting.

I scowled.

"What is it?" I asked, knowing he wasn't truly looking to bed me in a room full of people.

Colton considered me for a moment, then shrugged. "I want to see that book you were hoarding before we settled for sleep. I could take it by force, but I figured I'd be polite first and see where it got me."

I stilled, my eyes falling to the pack which lay beside my bed, its contents containing the few most precious things I owned.

My instinct was to refuse his curiosity but one look at his powerful body told me he hadn't been lying. He *could* take it by force, and then where would I be? Perhaps if I sated his curiosity over it he'd lose interest…

"Fine," I grumbled, taking a seat on my blanket and drawing my pack into my lap.

Colton sat beside me. Close. Too close, his knee butting up against my thigh and his shadow fallowing over me as it danced in the flickering light of the flames.

He was filthy. I was filthy. Hell this whole fucking place was filthy, and yet something about it suited him, like he was built for the roughness of the forest rather than the bustle of the town we'd left behind. I very much doubted the same could be said for me, but it didn't matter if I was suited to this place or not – my destiny lay beneath these trees and I wouldn't turn from it no matter how hard it proved to claim.

"It was no accident you ended up in here with us, was it?" Colton asked curiously, his gaze all too astute, his guess too close to the truth to bother denying.

I shook my head, poisonous memories slithering through my mind, a call unanswered, a fate which shifted so fucking unfairly-

"No," I admitted, banishing those thoughts. "I came here intentionally. It was always my plan."

"Then why not train as a Champion?" he questioned.

"My mother and father never would have allowed it," I said dismissively. "It would have broken their hearts for me to even suggest it. Besides, I'm not like you." I waved a hand at him and the rest of the Champions, indicating their brawn, bulk, preference for violence. "The way you plan to do this thing isn't the way I-"

The door thumped open, drawing our focus to Gunther as he sloped back into the room, adjusting his fly and grinning like he had something to be smug about. Helga didn't follow him but her words did.

"I'll be along in a bit – just need to finish what you couldn't, small fry!"

The grin on Gunther's face faded to rage and I quickly looked away from him, busying myself with drawing the larger of the two books I carried from my pack. It was the one I'd been studying when Colton had noticed it and the only one I was willing to share with him.

"Bitch," Gunther muttered, stalking back to his bedroll while Colton made no attempt at all to hide his laughter.

Gunther glowered at him but with one assessing look, he clearly decided he didn't favour his chances against the favourite of the Champions and truthfully, I didn't either. Colton Evast was a brute of a man and I was starting to wonder if I wouldn't be better off distancing myself from him sooner rather than later. Especially now that it transpired that he was actually paying attention to me.

Whatever decision I made in that regard would have to wait for daylight, however, so I gave in to the demand he'd made of me and placed the book in my lap.

"It's a book of the spirits," I said cautiously, my fingers skimming the embossed cover of the tome I cherished so dearly. There were metal coverings over the corners of the hard case to protect it, and each of the forest's spirits were represented on its face, all surrounding a single tree.

Colton eyed it, but as he reached out to take it, I quickly opened it and positioned it so that he could view it clearly from my lap.

Colton glanced at me, obviously knowing what I'd just done, but thankfully he didn't attempt to take the book from me again.

"There are chapters on each of the spirits," I told him. "Myths and legends recounted, descriptions, depictions." I showed him the first chapter which was titled 'The Stag'. There were pages of beautiful artwork showing its pelt of woven leaves, its moss-covered horns so tall and wide it was a wonder the beast could traverse the forest at all. "The Stag is the keeper of the forest's histories and the guardian of moss, fungi and soil. Where it steps, nutrients bleed into the ground, moss spreads across the trees and mushrooms sprout in honour of its passage," I surmised, pointing out the various images and notations, the ethereal stag peering out at us from the page as if it were listening too.

Colton nodded, reaching over me and turning the page. I tried not to wince at the dirt beneath his fingernails or the roughness of his grip on the ancient parchment and released a sigh as he managed to complete the task without tearing it. I curled my fingers into fists to stop them from smacking his hand from the precious parchment and watched him silently leaf through the chapter dedicated to the Stag before he paused on the next, which spoke of the Tiger.

"The Tiger was tasked with shepherding the wayward creatures of the forest and making certain that all paid homage to the Great Elm which lays at the heart of the labyrinth where the amulets must be hung if the curse is to be broken," I said while Colton studied the image of the huge spirit whose pelt was coated in small animals, mice, rabbits and squirrels riding on its back, foxes, badgers and hedgehogs roaming between its legs.

"So you prepared for the Great Hunt in secret," Colton surmised, turning another page and another. He didn't pore over them the way I had when I'd first gotten my hands on this book, but he did read the annotations, study every image. Perhaps he was more than just a brute after all.

"I prepared in my own way," I agreed.

"Because of Rissa?"

Her name on his lips was a dagger through my chest. I hadn't heard it spoken aloud very often in recent years. Mother and Father certainly never uttered it, and I'd long since fallen into the same pattern. People in town knew of course, but they didn't bring it up, didn't just spit her name out in a conversation as if it were nothing at all to do so.

"You remember her name?" I asked dumbly, and Colton drew his eyes from studying the pages which spoke of the Carp and looked at me intently.

"Do you really think me so self-interested that I didn't know the people of the town I grew up in, Ferris?"

"Truthfully?" I asked, and he narrowed his eyes before nodding. "Yes. I don't mean that badly," I hurried to clarify. "But you and all of the Champions were always so focused on your training. I hardly ever saw you socialising aside from frequenting the taverns for free meals and drinks-"

"I can't help it if people liked to show their thanks for our sacrifice by paying out for a few meals here and there," he protested, and I shrugged.

"I wasn't judging. And I agree. The chances always were that most of you, and likely all who entered this place wouldn't ever come back again. Every Champion chose to risk the forest in hopes of saving our people. Why shouldn't you have benefitted from some free drinks and easy company in the lead up?"

"Easy company?" he echoed in amusement, and I fought against the heat which rose in my cheeks as he leaned closer to me. "If you had no objections to offering me easy company, then how come you never did so?"

"Oh please," I scoffed, hiding the heat in my veins and busying myself by turning another page in my beloved book. "You were hardly short of offers and clearly had no need of one from me."

"That doesn't mean I didn't wish for one."

I snapped the book shut and he barely snatched his fingers away in time.

"Are you seriously flirting with me right now?" I demanded, meeting his gaze defiantly and finding nothing but a cocky smirk awaiting me. Colton had clearly gotten his way with far too many women, thanks to that smile, but I wasn't going to become another of them.

"Do you want me to be?" he asked.

"No. Go see if you can satisfy Helga in Gunther's place if you're looking for someone to fuck in the back room of a dirty tavern inhabited by all manner of woodland beasts. I came here to see this curse broken, not to become the latest of your nameless conquests, Colton."

"Ouch."

"Don't play the fool. You had no interest in me before we found ourselves together in this place, and I had none in you. Let's allow that to remain the bar we set our acquaintance at."

"Acquaintance? Is that all I am to you? Haven't I saved your life in here?"

"Haven't I saved yours?" I indicated the tavern we were currently sheltering in, and he conceded defeat by raising his hands.

"Fine. But you're wrong about me only paying attention to you now, Ferris."

"Of course I am," I replied scathingly.

"Always a book in hand, always a scheme in mind. You get that little crease right…there." He pressed a finger to the furrow between my brows, and it only deepened in response. "Always watching, always plotting. I saw you, Ferris, and you saw me. Only, I think perhaps you dismissed me a little too quickly."

I pursed my lips as he withdrew his hand, only to find him pressing that same finger to the cover of the book in my lap.

"This is Fae made," he stated. Not a question.

I sighed. "I traded for it."

"You can't trust a thing inside this," he pushed.

"I know." But I did trust it all the same. There were so many different accounts recorded in this tome, so many sightings recounted over a thousand years of the spirits when they'd wandered close to the edge of the forest and had been seen from beyond it. The legends of what they'd once been were all documented here too, from Fae who had been living before the magic of the forest was shattered and the curse sent the spirits who had once protected it into the frenzied state of loss they now embodied.

"You didn't show me the other book you're carrying," he said, allowing me my lie, or perhaps believing it too easily.

"It's not a book, it's a journal," I told him, making no move to show him it, and thankfully he accepted my rebuff.

"I'm sorry about Rissa," he said.

"I'm sorry about your parents," I replied, earning a hard smile from him.

"That's different," he grunted.

"It is and it isn't," I agreed, fighting a shudder as my thoughts slipped to the Hollows.

Colton looked away from me, his eyes on the edges of the window we'd blocked with a wooden dresser.

"If I survive this place, my next stop will be at the Necromancer's door," he growled, a menace to his tone which hadn't been there before. Despite our current predicament and the proximity we held to death, I couldn't help but shudder at that suggestion.

"You can't mean that," I breathed, looking over my shoulder as if someone might have overheard him, might pass his threat to the ears of the beast we all feared even more than these trees. No one dared speak ill of the Necromancer, let alone lay threats at his feet. You never knew what ears he might have listening, what foul creature he might send to your door.

"I can and I do," Colton replied without a flicker of fear. "What more can he take from me anyway? I'm not afraid of a coward who hides in his castle sending monsters out to do his dirty work."

"I heard someone say.the Necromancer is as dead as the army he rose in his image," I whispered, laying my hand on Colton's arm as if that might soothe the roiling fury which had been unmasked in his gaze at the mention of his parents' death. "You can't kill someone who wed themselves to death already, Colton."

It was said the Necromancer had once been a prince of the Fae who hoped to become king when the spirit of Providence decided to select a new monarch. But he'd been an impatient male and there were many princes and princesses who might be chosen for the throne. As the years ticked by and the immortal King Arthrun's reign grew ever longer, more heirs were born but no new monarch was selected, and it drove him to madness.

He coveted the crown the king wore with a fierce desperation and decided to claim his power in case the spirit chose another prince or princess to rise to the throne and disregarded him entirely. So one day, he crept into the palace and killed the king while he slept before taking the crown from his bedside, lifting the sacred relic and placing it upon his own brow.

The crowns of Fae weren't like the crowns of men. They held ancient power and would only yield to one owner at a time, granting power which aligned harmoniously with the soul of the one who wore it. But the power the crown had granted him manifested while he hid in exile, bestowing upon him magic more ruinous than any which had come before it.

By the time Bane Crownthief revealed his power over the dead, he'd already amassed an army and set it loose on the world at large. His anger was for the Fae but his Hollows struck at any living being they could find. My people had been hit harder than any. We'd been caught unawares and occupied with the forest's curse and we had no wall to hide behind. Thousands had fallen to his army of soulless dead, and we all knew well to run at the first hint of a Hollow.

Colton studied the fear in my expression, then sighed, shaking his head and waving a hand at our surroundings.

"No need to fear the Necromancer in here, Ferris," he pointed out. "We should focus on one foe at a time, don't you think?"

I relaxed a little even though it was madness to consider the spirits an easier foe than anything, but at least their power was born of nature, their curse something which could be broken. The Hollows and the Necromancer who wielded them were another matter, and one I planned never to come close to. I had my work cut out for me in this place and if I managed to win the forest's boon, then I would gladly allow my turn at adventure to pass and stay well clear of the Hollows, the Fae and anything like them for the rest of my years.

"Do you think we might find another spirit in the morning?" I asked, glad to change the subject.

"Tomorrow will be worse," Colton said simply, like the fact that we'd faced so much death and carnage already meant nothing at all. "That was just the welcome party coming to whittle us down and choose the real hunters it wants for this game of brutal chance. We'll find out the truth of this place in the coming days…assuming we're still alive to witness it."

He got up and rounded the fire to his own bed, taking his turn on watch while I carefully returned my book to my pack.

I said nothing more as I curled beneath my blanket and willed sleep to come for me, but I had the horrible feeling that he was right and our entry to this cursed place had been the easiest part of the hunt.

"Don't worry, Rissa," I breathed into the silence, even though I was beginning to doubt my own words. "I can do this."

HENDRIX

CHAPTER SIX

If there was a time when I'd cared about the fate of the world, it was long forgotten to me now. Call me selfish, greedy, a bane on the realms; I gladly wore the titles. I had no desires beyond my own gains in this hellscape of a reality anyway.

A cursed forest that would gladly devour me, body, flesh and soul didn't stoke fear in the remnants of my heart. My fears were few and far between - some would say I held none at all. But they would be wrong. There was still one thing that stirred terror into my bones in the dead of night, but I rarely put a voice to it.

Here on the verges of the world's consumption, who would I care to tell anyway? The Fae who had turned their backs on me? Or the worthless humans who were barely here for a blink of an eye, then turned to dust as if they'd never been here at all? Pointless beings. They were breathing one moment and gone the next. Barely worth a wasted thought of mine.

No, I didn't have time for humans, and Faekind could rot for all I cared. At least the mortals hungered for their day in the sun. The Fae squandered their endless lifetimes on political debates and drab merriment - I'd rather gut myself before attending either. Again. Because yes, once I had been a part of that bullshit, but I'd severed myself from their company long ago. My days of languishing at balls were dead and buried. The invites had dried up around about the time I'd killed a handful of my people.

They weren't so fond of shaking my bloody hands these days, and I was hardly scratching at their doors to be let back in.

I rather preferred my position as a loathed prince. But a prince I still was, they couldn't carve that name from me. My crown was made of blood and there was no tearing it from my brow while I still drew breath. Royal was royal, my blood was proof of it. They could cut my heart out raw and it would still beat blue. It was the envy of all, to be meant for a throne. There were few things the Fae craved more than power.

I gazed blandly at the forest around me, plant life veiling all paths and trying to confound me, but as I stepped toward a knot of vines, they parted.

Perhaps this place sensed what I was, the corruption of me mirrored in the ripe and tangible malevolence that hung in the atmosphere. This forest was ravenous, like a tankard with a hole in its base, filled tirelessly but never to find itself full. I knew the feeling well.

There was no birdsong in this part of the forest, no chattering little creatures. It was as if these trees were part of a larger beast, the moss between them its fur and the rough bark its claws. My task was to seek out its heart and drive a dagger into it - metaphorically speaking of course.

I walked along the silent path, the quiet all too pressing. But then – *there*, a scream. And another. A pitching wail that brought a twist to the corner of my lips.

"Hungry spirits," I whispered to the dark. "How many will you take before the next sundown?"

I had sheltered in an old cottage this past night, but I'd moved many miles from it the moment the sun had risen. In all those steps I'd walked, not one spirit had shown itself and the sun was already setting again. I'd moved cautiously, a predator well-versed in the hunt, but these spirits were no ordinary beasts. They sensed what I was and they were retreating from me, as all creatures tended to do.

The trees stirred in a wind I couldn't feel. Listening. They could hear my voice like lashes on their bark. They didn't want me here. Welcome I was not. But I had rarely been welcome anywhere in the latter half of my lifetime, so there was ease in the familiar rejection.

The forest acknowledged me as most others did: with caution. I was no meagre human tiptoeing through its boughs, nor a simple Fae whose wits might be bested. I was a beast in my own right, a monster fit for this trial. And these trees knew it.

"How easily you let me walk between your towering trunks, my lady," I taunted, talking to the creaking boughs. "But I know you're assessing the cut of me. Whatever death you've sent to those screaming Fae or mortals, you know it is not good enough for me." I raised a hand, brushing it over a knot in a particularly wide tree. It shuddered at my touch and the trunks groaned around me, roaring at my indifference to their power. "Come on, show yourself. Don't hide like this. I know you have a true form, let me see the real you. Stop hiding from me. Let me see your spirits."

A hiss drew my gaze skyward and movement among the thick canopy made me halt. I watched, waited, no weapon unsheathed. There was a crack of twigs, a heavy groan of branches as something large writhed between the branches up there.

"Hello, pretty," I purred. "Come to daddy."

I reached for the nearest branch, hauling myself up, using the gnarled trunk for footholds. Closer I climbed toward the hulking thing that slithered through the trees, the echoing power of it making my ears hum. The Serpent. Here she was at last. I couldn't see her beauty yet, but I was about to snatch a glimpse.

I'd trained in Summoning many hundreds of years ago, but I hadn't cared for the call of the forest until I'd finally realised its use to me. How the fair folk would shudder when they discovered who had claimed it. Their forsaken prince with all the power of the cursed forest to his name. It was worth the effort for that mere idea alone. But I had greater plans for it too.

A rustle to my left made me twist around and my fist snapped out, shattering the nose of the blonde male swinging through the trees. He yelled in pain, and his cries pitched higher as I launched myself at him, arms banding around his waist and sending us both tumbling out of the branches and crashing to the ground.

The air was knocked clean out of him but his soft body cushioned my fall. I grimaced as I was gifted the huff of his breath to my face.

"Caelan Havinger, fancy seeing you here," I growled, his yells quieting as recognition dawned in his eyes. He was part of the Coterie – the inner circle of the royals, a tight-knit group of ancient Fae who had lived longer lives than any of our kind. And they just so happened to be my favourite thing to kill.

Caelan scrambled for his sword, but I was faster, unsheathing it for him and tossing it aside, grabbing him by the throat in the next heartbeat and pinning him to the earth. "I'd say it's a pleasure seeing you again after all these years, old boy, but I always was a terrible liar."

"*You*," he rasped, unable to form much of a sentence as he clawed at my hand around his jugular.

Old boy was what I'd called him hundreds of years ago, and his hair had only just held a fleck of grey back then. He'd barely aged since in truth, but being a few hundred years younger than him had always been a point of contention between us. He might have been an Elder, but he coveted youth and beauty over all else. Time took a toll on our kind ever-so-slowly, but in reality, Caelan would never look a day over fifty – in human terms - no matter how long he lived.

"I always thought you'd end up trading with a Hag to get rid of those greys, Caelan." I plucked one out with my free hand, twirling the hair before his blue eyes. No Fae were ever unhandsome, but if I had to pick a face that was an irritation from mouth to brow, then it was his. "I guess you didn't think it was worth the price."

He threw his knuckles into my side, causing a nice crunch, the force throwing me off of him. We fell into a fist fight, all animal, but my new toy was trying to scramble his way free of me more than put me on my back.

"What would a fallen prince want from the Taking Trees?" Caelan spat as he regained his feet.

I lunged for his ankle, biting down with a feral snarl, and he screamed bloody murder. It was a wild overreaction but I guessed he had good reason, considering my appetite for death. And immortals tended to fear that more than all else. When you've lived hundreds of years, you tend to grow accustomed to living, so I rather enjoyed seeing the high class of the realm quiver in the face of death.

They gathered riches all their lives, treasures of infinite value, as if they might be able to take them into the black abyss beyond the grave. What a waste of living. And I'd know all about wasting life. Years of bleak, meaningless existence had seen me pursue all manner of follies. Nothing had quenched the monotony in the end. Not that there *was* an end. Unless you counted this shell my tired soul was trapped in as the conclusion of my existence. No, there was nothing to live for bar one thing now. The prize of the cursed forest.

Caelan kicked for my face but I was on my feet again, swerving in front of him as he tried to flee and pinning him to a tree with nothing but the firm muscle of my chest.

"You're a madman," he gasped, trying to push me away to no avail. "Why did you turn on your own people? What did we ever do to deserve your wrath?"

"What *didn't* you do, old boy? What wouldn't the Fae do for a little entertainment?"

His face paled with the understanding of what I knew of him.

"I saw you in your little den of vices," I sneered.

"W-well I may have my sins but yours weigh far greater than mine. The spirits of the forest won't let a black soul such as yours summon them. You'll perish in this place, and I'll damn well rejoice when-"

I stuck him in the neck with my dagger, his voice turning to a strained gargle, bubbles of blood rising to his lips and his eyes widening in delayed surprise. It was funny how close death could come to people before they realised it had snared them. Beautiful, foolish denial had kept Fae like Caelan merrily ignorant of his demise until his very last breath.

"Pity you won't make it to the celebrations, Caelan." I tugged the dagger free, ready to stab him some more to ensure he couldn't heal from that wound. But as he slumped to the ground, a tangle of vines crept over him, dragging him into a twisted mass of roots. He thrashed against them but they tightened their hold, wrapping around his throat and winding over his chest, stealing him away into a mass of bracken. It seemed the forest was happy to finish the job. And there he would stay I supposed. No grave to mark him, no one able to visit to leave so much as a flower. 'Poor Caelan' some insufferable wench would utter to the sky, but his soul wouldn't be there among the stars. It would lay here rotting forevermore. Because of me. And that suited me rather well. This day was already more interesting than the last, though to say my interest was piqued was still a stretch. Nothing roused me as much as the rush of killing.

I wiped my dagger on the moss by my boots and treaded on, my gaze skipping between the large leaves above, seeking movement among the branches. Nothing. All was still now, my beastie gone to ground. No matter. There were plenty more to find.

I walked a while among the whispering trees, certain they were speaking riddles to me. Sometimes I caught a word or two, a song to lure me east or west but I never wavered from my path south. Not that I knew what awaited me there, but I wouldn't risk following the call of the forest only to find myself in a trap.

At last, I reached a clearing, parting a fan of low-hanging branches to reveal a valley beyond. In it sat a trickling stream which coiled around an old castle of cream and brown stone. It must have been taken by the forest several hundred years prior. Its turrets were boxier than the modern palaces with their piercing spires but not as decorative, though their pale blue colour was striking in its own right. I strode toward the stocky building, finding it bigger than it had appeared from up on the hill. Vines were crawling across its walls and curling around its windowsills like clawing fingers, but the building remained mostly intact, despite the forest's touch.

The arched wooden door stood open, beckoning me inside, promising sanctuary. Or death. One of the two. And as no whispers summoned me closer, I risked the latter and walked inside.

The cold was apparent, but a fire would heat a room or two in no time. It was fine enough for a fallen prince - as Caelan had called me. He had loved the royals during his years of servitude, always gushing and following them dutifully. I'd never been fond of an ass tonguer, but Prince Koval in particular had adored the flattery. He was, quite unfortunately, my uncle. A male who had looked down on my father's choice to marry my mother – a Fae who had not checked the boxes the royals rather preferred for their wedded brides and grooms. The older the Fae, the better. The more connected they were among the inner circle of the Coterie, the more likely they were to find themselves a royal partner. Father had been a rebel. I had to thank him for that.

Royal I may have been, but my relation to King Arthrun who had sat on the throne during my time in the Fae realm of Rivenspire had been distant. I was a prince by blood, but there were plenty of others who had awaited a chance at the throne. The king himself had never borne children, but his sisters had, and some of those children had

had their own and so on until there had been a large pool of heirs with royal blood, all awaiting the moment the spirit of Providence would show up and select a new king or queen. But it never had. Usually, a monarch didn't reign longer than a couple of centuries – or if they were particularly poor at ruling, the spirit would crown another Fae promptly. One king had only lasted two years before being replaced, and he had lived in shame on the edges of society since. But Arthrun, he had ruled for over five hundred years, and there had been no whisper of the spirit stirring. And so the pool of princes and princesses had grown and grown, all hoping Providence might appear and select them. At least until The Last King was finally revealed and the crown finally found its place upon the head of the one destined to rule until the end of this age and beyond. Though I, like many of my kind, doubted that fated monarch would ever come.

Among my rather large family, my uncle Koval was one of the more insufferable of my relatives who had hoped Providence would select him for the crown. He always had been a prissy little tart, so I doubted he'd decided to step into the forest this time. Would he or any of my estranged family be joining me here in the Great Hunt? Perhaps my aunt, Princess Drava, might have had enough gall to test her mettle. The others? I highly doubted it. They held nothing of the ferocity my line of the family had possessed. Maybe my mother's rogue blood mixed with Father's rebel tendencies had been the reason for that.

The truth was, I hailed from two of the strongest Fae warriors of the realm, and I'd always found my extended family withering company. I expected I'd feel a touch more murderous if a reunion was on the cards. Funny thing about being branded as a psychotic outcast; you tended to live up to the reputation.

An old chair with a back so tall it was akin to a throne had been drawn up to a fireplace in a stone chamber away from the entrance hall and there I sat, plotting my next move.

Blood speckled my fingertips, and I examined the red tarnish to the deep golden hue of my skin. Silly things, weren't we? Immortal, so long as we didn't accidentally fall down a well or jab ourselves with something a little too pointy.

Death was inevitable, so she was good company to keep.

I'd rather make a friend of her than face her whimpering like a newborn pup. It was why I wore her fingers as a necklace. Two bony hands wrapped around my throat, tattooed there to declare her ownership of me.

I felt her creeping closer now, always brushing past, never quite catching hold of me, as if her grip was not yet strong enough to claim me.

"Yes, yes, you'll have me in the end, darling. But there's work to be done right now, and you'll want to see what's coming next. I'll put on a fine show for you. A bloody one. You know the type. Our favourite."

Stories told of Death's visage, the head of a falcon on the body of a woman. She was the spirit who would take the hand of all those passing into the afterworld and lead them to their fate.

She left me, as she always did, off to seek easier prey. But she'd be back. She couldn't resist the draw of me. Her little project.

The night was deepening beyond the stained-glass windows, the forest alive with groans and wicked wails. Someone was dying out there, screaming for mercy. They clearly hadn't made it to shelter in time. A human, most likely. The fleshy kind with bones so brittle, they'd snap like twigs. Why their kind came here, I didn't know. Proving nothing as ever. Trying to be remembered. What fools. But let them die for all I cared. Let them be hailed back home, only for those celebrants to die too one day, and on and on the cycle went. Stupid, fleshy humans. If I were so breakable, with a lifespan akin to a mouse, I wouldn't go squandering my death for glory. Spirits be, why didn't they die for something interesting?

Perhaps, I envied them a little though. Brittle as they were, they had something right. A beginning and an end. Clear cut and quick enough to give them one hell of a fire in their bellies. They lived truer and more keenly than the fair folk. We were the ones to squander life, lavishing in our palaces and draining the earth of all it had to give.

Now look; the forest was fighting back. It despised us, and so it should. I despised us too.

Rivenspire had deserved the scourge of the Hollows that had made the Fae hide, scurrying into their shining towers to wait out the storm. But it had never ceased, the dead still walked the land, roaming, devouring and ripping through lands that belonged to their lush realm – but that was before they'd built the wall. Their numbers increased with every passing day. Enough to climb that very wall perhaps. Or to crack clean through it.

I laughed. Dark and rumbling was the sound. Yes, that would amuse me greatly to see the Fae's palaces fall, to see them climb on each other's backs, brother on sister fighting to escape the purge. But there would be no escaping that end. The Hollows were death on legs, ever moving. An unstoppable tide.

If there was something worth living long enough to see, it was that. Oh how the Fae feared the Necromancer who had created them. How they whispered of the king of the wastelands who was sending his dead to finish them all. And oh how I would fucking laugh when their high castles came tumbling down.

Ferris

CHAPTER SEVEN

We'd been walking downhill for several miles, the forest now eerily quiet, the creatures which had been chittering and scampering through its boughs notably absent in this part of the woods.

An uneasiness crept along my spine, the sensation only growing more potent with each step we took.

Brian was whistling to himself utterly out of tune, the sound grating on my last nerve. I hadn't slept well that first night or the three following it. Whispers of my past kept rousing me since my talk with Colton, and between the cold and the hardness of the floor, I'd spent a long time staring up at the wooden beams above my bed, waiting for dawn to free us. Today, we'd chosen to venture deeper into the trees and abandon the tavern in favour of finding a new place to shelter once dark approached. I couldn't deny the nerves which twisted in my gut at the uncertainty in that decision, but we'd made no progress in the woods surrounding the tavern and had no choice but to widen our hunting ground.

A lot of the food I'd brought with me had been lost when my

pack had torn when I'd been dragged into these cursed woods and my stomach growled hungrily in protest to the meagre breakfast I'd afforded myself. The Champions may have been willing to share in each other's company but none of them shared supplies or provisions with one another. They certainly wouldn't be offering any to me.

I knew well enough how to forage for food, how to tell poison from sustenance, but that was out there. In here, I wasn't inclined to trust the plump blackberries I spied at the edge of our trail nor the wild mushrooms which appeared so innocently recognisable.

This place was a curse in itself. But I knew hunger would drive me to eat from it sooner or later. I couldn't survive forty days in here without turning to the bounty of the forest for nourishment. I just wasn't going to take that risk until my other options were all spent.

Our group of seven seemed in lower spirits than the previous days. Perhaps the reality of so much death and corruption had caught up to us at last. Either way, we made for a sullen and silent pack of hunters.

More than once, a whisper urged me to step from the path the group trod, the trees twisting and leaning aside to present a trail for me to take a chance on.

I slowed at each offering, a vibrant stillness falling over me as I stared at the passages through the greenery, the sweet scent of a summer's breeze urging me to take a fateful step. But each time, I lifted my chin and turned away from the passage the forest presented me with. I wouldn't soon forget what had happened to Emmy and Tyson when they'd been tempted by these malevolent trees.

The sun passed overhead, its passage only marked by the direction the light spilled down to us from above, beams of sunlight punching holes in the otherwise impenetrable blanket of greenery. There was no glimpse of the sky to be had down here. Only green and brown and the endless stirring of the leaves.

I tried to think over all of the tales I'd studied about the Great Hunt, the forest, the spirits. It didn't seem right for us to be aimlessly wandering through these trees in our search. Were we truly just supposed to hope that we stumbled across each of the spirits? Yes, it seemed as though that had happened with the Raven, but had that simply been chance? Didn't there have to be some method to finding them? Some rhyme or reason to their individual locations?

The Carp at least would have to be located in water. But aside from gurgling brooks and narrow streams, we'd come across nothing of a size capable of housing a powerful spirit such as it.

There was a puzzle here which tugged at the corners of my mind. Something we weren't seeing. Some way in which we were failing at this game despite having barely begun.

"Look," Esther hissed in a low voice which carried over our baleful silence.

We all stilled, moving closer to her where she stood at the base of one of the towering trees, its trunk at least ten paces wide.

Esther pointed and I couldn't help the sharp breath I sucked in as I noticed what she had spotted.

Several feet above our heads a body was bound to the tree. No… not bound. The longer I looked, the harder it was to tear my gaze away. The man, whose features were rough and frozen in a look of agony, had been consumed by the bark itself.

His legs and feet were little more than uneven lumps on the roughness of the tree's skin, but his chest and arms still protruded enough to hold their shape. One hand was yet to be claimed, the pale skin of his fingers tangled in lichen, reaching out towards us.

"You? Beware the slither of its belly," he croaked, and I nearly fell back on my ass as I lurched away from him in horror.

Esther cursed colourfully and Colton drew his sword.

"What manner of beast are you?" Colton demanded, pointing the tip of his blade at the jagged bark coating the man's chest.

"His ears," I breathed, blinking to try and un-see it, but there was no denying the slight point at their tip. "He's Fae."

The rest of the Champions drew their weapons too, muttering curses and spitting on the ground.

"Do it," the Fae rasped, his eyes pleading as he looked to the sharp tip of Colton's blade like it was his salvation in the offering.

Colton hesitated, though I could see how tempted he was to comply. The Fae were no friends to us. They hid behind their walls and scoffed when the Hollows came for us. Not to mention what they'd done to Rissa, to my family, to so many innocents, all in the name of protecting their own. We were the sacrifice they were willing to make and nothing more to them.

I stooped and marked an X in the soil at my feet before straightening again and taking a measured step forward.

"Answer our questions and we will reward you with death for them," I said, my voice coming out far braver than I felt.

"Fuck that," Helga growled. "Run him through or I will. The word of any Fae is worth shit to me."

Colton seemed inclined to agree, but I placed my hand on his elbow to halt his advance, giving him a stern look.

"We've been wandering aimlessly through these trees for days. There's something here we're missing. We need all the help we can get if we want to end this curse. Just let me-"

"Why are we wasting time listening to the one person here who holds no authority at all?" Gunther demanded loudly, and someone gripped my shoulder, wrenching me backwards.

"Wait!" I protested, shoving Damon away from me as I fought against everyone's arrogance, but it was to no avail.

Gunther swung his sword and severed the Fae's head from his shoulders with a solid smack. The head didn't fall though, the bark in its hair still holding it to the tree, the wild eyes of the Fae who had been consumed by it flying wide in a look of ecstasy as if death was the one and only thing he had ever desired.

Rage consumed me as I began to yell at Gunther for being a

pig-headed fool, but my voice was drowned out as the Fae male suddenly screamed. The sound which poured from him defied all reason, scattering my thoughts as it tore into my skull with sharp claws and tried to pluck the pieces of me asunder.

Gunther still grasped the hilt of his sword where it had embedded itself in the bark of the tree, but he was screaming too, throwing his weight backwards and heaving on the blade like his life depended on freeing it from the roughened bark.

I backed away, hands clasped over my ears while Gunther screamed and screamed. And that was when I saw the reason for his continued wails: the bark had crept over his boots and crawled along the length of his sword to capture his hands in it too.

"Help me!" he bellowed while the Fae still wailed with a noise that rattled the trees and awoke every beast and spirit for miles, beckoning them to this feast of fear.

Daniel lunged for Gunther, wrapping his arms around his waist as he tried to haul him free of the tree. I yelled a warning at him which went unheard beneath the volume of the screams.

The bark came for him too, his shrieks of horror tangling with the song of dread that shook the branches all around us.

"We can't stay here!" I yelled, backing away, knowing it meant abandoning the two Champions to their fate. But the forest had already claimed them. Inch by inch, the bark encased more of their flesh and hauled them towards the hulking body of that giant tree.

I could feel the desperate hunger of this place, the cloying scent of magic heavy in the air, iron and soot souring my tongue. It was too late for them. I knew it like I knew my own name, like the trees were whispering that truth directly into my veins and pumping it through my body.

The Fae's screams turned manic, his wild eyes meeting with mine in accusation, and I shook my head against the judgement he was passing on my soul. I had no part in his fate. I refused his condemnation.

Helga, Esther and Brian broke for the trees, sprinting away without a backwards glance, Damon yelling at them to wait for him as he broke into pursuit.

I backed away from the screaming men, apologies tumbling from my lips as their fate closed in on them without mercy.

My back struck a hard body and I turned, finding Colton with his sword still in hand, indecision lining his strong features.

"They'll become just like that Fae!" he shouted over the screams that almost deafened us. "They'll be left here to suffer in the grip of the trees for the rest of time."

I hadn't been certain if the Fae was still suffering his fate due to the longevity of his kind's lives, but with a sword cleanly severing his throat and his screams still ringing out endlessly, I had to agree with Colton. Whatever dark power had captured him, it relished in his agony, it kept him here to suffer at its will, and both Daniel and Gunther were headed toward the same fate.

I took my slingshot from my belt and loaded a stone into the hold. I'd never so much as shot a flea with it, had never wanted to use it to cause death. But that was the only hope of mercy I could offer the Champions now. Perhaps if death took them before the tree fully took root, they'd be able to escape into it.

I drew my slingshot taut and fired.

Gunther's head snapped back as my stone struck him in the temple. He slumped to the ground soundlessly, his cries for release answered.

Daniel met my gaze as I loaded my next shot, tears tracking down his cheeks and a single word forming on his lips even though I couldn't hear it over the screams of the Fae bound by that tree.

Please.

I gave him his wish in the next heartbeat, my pulse falling still as the weight of what I'd done struck me just like that stone. I'd killed him. I'd killed them both. For mercy or not, my hands were now stained with blood.

My horror had no time to hold me though, because even as the burn of that reality settled over me, the screams of the Fae turned wild with rage and a blast of energy exploded from the tree which held him.

It struck us like a force of wind, hurling us from our feet and into the trees, leaves and vines whipping at our skin as we were thrown away at great speed.

I hit the ground with a thump that echoed through my bones, pain exploding through my body as I rolled over in the dirt and spat leaves out of my mouth.

My limbs trembled at the shock of what I'd done, a breath catching in my throat and tears burning the backs of my eyes. *It was mercy*. I repeated that truth to myself again and again until the words tumbled together and spilled from my lips - although most of them got lost along the way and only one spun itself free of my tongue.

"Mercy, mercy, mercy…"

A sob racked my chest, the scent of iron and soot clinging to me like a second skin, electricity dancing in the air itself like the magic of this place was reaching out for me, its power roaming over my body in gentle, frantic exploration.

I couldn't stay here. We needed to run; I needed to get up.

With a shuddering breath, I managed to force my eyes open again, my pleas for deliverance falling silent, though my tears still burned a heated path down my cheeks.

I had to move. I had to find Colton.

I exhaled harshly, forcing the memory of Daniel and Gunther's deaths from my mind.

But if I'd thought the forest was done with me there, then I'd have been a fool, because as I pushed to my hands and knees with thorns digging into my palms and mud staining the tattered hem of my dress, a low and menacing growl let me know that I was not alone and this place had only just begun to break me.

Ferris

CHAPTER EIGHT

I froze, heart racing in my chest and palms slick against the roughness of the forest floor.

Something prowled closer between the soaring tree trunks, the chill of its powerful body taking hold of me in its shadow, coiling around me and choking the breath from my lungs.

The slosh of wet paws hitting the ground slowly advanced and a whimper rose in the back of my throat.

I turned my head. Slowly, so achingly slowly that I hardly dared breathe as drips of water hit my cheek like rain. But there was no rain.

A scream stalled in my lungs as my eyes roamed up the enormous body of the beast that stood over me, raised onto its hind legs, its head almost brushing the canopy of the trees far above.

The Bear.

My fingers shifted in the detritus beneath me, scrawling a shaking X into the dirt, though I knew superstition would do me no good.

The Bear growled in a low and menacing tone, its head cocking downward, more water spilling from its snout to rain down on my cheeks.

The spirit was a mixture of beast and element, its fur braided strands of pale blue liquid which moved endlessly across its hulking frame, making it appear as if in motion even though it stood still above me.

I reached for my slingshot with painful slowness, easing back onto my haunches, but it was pointless. My weapon had been in my hand when we'd been thrown through the trees and it had been lost in my fall.

I had nothing to defend myself against this creature of myth, and even if I had, what use would a slingshot have been against a behemoth such as this?

The Bear raised its snout, sniffing at the wind and looking skyward.

I didn't waste my chance, shuffling backwards, not daring to rise to my feet, hoping to find shelter at my back so that I might hide.

With a tremendous roar, the Bear slammed down onto all fours, the ground trembling beneath me as it landed, leaves kicking up as water splashed from its pelt.

The Bear had been tasked with keeping the forest nourished. Its job had once been to see to it that water reached every root, every sapling, every seed. Now, in its madness beneath the weight of the curse, I didn't know what it was capable of.

I stilled, fear eating its way into my soul as the Bear prowled toward me, every step of its enormous paws soaking the ground beneath it, its claws digging channels in the soil where the water pooled and dispersed.

"Don't eat me," I breathed, uncertain why I thought this monstrous creature might care for my pleas but unable to hold my tongue against them.

I hadn't even begun to do what I'd come here for. Each moment within these trees made my task fccl morc and more impossible. I didn't know where to start, and now it was all over before I'd even managed to-

The Bear's snout brushed my brow and I stilled entirely, sucking in a sharp breath as warm water trickled over my skin, roaming down my cheeks, washing the dirt from them. It didn't feel like normal water though, its touch was a caress, the swipe of a thumb to still tears, inquisitive, tender…

With a trembling hand, I reached for the Bear, uncertain if madness had claimed me in my final moments or if I was somehow finding a clarity which had been evading me from the first second I'd stepped into these cursed trees.

My eyes met the roiling blue tempests of the Bear's and a jolt of understanding struck me, like a pathway had opened up between us and now this creature wanted me to know the way its heart sang.

Iron and soot still sat on my tongue, but as I stared at this spirit of myth and legend, the taste didn't seem so sour anymore. It reminded me of days beneath the sun, splashing in the brook at the bottom of the hill beyond our house with Rissa. It gave me a taste of a joy I'd lost so long ago that I'd almost forgotten the feeling of it.

I stared into the eyes of this magnificent beast and for a moment, I felt what it had once known too, a forest so alive its heartbeat pulsed with each turn of the season. The gift of water so nourishing that the trees bowed in thanks for it as the Bear passed them by.

My lips parted as I caught a glimpse of what felt like both the past and something that might still be again, and my tears became one with the sorrow of the spirit which should have offered me nothing but fear.

I stared into those endlessly blue eyes and the Bear looked back at me like it could see me too, in a way that no other ever had. A low rumble sounded in its chest, but as it dipped its head lower, I found myself needing to know what it meant.

As if that one desire had been the key to a lock, the power of the bear swept around me in full, and its yearning for me to know its pain pressed into my mind without confine.

"Lost."

The word struck me like a blow, the echo of it tumbling through to my core and shifting everything around me on its axis. But before I could respond in any way, the Bear released a bellow which deafened me, a spray of water from its jaws crashing over me before its huge paw swatted me aside like a bug.

I hit the solid trunk of a tree hard enough to knock the breath from my lungs, pain exploding through my side, my terror turning to horror as I found Damon at the Bear's flank, his spear lodged in its thigh.

"Wait!" I scrambled to my feet just as Colton charged into the clearing, his sword held high and a warrior's cry on his lips.

The Bear bellowed as it swung a paw at Damon, striking him so hard that the sound of his spine snapping stuck me like a blow.

I cringed back as the spirit whirled around, water flying from it in every direction, saturating the ground, the trees and the leaves above us as it hunted for more targets to attack. But Colton had gotten behind it and he took a running leap as the spirit rose up onto its haunches with a furious bellow.

"Wait," I gasped, my moment having passed me by before I'd even realised it was upon me. I had no weapon, no way to defeat the spirit, but I had felt the need to claim it like a second heartbeat pounding in my chest.

Colton either didn't hear me or ignored me regardless as he swung his blade with deadly precision and the Bear bellowed mournfully as the blade sank into its heart.

Something cracked apart in my chest as the Bear staggered and then fell, its enormous body headed straight for both me and Colton, its weight sure to crush us both.

I didn't move, I couldn't tear my gaze from the woeful sight of that ethereally beautiful spirit being felled by something as commonly crass as an iron blade. I tipped my head back and stared up at the

Bear as it toppled straight for me, a cry piercing the air as it fell, the haunting beauty of it stealing my breath.

But we weren't flattened as we should have been.

Instead, a flood of water crashed down over us as the spirit disappeared, a swirling torrent of liquid hurtling through the trees and surrounding us like a whirlpool sucked toward a drain.

I staggered within the grasp of its power, my dark hair plastered to my cheeks, my heart breaking as my tears mixed with the water that rushed towards the centre of the clearing and almost swept me along with it.

Something heavy and solid hit the dirt, the last of the water seeming to disappear within it, and the world held its breath for several weighted moments like even the magic of the forest had felt the burden of the Bear's capture.

Colton recovered from the shock of what had happened faster than I could and strode forward to secure his prize.

He stooped, a victorious smile on his lips as he plucked a dark chain from the ground, a hexagonal locket swinging from it, about an inch in length.

I watched stoically as he placed the amulet over his head, the carved Bear on its face looking out at me with such intensity that I was almost certain the Bear itself was peering through the metal to survey me.

The weight of its stare felt like judgement. Betrayal.

I swallowed back the rising bile in my throat.

"At last," Colton said though panted breaths, his shirt clinging to his muscular body, his victory tangling with my bitter disappointment in the air that divided us. "The Hunt is coming to fruition."

I nodded, knowing he was right, that this was what had to be done. The spirits had to be vanquished before the amulets could contain them. Anyone wishing to Summon their power had to prove their worth in capturing them.

But as I followed Colton into the trees, the two of us alone in our hunt now, I couldn't help but mourn the loss of the Bear from these woods. Its existence was tied to the magic of this place, and I could feel an emptiness in the space surrounding us which hadn't been there before.

Worse than that, I'd missed my shot.

I needed to be the one to claim the most amulets if I wanted the forest to grant me its boon. The Bear should have been mine. Rissa was counting on me and I'd failed her.

I spotted my slingshot in the dirt as Colton led the way once more, and I bent down to take it. Bitterness consumed me as I stayed with him in our hunt despite the urge to turn tail and flee his wretched company. But I knew my chances were better with him than alone in this cursed place.

I'd come so close.

Next time, I vowed, I wouldn't let my opportunity slip away. Next time, *I'd* be winning a spirit for myself. I just had to pray that I could.

FERRIS

CHAPTER NINE

Six nights in the forest had done little to make it less daunting and everything to dampen my hopes.

I'd come here knowing full well that this task would be close to impossible but even so, I was being given a sharp taste of reality now that the task had begun in earnest.

I had no spirits to my name, not a single amulet to offer up in payment for the curse the forest suffered under. Worse, since coming face to face with two of the mystical beings which embodied the raw power of this lawless place, I had to question how I might ever hope to overpower one anyway.

I'd always known that defeating the spirits and shattering the spell that had abandoned them to madness would be hard, but now? Well, now I was having to admit to myself that the thought of overpowering one of them with my wits and a slingshot seemed almost impossible.

Not least because of the company I kept.

Colton was stoic in his loyalty to our alliance despite the fact that it seemed far weighted in my favour. But between us, we kept watch, prepared food and sought out shelter each night. We'd even dared to take a taste of the berries and mushrooms on offer between the trees and had thankfully lived to tell the tale.

I'd begun drawing maps of the places we explored, keeping track of the buildings we discovered and taking note of streams, locations with potential for foraging and anything else that might be of use.

I'd been marking out what we'd termed the 'Damned Ones' too. The trees that had consumed fallen Fae and humans alike, keeping them somehow alive while melding their bodies with bark and brush. The poor souls trapped in that fate hissed words of warning at us, speaking as if they knew us, their eyes staring endlessly, pain written in every expression.

I hated them. I knew it made me callous to think so cruelly of living beings suffering such a heinous fate but they only ever filled me with dread. I marked their positions to make certain we avoided seeing any of them twice.

"Do you hear that?" Colton's rough question had me stumbling to a halt, my instincts on high alert.

"What?" I hissed, but he only cocked his head to listen.

A distant cry made my heart lurch with fright, and I wrapped my fingers around my slingshot as I turned to try and determine the direction the sound had come from. There was something about the way noises moved within these woods which made it far harder than it should have been to follow them. We'd spent an hour chasing the trickling sound of a stream yesterday only to give up when the wind turned and it was lost. Not to mention the fact that the trees liked to play their tricks. A path one day could be a chasm the next.

"It could be a trap," I said hesitantly.

"Could be a spirit," Colton replied. "One that someone else has found. We can't risk that happening, we need to make sure it's ours."

I nodded, eyeing him warily. We hadn't spoken frankly about our plans for the remaining spirits but I got the impression he believed I would assist him in capturing them for himself. He knew my motivations for coming here, knew what it was I hunted for in every house we discovered and along every trail we explored, but I didn't think it had occurred to him that I might try to claim it by using the boon.

I supposed I seemed entirely unthreatening to him, the girl who read too many books and had too few friends. But if he truly thought that was all there was to me then he was a fool, and he'd soon come to realise the truth of it.

The cry carried on the wind again, and I bobbed my chin towards a bank on our right where the trees rose up and away from us. We hadn't intended to turn in that direction yet but as Colton nodded his agreement, we both slipped from the path we'd been taking.

Colton unsheathed his sword and I tugged my slingshot free of my belt, palming a stone in my other hand too.

We broke into a run, moving swiftly - though carefully enough to remain quiet. The cries came again, a chorus of terror on the wind, at least two male voices, possibly three.

I bolstered myself for what was to come, wondering if I was going to meet my end in the next clearing this time. It certainly seemed as though my death lingered in these trees, haunting my steps, waiting for its moment. I wasn't confident I would escape it, but I planned on trying my hardest.

We crested the ridge where a circle of huge oak trees were splattered with blood, a man's screams cutting off abruptly before I managed to locate him.

Two more figures had backed up to the edge of a stream, bloody swords raised before them, their shoulders butting against one another.

I made to run towards them, but Colton caught my arm, jerking me to a stop.

"They're Fae," he said gruffly just as one of the males noticed us. He had golden hair which shone even in the poor light beneath the trees, his features a perfect balance of beauty which momentarily startled me.

I'd seen a few Fae when they'd come to trade in our village, but they always kept their hoods high and more often than not covered their features in cowls or scarves. My father had told me it was because they didn't want to dazzle the humans who laid eyes on them, and I'd always thought that was ridiculous until this moment.

"Help us," the male demanded, his tone rankling against everything I was as he made commands of us so easily.

"Come," Colton ordered, turning away and catching my arm to make me follow him.

"You plan on abandoning them?" I asked, tugging out of his hold and tightening my grip on my slingshot. I had no intention of helping the Fae but there still might be a spirit here. We didn't yet know what they were running from.

"That's exactly what they did to us when they built their walls," Colton bit back.

"I don't mean to help them," I hissed, and the golden-haired Fae spat a curse our way as though he'd somehow heard that. "But what if there's a spirit, like you said?"

"I don't like our chances of claiming it from two Fae," Colton grunted, his irritation at that fact clear. "Besides I-" Whatever else he'd been going to say was cut short as his eyes flicked toward something behind me.

A chill slid right through my core and I stilled, like some primordial instinct already felt what was happening before the rest of my brain caught up to it.

I turned just as a guttural shriek burst from the lips of the thing which was running at me through the trees.

My heart leapt into my throat, terror compounding in my veins as it exploded through me on a wave of adrenaline.

The Hollows were in the forest.

I'd come here knowing I would be forced to face all manner of beast and monster, malignant magic and scorned spirits. But the one thing of terrors which I had counted on being able to leave beyond the border of these trees had been the dead who rose at the command of the Necromancer Bane Crownthief and haunted all corners of Rathian for ruinous sport.

The Hollow ran at me with a ferocious want in its faded grey eyes, the beast which had once been a human man now nothing but a feral creature set only on the desire for bloodshed. Rot had begun upon the face of the corpse, a pale blue light clinging to its grey skin where the foul magic which summoned it into being had imbued it.

I turned and bolted, fear blinding me and my instincts taking hold. A Hollow could not be felled by a stone from a slingshot and I had no blade to strike for its heart.

Colton ran too, both of us racing down the hill toward the Fae who clung to the edge of the lake like it was their one hope of salvation. Neither made a move to help us and I cursed myself for ever having come in search of their cries.

The Hollow screamed and slammed into me, knocking me from my feet with the full weight of its decaying body and sending us flying down the bank.

The band of my slingshot caught then ripped free of its holding on one side as I tumbled over the dirt and leaves, kicking and thrashing as the Hollow's fingers bit into my arm and shoulder.

We struck a tree, and I thanked all the spirits in the woods as the beastly thing was knocked off of me and I skidded through the leaves towards the booted feet of the two Fae.

One of them lunged, swinging his sword so close to me that for a moment I saw my death in the reflection of the sharpened steel, but then the Hollow screamed in raw frustration and a severed arm fell to the dirt before me.

I scrambled backwards, kicking out at the creature as it lunged for me again, its dull eyes pinned on me, its want for my death so compelling I could feel the grip of its fist around my soul.

"Not yet," I spat. I'd come too far to fall here now.

The other Fae with dark hair and golden eyes yelled a warning to his companion and leapt over me like I was nothing but a stray log in his path. I didn't care, I was all too happy to allow them to place themselves between me and that monster.

A second Hollow shrieked with violent desire as it ran at us from the trees, this one female, her ragged dress tangling around her long limbs, though she paid it no mind, her sole intent to bring more death to pass.

I backed up further, pushing my useless slingshot back into my pocket before shoving to my feet and hefting a large rock into my grasp, the cold stone weighting me in the moment as my boots splashed into the water at the edge of the lake.

I hunted for Colton in the dim light, finding him fighting yet another of the heinous creatures, his sword swinging with ferocious force that struck the Hollow in the neck and almost decapitated it. Still the beast threw itself at him and I broke into a run as he fell beneath it, hefting my rock in my fist.

Blue light exploded from him before I could reach him, the roar of the Bear echoing from the trees as he Summoned the spirit he had captured to his aid.

The Hollow was thrown clear of Colton, its spine snapping as it struck a tree, but it dragged itself back towards us again.

The Fae males exchanged looks of surprise, but their attention was quickly stolen by the Hollows once more as six more of them burst from the trees.

I turned, hope dimming as I took in the weight of our peril, but Colton had made it back to his feet and the Bear bellowed as it charged between the trees, hunting the Hollows at his command.

The Bear collided with the first corpse, its claws ripping through rotten flesh, water spraying from the spirit's body to pepper the trees and undergrowth, and when it finally leapt free of the Hollow, the monster moved no more.

The two Fae were closing in on Colton, and I broke into a run, wanting to join with them too, but a hard body slammed into me before I could take more than a handful of steps.

I hit the dirt beneath the weight of the Hollow, rancid breath flowing over rotten teeth as it lunged for my face and worked to rip into my skin.

I cried out in pain as its fingernails carved into the flesh of my chest, my hand closing around its neck as I fought to force it back.

The rock still filled my other hand and I swung it with all my might, a sickening crack confirming its impact with the Hollow's skull, though I knew that wasn't the way to its demise.

I thrashed and fought beneath my foe, calling Colton's name in a desperate plea as the Bear raced through the trees, ripping the Hollows to pieces and claiming their destruction one by one.

"I'm coming Ferris!" he yelled, and I caught sight of his boots pounding through the dead leaves, a second set of heavy boots right behind him.

"Colton," I gasped as the Hollow's hand pressed down on my throat, its weight crushing the air from my lungs.

I swung my rock again and again, but the Hollow paid it no mind, its attention never wavering from the prize of my death as it fought to rip me apart.

Water crashed over me and the Bear bellowed as it tore the Hollow off of me, its powerful jaws snapping the corpse in two and puncturing its heart at last so that the rotting remains fell still.

Colton reached for me but as he bent low, hand outstretched, the dark-haired Fae slammed into him, knocking him straight into the path of a pair of Hollows.

I screamed in horror as the living dead took hold of Colton's arms, tearing at him with inhuman strength, hauling him in differing directions as they fought over their prize.

The Bear ran back through the clearing, racing to the aid of its master, but with a sickening scream, the Hollows claimed Colton's death before the spirit could save him.

A cry ran ragged through my throat, horror engulfing me as my one true ally in this place was torn away in a flash of bloody violence which left me reeling in shock.

The Bear exploded in a wash of water, its energy spiralling away, sinking back into the amulet which had fallen to the forest floor, useless without anyone to Summon its power.

I stared up at the dark-haired Fae in horror as he grinned triumphantly and stalked forward to take the amulet as his reward for that murderous act.

But the bastard had struck too soon and three Hollows still stood, seeking our demise.

Two of them charged for the blonde Fae, knocking him from his feet, his panicked screams ringing out through the trees.

The bastard who had killed Colton ran to his aid, his duplicity clearly only stretching towards my kind and not his own. My pain and fury over the death of the one Champion who had stood by my side roared within my skull and a want for his murderer's death rose within me.

The last Hollow chased him, every monster in the clearing forgetting the pathetic human who still drew breath among them.

Tears burned the backs of my eyes as I took in Colton's mutilated corpse, then my gaze spilled to the amulet which had cost him his life.

I got to my feet, meaning to claim it for myself, but as I reached for it, my eyes caught on a dagger at Colton's belt instead.

My fingers curled around the blade and I tugged it free, my chest rising and falling with heavy breaths as I looked to the bastard who had killed my friend.

He fought his own foe with furious panic as the blonde male screamed his death cries beneath the weight of the Hollows who had pinned him to the dirt.

I watched, a deep coldness settling over me as they fought for their lives. The blonde male released a strangled scream as a Hollow tore out his throat and Colton's dark-haired murderer cried out in anguish. His pain did little to stifle my own.

He cut down the Hollow he was fighting, then ran through another but the third tackled him, taking him to the ground.

"Help!" he begged as the Hollow clawed and ripped at his face, shredding the beauty from him and revealing the monster beneath.

"No," I spat, backing away, leaving him to his death in payment for Colton's.

The forest loomed around me and I turned, meaning to run from this place of horrors and instead colliding with another of the deadly Hollows.

I was knocked against the thick trunk of a tree, the back of my head connecting with it and my vision shuttering as I swung a poorly aimed stab at the creature intent on my death.

Rotten teeth and a ghastly face void of a nose lunged for me, my demise burning in its shadow-coated eyes.

I screamed as I stabbed at it wildly, rancid blood spilling over my fist and doing nothing at all to halt the monster as it pinned me to the tree and lunged for my throat, my forearm crashing against its neck as I fought to hold it back.

Again and again I stabbed at it, my screams echoing off the branches of the uncaring trees, the forest leaning close to watch as my death rushed closer. And in the depths of their rustling leaves and tangled limbs I found my name whispering between them, beckoning me close, making their claim.

"Come, Ferris. It's time. Ferris...Ferris...Ferris..."

I stabbed and stabbed, hunting for a heart I couldn't find, every second punctuated by the frantic thundering of my pulse as I fought with all I had for a life I'd barely begun to live.

I cried out for help that wouldn't come, fighting with a feral determination I'd never known I had, desperate to survive despite the odds promising I wouldn't. For my parents, for Rissa, for all I hadn't yet done.

With brutal ferocity, I kept stabbing even as my arm ached with fatigue and the Hollow crushed me to the tree, even as my reason for entering this cursed forest taunted me and my chances of doing what I'd sworn to do diminished with every passing second.

But still I fought, and I would keep fighting, on and on and on until my dying breath left me and even then, I'd resist it with all I had and all I was. For her.

HENDRIX

CHAPTER TEN

I'd been tracking a spirit all day. The clever beastie was made for stealth, outwitting me time and again. But I'd caught a glimpse of its blazing red tail, had almost grasped a handful of its flaming fur once before it had slipped through my fingers like a ghost. But at last, I had it cornered.

A great waterfall thundered down a rockface before me, the sheer walls reaching up far too steeply for even the Fox spirit to climb. That was my hope anyway.

I crouched in the long grass, legs cramping from how long I'd maintained the position, waiting for it to show itself. Surely it thought it'd lost me by now.

I was reminded of a time long ago, a hook of a memory catching in my brain, of me stalking my little brother in the grass, capturing him by the ankles and tickling him until he couldn't breathe. That image of me was like viewing another person through a faraway lens. It was distorted, not marrying up with who I was now.

I didn't indulge in child's play anymore. Those desires had been gutted out of me, the hands of reality carving away the goodness

I might have once claimed and leaving only rot behind. I couldn't deny how much I'd festered since. I supposed when you lived long enough, eventually the bad things began to pile up. One on top of the other until something so terrible came along that it cracked the mind and shattered the peace for good.

The raging falls concealed the sound of my approach as I crawled toward the spirit through the grass. It was difficult to hear much beyond the crashing of the water, but every now and then I thought I caught the yells of a woman in the distance. I didn't turn my head from the Fox, gaze fixed unwaveringly as I became nothing more than a hunter in the grass. It may have been powerful, but it hadn't met the likes of me yet.

The Fox's strength was great, the air alight with it, and I knew possessing it would put me in good stead for gaining more amulets. There it waited for me, a thing of wild beauty, its fur a swirling storm of fire. Flames of red, orange and gold fluttered from its body in an ever-fluid movement and embers spiralled upward, only to be recollected by the spirit's eternal fire. The power of this spirit thrummed in the atmosphere, clogging my lungs. And it was still unawares of my presence.

Now was the time to seize it.

Just as I shifted forward, a scream cut through the air sharp enough to break through the roar of the waterfall, startling the Fox and making my head turn too, a growl rolling up my throat.

My spirit darted, rushing toward me, and I lunged to grab it with a curse, the movement clumsy in my distraction. It leapt aside and darted past me in a whirl of fire, racing away through the grass in an instant. I watched as it leapt between two trees, a flash of golden flames spilling away into the shadows. Then it was gone.

A snarl tore from my lips, and I turned my gaze in the direction that female scream had come from, back through the dark forest behind me.

I shoved to my feet and stalked toward the sound, unsheathing my dagger as frustration ripped through me.

"Your screams will be all the louder when I find you," I bit out, the words muffled by the mask I had pulled up over my face. I'd decided it was best to remain anonymous in this place so as not to draw attention to my presence. I knew the hatred for me ran deep enough that the fair folk would likely unite against me if they learned of my presence here.

That didn't mean I was playing coward. I planned to snatch as many amulets as possible from this forest, then show myself to my old kin and watch the smiles crumble from their faces. I'd once had a flair for the dramatic and it liked to rear its head occasionally.

It wasn't difficult to follow the commotion, the sounds drawing me along the river which spilled away from the waterfall directly towards a lake where my screamer must have been. I'd snap her neck - or I might make it slower if she was Fae. Perhaps it would be Princess Drava herself, in dire need of assistance only to find the Fae she had summoned to her aid was a greater monster than the one she faced between these trees.

I made it to a clearing between two towering oaks, finding a human woman on her knees in a sludge of mud, shaking the arm of a dead-looking mortal man who had been ripped apart by some beast. Blood stained her body, her once-green dress more red and brown because of the muck. There were plenty of body parts strewn around that spoke of recent carnage and I recognised Hollows among the gaunt faces of the dead. The destruction was a familiar sight to my eyes, the violence these creatures could reap upon human and Fae alike was unlike any other. I'd known the Hollows were here, chasing death between these trees, but I hadn't witnessed their bloodshed until now.

Darkness settled over me, sinking into my bones and painting them black. This was the plague of Rathian, the one feared more than any other. Even more loathsome to its inhabitants than the bane of the cursed forest.

I regarded the woman who was yet to note my arrival. Her hair was long and brown, hanging around a face I couldn't get a decent look at from this angle.

I whistled to catch her attention and she whipped around, causing me to cock my head and study her even closer. She was an intriguing thing indeed. Her heart-shaped face held the beauty of Fae but without the perfection of my dull kind. She had a wild look in her uniquely violet eyes that told of her mortality, and I could almost taste the fear on her, the uncertainty of the big bad world she found herself in. But then she lifted her chin, rose to her feet and pointed a stick at me. Not even a branch. It was even more breakable than she was.

Those eyes continued to blaze at me and I frowned at their brilliance, how they shone with a near-ethereal light. I had only seen that colour once before in my many years of life. In a place I'd had no right to enter. In the presence of a creature so mighty, it had undone the threads of my heart and broken me apart piece by piece. I could have sworn I was standing before that very beast now, the spirit of Providence itself. Intriguing indeed. How did a human girl go about possessing eyes the colour of fate itself?

"Who are you?" she demanded, and it was so forceful a command it made me bark a wicked laugh. But the smile on my lips dropped to a flat and cruel line as I took a step toward her and she stumbled over a rock, falling onto her ass beneath me. It felt good to have her there, and I revelled in glaring down at the useless little human who was still pointing a stick at me.

I was struck by her ferocity, the set of her jaw reminding me of the warriors of my family. The keenness they had possessed for victory. My gaze fell to her lips, the curve of them making my throat tighten and my fingers flex with the desire to touch her. I could break her neck, that would be the quickest way to do it. But I rather liked the thought of punishing her first. Slowly enough to hear her scream for me. Only for me this time.

I mulled over the answer to her question, uncertain why I'd decided to give one instead of killing her immediately.

"My name is Hendrix Draven, I hail from Mithelnore in Rivenspire," I told her. "And who are you, little mud-dweller? A pig come to wallow in the dirt?"

I stepped toward her again and she shoved to her feet, stick still very much pointed at my heart. Was she planning to skewer me on a twig?

"I'm Ferris Creed," she said firmly. "The people I was travelling with are dead."

"Yes, I see that. Never mind, another few humans will be born this hour to replace them easily enough. Your kind breed like rabbits."

I swept a hand out indicating the dead I was speaking about, my gaze tracking over them coldly, then halting on the faces of the deceased Fae. I recognized one of them with a breath of amusement passing my lips. Jarta Cageworth with his floppy brown hair and too-smiley mouth had been the type of male who had enjoyed watching his enemies get whipped until the flesh was flayed from their bones. His casual jovialness had never married with the harsh cruelty he could so easily deliver to those who wronged him.

The crimes he named could be as little as a snigger in his direction. Spirits help the servants who had doggedly tried to please him. I supposed they were free of him now though and I was rather glad I'd never have to endure his haughty laughter again either.

The other Fae was unknown to me, more youthful than I was no doubt. Perhaps born after I had been run out of Rivenspire.

"You're lucky to have survived the Hollows," I commented. "Perhaps a flock of lightwings brushed you with their feathers moments before the attack." I glanced around in amusement, as if looking for the small bird-like spirits which granted good fortune to those they came across.

"Lucky?" she snarled. "My friend is dead." She gestured to the bloodied human man on the ground and I blandly offered him my attention.

"Unfortunate," I said dryly.

"Fuck you," she growled.

My eyebrows arched as I spotted an amulet on the ground near to the dead human, the image of the Bear carved into its surface. I dropped down, snatching it but finding a soft hand grabbing hold of mine, nails trying to tear into my skin.

I looked to the human in surprise and she released a yell then jammed her stick into my kidney. It snapped of course and I threw my forearm against her chest, knocking her to the ground from the force.

"That's mine," she spat.

I ignored her, the rush of seizing an amulet at last bringing a heady sensation with it. It shimmered like water, glittering as if sunlight lay upon a pool. The Bear was a powerful spirit, a true prize.

I placed it around my neck and as its weight settled against my chest, a rumbling sense of magic coursed through my blood. It built like a thunderous river running through my veins and the Bear's roar resounded through my skull like the crash of a raging waterfall. The power was immense, the amulet trembling as if it could barely contain what lay within it, but it held. The power of the amulets was as ancient as the sky, a force forged of nature itself and this forest and all its spirits could do nothing but bow to it.

My pretty little human lunged up from the mud again, reaching for the amulet but I grabbed her by the throat, stalling her in her tracks, easily lifting her feet from the ground. Her eyes widened and death drew closer, seeking to claim my prey.

"So breakable," I commented, feeling her pulse thrash beneath my fingertips.

She didn't give up fighting, clawing at my arm and cursing me with strangled breaths. She even swung for my mask to unveil my face to her, as if that would do anything at all to help her. I was a cat with a bird between its paws. One bite was all it would take to end this creature, but instead I decided to play with my food. Though perhaps it was more than that, something holding me back, that fight in her igniting an ancient longing in my heart – though I couldn't put a name to it.

Movement to my right made my head whip around and a glint of large claws in the trees told of some spirit there. But the moment my gaze fell on it, it shrank away into the shadows again. I itched to follow, but dusk was already drawing in and a pursuit now might just spell the end for me. A thought crossed my mind that made my fingers loosen on my captive's throat. Had a spirit come to investigate the human's screams? Well, well. That could be useful…

I dropped my thrashing human girl and she landed heavily on her feet, almost falling again but righting herself at the last moment.

I caught her hand in mine, soft fingers snared tight between the roughness of my own.

"I've decided to let you live," I announced, tugging her close and drowning in the stormy nature of those violet eyes of hers. They were like the ocean, a calm and rolling ride one moment, then a violent cyclone the next.

"For what purpose?" she hissed, trying to hide the fear in her eyes, but she knew I could have no decent intentions towards her.

"For company," I deadpanned, and she glowered at me, trying to pull her hand free of mine but there was no doing that.

"Let go of me," she demanded, starting to fight again, but her strikes were barely more than butterflies' wings against my skin.

"I will not."

"I'm not going anywhere with you," she snapped.

"I do not need to ask," I said darkly and a little shudder ran through her shoulders, though she didn't stop fighting.

"I will fight you every step of the way," she hissed.

"Then fight. It means nothing to me." I dragged her along,

sending her feet stumbling over each other, but she stayed upright thanks to my grip.

"Your kind are the reason my friend is dead," she snarled, her nails tearing at my hand around hers. "I despise you. For that and far more. I will never let you take me."

I rounded on her, my gaze cold and unrelenting. "You will follow me, lightwing, because it's getting dark now, and you don't want to be left out here when the forest comes for you at dusk. Better to stay in my shadow because there is one thing the Taking Trees fear in this dark and harrowing world, and that's me."

"*I* don't fear you," she hissed, the lie so apparent it was almost laughable.

I smiled beneath my mask, knowing she couldn't see it, but her face paled all the same.

"Yes, you do. But not nearly enough. Because soon you will have no greater nightmare than me, Ferris Creed."

Ferris

CHAPTER ELEVEN

The Fae dragged me through the forest, ignoring the way I tried to prise his fingers from my hand and dig my heels into the mud.

I cursed him, kicking out at his knee, but he only turned a savage glare on me before hauling me onwards again.

It was impossible to tell much of his expression with the hood shrouding his eyes and mask pulled up to cover the lower half of his face but there was no mistaking the prowling, powerful body of this beast. He was twice my size and then some, his height towering over my own so that I was forced to tip my head back to look up at him. His body was thick with muscle in a way I'd never seen on a human man and something in the depths of my gut made my hackles rise at his mere presence.

Every instinct in me was screaming a warning to run the hell away from him, telling me that this male was one thing and one thing alone.

Hunter.

And I wasn't going to become his prey.

I stopped fighting, allowing him to tug me further into the trees, away from the clearing and the pool of water where my last ally had met with death. I was alone out here now. Colton's death was a brutal, harsh stab of reality which had burst my final bubble of security like the flimsy fabrication it had been. Because of course I hadn't been safe in Colton's company despite how powerful he had seemed. And now I was going to have to face the horrors of this cursed place alone. But maybe that was for the best. I hadn't come here expecting any form of help. I'd come to win the forest's boon for myself and I needed to be more ruthless in doing so.

I may have been trapped in the company of this beast, but I refused to remain so for long. I could have wept for my stupidity in not claiming the Bear faster but snatching it while Colton's body was still warm had felt like a betrayal. I wouldn't allow such soft sentiment to rule me again.

The moment Hendrix's posture signalled his belief in his victory over me, I lunged forward and sank my teeth into the fingers which were coiled tightly around my wrist.

The Fae cursed, snatching his hand away and I wasted no time in launching myself into the trees, his blood staining my lips and adrenaline flooding my limbs.

The forest shivered and hissed amusement, the leaves whispering with each other like a thousand expressions of laughter.

Hendrix's footsteps pounded after me but the trees seemed keen on encouraging this chase, roots slipping out of my path and then snapping into his. I chanced a look over my shoulder as his boot snagged on one and he almost tripped, his hand colliding with the thick trunk of a tree as he caught himself.

"Stop!" he bellowed in a tone which told me he expected the entire world to bend to his commands, but I was no follower of Fae.

Grief clung to me as I ran on, the memory of Colton's corpse and the Fae who had caused his death spurring me on faster, urging me to escape. I wouldn't bend to whatever ploy that bastard had in mind for me and I would face the darkness of the forest before I bowed to his orders.

But his footsteps were gaining on me.

"Please," I begged the spirits, the trees, the dirt beneath my feet, anything which might heed my plea in this place of powerful magic. "Help me."

Shrubs parted, vines whipping aside as the forest opened up a pathway for me to follow and for once I was willing to take its lead. Whatever these trees might have in store for me couldn't possibly match the wild wrath I found burning in the eyes of my pursuer as I glanced back to find him hindered by the same plants which were helping me.

I leapt over a fallen log, vaulted a small stream and weaved through a coppice of saplings which tangled themselves together in my wake, blocking me from his view.

"You can't think you can truly outrun me!" he roared, but his voice was wrapped in the whispering of the trees, a flash of darkness overhead making me wonder if more than just the forest was watching me flee.

"Thank you," I gasped between laboured breaths, uncertain if it was madness to converse with the trees or simply good manners. They were helping me after all.

I almost screamed as I came upon one of the Damned Ones, the woman's body almost entirely engulfed in the bark of a large horse chestnut tree ahead of me.

"Beneath these trees your fate will rise. Beware the one with silvered eyes!" she wailed at me.

I lurched away from her at speed, rounding a great, weathered oak and spied a ramshackle building with a mouldering roof and walls of grey stone. It looked to have once been a stable if the row of stalls was anything to go by and I wasted no time in hurling myself through the closest door.

Darkness was encroaching on the forest, night drawing near, and if I had any luck at all, then perhaps he wouldn't find this place and would be caught out there when it fell, the beasts of the midnight hours consuming him for me.

I crept deeper into the stall, my feet snagging on mildewed hay as I sought a way into the rest of the building. Thankfully there was another door at the back of the stable, leading into a wide hall where saddles coated in mould and bridles with rusted bits hung forgotten.

"Do you really think you can escape me?!" Hendrix shouted from somewhere in the trees and I flinched, pressing deeper into the dim building and spying a ladder which led to a hayloft above.

I gripped the ladder, feeling the silken moss on the rungs beneath my fingertips. The wood flexed beneath my hold and a pang of dread resounded through my bones. But it would have to do.

Without allowing a single doubt to cross my mind, I began to climb, my eyes on the square opening which led into the hayloft beyond. Six rungs, seven, eight, nine –

I barely stifled a scream as the tenth split beneath my weight and fell with a clatter to the flagstones below, leaving me dangling by my fingers above a drop which may not have killed me but would certainly hurt like a bitch.

My legs swung wildly as I fought to heave myself up and get a foot on the next rung.

Footsteps crunched across dead leaves far too close for my liking and I prayed to all the spirits in the forest for aid.

With a surge of strength, I managed to pull myself higher, my foot finding purchase at last and allowing me to reach for the edge of the hayloft's entrance.

I scrambled inside and then dragged the ladder up behind me, cursing as it groaned at the imposition and made my arms strain at the effort. I dug my heels into the wooden platform beneath me and with a final haul, the ladder thumped down on the mouldy hay beside me, knocking me back with it.

My breaths came in shaky rasps but I froze in place as a solid thump punctuated the opening of a nearby door.

"Has no one ever told you that its foolish to run from a Fae?" he rumbled, his low baritone sending a tremor of fear through my flesh. His question was a taunt but I knew better than to answer it. He couldn't be certain I was here. I'd been too far ahead of him and the dry ground hadn't provided a place for me to have left tracks. All I had to do was stay silent and wait him out.

His boots thumped slowly across the floor, his pace a prowl, his aura oppressive. It was like the air itself was shifting aside to make room for him as he entered, knowing that it was nothing in comparison to him. He oozed power like a physical force, its weight cloying, suffocating.

Strands of hay tickled my face, trembling against my lips with each stilted breath I allowed past them. My bed was far from comfortable, every stalk prodding me with purposeful precision while the scent of damp and mould choked me. But I refused to move an inch. He'd hear me if I did. I knew that much about his kind. Their senses were razor sharp, their instincts more like a beast's than a man's.

They had powers too, each of them born with a single gift which manifested itself when they reached adulthood. I'd heard of Fae who could call the light of the sun from their palms, converse with animals and bend them to their will, toss shadows from their fingertips or spin silk from nothing but the wind. I only hoped the brute hunting me didn't possess the ability to track down prey at will because it certainly felt like he was doing just that, his presence encompassing this entire building like he might scent me in the dark.

His boots thumped slowly around the stable and he hummed a low tune which turned my blood to ice in my veins. I painted an X in the scratchy hay at my side but superstition had never saved me before.

Something scratched against the walls, the roof, like the scurrying of tiny claws moving closer.

In the rafters overhead a shadow moved and my heart leapt in fear as I felt eyes upon me. But he couldn't be up there. It had to be a rat or a mouse, the scratching marking its movements. But if he were anointed with the power over creatures-

Something struck the rotting wood of the hay loft right beneath me, the jolt of the impact rattling through my bones before the whole thing groaned and began to give way.

I scrambled to get up, reaching for a knotted rope which hung against the wall. My fingers brushed it as the floor beneath me collapsed and I leapt for it, a small window beyond offering my only chance of escape.

My foot struck the beam at the edge of the window but my boot slipped on the coil of rope. I screamed as I pitched backwards, my fingers knotting in the rope like it might somehow save me - and in a way it did. I still fell but as I yanked the rope tight it snared my foot and hoisted me skyward by my ankle before jamming against the rafter.

I jerked to a halt upside down, dangling by one foot, a swathe of dark hair filled with strands of mouldy hay blanketing my face.

I spun wildly before a hand caught my shoulder, jerking me to a halt.

My hair tumbled out of my face and I found myself eye to eye with the beast who had hunted me here, and I glared at him while dangling upside down.

"Are you done yet?" he drawled and I spat in his face, saliva striking his mask before my fist followed it.

He jerked his head back in surprise, the black fabric of his mask falling down to reveal the sculpted lines of his features. I glared at him while he scowled right back, his brow low over eyes that were as deep a green as the forest we were trapped within. His chiselled jaw was rough with inky black stubble to match the strands of hair which had fallen from his hood to surround his roughened features.

My breath caught as I studied him, my eyes tracing a tattoo

which framed his left eye roaming from his temple down to kiss his sharp cheekbone. It resembled a figure of eight with a line striking it through and small fragments of twisted symbols surrounding it. Just looking at the mark made a shiver burn through me, that oppressive power of his flaring at the attention I offered it.

"Let me go," I snarled.

"Gladly." He took a dagger from his belt and hurled it with such speed I barely had time to flinch, my gut bottoming out as I found myself falling a moment later.

I threw my hands up to try and shield my face but strong arms caught me a moment before I could strike the ground and then swung me up and over his shoulder.

"Put me down!" I yelled, my fists thumping against his back as I squirmed and kicked to get free but he only grunted in annoyance and clamped his arm more forcefully around my legs.

"No. I think I'll find a use for you, lightwing. Besides, you walked so willingly into my domain, I can only assume you were seeking a place to stay."

Hendrix strode from the stables and circled it in the dim light of the evening. I cursed him, still trying to fight my way free, but he paid me no attention whatsoever as I thrashed and struck him, then began calling him every foul name I could think of.

I barely even noticed as he took a winding stone path through a set of open, rusted gates choked with ivy and rusting beneath the sway of the forest, but I felt the heavy shadow of a large building fall over us and turned my head to look at it.

Hidden within the depths of the trees was a castle built of brown and cream stone, topped with pale blue turrets which tapered to spires as they reached toward the sky with a coat of vines and ivy draping from every angle. Green algae clung to the walls beneath the windows like tears spilling from the eyes of a forgotten giant, dripping to soak the ground with the evidence of their grief.

Clearly Hendrix was familiar with this place because he strode straight for the heavy wooden doors and pushed them open, causing a low groan to echo out into the empty building.

He carried me inside before kicking the door closed and moving to secure it with the turn of a key in an ancient lock.

"What is this place?" I demanded, though his silence up to this point implied I'd get no answers, but he did in fact reply.

"This was once the home of a Fae family. One of the most powerful bloodlines of our kind. The forest doesn't care for such claims however and took it nigh on fifty years ago now."

I'd known the place was Fae-built before he gave his answer but my skin still prickled at the news. There were no human properties such as this. The only castles my kind had built were squat and practical, intended for defence not beauty. But of course we'd never been able to indulge in the luxuries the Fae delighted in with frivolity. We'd been out there fighting the forest on one side and the Hollows on the other for so long that none of us really knew how to indulge in anything at all.

Hendrix kicked open a door to the left of the wide hallway and strode into a plush lounge with dark green armchairs arranged close to a dominating fireplace. There were tapestries hung on the walls along with beautifully-crafted glass braziers that had been sculpted to look like tulips. A red rug adorned the dark wood floor and gilded candlesticks decorated the mahogany side tables.

The world flipped as Hendrix tossed me down into one of the chairs and I fell into it with a heavy thump.

I kicked out at him, my boot catching his shin. He lunged at me, his hands crashing down on the arms of my chair, his face leering so close to mine that we might have been lovers a breath from a kiss.

He snarled at me, baring his teeth like a beast, and I bared mine right back, though I didn't strike at him again.

"Stay," he growled, jabbing a finger at me which hit my shoulder and knocked me back against the plush cushion of the chair.

I only scowled as he straightened, watching him while he stooped before the fireplace and deftly set a mound of kindling aflame before adding some larger sticks to the blaze.

The crackle of the building fire was the only sound while its orange light crept from beneath the mantlepiece and brushed across the room in measured inches. My eyes drank in the details of everything it illuminated, slipping across the room towards the heavily-shuttered window.

Hendrix finally placed a larger log on the fire and then stood, removing his cape and revealing the full length of his hair beneath the hood. It was as dark as night itself, running down his spine in twisted tangles which only seemed to draw more attention to the breadth of his powerful shoulders.

He tossed the cape and the mask he'd worn onto a chair a little further from the fire and I caught a glimpse of more tattoos around his throat, skeletal fingers ringing his neck like death itself was trying to choke him and failing.

He said nothing as he turned and strode from the room, leaving me coiled in my chair like a spring ready to explode into action.

I counted his footsteps as he headed away down the hall beyond the room and when I reached double digits I sprang upright and ran for the shutters. They were locked, metal rods holding them in place and it took me several seconds to figure out how to open the contraption before finding a handle and turning it.

The rods twisted, shifting apart and I yanked the shutters wide, reaching for the latch which secured the pane of glass, my fingers grazing it just before a rough and calloused hand clamped down over mine.

"Do you covet death, lightwing?" Hendrix cooed, his solid body a wall at my back, his pulse a drum against my spine, so slow, so steady, while mine was the frantic flutter of a hummingbird's wings.

I opened my mouth to reply and then stilled as movement in

the darkness beyond the window stole my focus. The trees were thrashing as if a storm hounded them, though no rain spilled down to crash against the dirt. A deep, guttural roar shook the air and Hendrix tugged me away from the window, slamming the shutters and barring them once more.

"Have you forgotten the rules of this game you so foolishly chose to play?" he asked in a growl, releasing me from the heat of his flesh as he gave me a rough shove back into the centre of the room. "The night will swallow you whole and spit your bones out again within minutes."

"As if I'm any safer in here with you," I hissed, retreating from him, and he broke a dark laugh.

"At least you're quick on the uptake. Yes, I am just as terrifying as the things that lurk beneath those trees, my sweet savage, if not more so. But luckily for you, I don't feel inclined to feast on your flesh. For now."

The way he said those words made heat rise in my cheeks, my stomach knotting at the implications behind them. My gaze darted to the window once more as I considered whether I would be better off taking my chances in the trees at night than locked up in this castle with him.

"There are clean clothes in the rooms upstairs and water to bathe yourself should you wish to rid us both of the stench that clings to you," he said dismissively, waving a hand towards the door. "Unless of course your hatred for my kind extends as far as refusing the hospitality of a long lost castle in the middle of a cursed forest?"

"I'll gladly steal from the Fae," I told him defiantly, backing up towards the door, refusing to give him my back. "After all, you owe me that much."

"Do I now?" he mused, a hint of taunt in his molten jade eyes.

"Yes." I backed out of the door and closed it for good measure, wanting to put as many obstacles between us as I could.

I instantly missed the warmth of the fire but I would gladly forgo it in payment for leaving his company.

Fucking Fae. I hated them. I hated them more than the forest itself - which was saying a whole hell of a lot after what these cursed trees had taken from me. But it was the Faes' fault in the first place. Their kind who had caused my loss and stolen Rissa from us. Their kind who I hoped would pay for it in the end. Though not before I got what I'd come here for.

I backed away from the stairs and glanced around. The hallway was lit from the glow of the sconces, the flickering light casting dancing shadows on the ceiling, highlighting a mural which had been painted there of a Fae female surrounded by pink and peach peonies. There was no sign of mould or damp despite the amount of time which Hendrix had claimed this place had spent within the grips of the forest and I had to wonder if the Fae had ways of protecting against such things.

I stifled my curiosity on Fae architecture and hurried up the wide, pale marble staircase, my fingers trailing along a banister carved to look like a winding grape vine complete with plush bunches of fruit which made my empty stomach growl.

At the top of the stairs were at least ten rooms, all hidden behind wooden doors carved with symbols of the sun at their centre. I pushed open the first one I came to, finding the sconces lit in there too and a bedchamber which was larger than the bar at the tavern in my town. The bed itself was a monstrosity, a carved four-poster with gauzy blue drapes hanging around it and plush cushions whispering for me to join them.

I pressed the door closed at my back, releasing a slow breath as I finally gained some more distance from my unwelcome housemate. I was going to have to stay here tonight but at dawn I'd be gone. I'd plan my escape before curling up in that beautiful bed and stealing what rest I could while I had the chance, then I'd be out of here at the first shard of light over the horizon.

I moved to the dresser where a pitcher of water stood beside a shallow, golden bowl, a bar of apricot-scented soap making me groan with longing. Hendrix may have been an ass but he was right – I was covered in filth and gore, blood dried beneath my fingernails and in my hair too. I needed to bathe. A tub would have been a dream but clean water and soap were the next best things. There was even a stack of washcloths.

A heavy armoire stood to the side of the shuttered windows and I inched toward it, wondering about the promise of clothing he'd mentioned. My green dress had been ruined my very first day here and I would gladly burn the tattered, stained and stinking fabric in the closest fire given the chance.

I eased open the door to the armoire and drew in a sharp breath. There were all kinds of clothes intended for a Fae who had clearly lost her home without enough warning to gather her belongings from it. There were trousers and tunics, boots and warm cloaks, all things which would definitely be practical and well-wearing for the coming days in the forest. But there were gowns too. The kinds of gowns that dreams were made of and no mere human had ever so much as gazed upon, let alone been given free access to.

I ran my fingers over the fine brocade of a navy blue dress which had tiny sapphires inlaid in its skirt and grinned. The clothes had been made for a Fae and would be long on me, but I was tall, and aside from that, they looked like they'd fit me well enough.

So, a Fae had kidnapped me to his castle and planned to torture me with extravagant clothes, a place to bathe and a bed larger than the room I grew up in? Did he expect me to baulk at such a thing? How utterly awful of him. I would have no choice but to take full advantage of the opulence at my fingertips in defiance of the pointless pride he might expect me to have. Would I deign to wear the clothes of my enemy? Would I deign to take comfort in their castle? Why yes, yes I would. And I planned on doing so as utterly obnoxiously as possible.

HENDRIX

CHAPTER TWELVE

Despite my failures in this cursed place, it felt good to strive for something again. I'd hungered for an answer all these years and finally the forest had provided it. A boon which I had long underestimated, not realising how powerful it really might be until I'd bargained with a Hag for an answer to my dilemma. Yes, she had taken a wicked price from me in payment. But it had been worth the knowledge that the forest could be the answer to my desires.

It was strange that the answer had laid here of all places, because since the Great Hunt had begun all those years ago, I had often felt the urge to take part in it. Every fifty years as the Hunt approached, the pull had been almost irresistible, but what use would such a trial have been to me? Back then, I'd dismissed it, putting it down to the forest's twisted magic, but perhaps it had been trying to tell me what the Hag had told me in the end.

After so long feeling lost, I was finally on track to my goal. The emptiness that had taken up residence in my bones felt fuller than it had in far too long. But something was missing even now. I experienced life like I was one of the Hollows, as dead as them inside but still moving, seeking something alive to sustain myself.

These past decades, the world had become a dreary artist's palette of greys and darkest blues, set to depict a gloomy, soulless sky. And here in this painter's landscape, I remained trapped.

My mind turned to the human girl and all her untamed desires. Ferris Creed. Life had likely been harsh to her - as it was to most humans. She didn't have the roughened look of a land worker, but she was not so delicate in appearance as a seamstress. Those were common trades among her kind, yet she didn't strike me as common. I could ask of course, if I cared to. But I did not.

"Henry?" Her voice. She repeated the name. Three times more in fact.

I didn't know who this Henry was or why she was calling for him now, but she was disturbing the quiet. Perhaps she had named a dormouse and lost the thing when it scampered down a hole. They liked their pets, the humans. They lived shorter lives than even them. I supposed it gave mortals a taste of the immortal life. Watching their little friends die well before their own time came.

Ferris entered the room, walking over and snapping her fingers in front of my face. Ever so slowly, I dragged my eyes away from the blazing fire and regarded her.

"My name is Hendrix."

"My mistake," she said innocently, though she was sharp enough to have not forgotten it.

My jaw flexed at the creature staring down at me. She had chosen to dress herself in a silk gown, the navy blue fabric clinging to her body and drawing my gaze to the enticing curve of her hips. Her brown hair was freshly washed, hanging in loose curls over her shoulders and tumbling down her spine, caressing a slender neck which begged for the touch of roughened fingers.

The scent of apricot hung on my captive and anger coiled in my chest at her clear mockery of my imprisonment. Dressing herself up as a damsel, but the hardness to her eyes dared me to reveal her true nature.

I rose abruptly to my feet, knocking her back a step, but my hand landed firmly on the base of her spine and a taunting grin lifted my lips. I snatched her hand in mine, raising it high and yanking her firmly against me, forcing her to waltz with me, though her feet stumbled over my own.

"Let go of me," Ferris hissed, alarm rising in her eyes, but she had started the game.

"You come to me dressed for a ball and you won't even dance with the only other guest here? Tut tut, lightwing, perhaps a punishment is in order." I let my smile drop, showing the monster beneath the mask, and she tried to pull back again, a shaky breath fluttering across her lips. Lips which drew my gaze and made me wonder what a mortal mouth would feel like against my own. Her kind were often obsessed with mine, our appearances far more appealing to them than each other were. But the fact she that was drawing my attention in kind invoked a deep rage inside me and I wouldn't be tempted to take a bite. No female, human or Fae had ever had that kind of power over me. I was always the one in control, the one who could cut the cord at any moment, and that was how it would stay.

I forced her to spin beneath my arm and then tossed her haphazardly toward the chair. Her ass hit the arm of it, but she caught herself before she fell backwards into the seat.

"I'm hungry," she blurted, a demand to her tone.

I arched a brow as she righted herself, chin lifting, determination sparking in her violet eyes. I took my time to answer, peeling her apart with the lingering look. Pretty thing she was. But she carried a burden on her. Perhaps just the weight of a mortal life, but it might have been more than that. A mouth as sweet as hers should have worn a thousand smiles, but I suspected it had worn less than she had hoped to win from life. Pity.

I supposed I needed to feed my bait if I was going to keep her living long enough to capture me a spirit. I turned my back on her, heading from the room with her quick reply following me.

"You'd better make it a feast. I'm famished."

My teeth ground together. I couldn't recall the last time anyone had ordered me about. I had a mind to spank her raw for it, but she would likely cry and if I planned on sleeping a wink tonight, I didn't need the headache.

I passed through the kitchen where mottled stone and a seven-foot fireplace greeted me, then stepped into the larder. The shelves were full, practically overflowing with fresh produce. At least one of the Fae who had owned this castle had been granted the Art of protection, it seemed, because this place had not withered in the grip of the forest and neither had the food.

"Looks like you'll have your feast then, lightwing." I sneered, grabbing handfuls of bread and cheese, along with a basket of fruit and some baked pastries.

She had no idea who she was dining with tonight. Her little dressing up game had ignited the spark of madness in me and awoken my demons. If she wanted to play house with a monster, then let us see who would break first.

I stalked from the kitchen, making my preparations before returning to her dressed in a fine suit I'd found in the old master bedroom. My long hair was a mess of wet strands from a recent bath and the scent of jasmine now hung upon my skin too. Sweetness to veil the bitter creature beneath.

Ferris was facing the fire when I returned and I waited for her to acknowledge me. Perhaps she was lost to her thoughts because she didn't turn and I managed to close in on her from behind, a prowling animal in the long grass with his gaze set on unaware prey.

"Tell me, how did you survive this long with wits so dull?" I uttered.

She didn't whip around in alarm as I'd expected but kept her gaze on the fire instead.

"If you wanted me dead, I wouldn't be here, would I?" she clipped, still not looking at me. My ire grew. Why did she not turn her eyes upon me? I was a male who made fiercer hearts quake than this breakable creature's.

My gaze slid to where her fingernails were biting into the arm of the chair and I cocked my head, a dark satisfaction rolling through me. She was hiding it, trying to play the big bad wolf at his own game. Well then, I would have all the more fun unveiling the truth of her terror. Let's see how long she could keep up this ruse.

I approached her from behind, laying a hand on her shoulder, her skin as soft as fallen rose petals. Goosebumps raced across her shoulder as my fingers dug in just a little and I lowered my mouth to her ear.

"Dinner is served, lightwing. You'll join me in the dining room. Come."

She pushed to her feet, forcing my hand from her, and I straightened to assess her. Small mouse, too delicate for a place like this. But those eyes. I couldn't get past the spark in them. What kind of mouse held the eyes of a wolf?

I offered her my hand, a mocking tilt to my lips as I waited to see if she would dare continue this game.

Her jaw ticked, throat bobbing. This act would shatter soon enough. If only she knew who she was playing with, she would sob and claw at the windows and doors. She would beg for freedom but I would never grant it.

Ferris stepped forward and placed her hand in mine, my fingers closing firm around hers. My heart thumped quicker than it had in some time. Power had always been my favourite pursuit. She would bow to me this very night. And oh what a delightful thought it was to picture her on her knees, her eyes on me as I stood over her and her pleas for mercy filling my ears. She would make my time in this forest a less dreary task, a plaything for a bored Fae.

I led her to the dining room where long red drapes hid the deadly night from view beyond the high windows. The table was long and oval, but only two chairs had been placed there by me. One at the head – mine, of course - and one to its right.

I guided her to her seat, pulling it out for her as if I were some gentlemen and gestured for her to sit. She did so, eyeing the food I'd laid out with suspicion.

"Where did you get all of this?" she asked, frowning at the fresh cheeses and breads, then to the display of fruit beyond it and the wide selection of pastries which looked as though they had only recently been baked.

"Do you know nothing of the magic of my kind?" I drawled, standing close as I reached past her, lifted a bottle of red wine and poured us each a glass.

She shivered, just a little, but enough to draw my attention. I was pressed to her back as I leaned over her, and I couldn't deny that the warmth of her stirred my intrigue. She was enchanting in an imperfect way. Only the humans could manage this kind of beauty. But she possessed a mortal allure that I had never witnessed in another of her kind. A part of me itched to explore it.

"The Fae are granted magic by the spirits of the sky when they reach maturity," she said in answer to my question. "You call them Arts. Fire wielding, storm brewing, metal moulding-"

"Of course your kind would focus on the brutish Arts when whispering about the Fae," I scoffed. "I suppose you tell tales around the fireplace of how your people have suffered at the hands of such power?"

She scowled up at me, not flinching beneath my scorn. "They aren't tales; they're warnings. We may have short lives but we have long memories and none of us will forget the horrors your kind have laid at our doors in centuries past."

My lips twitched in amusement which I didn't bother to share with her because we both held the same scorn for Fae who practiced cruelty with the Arts the spirits had granted them.

"Well there are plenty of other Arts besides flame and lightning. Like preservation." I waved a hand at the bountiful table before us in demonstration. "Perhaps you should educate yourself further before passing judgement on all Fae based on campfire tales."

"Perhaps I will," she replied, surprising me again. "What Art were you granted then?"

My mocking smile flattened and I simply shrugged. "That would be telling," I growled, ending the conversation.

She reached for her wine, but I caught her wrist, tugging her arm firmly behind her back before snaring the other one.

"Let go of me," she gasped, trying to rise, but I didn't let her. With one hand, I held both her wrists at the base of her spine, then took a coil of rope from my pocket and began to bind them. Tight. Enough to make her wince. I waited for a murmur of fear to pass her lips but it didn't come and I couldn't deny my disappointment.

I rounded the table, taking my own seat and lounging back in it, my knee bumping hers while my gaze fixed on her face. Yes, there was a flicker of uncertainty in those unusual eyes, but when her lips parted on a plea or perhaps some desperate questions, she snapped them shut again and pressed them into a tight line.

Interesting.

"You'll eat and drink without your hands, I've decided." I smirked, lifting a sharp knife from beside the bread and leaning back in my seat again to toy with it.

"How will I do that?" she scoffed, all anger instead of uncertainty.

I shrugged, then stabbed a wedge of cheese hard enough to pierce the table and she flinched at last. I yanked the blade free of the wood and brought the cheese to my lips, taking a bite of it. She wetted her lips. My hungry little beastie.

"What game are you playing?" she hissed.

"You're the one who started it, lightwing. I'm just making up a few rules of my own."

"I only asked for dinner," she said innocently.

I barked a laugh that made her spine straighten, the sound entirely unfriendly. "You asked for more than that when you played dress up and made demands of me. You're either a halfwit or brave and I can't work out which one it is yet."

She glared at me.

"Come on, eat up," I insisted. "I didn't prepare all of this for it to go to waste. You don't want to displease me, I assure you. Those who displease me tend to end up choking on their own blood and this food will taste far better than that."

"How?" she growled again.

"You know how." My smile dropped to a callous taunt as I took another bite of cheese.

Silence.

Dawning comprehension.

Anger.

Yes, she understood now.

"You want me to ask for your help," she sneered.

"No, lightwing." I leaned across the table, knife speared with cheese a little too close to her throat. And still, she didn't quake. I could tell her what I was, tell her the darkest secrets I knew and then she'd cower. She'd run too. But there would be no escape. "I want you to beg for it."

I slumped back in my chair, grabbing a loaf of fresh bread and tearing it in two with my hands.

"Is this how all Fae eat?" she goaded, watching the crumbs fly as I tore into the bread with my teeth.

I swallowed and shed the cheese from my knife onto my plate, dropping the lump of bread onto it too. Then I tapped the infinity mark on my temple with the tip of my blade. "See this?"

She nodded, a frown creasing her brow.

"That's the mark of an outcast. A Fae like me doesn't attend balls and dinner parties. Not anymore. I'm one of the black sheep of Rivenspire. A Fae who pissed off the Coterie. So when I want to eat, I eat with raw abandon, because when you're called a savage long enough, you tend to start acting like one."

"Are there many outcasts among your kind?" Her eyes narrowed, suspicion rising like the tide, and I realised what might just be stirring in her mind.

"Hundreds," I lied dismissively. "We're not all honey and sugar, sweetheart."

I moved to take a bite of my food when I was halted by a sharp command.

"Feed me." She stared at me, hard and unblinking. Her tone wasn't a plea as I'd requested, but I found my hand moving toward her lips in offering all the same.

She took a bite and I watched her mouth move as she chewed and swallowed.

"Another," she demanded.

"Ask nicely," I growled, holding the food out of reach.

Quiet.

One second.

Two.

Three.

"Please."

My pulse hitched, that word a sin on her tongue. It didn't sound submissive though, it sounded mocking. She was playing me and spirits help me, I offered her the bread and cheese once more. But this game wasn't won yet.

I offered her the wine next, watching how her throat bobbed as she drank it and liking the show she was putting on for me. She was a more seductive thing than I'd realised. Every movement demanding I study her. And like this, with me in charge of every bite and every sip, I could.

I fed her grapes next, one by one, and slowly too. Her lips brushed my fingers on the fourth one and a low growl rolled up my throat. When I offered her another, her eyes met mine and she did it again, just for a moment, perhaps unaware of it, her lips skated against the pad of my thumb and sent a ripple of potent desire through me. My gaze slid to her soft lips and that ache grew, my body shifting closer to hers without me telling it to do so. Then I offered her another grape.

"I'm done eating," she said.

"You're done when I say you're done."

Ferris bit me, her teeth digging in hard, and my other hand flew out to fist in her hair.

She released me and I yanked to force her head back and expose her throat. I could practically see the thrumming pulse in her neck and I lunged forward and sank my teeth into that very spot, giving her a taste of her own medicine. She gasped, arching against her chair, but into me instead of away. She tasted like life itself, a heady concoction of wants and endless yearnings.

I leaned back, my hand still in her hair as I stared at her, almost nose to nose. Her breath fluttered against my lips, ragged and fearful at last, but there was still that defiance there. A hatred for everything I was.

"Why do you really hate my kind?" I asked with grit, giving no heed to her personal space.

"Because you take what you want. You take and take because you think you're above us. You think because we're mortal that we're expendable." The wrath in her voice was tempered with pain and at last I saw the crux of her. This was personal.

"So what is your plan, lightwing? You seek the forest's boon to destroy my kind for good?"

She laughed coldly. "As if I'd waste the boon on revenge. I have deeper desires than that."

"Then we are not so different after all," I muttered.

"I am nothing like you," she hissed.

I considered that and nodded. "You're right, I am a hunter and you are prey." I shoved the chair she was sitting on and it collapsed to the floor, my hand moving from her hair to grab her waist and force her to her feet so she didn't fall with it. The clatter stirred up a tempest in her eyes and I smiled that villain's smile I was so used to wearing.

I cut the rope from her wrists, tossing it aside.

"Run, lightwing. Run and hide. Because I am in the mood to hunt. And perhaps if I find you, I won't feel so merciless. Perhaps I will change my mind on keeping you alive."

I released her but she didn't run, so I turned and flung the entire table over, sending food and cutlery flying everywhere. I turned back to her and bellowed, "Run!" and she stumbled away from me, nearly tripping over the chair behind her before she raced from the room as fast as she could go.

I stared after her with vitriol coating my heart, my throat soaked in it too. I wasn't going to follow her. I just wanted her out of my sight. Because I hated her. Not for who she was but for what I wasn't. For the mirror she held up to me. I wanted her to fear me as all others did, not look at me with those infuriating eyes which never dropped from mine in submission.

And yet…and yet, and yet…how I didn't want that too.

FERRIS

CHAPTER THIRTEEN

I woke with a jolt as if a phantom hand had shaken me and I pushed myself upright in the enormous bed as I worked to take in my surroundings. I groaned, my luxurious sleeping space calling me back into its embrace. Never had I slept so soundly or so comfortably in all my life. Despite the dangers surrounding me, the bed I'd chosen for my place of rest had been nothing short of sinful in the way it had caressed my body all night long.

If only I could have brought it with me, I certainly would have done.

The room was dark, only the faint glow of light from the embers in my fireplace offering illumination. But something told me that dawn was close. My slumber had been disturbed by the distant sound of singing and I frowned as I recalled it, wondering if it had been real or just a part of my troubling dreams.

I gathered up the second and most precious of the two books I'd brought with me into the Taking Trees – Rissa's childhood journal. The pages were dog-eared and grey from the amount of times I'd fallen asleep reading over her words, pretending I could hear her voice between the letters, imagining she was a little closer when I consumed them. They contained nothing of real value to anyone else, but to me, they were the most precious thing in all the world.

I stood, shivering a little as my bare feet pressed to the cold floorboards. I glanced at the door, relaxing as I found the chair I'd wedged beneath the handle still firmly in place.

Hendrix may have kept his distance during the night but I knew he had some scheme in mind for me yet, and I was going to be far away from here before he had the chance to act upon it.

I'd run from him last night, fled like the pathetic human he judged me to be and proven to him that I feared his wrath despite my attempts to conceal it. My heart had still been pounding when I'd finally accepted that he wasn't going to hunt me after all and I'd taken my opportunity to sleep.

I swallowed as I thought back on my meal with the brutal Fae, my fingers pressing to the tender skin where he'd bitten me like the beast he was.

Heat flared in my veins at the memory, the way his stubble had grazed my throat, his fingers pressing against my skin, his lips lingering for just a moment as his teeth withdrew…

He was a monster of the deadliest design and I needed to escape him before I fell prey to his madness again.

I tiptoed to the heavy drapes which hung before the windows and twitched them aside to reveal the shutters beneath. A small crack at their edge allowed the faintest whisper of deep grey light to shine through it and I was relieved to find that my instincts had woken me right on time.

I hadn't intended to sleep right through the night. My plan had been to nap for a couple of hours at most so that I wouldn't miss the sunrise. Truthfully I hadn't wanted to do that, but the exhaustion in my bones had demanded it. Either way, I'd slumbered for what must have been ten hours. I wasn't entirely certain how I'd managed to wake right at the crack of dawn but I was endlessly relived to have done so.

I hurried back across the room, dressing myself in the Fae clothes which were more suited to traversing the forest. The material was as soft as butter against my skin, the black trousers fitted yet supple, a warmth to them which defied the thinness of the fabric. I added a white tunic to the outfit, its billowing sleeves a little more decorative than practical but it was comfortable and easy to move in. The boots fit me surprisingly well and I laced them tightly, wondering if the forest itself had meant to lead me here so that I might find the supplies I'd been in such desperate need of.

I wrapped a dark green cloak around my shoulders last, the material sumptuous and warm while the colour promised me anonymity within the folds of the woodland. All I had to do was make it into the embrace of the trees and I'd quickly be lost within them, leaving Hendrix and his brutish disposition far behind in my wake.

The bag I'd stuffed full of supplies was heavy but I refused to second guess what I'd packed and quickly secured Rissa's journal inside it. I'd snuck back out to the pantry once I'd been certain my Fae captor wasn't actually hunting the halls for me and had filled the pockets of my fine gown with food from the kitchen. I'd stolen a few sharp knives too, meaning to use them against him had he come for me, but now they would accompany me in my escape.

In addition to that I still had the remains of my old supplies, my books and now some spare clothes and a blanket too. I doubted I'd find shelter in a luxurious castle again tonight and though I would sorely miss the comfort of this place, no meal nor fine bed could make up for the abhorrence of Hendrix's company.

The shutters groaned as I unbolted them and eased them open, the low whine making my pulse spike as I glanced back towards the door and the chair which remained stoically wedged before it.

There wasn't a breath of sound from anywhere in the castle and

I could only imagine that the great Hendrix was resting his massive head on plush pillows of his own. No doubt maintaining such an alarmingly over-inflated ego was hard work and he'd exhausted himself in hauling it around so much at dinner that he would sleep on for hours yet.

"I hope you don't choke on your own drool," I muttered in place of a farewell to the obnoxious Fae, then reached for the latch to the window.

My fingers brushed the cool metal and I couldn't help but hesitate as I peered out through the glass. Years in the forest had allowed a green film to build up over the square panes and I had to squint through it to gain a look at the walls and tangled rosebushes that made up a long-neglected garden below.

It was only a breath beyond pitch darkness outside, the slightly-paling light filtering through the trees all too slowly. Would the beasts that roamed the forest at night have retreated yet? Did this teasing whisper of dawn count as daybreak?

I swallowed back a lump of fear in my throat, counting slowly back from ten and painting an X against the glass with my forefinger.

"Spirits, please let me pass," I begged in a low whisper. Then I turned the latch and thrust the window wide.

I braced, my muscles tensing and features pinching in anticipation of an attack, of some unseen monster lurching from the trees to devour me for daring to step out into the night.

But nothing happened.

Cool air fragranced with the scent of the roses that littered the forgotten garden below my window washed over my face in an amused greeting and I forced myself to relax.

It was going to be okay. Dawn was breaking. It was time for me to move.

I leaned forward, peering down at the drop which seemed so much further than I'd been expecting. I was certainly high enough to break my neck in a fall but I couldn't back out of this now.

I closed my eyes to centre myself. I'd snuck out of my own bedroom window many times and clambered over the little lean-to beneath it before scrambling to the ground and hurrying out to practice with my slingshot or run laps around the village while no one would be awake to watch me.

I was well used to seeing this time of day and well used to the fear that came with risking the wrath of the night, though admittedly my village held far fewer threats than this place did even with the risk of Hollows and the creeping trees.

With a steadying breath, I hunted for footholds and planned a path to the ground. There was an iron drainpipe around six feet to the right of my window which ran to the garden below. Between me and it was little more than crumbling stone and some overly enthusiastic vines but I would make it.

I clambered onto the windowsill and turned to grip it as I lowered myself over the edge.

The toes of my boots scrambled against the brickwork, hunting for the gap I'd spotted in them. My arms trembled as I fought to find it and lowered myself further, my muscles straining with the effort as I cursed and swung my legs, still trying to locate it.

I'd promised myself I wouldn't look down, and the moment I broke that oath I almost cried out in fear, my boots still scraping against flat stone, my fingers slipping as my weight threatened to undo them, the fall beckoning with glee-

My toes struck the edge of the gap I'd spotted and I finally managed to push some weight into my leg.

"Fuck this castle," I hissed to the wind. "Fuck this forest and the Fae – one Fae more than the rest. Fuck all of them and please, for the love of the spirits, don't let me die while trying to climb out of a damn window."

I reached towards the drainpipe, my fingers thankfully finding a gap to cling to at a midway point between me and my promise of salvation. Bit by bit, I eased closer to the black iron, clinging to the castle wall like a damn spider - though with far less grace to my descent.

When my hand finally met with the cool metal, I nearly sobbed with relief. I lurched across to it, my toes wedging against one of the fastenings which held it bolted to the wall before my other hand made it to the pipe too.

I clung to that rusted, iron pipe like a babe to its mother's breast and tried to pretend I was shaking from the cold rather than the fear of the fall. I chanced a look down again, the drop still the same but somehow much less terrifying with a clear path to the ground now laid out for me.

I began to shuffle down the drainpipe, inch by inch, making my escape like the world's most determined sloth. I didn't care. This was my path to escape and it was all going to plan despite the odds.

The light was gradually paling, easing my concerns about being in the forest at night, and a grin slowly spread across my face. I could do this. I could make an escape in the dead of the night and I would find a way to hunt the spirits of the forest and seize them too. I was going to do what I'd come here for, no matter the cost. I would prove that I was no weak-

I cried out in alarm as something sharp pierced the skin of my hand, some small beast taking a bite out of me in my moment of triumph.

I snatched my hand free of the drainpipe before I could think better of it, my cry turning into a shriek as I pitched backwards, my arm flailing wildly.

With a surge of will, I threw myself back towards the wall, grabbing the drainpipe again, though the jolt of movement saw me slipping several feet towards the ground.

I tightened my hold and jerked to a halt, my eyes clamped shut against the oncoming demise I'd somehow avoided.

As I peeled my lids back, I turned my injured hand, expecting to see the tell-tale double piercings of a drath spider's fangs, knowing my end would be rushing for me within the hour without antivenom to save me.

I blinked at the large, brown thorn which stuck out of my skin, a tiny spec of blood ringing the small wound.

I arched my neck and spied the rose vines a few feet above me where they'd tangled with the drainpipe, their pale pink blooms seeming to laugh at me as I found myself not in the hands of death but suffering from a pricked palm.

Groaning at my dramatic imagination, I plucked the thorn free with my teeth and continued my slow descent with shame clinging to me and the definite relief that there had been no witnesses to me panicking over a thorn. Though in this forest, who was to say a rose couldn't be lethal?

I pushed my thoughts away from that path before I could allow myself to believe I was dying again and thumped down onto solid ground with a cocky smirk. Who was a prisoner now?

I looked about, the spot I'd descended into surrounded by low walls, rotting trellises and decorative statues which represented various woodland animals. I didn't linger to inspect it more than that, needing to lose myself in the depths of the forest before that boorish Fae realised I was gone.

My steps led me back and forth through the rose garden, their sweet scent cloying as if it had puddled here and couldn't escape. I rounded a wall, then ducked beneath a trellis which sagged with the weight of the white roses that had utterly smothered it and finally found myself looking out into nothing but trees.

"So long, you arrogant ass," I told the castle at my back. "I'll miss the way your vulgar personality almost made me want to gouge out my own eyes and stuff them in my ears." I held my middle finger up over my shoulder and strode triumphantly into the trees.

"I would say I'm impressed but you were painfully slow in that descent and almost lost your life to a thornbush," a low voice drawled behind me, and I whipped around in alarm.

Hendrix stood leaning with his back to a towering ash tree, his foot kicked up nonchalantly while he slowly sliced a pear with a hunting knife and peered at me from within the depths of his hood like I was little more than an irritation to his day.

I stilled, my hand going to my pocket and curling around a stone while I snatched my slingshot from my belt with the other. It had been little work to fix the band back into place and I felt better with my weapon in hand, no matter how meagre it might seem in the face of the enormous Fae.

"I'm leaving," I growled defiantly, and his posture didn't change while he lifted a slice of pear to his lips and ate it.

"Are you?"

"Yes," I growled.

He said nothing, didn't move to stop me, didn't do anything at all other than eat another slice of that damn pear.

I scowled at him, then took a step further into the trees. Still, he made no move, did nothing at all. In fact, his focus wasn't even on me anymore while he just ate his pear and leaned against that tree like a psychopath.

Good. That was good.

I started walking, my pace increasing with each step, my head turning to keep him in my line of sight until too many trees divided us to make that possible and I finally broke into a run.

There was no sound of pursuit, no cries for me to stop. I was free. He was letting me go. I didn't know why or what reasoning he had, but I didn't care because I was going to run and run until the distance between us was impossible for him to breech and even if he changed his mind there would be no finding me.

I shoved my slingshot back into my belt and raced into a wide clearing in the trees, birdsong falling to an abrupt halt at my arrival and just as victory sung my name in a sweet and breathy voice, I crashed headlong into an enormous body built of water and ice.

The Bear spirit became incorporeal as I collided with it, my cry of surprise turning into a splutter of alarm as I was engulfed in icy water and washed right off of my feet to slam down into the dirt.

The Bear disappeared in a rush of water and through dripping lashes and heaving coughs, I found a pair of boots striding towards me, kicking up water and leaves.

Hendrix tossed the core of the pear aside and strode closer like he was simply out for a morning stroll, his hood shrouding his eyes and making him appear as little more than a demon.

I cursed him, flipping over and scrambling away, trying to make a run for it, but I didn't even get on all fours before his hand locked around my ankle and he started dragging me back towards the castle with a dry melody rolling from his throat.

I kicked and fought, spluttering and coughing in the muddy froth the Bear's water had created along the forest floor, but nothing I did made the slightest bit of difference. He hauled me all the way back to the castle before depositing me on the floor of the dining room beside the fire.

"You're late for breakfast," he clipped, taking his seat at the head of the table.

I fought against the sodden weight of my cloak and was forced to drop both it and my pack to the ground before I could claw my way upright again.

"What the fuck was that?" I demanded furiously, my tunic clinging to my body, hair and clothes dripping mud and water in a puddle which was slowly spreading to consume the rug.

"That was tame compared to what I could have done. So stop whining and eat. I don't need you fainting on me while we're out there in the trees, and you know now how futile any attempts at escape will be. Why don't you just do us both a favour, give up and remain silent unless speech becomes utterly unavoidable."

I looked back towards the door which he hadn't bothered to close behind us, then glanced at my drenched pack and cursed as I hurried to open it, tossing the clothes and sodden food aside before finally hauling my precious books out.

I sighed in relief as I found the bindings around them had proven their worth yet again, keeping them dry and saving them from ruin. With a huff of irritation, I sat down heavily in my chair, placed my books beside my plate and proceeded to eat as much of his delicious food as I could manage in the most obnoxious way possible. At least he didn't seem inclined to tie me up and make a show of feeding me. His moods were as changeable as the wind though, so I was going to devour it quickly before he reconsidered letting me eat freely this time.

Perhaps he'd won this round, but clearly he wasn't looking to hurt me and wanted me for some other purpose. So I'd simply have to try and get away from him again. And again. And again. However many attempts it took, no matter how hopeless it seemed. I'd find my way free of him and claim every spirit remaining in this forest for good measure.

"I believe I know where the Fox is hiding," Hendrix said, pulling me from my mutinous intentions. "And I'm going to take you with me while I hunt it."

I scowled at him while ripping into a bread roll with my teeth.

"Why?" I asked through a mouthful of food, and he sneered at me in a way which only made me want to irritate him further.

He cocked his head at me like I was a flea he was contemplating squashing and I reached across the table to take another roll and some fruit. Surprisingly, he did answer me.

"You're to be my bait," he said, amusement coating his tone, and I bristled at the implication, the word setting me on edge. What did he mean? Was his plan to tie me up in a clearing like a sacrificial lamb and pounce upon the spirit while it was preoccupied with devouring me?

"Bait?" I asked slowly, lowering my roll while trying to stay calm.

His lips curled with amusement at the change in my tone, and for a moment, I was startled by the difference that small smirk made to his cold features. He was Fae, so of course he was beautiful, but until that moment all of his expressions had seemed forced, like he was a vessel void of true emotion, a statue with a breath of life within him, the artist who had carved him too caught up in creating perfection in his lines to waste time on offering out any humanity. But that smirk revealed a slight imbalance to his smile, a dimple in his right cheek, a glint of something wicked in his green eyes, real feeling behind the words, even if that feeling was cruelty.

"You do scream so prettily, lightwing. I believe every feral beast in this forest may be drawn to the poetry of your cries. And I intend to be waiting in the shadows when they arrive."

I shifted in my seat, refusing to show fear at his plan, but the thought of it set my teeth on edge. I lifted my chin in defiance.

"You aren't here to hunt beasts. You're in pursuit of spirits," I reminded him. "And they are not motivated by death and ruin the way other monsters are."

The scathing look I offered him made it clear that my jibe had been intended for him but he only lifted his glass of water to his lips and sipped it slowly, his piercing eyes never straying from mine.

I stared back at him despite every instinct willing me to break the contact.

Hendrix thumped his glass down onto the table and I flinched at the sudden sound, making him snort in amusement.

"The spirits lost their minds when the curse was struck. They're just as feral and bloodthirsty as every other monster in these woods."

I rolled my eyes and reached for an apple, uncertain why I was surprised. The Fae may have played at being sophisticated and highly knowledgeable but they were as ferocious and spiteful as any other monster. In fact, they were worse. A beast had no way of knowing it was a beast. It couldn't reason or try to justify its actions. It worked on nothing but instinct and need. Hunger, shelter, territory. The Fae were vicious out of selfishness.

"What is that look for?" he asked when I failed to expand on my judgement of his assessment.

"You really care? I was under the impression that I was an irrelevant human whose opinions meant less than dirt to you."

"Well yes, obviously, but you might as well fill the silence with your irrelevance rather than letting it fester."

I pursed my lips, choosing not to comment on my feelings about him and his kind and instead focusing on his dismissive assessment of the spirits. "The spirits here may have lost their way, but they were born of pure magic with the sole purpose of protecting this forest. I don't think those instincts have diminished completely and neither do I believe that they are entirely without thought or reason in their current state."

"So what are they then?" he asked, though clearly he didn't think much of my assessment.

"Lost," I muttered, the word a sting on an old but unhealed wound. "And in need of our help."

Hendrix snorted, shaking his head at me like I was some foolish child, and I bristled at his arrogant sense of superiority.

"The forest literally told us so when we arrived here. They need to be found and reunited. Doesn't that sound like a mother in search of her children or at least a queen missing her army?" I pressed.

Hendrix considered my words while he chewed, then shrugged. "What mother requires their children to stop them from devouring the entire world the way this forest is attempting without its spirits to hold it in check?"

I stared at him in complete disbelief. "That's precisely what a mother would do if she lost her children. She'd tear the world apart in her desperation to retrieve them and damn the ones who fell to her wrath."

Hendrix still appeared unconvinced, so I grabbed my precious book from its place beside my plate and opened it with enough force to make the cutlery rattle, pausing on the chapter which spoke of the Dragon.

"At its heart, the Dragon is a protector," I read. "It patrolled the trees at dawn and dusk, circling them and catching up to any who might think to creep beyond their bounds. With scales lit by starlight and dancing on the powerful heart of a storm cloud, its mighty roar would make the leaves bristle and shiver, requiring every bough, branch and trunk to stand and account themselves upon each sweep it took between the-"

"So the Dragon could summon a storm to fell any tree which wandered beyond the boundary of the forest and without it they roam free, yes, yes," Hendrix said, waving a hand like he wanted to brush my words from the room. "I've heard those pretty little fairytales before, though you do realise there is no proof to them?"

"You weren't listening properly," I growled, my hand splaying protectively over the silvery depiction of the Dragon in my book. "It didn't just command storms, it had a job to do which kept the magic of this forest in check. All of the spirits had a job just as important to this place and to the rest of the world too because without them doing what they should, we are all at risk of being consumed by these trees and the malevolent things which dwell within them."

"Don't lecture me on what the forest has taken, girl," Hendrix sneered. "I know far better than you because I've lived it. I've watched it consume the world bite by bite and-"

"Do not presume to know more than me about what this fucking place has taken!" I yelled at him, my fingers crumpling the page of my precious book in my utter fury at his cavalier claim that his years spent living in this world somehow trumped my experience of it.

Hendrix fell silent, sitting back in his chair and staring at me for several long seconds which were filled with vitriol from my end and blatant curiosity from his.

"What has it taken fr-"

I cut off his words with a bark of my own. "I thought the point here was to find the spirits, not get to know one another? Because I can assure you I have no interest whatsoever in getting to know you nor divulging my past or my motivations to you. You are a stranger wishing to use me as bait in pursuit of the lost spirits. I am simply trying to inform you on how best to go about seeking them because I do not believe they are solely interested in eating human women."

"I'm willing to take a chance on disagreeing with you there. Besides, you have a vested interest in dissuading me from my planned course of action and I may as well tell you now that I will not be dissuaded," he drawled, and if the table had been smaller I might have kicked him in the shins for his hubris. He really was the most aggravating, infuriating man I'd ever met. And he wasn't even a man.

"You truly are so bloated with your own ego that you won't even consider what I'm saying to you?" I demanded, but he only shrugged nonchalantly.

"You cannot honestly believe that all of the spirits were only born to serve the forest? What of the Fox? What use is fire to trees? In its very nature it is their greatest threat."

"The Fox's job was to protect the forest from the threat of flame by consuming all it found and adding them to the length of its tail. So no, having a spirit born of fire was not a foolish choice on the forest's behalf. It was a clever one. And you might do well to take note of cleverness whenever you come across it."

"Is that so?" he challenged in a rough growl which was all malice. But I had the measure of him now. I was useful to him. At least until the amulets were reunited. And that meant he wouldn't be harming me.

"You do seem to be lacking in it," I agreed.

"Regardless of your irrelevant opinion, you may wish to eat faster. I've heard your kind wilt quickly without sustenance, rather like a flower in the spring – so vibrant and beautiful, but only for a few days. Then its petals tumble to the dirt and it is nothing but fodder for the worms to feast upon. Much as you humans live for so short a span that you barely get to know who you are before your time is done and your bones become ash. So come on, the sun is hastening towards its zenith, and I have a spirit to capture."

I smoothed out the page of my book and closed its cover before returning my focus to my food.

The Fox? Yes, I would happily go with him in pursuit of that spirit. And I'd steal it out from under him while he wasn't looking too.

HENDRIX

CHAPTER FOURTEEN

"What makes you think you know where the Fox is?" my little captive demanded as she tried to keep pace with me. My stride was plenty longer than hers even though she was tall for a human, but the persistent creature managed to stay at my side.

"There is very little in this world that cannot be found when you are watching closely enough."

"That's not an answer," she huffed.

I had to hand it to her, lesser humans would be out of breath by now from the pace I'd set, but she was fit enough. It was funny how some humans worked all their lives to be strong, yet I could still snap their necks with my bare hands in two seconds.

"I climbed a ridge the other day and watched the trees for signs of smoke. It came thrice from the same place and that was where I found the spirit. Where there is fire, there is smoke. Where there is smoke, there is likely the Fox. So we will seek it in the area I last saw the smoke and hunt for it from a viewpoint if it cannot be found there."

"Great, how about you drop the patronising tone next time you answer a question?"

I ignored her griping, pushing though a mass of vines and finding a mossy hill dropping away beyond. The dark was heavy here, the canopy so thick above that it blotted out most of the sunlight, and there was a weight to the air that spoke of magic.

I wondered if the human could sense it too. My eyes drifted to her and I noticed her boot slip on the moss as we began our descent. My hand flew out, landing firmly on her back to steady her and her palm fell on my arm, gripping tightly as she righted herself.

"Watch your step, lightwing," I muttered, glancing at her hand on me, the buzz of her humanity skipping beneath her fingertips, dancing against my skin. Even a fall could kill her kind if they hit their head hard enough.

Her eyes met mine, two bright violet fires blazing with the intensity of the stars. That unique tone to her irises seeming brighter here beneath the canopy of the trees, something sparking in her gaze which appeared so much older than she possibly could have been.

She snatched her hand away from me and walked on without a word of thanks, taking the lead down the hill with assured footfalls. I followed, head tilted down, a wild animal at her back. If only she knew who stalked her footsteps she would run and never stop running.

The unusual interaction irked me. I should have let her fall.

"How will you lead the way when you have no idea of the direction we are heading?" I called to her. There was a hill near here that I had found a few days back which should give a good view across the forest and hopefully a glimpse of the Fox's smoke.

"Poor, dumb Fae," she cooed, and my teeth locked together. "You're the one who gave me the answer, has your aged mind forgotten it already?"

The scent of smoke reached me as I joined her at the base of the hill and I cursed myself for not having noticed it first.

"Perhaps I'm testing you."

She gave me a dry look that said she didn't believe my bullshit for a single second and I marched on past her, taking the lead once more.

The brush was dense here, slowing our progress, as if the forest was willing us to turn back...or at least that was how it appeared to be treating me. But when my gaze fell to the human who should have been helplessly stumbling along in the path I was forging, I found her striding between brambles which slithered aside for her boots and passing beneath vines that lifted to accommodate her of their own accord.

"Playing favourites, are we?" I grumbled at the trees, but only the shiver of the leaves above my head came as answer.

Between my sword and sheer force, I cut a path toward my Fox and at last found it waiting for me. Luck was clearly on my side today, the spirit wandering right into our path without us needing to seek smoke from the treetops at all. It appeared I might not even need to use my bait this time to lure it, but no matter, the human would come in useful for the next one. Maybe she really had been touched by a little lightwing spirit before I'd found her and granted with its fortuity.

The Fox was curled up sleeping in a clearing, the grass flattened out from how many times it had slept here before. Coiling up from its fiery fur was a gentle plume of white smoke. Perhaps it only happened when the creature slept because I had not seen the smoke rising from the trees often enough to believe it was constant.

I crouched low, assessing the area for traps, expecting the forest to strike at me before I could lay my hands on my prize.

"It's beautiful," Ferris breathed, lowering down at my side. "Fire embodied."

I remained silent, letting the doe-eyed human focus on the Fox's splendour while I concentrated on how to seize it.

I sheathed my sword and took a knife from my hip, creeping closer, ready to hurl it at the beast and claim it at last. My foot snapped a twig and I stilled, the Fox's head flying up and its eyes meeting mine.

I hurled my blade, but it was gone, the knife driving into the ground right where it'd been.

"Shit," I growled as the Fox darted off into the trees, a swish of its burning tail signalling my loss. I yanked my knife from the ground as Ferris sprinted past me, snatching a handful of dry pine needles from the forest floor and disappearing into the brush.

"What's your game?" I bit out and chased after the Fox, forcing a path through the tangled thorn bushes and earning myself a line of scratches along my arms.

I quickened my pace, hearing Ferris just ahead as I broke into another clearing between two enormous oak trees with high roots that covered most of the ground. Ferris was bounding between the roots with ease while I was forced to slow down, my bulk making the task harder.

There was no sign of the Fox and I guessed Ferris had given up when she abruptly sat down on the ground between two large roots.

I caught up to her at last, overtaking her and throwing a glance at the ground where she was crouching over something. She'd bundled the pine needles together and was striking two flints above them, but I didn't have a thought to spare to her madness as I continued on, barrelling off into the closely-gathered trees beyond the oaks.

I forged deeper into the forest, but there was no more scent of smoke to follow now. No flicker of a burning tail. Disappointment burned on my tongue like acid, a curse tumbling from my lips as my hopes diminished.

I hunted the area, desperate to find my Fox, furious I'd lost my chance at it yet again. But just when I was about to give up for good, the scent of smoke reached me once more and I turned keenly, racing through the trees, pushing on with an unforgiving determination.

Everything depended on me returning the amulets to the Great Elm at the heart of the forest.

The path I sought might have been layered in death, but it was what I wanted more than any other thing. No material item or petty desire could outweigh the reason I had come here. The boon would be *mine*.

I shoved through the brush and stumbled beyond the tangle of thorns, finding myself back between the two oak trees. The smoke wasn't coiling up from the Fox after all, but from Ferris's fire.

I was about to unleash my inner demons upon her and punish her for the mindless action, but then I saw it. The Fox, pawing its way toward my captive.

Ferris knelt before the flames, offering her hand out to the spirit like she expected the monstrous beast to come and nuzzle her palm. The spirit drew closer, its eyes alight with the fire and the need to consume every flame. I frowned, seeing more to the spirit than I had allowed myself to before. It didn't seem like a vengeful monster in that moment, at least not when it came to her. Perhaps there was something to Ferris's beliefs about them after all.

My human was no ordinary creature, it seemed. She was clever, sharper than I had been in my moment of desperation. She'd lured the Fox right to her with her wits and now it was looking at her as if she might be the answer to all its problems. But we weren't here to comfort the spirits of the cursed forest. We were here to capture them. So while she was seeking a bond with the Fox which was regarding her with gentle intrigue, drawing closer to her outstretched hand, I took aim.

"I won't hurt you," Ferris whispered to it just as I threw my knife.

It spun end over end, then slammed directly into the Fox's chest, making it yelp in pain before it vanished in a swirl of smoke. An amulet fell to the forest floor in its place, a fox carved in fine lines upon its front and smoke coiling around it before finally slipping inside, making the locket glow like embers before it fell dark.

I smiled wickedly, picking up the amulet and relishing in my victory as I placed it around my neck. The flood of a fiery power ignited in my veins, embers flickering along my limbs and winding through my chest. The beast connected to me in a flood of furious flames but they didn't burn me, their heat a balm instead of a bane. I was so caught up in the moment that I didn't even notice the branch swinging for my head. Ferris whacked the thing against my skull hard enough to knock me back a step. I snatched her wrist with a growl, forcing her to drop the branch and baring my teeth at her, reminding her who she was striking at.

"The Fox was mine," Ferris snapped, feral rage burning through her as she glared at me like she might truly be a match for a prince of the Fae. Not that she knew my true heritage.

"Don't be a sore loser, lightwing. Your plan was pretty but your execution was poor. Touching the spirits won't make them yours."

"Fuck you," she snarled, trying to yank her wrist free of my grip, but I didn't let go. How easily I could break her bones, just the right amount of pressure and I could snap her wrist. Did she have no sense to protect herself from me? Did she not understand the threat I posed? She'd made it clear enough that she was no fool, so why then did she challenge me as if I were some mortal man?

I lifted her clean off the ground by her wrist, reminding her of my strength as her legs kicked at me. She struck me in the thigh and I held her further away from me, shaking my head.

"My guess is, you have survived this long out of sheer luck. And you only still live because I decided it. You're not here to offer me your opinions on the Great Hunt, you are here to be my tool, and while you are not being useful to me, you'd best keep your mouth shut." I dropped her and her feet hit the ground hard but she didn't fall.

She didn't cower or drop to her knees to grovel as I'd hoped, but instead, she laughed. She laughed openly at me, mocking and cold. "You can't silence me and need me in the same sentence. You said it yourself, I'm alive because you're keeping me so. That means you have to put up with me as I am. And I will speak my thoughts whenever I like, *bastard*. I might just be bait to you, but I'm far more than that. I'm human, and we're more than your kind could ever hope to be."

I scoffed a laugh back at her. "How so? Do your people possess our strength? Our ferocity? Do you outlive all other beings? Do you possess magic in your veins that can wield the very forces of the world we live in?"

Her jaw flexed and she stepped toward me, eyes never leaving mine. Despite her humanity, she appeared surprisingly powerful in her stature. "We possess none of that meaningless tripe."

"*Tripe*?" I echoed, affronted by her insanity. "What more is there to this world than power?"

"Humans have fallen for that trap too, but many of us know the real meaning of life. The brevity we have gifts us something you'll never understand. We live for each moment, we wring the goodness out of our days and we strive to make everyone we love know they're cherished because we don't know when we might lose each other. It makes life meaningful. You, on the other hand, hold no meaning. You cherish nothing but your precious power and in the end, you'll find yourself hollow."

That word struck me like an anvil to the chest. Hollow.

Hollow.

Hollow.

Hollow.

No one used that word lightly; she was inferring I was just like the undead who walked this plane with us. The thought was one I'd had myself. How could she possibly see the emptiness in me? How could a creature like this know anything of what my long life had led to?

"Your silence says I'm right." She turned her back on me, heading for the trees, moving fast like she planned on running from me again, the forest once again bending around her like it found amusement in aiding her against me.

I clasped the amulet of the Bear, turning it in my palm to face the forest and urged it to show itself. The locket shuddered and a thunderous flood of power rattled through me as the Bear spilled from the amulet, pouring free in a swirl of water that formed its huge figure.

Ferris glanced back and I didn't need to make the spirit chase her, her eyes hardened and she fell still.

"Back to my prison then," she conceded. "For now."

"For as long as I bid it," I hissed, hatred spilling from me. Yes, I despised her now for how easily she saw through me. How starkly she had bared the truth.

I hated her because she was right. Her brevity was, impossibly, her greatest gift. Because in a timeless form, there was only one fate on offer when you had walked the path I had. And that was an empty, lonely nothingness.

FERRIS

CHAPTER FIFTEEN

Bitterness coated my tongue as Hendrix manhandled me back to the castle, and it didn't sweeten as night fell and I once again found myself trapped in his company.

"You're even more useful than I thought you'd be, lightwing," he drawled in what was clearly an attempt to bait me into a fight, the pair of amulets he'd stolen from me clinking together around his neck.

Furious didn't come close to how I felt as I scowled at the matching amulets, one carved with the figure of the Bear, the other of the Fox. He hadn't deserved either prize, though the way he was acting told me we didn't agree on that. He clearly believed that stealing one from the corpse of my friend and snatching the other from between my outstretched fingers wasn't a problem at all. The Fox had been *mine*. It had been drawn by the fire I'd lit and had only been captured by that dull-witted brute because it had paused to regard me when my trap was sprung.

I hated him. Him and his whole fucking realm full of Fae. He was right to question whether I might use the boon to rid myself of the lot of them because in that moment, I felt like it wasn't such a bad idea.

But I had a far more important use for the boon, one which I couldn't allow myself to take my focus from.

I ripped my arm out of his grasp and strode away into the luxurious castle, heading for the kitchens where I planned on claiming my own meal. I had no appetite for sharing a place at his table and the sight of his smug face, for even a moment longer would certainly make me hurl.

"You did well, beastie," he called after me, clearly still hoping for a fight, but I wasn't going to play his game. "The perfect tidbit for a hungry spirit. And you even managed to return here with all of your limbs – aren't you going to thank me for keeping you alive out there?"

My blood boiled and I stalled for all of half a second, meaning to turn and embark on the war of words he was hoping for, but that was just it; he wanted my ire, my wrath, my fury. It amused him. So he wasn't going to get it.

"Your company is so dull I fear I might fall asleep should I remain within it a moment longer," I called over my shoulder dismissively. "So I plan on removing myself from it lest I end up sleeping right here on the floor."

"And I suppose you think yourself to be a riveting conversationalist, far above conversing with the likes of a Fae who is over six-hundred years your senior?" he called, but I'd already made it to the kitchen door and even his diabolical claim at longevity wouldn't rouse a reaction from me. "You know, if I wanted to, I could have you-"

I let the door thump shut between us and thankfully missed whatever audacious statement he'd been so keen on making. I knew he wouldn't leave it at that though, so wI grabbed a broom from the closet beside the door and wedged it beneath the handle to slow his pursuit. He was like a dog with a bone when it came to harassing me and I wondered whether he was truly so desperate to infuriate me or if he was simply so oafish that it had been a long time since anyone else had deigned to endure his company.

Either way, I wasn't inclined to become his new confidant or plaything. I was going to get away from him whatever it took.

I grabbed a picnic hamper from beneath the large kitchen table and hurried to start filling it with all manner of delicious food and drinks from the pantry, making my very own feast which I planned to enjoy in solitude. I couldn't fathom the powerful magic which had been used to preserve this place and the food within it in such a perfect state but I certainly wouldn't have minded having the ability myself. Either way, I was going to take full advantage of its use.

The door rattled as Hendrix reached it, his muttered confusion only offering me brief satisfaction. I doubted a broom would waylay him for long.

I grabbed my supplies and hurried across the huge room, heading for the door I'd spied in the corner there and pulling it wide with hope blossoming in my chest. A second staircase greeted me, this one narrower and darker than the grand thing in the heart of the house, likely meant for servants and certainly welcome for use by me.

I closed the door at my back and hurried to ascend the stairs in the dark just as the sound of a broomstick shattering and a door banging open against a wall caught up to me.

"Playing hide and seek?" Hendrix taunted, back on the hunt for me, but I ignored him, climbing higher and higher in the dark until I found another door which let me out onto the second floor.

There were countless doors on either side of the corridor I emerged in but I hurried past all of them, ignoring the stares of the Fae woven into tapestries and brought to life in oil paints. The corridor veered sharply right and I selected the second door I came to, slipping through it while working to ignore the sound of Hendrix flinging doors open deeper in the house.

This place was huge. With a bit of luck I could at least avoid him long enough to eat. With a *lot* of luck I could stay clear of him until the sun rose again and I took my next chance at escaping.

I hurried further into the room, unable to make out much more than shifting shadows in the gloom.

The brush of a silken leaf slipped across my cheek in the darkness and I stilled, my heart lurching. I wondered if I'd somehow made it outside or found my way into a room that had been breached by the trees.

I reached up to knock the fronds aside and my fingers grazed against more of them. But there was no wind here, no chill from between wide trunks or rustle of small critters in the foliage.

I could still hear Hendrix hunting for me and perhaps it was madness but I pressed on, eager to avoid him.

More leaves brushed against my arms, my face, tangling in my hair and tugging at my cape. The scent of earth and dampness surrounded me and my fear over the forest spiked again until I stumbled out into a small space where the room widened and silvery light pooled down from the roof to surround me.

My lips parted as I peered up at the glass structure which loomed over my head, moonlight illuminating a grand conservatory abundant with beautiful plants and luscious blooms. They flowed into every spare inch of space, flourishing with life and vitality.

I was standing upon a wide balcony, wrought iron staircases descending into the conservatory on both my right and left, this monstrously huge addition to the palace spanning all four of its floors and extending out into the gardens to the rear of the building.

I almost began to question how they had survived in here without anyone to care for them but I could hear a low trickle of water, and as I stepped up to the edge of a balcony, I spied a beautiful pond at the heart of the room, small rivulets running from it in every direction.

This place didn't need anyone to care for it. It was an oasis all of its own. And the magic which preserved everything in the castle had clearly helped it thrive.

My feet chose their own path as I descended the stairs, slipping beneath overhanging branches with orange flowers bigger than my head. There were paths between the fauna, little gravel tracks which I could just about navigate by stepping over or around the occupants of this miniature nirvana.

I didn't follow any particular path but I ended up standing before a wooden hut which was hidden beneath a swathe of leaves so big they could have been bathing tubs. There were a pair of chairs nestled inside with cosy blankets draped over them and a firepit waiting expectantly between them.

I dropped into one of them with a sigh, lifting my picnic basket onto my lap and taking out the first piece of my feast. The vegetable pie was creamy and delicious, the tomatoes bursting against my tongue and making me groan. I was used to plain, hearty fare and though we'd never been at the point of starvation, I was more than accustomed to difficult winters with monotonous simplicity on the menu. The kind of food the Fae had left behind made me certain they'd never faced that type of hardship, which only made me hate them more.

I devoured another slice of the pie, then a third, grinning while I ate because there hadn't been another and I knew Hendrix would get none. Then I settled back and took the sweet pastries from my hoard. One filled with blackberry and apple, the second with strawberries and cream, and the last smelled of the finest chocolate.

But before I could lift any of them to my lips, something hard dug into my side from a gap between the cushions of my seat. I leaned to the left, rooting around for whatever was ruining my moment of petty victory before finally pulling a small diary free.

I frowned as I looked at the pale grey book, the journal loosely bound and nowhere near as fine as the rest of the items I'd seen in this house. In fact, if I were to guess, I would have to say that it looked distinctly…human.

I released my hold on the pastries, letting them tumble back into my hamper before carefully opening the book to discover its secrets.

A small chill ran down my spine as I cracked the pages open. I'd always loved that feeling, the moment of delving into a new world, mysteries whispering their way out of the ink for me to consume.

The book fell open on a page a little more than half way through, the spine bending there as if it had been waiting for my arrival. I frowned at the handwriting, finding something comfortingly familiar about it as I began to read.

Day thirty-seven.

I heard singing in the trees again. The Lost Children are hunting me, there is no denying it now. They don't wait for nightfall any longer but start creeping through the shadows in my wake for at least an hour before dusk.

I don't think they wish to harm me, but they want to lead me somewhere and I'm uncertain how many more times I'll be able to resist their calls.

I realise now that I should have spent time finding the other Champions. What point is there to us all trying to gather the amulets alone – how are we supposed to know when all thirteen have been found??

The Unicorn and Rat amulets no longer feel like accomplishments where they hang around my neck but rather burdens to bear. Time slips by and the only other spirit whose location I know of is impossible to capture. That monstrous beast will not be tamed by me, I know it now. Perhaps it would take an army to vanquish such a being. And perhaps that means I must leave this place to find one. I am not sure there has ever been a creature more powerful in this world. Even the Fae tremble at the mention of it.

I cannot be the only Champion still living. I no longer covet the boon. What good will my unfulfilled wishes do me when we run out of time and the forest consumes me? So I plan to set out and find whoever else still lives within these cursed trees, though it pains me to abandon this sanctuary I found. But what other choice do I have?

I can only hope that the rest of the spirits have been captured by now, and if all the Champions unite, we may yet claim the final beast and break this curse together.

But my hope for that is dwindling, hence my abandonment of this journal. Herein I have documented all I've learned during my tortuous weeks in this cursed place. I cannot say I am glad I came. The prestige and renown I'd so coveted when coming here has lost its shine. I do not wish to break this curse so that I might be hailed as a hero for the rest of my days and beloved by all people any longer. Those were the wants of a foolish woman, convinced of her own self-importance. I am now simply a being who wishes to survive this place but fears I will not.

The map may guide you, though I wouldn't trust it fully – these trees are no mere lumber awaiting the axe but living, feeling spectres with minds of their own and no spirits to rein in their malignant intents.

I have noted all I've found and all I suspect as well. I compete in the eighth Great Hunt. I hope on all I am that it is the last and my plan to unite with the other Champions works. If not, then I pass my hopes to whoever finds this journal and offer you my wishes that your hunt is more fruitful than my own.

A shiver ran through me which had nothing to do with the cold and everything to do with the author of this journal. I was currently taking part in the thirteenth Great Hunt. Her plan had failed and she'd been claimed by this place.

I'd been so caught up in my reasons for needing to join the hunt that I supposed I'd never given enough thought to how hopeless a venture this had been for so many before me. People who had trained their entire lives for this challenge had succumbed to it time and again, human and Fae alike.

The forest was the only victor in this game, yet still we kept playing. Still I'd chosen to play.

And as my thoughts slipped to my reasons for doing so, I knew I wouldn't have ever made a different choice.

A note of melancholy song started up in the distance, a feminine voice which made the hairs raise along the back of my neck and my heart jolt to attention. I sat up in my chair, seeking out a window between the tangled vines and flowers filling the conservatory.

There was a flicker of something pale as it darted between the trees and I was on my feet.

I ran between the wildness of the plants, my boots splashing into one of the small streams and sending spray up around me as I raced toward that tiny offering of a clue.

"Rissa?" I called, my voice loud and echoing, but I didn't care.

I slapped large leaves out of my way and ran until I finally came upon the towering pane of glass which divided me from the forest beyond.

There was a door to my right, a key in the lock, a finger beckoning me closer as if to make it all too easy for me to step out there. I reached for the key, heart pounding as I scoured the trees for what I thought I'd seen, my ears straining for another note of song.

Nothing.

The trees bowed and bent in a wind that seemed intent on changing direction over and over, creating a dance with the leaves which had been torn free from the canopy above.

I almost turned the key. Almost stepped out into the dark. But there was something in my hand already, something warmed by my touch and grounding in a way I'd always found so very reassuring.

I glanced down at the book I still clutched in my fingers and stepped away from the door. It was madness to go out there at night. I hadn't seen what I'd thought I'd seen, hadn't heard it either. And even if I had, I couldn't risk the trees at night. I knew that.

"Rissa?" I called again, my hope fading, that old ache rising to consume me. Was she here? Were my hopes weighted in anything real at all? If I failed in this task, then everything I had dedicated my life to would come to nothing, the fear and grief I had exposed my parents to when coming here would be nothing more than a cruel and callous act.

Tears burned the backs of my eyes and my breaths came unsteadily.

"I'm here," I told her. Or told no one. Perhaps I was chasing a ghost which had no desire to be found.

I took another step back, forcing myself to ignore the call of the forest, and dropped down in defeat to sit beneath a leafy canopy of wisteria, the purple blooms perfuming the air and drawing me back from the madness which had almost consumed me.

I leafed through the pages of the journal, flipping back through the book past the neatly written words penned there by an author long since dead and lost to time two hundred and fifty years ago.

Finally, I made it to the front of the book where a sheaf of parchment fell free into my lap.

I took hold of it, my fingers trembling lightly as I unfolded it, like I could already tell that it was important.

I bit down on my bottom lip as I took in the map which had been drawn there, the detail and talent which went with it putting my own rough sketches to shame, though I found some similarities to my own work in it. There was the well I'd almost fallen into when encountering the Raven and there, just to the north of it, a dell had been marked with a little image of a midnight black bird upon it.

My breath caught as I took in its implication and my eyes darted over the rest of the map, drinking in the details. There were notes, questioning and dismissing the locations of the various spirits, making it clear that the author of the journal hadn't been certain of many of their locations but had made guesses based on what she'd gleaned from other Champions or had witnessed herself.

I noted the positions of both the Unicorn and the Rat, knowing that she had captured those spirits. If there was any truth to her theory that they had secured their own dominions within these cursed trees and that they haunted specific places then I would need to head there. She didn't have all of the spirits marked but her guess for the Raven made my pulse quicken because it aligned with my own experience too perfectly to be a coincidence.

And there…the Fox was marked in a position to the west of this castle too. My heart pounded faster in my chest, hope a spark that built and burned more brightly with each aspect I took in.

I scoured the page, drinking in every detail. This could be it. Precisely what I needed to be able to win the boon and do what I'd come here for.

As I hunted the neatly drawn lines and worked to commit it all to memory, my eyes snagged on an image above a network of caves to the north of the castle we were in, showing a reptilian beast with gleaming eyes and scales that shone silvery even in the tiny sketch.

The Dragon.

"Ferris." Hendrix took his time over my name, the deep baritone of his voice making each letter rumble like a new secret to be discovered.

I flinched, folding the map hastily and shoving it back into the journal before pushing both beneath my crossed legs and glaring up at him.

"Oh good, you found me," I deadpanned, everything in my

expression urging him to get lost again, but he simply shrouded me in his shadow, a scowl descending over his features.

"If you were so keen to play prey for me you could have at least hidden yourself better."

"The only thing I'm determined to do where you're concerned is leave," I muttered.

Hendrix smiled that predatory grin which he favoured so often, bending low until his face was level with mine and I was utterly drowned within his dominant aura. I wasn't afraid. Not because he wasn't terrifying but because it was so painfully obvious that he could kill me whenever he wanted to. Fear seemed utterly pointless in his company. Fight or flight would get me nowhere. I doubted it would so much as delay the inevitable. So I gave him neither and awaited my chance to slip away from him.

"You played a better role than I gave you credit for today," he said, goading me, and I couldn't help but drop my gaze to the twin amulets which hung around his neck, the pair of them dangling before me as if daring me to snatch them. Not that it would do me any good to do so.

I pursed my lips, leaning closer to him, refusing to recoil.

"And you played yours so predictably," I said. "The Fae always were treacherous, scheming creatures, willing to connive and steal whatever they couldn't claim with honour or dignity."

"I suppose the humans are rife with honour and dignity then? As we are so despicable to you, you must have grown up in quite the paradise where all are treated so well and so fairly."

My silence answered him on that and he snorted derisively. "Are you going to make me take it?"

I stiffened. "I don't know what you mean."

"You don't know what I mean?" he parroted, leaning lower, his rough fingers brushing the outside of my thigh and making my skin burn beneath my trousers. He lifted my leg with the back of his hand, tugging the journal free, and I had to force myself not to snatch it away from him again.

"That's mine."

"Liar."

"I found it and the original owner is dead. Same difference."

"Then I took it, so I suppose its ownership has changed hands once more. Didn't you say that my kind are all thieves and scoundrels anyway? Please, dear Ferris, let me play the villain you so keenly paint me out to be."

"You clearly paint yourself as such," I sneered. "And your people did too." My eyes flicked to the tattoo which curved around his eye.

He snatched my chin into his grasp and forced my eyes to meet his again, the green so dark it appeared black in this light. "If you had an ounce of real understanding about this mark I carry, you wouldn't be scowling at it, lightwing. You'd be screaming and running out into the night, begging the trees to claim you before I do."

"I thought you'd already claimed me," I replied, though his words sent a chill to my core and made a thousand questions blossom on my tongue. But I knew he wouldn't answer any of them. He only ever spoke about who he was in riddles and lies.

Hendrix chuckled, straightening suddenly and releasing my chin from his grasp. His fingerprints left a burning impression on my flesh where they'd departed and the coldness of the room crept closer in their absence.

"You'd know if I had." He fell silent as he opened the journal and I bit down on the inside of my cheek to stop myself from demanding it back. "These are just the ramblings of some poor bastard who failed to do what I will succeed at. What use is it to you?"

"Perhaps I can learn from her mistakes," I said, wondering if my Fae captor might just lose interest in my discovery before realising what a great treasure it had the potential to be.

Hendrix scoffed dismissively, snapping the journal shut before tossing it back to me.

"Come. I'll not have you wandering the corridors like a mouse scurrying between the walls. You'll join me for dinner willingly or I'll tie you in place again. Perhaps you have a taste for that treatment now?"

"Fine." I pushed to my feet, slipping the journal into my pocket before he could think any more of it.

I'd play his games for now. But soon, I'd find a way free of them and the moment I could, I'd disappear into the forest once more.

HENDRIX

CHAPTER SIXTEEN

Dawn arrived in shimmers of colour that spilled through the stained-glass window at the far end of the dining hall while I ate my breakfast. I took my time over my food, pondering my next moves in this forest and all that was to come, then I headed outside and walked the perimeter in case my human had decided to attempt escape again.

She was nowhere to be found though, and one sweep of her room inside told me she had scurried away to her favourite place in the castle again. So I headed for the conservatory that was lush with plant life and predictably, there I found her, laid on some cushions strewn on the stone floor as she poured over the diary she'd discovered.

She hadn't noticed my arrival yet and I decided I didn't want her to. I prowled a little closer in the shadows, noting the crease on her brow and the way her finger tracked delicately over certain words or images.

She studied every page meticulously before she moved on to the next, and something about the persistence of her soul captivated me. Her best chance at surviving this forest was assisting someone like me in the pursuit of the spirits, but instead, she still harboured a fascinating desire to do it herself.

Did she really think she would be the one to earn the boon of the forest? It was laughable. A human wouldn't survive the brutality of this place and it wasn't just the cursed trees she had to fear.

Even I, the outcast prince, had doubts over who I might meet among the Champions. There had been whispers that Islasees Bellatorn was going to enter this Hunt in hopes to end the curse – and no doubt seek the boon for his own devices. A Fae who had built a ferocious army in the name of King Arthrun over six hundred years ago. Islasees had used his warriors to conquer a rebel faction of Fae who had made the darkest brand of deals with the Hags. If he had deigned it worth his time to take on the forest and we encountered him here, we may not even make it to the Great Elm.

His hatred of me ran as thick as oil in his veins - and I was inclined to feel the same. I had been the one to kill his precious king after all, and he had been the one to run me out of Rivenspire.

There was one other thing that Ferris had no idea about in this game. Before we made it to the Great Elm, we had to pass through the labyrinth, and as far as I knew, I was the only person who had discovered what was required to gain entry to it. The Hag I had bargained with for information had not just told me of the boon's capabilities but of a secret none besides I was privy to. The labyrinth was locked. And the key? Well, that was in my possession.

I stepped up behind Ferris, tilting my head as I took in the map she was poring over. My brows lifted as I noted the location of the Dragon marked so clearly upon it. North of a winding cave system – its only access through that twisting passage. But it seemed the dead man who had drawn this map had charted a path through it. Or at least, he had obtained the knowledge from someone who had. It was a gamble. We could end up stuck in those caves following the meandering trails of a human who had lost his mind during his time in the forest. Or…

"*Up*," I barked, and Ferris nearly jumped out of her skin as she leapt to her feet. I snatched the diary from her hands and she cursed me as I took a closer look at the map.

"Give that back." She clawed at my fingers, trying to get it free, but she was as much a bother to me as a mosquito. When I'd had my fill of looking, I tossed it back to her and she caught it, hugging it to her chest and glaring at me.

"You said you weren't interested in it," she growled.

"Feisty little thing this morning, aren't you?" I drawled. "I have decided to put some stock in your dead human's diary. So come, lightwing, let's go see if we can find ourselves a Dragon."

With that, I turned and left her to decide her fate – though it was obvious she would join me. Her foolish ways would lead her to continue her plight in seeking the spirits and that suited me well. At least I didn't have to keep rounding up my bait when it walked so willingly after me into danger.

I marched through the castle, exiting into the wilderness where the cicadas pulsed with a rhythmic, high-pitched droll that came from every direction. Small critters and birds chattered this morning too, telling of no magic disturbing them. No spirits close to seize.

My pet human didn't appear right away, taking her sweet time to follow, and finally arriving with a pack fit to bursting with supplies. I could go days without food if necessary, but of course, the human could not. Such delicate things. She never went anywhere without those precious books of hers either. If they held the potential usefulness of the one I'd just caught her studying, I might just have to take more of an interest in the others. But I'd wait to see if the Dragon was where the map indicated before I put any true stock in her human scribblings.

I made a fast march for the north of the forest and Ferris stayed beside me, jaw set.

We walked for over three hours in silence, nothing but the

company of the wildlife breaking the quiet between us. She never once asked to stop, not a single complaint passing her lips even when I led her up a sheer hill. And still nothing when we began down the other side, heading into a treacherous valley lined with jagged rocks. Those violet eyes never missed a beat though, drinking in her surroundings, studying every tree and vine we passed. What went on behind them was a mystery she wouldn't share with me and it irked me that I was curious enough to care.

We were close now. Our cave was just on the other side of this valley. The Dragon potentially within my grasp.

"Wait," Ferris hissed, finally breaching the wall of quiet between us.

I looked to her with a bored expression, expecting her to complain of her aching feet and demand I let her rest.

"Hollows," she breathed, an edge of fear slicing her voice apart.

My head whipped around in the direction she was staring and I spotted them at the base of the hill, their grey pallor and worn clothes blending them into the landscape. But I should have noticed them first. My mind was sharper than most Fae's, let alone a human's, especially when it came to damn Hollows. But she and her maddening eyes had drawn my focus once again.

Fuck.

It was a large group of the dead, fifteen of them at least, and there were certainly more lurking in the surrounding forest.

"They're blocking the entrance to the cave," Ferris hissed, lowering down to a crouch to remain concealed from them.

I gazed beyond the Hollows who roamed the rocky terrain, finding she was right again. Our passage lay there, and between us and it were the Hollows.

"Get down," Ferris insisted, and I lazily lowered to a crouch beside her, taking in the fear in her eyes. The terror that ran so deeply in her and every other being across the lands because of these monsters.

"We have to distract them somehow, lure them away from that cave," Ferris said, her hand closing on a rock as she weighed it in her palm, her brow creasing with thought.

"Yes, indeed," I said darkly, still drinking in her terror. "Have you met with them before, lightwing?"

Her eyes locked on mine, her throat rising and falling. "Yes. They hunt the human realm just as they do yours."

"They hunt nothing," I said, my voice a cold, malicious thing. "They kill blindly, without thought or feeling. The hungry ones do anyway, once they have truly lost themselves. Keep them fed and they stay a little sharper."

"Well these look ravenous," she said, her eyes darting back to our minor problem in the valley while her fingers painted an X in the dirt.

"Have they ever come for you, Ferris? Have you felt their nails on your skin? Smelled their rancid breath? Seen the manic nothingness in their eyes?"

She turned to me again, recoiling at my words. "Yes," she whispered. "And you?"

I looked to the Hollows, saying nothing. *Oh Ferris, if only you knew what I had been through. The twisted fate this world has handed me. Spirits be, how you will tremble in my presence once you learn the truth.*

Ferris gained her feet, creeping up to a large boulder and positioning herself behind it as she took out her slingshot. I watched in amused interest as she placed the rock in it and readied her shot.

With a whoosh, the rock was released, pelting away over the heads of the Hollows and crashing into the trees beyond. But that would hardly be enough to draw them away. I got to my feet, ready to deal with them myself, but a second rock flew from her sling and surprise gripped me when it hit a bees' nest hanging up in the same tree her first rock had fallen close to before. The nest fell and smashed in an explosion of bees, the sound drawing the attention of the Hollows who ran clumsily and desperately toward it, clearing a path to the cave.

Ferris said nothing as she took off down the hill, traversing the jagged rocks faster and faster as she ran for the cave. I had no choice but to follow in her stead, a wild laugh escaping my chest as I raced to catch her. Clever thing, there she went again, surprising me after all.

We made it to the cave together, sprinting into the dark side by side and leaving the Hollows to seek sustenance elsewhere. My laughter was echoed by hers and we shared a look as we slowed our pace, our faces lit by the shimmering bioluminescent glowworms lining the cave roof.

Our laughter fell away and I stepped closer to her, drawn to her inexplicably as magic pulsed around us in the air.

A spirit was close, its power so thick and so omnipotent that it made the hairs raise along the back of my neck. But nothing called my attention more than the human right then. Her dark hair was wild about her shoulders, her eyes full of unspent life, so bright they almost burned.

I moved closer, close enough that her back pressed to the cave wall. I had her cornered but she didn't try to run, and maybe I was deranged by all the years I had spent alone, but I could have sworn she was looking at me the same way I was looking at her, drunk on the energy in this place, and perhaps on each other in some confounding way.

"Pretty thing, if only you knew…" I captured her chin between my finger and thumb.

"Knew what?" she asked, her voice a rasp, a plea and a demand.

"What a monster I can be."

"I'm still not afraid of you, Hendrix."

"Then you are a fool."

"I fear things that will hurt me. And I know you won't do that. You need me too much." She caught my wrist as if to remove my hand from her face, but instead her fingers flexed against my skin and she frowned like she didn't have an answer as to why she lingered there. I certainly didn't have one for her.

"And what happens when I stop needing you?" I growled, the truth of what was coming far too stark.

"You'll let me go," she said assuredly, her chin lifting.

"I wish to never let you go," I admitted, the truth a sin that marked her as my captive. One which I had a mind to keep. As I closed the space between us, mouths hovering an inch apart, she didn't recoil like she should have. She made no move at all as those violet eyes connected with mine, seeing into the depths of my soul, finding the rot within and yet still not shrinking from me.

"I'll escape you one day," she whispered.

I coiled a lock of her dark hair around one finger, revelling in how the silken strand glided over my skin. "Maybe you will not wish to."

Her throat bobbed, jaw ticking and a heated hatred mixing with the sultry look in her eyes. But she didn't run away.

Her breath was as sweet as honey on my mouth, a temptation so blinding I couldn't recall where we were or why we had come. I only had a mind for the presence of *her*.

She tugged my hand away from her face, but my body still caged her against the wall. Energy buzzed between us, a push and pull of power that thrashed inside my chest and demanded an answer.

I was suddenly very aware of what was coming. Only death awaited her in this forest. Be it at my hand or another's. She would perish, as most of them would. Because this game only ended one way. Just as all games I entered into concluded. I was not going to get my wish of keeping her.

"Move," she commanded, the moment fracturing as her softened eyes hardened in an instant.

My jaw gritted and my thoughts jarred. What was I thinking? Had I really intended to seduce the human? Was her temptation so great that I was going to be distracted from the task at hand time and again?

Rage blossomed through me and I gestured for her to go ahead of me with a grunt of irritation. "Hurry up and chart the way, lightwing. You're wasting my time."

"I'm wasting *your* time?" she scoffed. "You're the one who-"

"Who what?" I sneered, daring her to say it, but she only pursed her lips at me. I took the opportunity to shove her further into the tunnel. "Move then. The caves await us. And you are the only one with a map."

FERRIS

CHAPTER SEVENTEEN

There was an energy to these caves which made the hairs along my arms stand on end, my skin prickling like static was striking every part of me. The dark walls smelled of iron and petrichor, and despite us being beneath the ground, I felt as though a storm might break out at any moment.

The glow from the blue worms which pulsed softly across the ceiling and walls was eerie, and no matter how carefully we stepped, our boots echoed loudly in the silence.

My skin prickled with electricity as though it danced in the air all around us. I felt flushed to the point of dizziness, and there was an ache in my flesh which was present right down to the air I inhaled.

My body was responding to the heavy power here, nothing more. It certainly wasn't a reaction to the proximity of the Fae who had just looked at me as though he was thinking of devouring me whole.

Every instinct in my body was warning me to beware for more reasons than one, and perhaps a less foolish woman might have turned back. But despite the warnings hanging in every part of this place, I felt only the desire to keep going, to seek its end and what might lay there.

The ground rose steadily beneath our feet and a rush of cool wind brushed over us, whispering of an opening up ahead.

Hendrix shouldered past me, drawing his sword and falling into a warrior's stance which only made him appear more lethal than ever.

I eyed him warily, knowing he had plans for me once we arrived at our destination and trying to figure out what they were. He was so certain that he could trick the spirits by using me as bait, and I supposed with his strength he would only need a moment of distraction on their part to claim the upper hand. Still, the two amulets he wore should have been mine.

I refused to accept that he had rightfully earned either of them. The Bear had been won by Colton and in his death, he would have wished it to go to another human Champion, not a Fae. I may not have been a Champion by design but I had become one upon my entry to these woods and had been the only human with him when he was ripped from this world. I was sure he would have expected me to take up his prize. Instead it had been stolen by the Fae bastard just as so many other things had been taken from us by his kind.

The Fox was a sting that cut deeper. Hendrix had blundered that catch, racing after the spirit like a charging bull and quickly losing sight of it. I'd been the one who had figured out how to lure it back to us with fire. I'd been the one sitting before it when it had returned and I'd been mere moments from striking and seizing it for myself when he'd strode up and stolen it.

But like a fool, I'd hesitated. I'd had my shot right there before me but I'd found myself staring into the flaming eyes of my quarry and had been lost in the pain I'd discovered there. I wasn't certain how I'd known it, but I'd felt a weight of grief clinging to the spirit which mirrored the pain in my own heart so keenly that I'd been rendered still by it, shocked to find anything in a creature born of magic which might resonate so deeply within me.

Yes it had been terrifying, its teeth bared over flaming lips, the heat of its fiery body wrapping around me so tightly that the air in my lungs had seared its way through my chest. But the Fox had been so sad. And then Hendrix had thrown his blade at it like a damn beast and my chance had been lost just like that.

I was determined not to hesitate again. I had no idea how I might hope to claim the most terrifying spirit of them all, but I was set on trying. The Dragon was ancient, all lore about it cloaked in myth, but some strands of its history aligned time and again in the books I'd studied so desperately.

The Dragon's task had been to protect the forest from all ill and herd the trees back together if ever they began to wander at will. It was strong and fierce, wild and wary. And it would rain down terror upon any it saw as a threat to its charge.

We turned a corner and light finally spilled into the caves, a shimmering silver glow which spoke of thick clouds beyond the canopy of the forest outside.

I took a steadying breath and crept towards the cave's exit, the static only growing heavier in the air, a few strands of my dark hair lifting around my face.

Hendrix led the way as we crept out into a clearing beyond the caves, the grey sky just visible between the outstretched branches which leaned over to hide this place from view.

A great wall of braided sticks and branches blocked our way on, the side of it extending up just above our heads. I stared at the structure, trying to understand what it was and spying a glimmering silvery-white feather threaded within the twisted sticks.

I edged forward and took hold of the end of the feather, a small shock sparking against my fingers and making my hand jerk back again.

Hendrix turned a withering look on me, arching a brow. "Scared, human?"

I scowled at him, not bothering to dignify his question with an answer because only a fool wouldn't be frightened in this place. Wherever we were, it was thick with magic, the feel of it humming between the branches of the ancient trees and whispering its way through every twisted vine, every blade of grass.

We were being watched. I felt it in my bones, though I couldn't see anything in the surrounding glade to prove it.

I gritted my teeth and grasped the feather again, ignoring the zap of electricity that bit at my fingers as I tugged it free of the twisted branches.

I gasped as I held it aloft. The feather was almost as long as my arm with trails of zigzagging silver light slipping across its pearly white surface. It was soft but also strong, the silken strands which surrounded its shaft only bending slightly under the pressure of my thumb before springing back into place.

"Hendrix," I breathed, holding my prize out to show him. "I think it's really here somewhere. This feather could only be from a creature born of pure magic, one who-"

My words cut off as Hendrix grabbed me, an 'oof' escaping my lips as I found myself flipped upside down and tossed over his shoulder.

"That's all very fascinating, lightwing, but I'm ready to get to the punchline."

I kicked him in the stomach as hard as I could but he only grunted once, then clapped his arm over my legs to still them before starting to climb the wall of braided wood.

"What are you doing?" I hissed, punching him in the kidney to no avail.

"What we came here for," he replied darkly, no hint of hesitation in his voice.

I continued to strike him while he climbed but he ignored me, vaulting over the top of the braided wall and dropping down on the other side of it.

Hendrix dumped me onto a pile of the twisted branches, and I sucked in a sharp breath as I took in the bowl I found myself in, moss and more of those beautiful feathers woven between the sticks and making it clear what this was.

"It's a nest," I breathed, looking around at the beautiful structure we'd climbed into.

"Yeah. A nest where a Dragon lives. You're up, lightwing. Time to play your part," Hendrix grunted, taking a coil of rope from his pack and moving to loom over me.

"You're not seriously going to-" I shrieked as he lunged for me, kicking out and managing to strike him in the jaw hard enough to make him stagger back a step.

I scrambled away, trying to escape him, scrabbling to get up, but he caught my ankle as I flipped around and dragged me back beneath him again.

Hendrix hauled my arms behind my back and the rope cinched tight around my wrists a moment later. He flipped me onto my back once more and grinned down at me like a maniac.

"Are you going to scream for me, pretty human, or will I have to make you?"

"Fuck you."

"The hard route it is then." He took a dagger from his belt and knelt over my waist as he brought it down towards me.

"What the hell are you doing?" I gasped before his blade cut into the flesh of my shoulder and a cry of pain escaped me.

I bucked and fought beneath him but he ignored me, pinning me down with a hand on my chest, his eyes moving to the trees above.

"Again," he growled before slapping his hand down on the cut he'd given me when I refused to comply.

The bite of pain tore another cry from my lips and a crack of thunder boomed through the sky.

In less than a heartbeat, Hendrix was gone, racing away and leaping from the nest before disappearing into the trees.

My heart pounded violently as I fought against the bonds which tied my hands at the base of my spine. There was no way I was climbing out of this giant nest without them, and as thunder crashed through the sky once more, I couldn't help but cower against the oncoming presence I could feel between the trees.

The Dragon had heard us. It was here.

Rain crashed from the sky and pounded a path through the canopy, drenching me within minutes, plastering my clothes to my frame, the downpour turning torrential so that even the trunks of the trees became hazy and undefined.

A low growl rumbled through the forest.

I stilled, my head whipping back and forth as I fought to spot what approached, my muscles straining as I tried and tried to break free of my bonds.

Lightning split the world in two, forcing my eyes to snap shut, a shimmer of electricity sparking across my body as the power of the strike resounded through everything in the clearing.

My eyes flew wide and I screamed as I found the Dragon bursting from the trees, lunging right for me, its luminescent, serpentine body a mixture of white and silver with trails of teal-coloured electricity scoring paths between its scales.

I recoiled into the hard sticks beneath me, unable to look away as the Dragon came for me, my death a certainty glimmering in its silver eyes. Feathers clung to it like a mane, coating the backs of its legs too, though the talons which were outstretched and aimed my way drew more of my focus.

I really did scream then, fear and failure coating the sound as my end rushed towards me with such certainty that I could do nothing to escape it.

But just before the spirit could attack me, Hendrix leapt from the trees, swinging his sword and colliding with the beast so hard that they were knocked aside.

The two of them hit the edge of the nest to my left and the entire thing rocked violently as if it might flip over.

A sharp branch snagged in the rope which bound my hands and my desire to survive this place took over as I began to tug and saw at them.

Hendrix swung his blade again but the Dragon twisted to meet it, claws swiping with a savage blow which knocked the sword from his hands.

The Fae didn't even flinch, ducking beneath the strike of the enormous beast and ripping a pair of daggers from his belt instead.

I cursed him as I watched him holding his own against a Dragon with a brutal efficiency which defied humanity. He moved so fast that the Dragon couldn't catch him, parrying strikes from its razor-sharp claws and ducking low as it whipped its feather-lined tail straight for his head.

With a jerk, my bindings loosened as something snapped and I ripped my hands free of them, scrambling upright just as the Dragon lunged for Hendrix once more, its talons making it beneath his guard at last and striking him savagely across his chest.

Blood flew in a wild arc, splattering the tangled sticks and twigs which made up the creature's nest, and Hendrix's bellow of pain set my heart racing.

He fell back with another agonised cry and the Dragon pounced, its talons sinking into the nest either side of his head as it released a bellowing roar which made the forest shake.

Lightning exploded from its jaws as the rain pounded down on us even more forcefully and Hendrix jerked and roared as it slammed into him.

My lips parted in shock. He was going to die. The great Fae warrior had been felled by a spirit of these cursed woods and I was watching as it stole his final moments from him.

I stared at the Dragon, its focus fully on my enemy, and in that moment I fell prey to what I could only describe as a madness of my own.

I broke into a run, a cry parting my lips as I took a running jump and leapt onto the back of the Dragon, landing squarely behind its shoulder blades, its thick, serpentine body jolting beneath me as it reacted to my presence.

Electricity coursed over its skin, lashing every inch of my body through my saturated clothes as it wheeled its head around and snapped at me. But I held on, my position too close to its head to allow it to reach me, the smooth scales beneath my palms flexing and rippling with effort.

The Dragon roared in fury, but beneath that I could feel a hollow ache in its soul. I didn't know how else to describe it, but I knew the loss which clung to it. The spirit was lost, empty, aching and alone and I understood all too well how that felt.

I was gutted by that feeling, the weight of it humming in the air around us, my chest hollowing out at the emptiness this poor being endured. I was one with the spirit in that second, every moment of sorrow, regret and guilt which had plagued me for so many years humming throughout my body, my pain a mirror to the agony encompassing this creature of legend.

"I'm sorry," I whispered, my grip on it tightening, my hold becoming an embrace as the purity of its heartache washed through me and my own grief sharpened in reply.

My fear shattered and reformed in pain, my breaths coming as sharp stab wounds which stuck at my aching heart.

A tear slipped from my eye and rolled down my cheek, mixing with the rain before spilling from my skin and falling against the shining scales of the Dragon beneath me.

A jolt rocked through my body and I gasped as a blast of wind barrelled over me, whipping my hair away from my face and almost tearing me from my position on the Dragon's back.

The spirit stilled, its head tipping back and a note of song escaping it which echoed out into the trees, everything falling eerily silent in its wake as even the rain paused to hear it.

The scale where my tear had fallen shimmered and sparkled before my eyes, and I stared as the white darkened to lilac beneath me, that single scale becoming something new.

My spine arched as a jolt of power raced through me, my vision sharpening on the sky above, my veins buzzing with unknown energy, my world dividing and reforming in a single heartbeat.

I sagged forward as the power released me as fast as it had come, my arms locking around the spirit's neck as I choked down heaving breaths and tried to get my bearings in a world which seemed to have flipped on its axis around me.

Something white fell against my cheek in a soft embrace as if trying to soothe my trembling soul, but before I could turn to look at it, the Dragon leapt from the nest and burst into the sky.

I screamed as it took off, needing no wings to propel it toward the heavens but instead riding the wind as if it were born from it, its long body undulating in a current I couldn't feel but which pulsed in the air all around us.

The outstretched branches of the trees slapped at my skin as we raced higher and higher, my grip so tight I was afraid I might choke the beast in my desperation to hold onto it and not plummet to my death.

My screams didn't let up as we tore through the canopy and exploded into the sky beyond it, escaping the clutches of the forest as if we were breaching the surface of a great ocean.

The Dragon straightened, stilling in the air as it released another note of its sweet song into the sky.

I peeled myself upright, blinking as the rain slowed, then stopped, the forest revealing itself beneath us. We were so high that only the clouds remained above our heads, and I had to fight the swaying sense of vertigo as I forced myself to look down.

The forest extended in a great ring at the heart of the world below, the trees roaming in all directions, taking up so much of the land that it took me a moment to pick out anything which lay beyond its borders.

To the east, the glimmering wall the Fae had built divided their realm of Rivenspire from the one I'd grown up in, Arringfall. The Fae and human lands extended beyond it, ringing the edges of the Taking Trees in a terrifyingly narrow band which ended abruptly at the edge of the ocean that surrounded Rathian on all sides.

I'd already known that we didn't have another fifty years to break this curse but seeing so plainly the way the forest had devoured the land was chilling to behold.

I forced myself to look to the northwest where the Blight lay; the dark and barren lands where Bane Crownthief and his army of Hollows resided. The Necromancer the only thing in this cursed world which may have been worse than the forest.

I swallowed thickly as I took in the shadow of the lands he'd claimed for his army of the dead, hating to see how much of this narrowing world he'd managed to steal for his own. He was a monster which devoured the land and gave no heed to Fae or humankind. I'd gladly see him destroyed by this forest. He deserved the worst kind of death for his heinous deeds.

I turned my gaze back to the trees as the Dragon cried out again, spotting a few turrets and roofs, a windmill and even a flagpole still flying a tattered flag between the leaves.

Mostly there was nothing but greenery to see, but my gaze fell on an enormous elm tree which stood taller than all the rest, set right in the heart of the forest. There was a presence to it that made me feel as though it was watching me, the impressive branches fanned out and reaching for the eternal sky. The tree didn't sway or twist in the wind like those surrounding it. In fact, it was eerily perfect, and the light reflecting from its golden-hued leaves in a shimmering glow made my chest tighten.

"That's where we have to go to reunite the amulets?" I asked, uncertain why I was asking anything of a wild spirit. But as the Dragon turned its head to look at me, I found a deep wisdom in its eyes which resounded within my soul.

The spirit bellowed again and I screamed as it plummeted back into the trees, my arms locking tight around its neck as we shot towards the ground at an alarming pace, and I couldn't help but clamp my eyes tight in fear.

The spirit halted with ethereal grace, and I peeled my eyes open to find it landing softly in the heart of its nest.

I slid from its back and it turned to look at me, pinning me in its silver gaze as my heart rose to pound in my throat.

A long moment passed between us, an understanding so primal that I felt it in the roots of my soul. We shared a loss too hard to bear and we shared the same desire too. Somehow, the Dragon knew I needed to win the boon the forest had to offer its saviour, not for me, but for something so much more.

The Dragon dipped its head, its brow pressing to mine, the cool scales sending zips of static across my skin. I didn't dare breathe. I reached out to place my hands on either side of its enormous face and it allowed its eyes to fall closed.

"Don't fail me."

Shock splintered through me at the echoing voice inside my own head, but then the Dragon spilled away into a gust of wind, my hands closing on nothing as an amulet fell into the centre of the nest where it had stood just moments before.

My hand shook as I bent to take hold of it, the metal cool between my fingers as I lifted the amulet to inspect the carved dragon upon its surface.

I released a shaky breath as I looped the chain around my neck and a trembling laugh escaped me.

I'd done it. I'd claimed the Dragon. I wasn't sure whether to descend into hysterics or sobs, but a low and agonised groan stole my focus before I could decide between the two.

Hendrix lay in a puddle of his own blood, smoke rising from his clothes as the lingering burn of the lightning smouldered against his skin.

I gritted my teeth as I moved closer to him, crouching down to glare at the bastard who had so flippantly risked my life for his own gain.

I had assumed he was unconscious but his eyes flickered beneath his lids before opening, his green gaze meeting mine before slipping to my hair.

"It's silver," he wheezed, gripping a lock of my long, wet hair in my fingers and tugging it forward.

I frowned, then blinked in surprise as understanding filled me and I simply stared at the lock of hair tangled between his bloodstained fingers.

"How..." I began, staring at my hair which was no longer dark but that same, silvery opalescent hue of the Dragon's scales. It had marked me when it had chosen me to be its Summoner. I really was its keeper.

Hendrix wheezed a cough, blood trailing from the corner of his lips as he stared up at me, his fingers slipping in the strand of hair he still clung to.

"You're dying," I told him as I surveyed the jagged wounds across his chest and abdomen where the Dragon's talons had ripped into his flesh. I should have been glad, should have spat in his face and taken sick satisfaction in his demise. Instead I felt as empty as I'd declared him to be. Hollow. Void of any feeling on the matter of his death aside from a bite of contempt because he had been so willing to risk my life only to have ended up losing his own.

He bit out a laugh laced in agony. "If only."

"I should finish you myself. But then I wouldn't be able to take back those amulets you stole from me," I sneered, rising and taking a step away. His fingers were forced from my hair and his hand thumped down against the bloodstained branches beneath him. "I suppose I'll just have to come back to claim them from your corpse."

I made to turn away, fully intending to leave him there to die, though the thought had my stomach twisting with bile. But he deserved it. Deserved worse than that. He'd been more than willing to watch me die if it served his ends, had been happy to be the cause of my death. I was only allowing nature to take its course. I had no reason to feel any guilt about it.

Hendrix's hand snapped out and he grasped my ankle.

"You can't leave me here," he rasped, and I sneered at him.

"Watch me," I said cruelly, though my heart was racing frantically, but I refused to let him see even a flicker of hesitation in my gaze.

"Not because you might be burdened with guilt," he grunted, still maintaining his grip on my ankle. "But because you can't complete this task without me."

"I don't need you," I hissed.

"No," he chuckled as if the pool of blood that surrounded him was nothing but a mere inconvenience. "But you do need the key to the labyrinth."

I'd yanked my ankle from his hold while he'd spoken but I stilled at his words, a chill seeping into my bones as they sank in.

"There's no key," I muttered, trying to dismiss the strange chill which had run down my spine at those words, the whispered warnings hissing from every leaf above our heads. Some innate sense was warning me not to ignore his words, to listen despite my desire to scorn them…

"There is. And I possess it. Are you willing to risk reaching the labyrinth alone to find your passage barred and only regrets of my death for company?" Hendrix pressed, a smug smile on his face even as he lay dying at my feet.

"You don't have it."

"I do."

I crouched down and started tugging at his clothes, feeling for pockets, pulling blades free of their hiding places but discovering little else.

Hendrix laughed again, more blood slicking his lips. "If you'd wanted a chance to remove my clothes, you only needed to ask."

"In your dreams," I spat, shoving away from him and standing again. "Where is it if not here?"

"I really will die before I tell you, lightwing," he replied smugly. "But if you help me get back to the castle, then perhaps we can come to a new deal."

"What deal?" I snapped, not wanting a part of any agreement with this bastard.

"An alliance," he said as if I'd ever wish for such a thing with him. "You've claimed the Dragon. Perhaps there's more to you than I wanted to admit. I, in turn, have the Bear, the Fox and the key. If we work together, we can find the rest and end this curse."

I shook my head, wanting to deny him, to tell him to take his offer and shove it up his ass because he hadn't thought me worthy of one before. He only wanted this deal with me now because I'd seized what he could not and he was bleeding out in this cursed place with no hope of escape before night fell without me.

I could still leave. I could go and come back here tomorrow to take his two amulets from his corpse…assuming nothing stole his body in the night. But the key. If he really did have the key and it truly was the only way to gain entry to the labyrinth, then none of this would matter without it. I could find and capture all thirteen spirits and still die here in these cursed woods without ever winning the boon.

"I hate you," I growled as I gave in to the inevitable.

"I'm yet to find anyone living who doesn't," he said as if that were a declaration to boast of.

I crouched down and held my hand out for his. "An alliance. Equal partners or nothing."

"Equal," he agreed, clasping my hand, though I didn't miss the clear amusement in his green eyes at the statement.

By the spirits, I despised this male.

With a curse, I took hold of his hand and hauled him to his feet. He swore and staggered but managed to loop his arm around my neck and let me support him as we began what was certain to be a laborious trip back to the castle.

I couldn't ignore the wet slick of blood which soaked into my skin, nor the drops of it he left in his wake at every step. He'd be lucky to make it halfway back to the castle on his feet and if he fell, I had no hope of being able to drag him the rest of the way myself. We'd have to move fast and lay our hopes in the hands of the spirits.

"Would you like to hear a tale of my prestige?" Hendrix asked as we stepped into the shadow of the caves once more, his words a rough grumble against my ear which sent a shiver tumbling down my spine.

"No," I hissed in reply. "I simply want this over with as fast as humanly possible."

"It will be a slow journey indeed then." Hendrix barked a laugh which only made his wounds bleed more, and I winced beneath the weight of him as I led him back through the caves.

I had no idea if he would even make it to the castle, let alone survive the night once we got there, but I had no choice beyond helping him now. At least until I got what I needed from him because then, all deals would be off. And I would forge my own path once more.

Hendrix

CHAPTER EIGHTEEN

I was in the company of not one, but two others as my pretty human bore the brunt of my weight and worked to guide me back to the castle.

Ferris was the only visible member of our trio, the third being Death herself. Drawn close to me once more, fingers grasping, ready to steal me away and boast of her prize. What a trophy I would be to her. She would parade me before the dead souls and offer me up to the ruling spirit of the underworld. The dreaded Hawk of Woe. He would sink his talons into me and see me torn apart before scattering my pieces into countless sanctums of torment.

I would burn and freeze and break all at once until my soul was dust and I became nothing. How long I suffered would be decided by the mighty spirit of woe, and the stories described him as a merciless being that made Death herself quake in his presence. Considering my misgivings, I doubted I would be fortunate enough to be handed oblivion quickly.

Still, death would certainly make a change from this wearisome thing I called life. But even with blood slicking my chest and my vision growing hazy at the edges, her hand never touched mine. I couldn't leave this world without seizing the boon of the forest, and she knew I'd go through a thousand plagues to see my task done. She knew me better than any, actually. But her presence told of her doubt in me.

"Just a little further," Ferris grunted, struggling with the effort of holding up my considerable bulk.

We had somehow made it through the cave system and out of the valley, but we still had to traverse the forest for spirits knew how long. I couldn't tell how far we were from the castle, but I had the feeling Ferris's words were in aid of bolstering her own confidence in making it there. The sun was already descending. It was taking too long. And if night fell, it was game over.

"You have to move faster," I growled, gritting my teeth through a wave of agony.

Every step jolted my injuries, and I was losing enough blood to make my movements particularly clumsy. Between each hazy blink, I caught a glimpse of Death, just there on the periphery, her Falcon's head angled towards me, her long, ebony cloak trailing over the moss and those beady eyes ever watching me. Waiting for her moment.

"I'm moving as fast as I can, considering I'm carrying the two of us. You're the one who weighs as much as a damn tavern."

I chuckled through a pool of blood in my mouth, my wounds invoking my mania. I should have been furious knowing the human had stolen the Dragon right out from under me, but the way my head was spinning made it seem pretty amusing instead.

Look at her, with her pearlescent silver hair, gleaming with hints of teal when the dying sunlight hit it just so. Why had she been marked like this, I did not know. But it suited her somehow, the way it flowed around her shoulders and gave her a magical quality. I'd never seen a human possess any such thing. Her fragility was mirrored by power.

She had no idea what strength she now held and perhaps it was better not to let her know. With the Dragon answering her whims, she wasn't just a match for me, she was a match for every Champion between these trees.

So that meant…

Yes, I knew what I had to do now.

I laughed harder, the sound a wicked, foolish thing. Oh what a turn in fate. How the weak had risen among our ranks of grand warriors. She held the greatest gift here, even those with multiple spirits to their name would struggle to counter her now. But only if we could make it to shelter before night enveloped us.

I called on what little energy I had left and gritted my teeth through the pain, releasing some of my weight from Ferris's shoulders, but my fingers dug tighter into her arm.

The Dragon may not have been mine, but the human was. And I would defend her with everything I had left.

"We won't make it, weakling," I growled, knowing it would rile up a storm in her. "Not with your feeble legs trying to move us."

"Shut your mouth," she hissed and put on a spurt of energy.

A smile toyed at the edge of my lips at the response I'd gotten from her.

Once again, the forest seemed to bend and twist to allow her an easier passage, though it was unclear if she noticed the aid it offered. What was it about this human which had the cursed trees so enraptured? Did they find amusement in aiding the weakest Champion to have entered their domain? Was it a taunt for my benefit?

"We're so damn close," she exhaled to herself. "Come on, come on."

The light was trickling away between the leaves above, the dark growing thicker and the magic around us stirring to life. The forest was so very hungry, and at night, its power was more malignant.

I could feel the forest's roaring fury in the air, so palpable it was like blades swinging through the space before us. It wanted us to fail, it wanted to feast on us. And by the spirits, it looked like it might just have its wishes fulfilled.

"*There*," Ferris gasped, and I looked up from my stumbling feet to find the castle looming between the trees ahead. Our sanctuary just a hundred yards away.

My foot hit a root and I staggered, knees hitting the ground before I could catch myself, and Ferris was almost dragged down with me.

"Get up," she gasped in horror, the fading light a promise of our certain demise.

She tugged on my arm, trying to heave me to my feet, but I found I had no strength to summon. My head hit the moss and above the alluring face of my human, I saw a giant, writhing snake slithering through the trees above. The Serpent. The most cunning of the spirits, the one who could outwit even the Dragon.

My desire to seize the forest's boon drove my movements as I reared to my feet with a surge of agonised effort and somehow managed to unsheathe my sword. I swung for the branch, but the movement made my injuries scream in protest and my knees crashed to the forest floor once again. But I couldn't give up.

"Hendrix!" Ferris barked at me, catching my free arm and trying to pull me toward the castle.

"I must have it," I snarled through my teeth, resisting the tug of her hands despite the roaring pain ripping through me.

"The sun is setting!" Ferris cried.

The forest was alive around us, creatures of the night screeching as they sensed the true malevolence of the trees awakening. I staggered upright again, raising my sword, but the Serpent slithered up and away to evade me, its silken scales like woven gold, threaded with shining minerals and hardened rock. It was the foundation of this earth the forest stood upon, a forger of the ground. It could cause quakes, shift the stone and mud to cause utter devastation if it wanted to. I could feel the ground tremoring beneath me now, the spirit's ire invoked. But I was coming to claim it between roiling tides or falling skies. It could not escape me.

Ferris tugged me on again but I snatched my arm away, pain the only presence in my flesh as I focused on the Serpent.

Ferris released a yell, but I couldn't turn to look at her, stumbling forward to brace myself against the tree's trunk. Wooziness clouded my thoughts. My arms were leaden. My sword would not swing.

I blinked up at the Serpent as it slithered away into the canopy, knowing if I was healed, I could scale this tree and hunt it well.

My fingers clawed at the bark, the thought igniting determination in my soul. Everything depended on me returning the amulets to the Great Elm.

But the sun had fallen.

And Ferris was screaming.

I dragged my eyes from the Serpent, finding Ferris on the ground, a tangle of vines trying to drag her toward a hole beneath a fallen tree. That gaping mouth of darkness was about to consume her, bury her in the earth and steal her from me for good.

She grabbed a sharp flint from the forest floor and hacked at the vines, but every one she broke was replaced by another.

The Serpent hissed once more, drawing my attention to it again. So close. I could bury my sword in it if I could get a little closer.

Ferris's scream cut through me again, and then I was moving without even knowing when I had made the decision. I abandoned the spirit and heaved my sword above my head, swinging it down with the very last of my energy and severing every vine that had hold of my human.

Ferris scrambled to her feet just as I lurched into her, nearly crashing to the floor once more. But she had me. An arm looping around my waist, a strength and determination in her violet eyes which made it into the roots of my own soul. Then, somehow, we moved. And we kept moving until the forest was howling at our backs and we were falling through the castle door.

Ferris kicked it shut as we slumped into a heap on the flagstones, her arm crushed beneath me and my own resting on her lower back.

I drew her close as the scent of my own blood tainted the air between us. I could see her mouth painting my name, but I could no longer hear the word. Because darkness was coming for me and there was no escaping it. It stole me away and I was left at the mercy of a human, knowing my life depended on her and only her.

FERRIS

CHAPTER NINETEEN

I lay panting in the grip of my enemy, his bulk pinning my arm to the flagstones in the wide entrance hall, his hot blood soaking through my shirt.

"Get up," I hissed, the adrenaline fading and my racing heart painting a rapid tempo against my ribcage.

Hendrix said nothing, did nothing.

I turned to look at him, the darkness of the castle making it near impossible to make out his features, but I found his eyes closed, that penetrating glare at last removed from my skin.

"Hendrix?" I breathed, rolling towards him and shaking his shoulder to try and rouse him, but it did nothing more than stain my hand with more of his blood.

My other arm was still pinned beneath him, his bulk immobilising me as I lay in the deep shadow of his muscular frame.

"You need to wake up," I grunted, trying to tug my arm out from under him and gasping in alarm as he slumped over, his weight falling onto my right side, his face pressing into the crook of my neck.

The heat of him drowned me, my throat bobbing as the rough

graze of his stubble caught against my ear, a knotted lock of his hair brushing against my lips.

"Hendrix," I grunted, trying to push him back, my skin too hot beneath his, my body prickling at the contact. Still he didn't rouse, didn't speak, didn't do anything at all other than crush me into the flagstones and bleed all over my clothes.

The sound of metal clinking together drew my attention to the amulets which had tangled with my own. How tempting it was to just let him die, let him succumb to his wounds and relinquish his hold on the Bear and the Fox. I could be the owner of three amulets by morning.

But as the thought occurred to me, my gut twisted in denial.

The key. I needed his key. That was all there was to it.

I drew in a deep breath, then with a surge of effort managed to shove him back enough to allow me to crawl out from under him. His forehead thumped against the flagstones, and I felt a little guilty before remembering the sting of his blade when it had cut into my arm.

With a curse, I turned from him and hurried away into the castle. I was familiar enough with it to be able to gather what I needed from the kitchen, then I ran to the drawing room where I made quick work of lighting a fire in the hearth.

I laid out the bandages and tinctures I'd pilfered, then returned to find my patient still lying face-down in the entrance hall.

I tried calling his name again and got nothing. I poked and shook him, even managing to roll him onto his back and slap his smug face, but there was no satisfaction to be had from the strike as his head only lolled to the side.

"Shit," I muttered, wondering if I was already too late to save him. He'd lost a hell of a lot of blood and his pallor was more than alarming.

There was no way I was going to be able to carry him, so I took hold of his wrists and started pulling. By the spirits, he was one heavy bastard. I grunted and cursed from the strain of tugging him along, my heels digging into the floor and muscles bunching from exertion as I hauled his ass back into the drawing room.

The fire was crackling in the hearth, growing nicely and beginning to warm the room while illuminating it with its orange glow. I hauled Hendrix over to it, depositing him on the rug and dropping down to kneel at his side.

I picked up the knife I'd grabbed from the kitchen and quickly sliced his shirt open, cutting the sodden black fabric off of him to reveal the extent of the wounds beneath.

I hissed a sharp inhale as I took in the injuries across his chest and abdomen, his powerful body sliced open in six lines which marked the passage of the Dragon's talons across his frame in two groups of three.

The first strike had carved a path from the ribs on his left side across his chest and up to the shoulder of his right arm. The second had scored a path across his abs, curving down towards his right hip.

Blood oozed from the wounds, and I snatched the bottle of iodine I'd found, dousing them all with it and recoiling as Hendrix flinched, a grunt of pain escaping his lips, though he remained unconscious.

"You deserve this," I told him, the cut on my arm burning as if to remind me of the truth to my words. "You're a mean bastard who uses other people for your own gain. It's no wonder the Fae cast you out."

My gaze flicked to the tattoo which framed his eye for the space of a blink before I snatched it away again. Lying there he looked too fragile, too perfect, to be worthy of the insults I flung at him. It wasn't right that he was so beautiful. His face was a lie. Hell, his body was a masterpiece of deception too.

I swallowed thickly as that intrusive thought pushed its way through my mind. I hadn't removed his shirt so that I could become distracted by the allure of his powerful body. It didn't matter how attractive he was. He was still a beast no matter the frame his monstrosity was packaged in.

I inspected the newly cleaned wounds and was relieved to find that only two of the gashes were deep enough to need closing. The others would heal on their own with bandaging and time.

I had no thread or needle to stitch his wounds and no real knowledge of how to do so even if I had. Instead, I placed the blade of his dagger into the heart of the fire and waited.

Hendrix remained still beside me while the blade slowly began to glow with the heat of the flames until I finally drew it out again.

"This is going to hurt like a son of a bitch," I warned him, but of course he remained unresponsive. For his sake, I hoped he stayed as such.

I took a steadying breath and moved closer to him, aligning the flat of the blade with the still-bleeding wound before gritting my teeth and pressing it down.

Hendrix bucked beneath me, a cry of pain escaping him as he lurched upright, his green eyes flying open, hand lunging for me wildly. I jerked aside but he caught a fistful of my hair and tugged me so close that his forehead pressed to mine.

"If your aim is to kill me then I suggest you do it faster," he snarled as the scent of burning flesh rose between us and I pulled the blade from his skin.

"What's wrong, did the scary Fae need me to hold his hand while I fixed him up?" I bit back.

He bared his teeth and I bared mine in reply. Several seconds passed between us, the air in the room sparking with tension and hatred, his abhorrence for my kind warring with my despisal of his until he finally broke our stare and looked down to his wounds.

"One more to go," I told him, and he spat a curse.

"Get on with it then." He slumped to the rug once more and I thrust the dagger back into the flames.

I said nothing, only watched the blade until it glowed and I tugged it free again.

I positioned it over his chest, glancing up to find him watching me with sharp intensity. Sweat slicked his inked skin, his whole body tense with agony, but he said nothing to stop me as I prepared to cauterise his next wound.

His fingers flexed at his side as I lowered the blade and some madness struck me because I clasped his hand in mine a moment before pressing the searing metal to his skin.

Hendrix bellowed in pain, his body tensing, spine arching and hand snapping closed around mine so tightly I was afraid he might break bones. I withdrew the blade and tossed it aside, a shudder rolling through me at what I'd done.

The Fae slumped back onto the rug, unconscious once more though his hand still kept mine captive.

I hesitated before pulling my fingers free, offering him a final squeeze as I withdrew. It was more than he would have done for me, but I didn't have to lower myself to his level. The Fae were cruel and heartless but humans were not, and I wouldn't allow him to take my humanity from me no matter how little he was deserving of it.

I focused on cleaning the blood from his skin and bandaging his wounds. He didn't wake again.

When I was done, I cleaned the cut he'd given me too, finding it thankfully didn't need stitches and wasn't all that deep. Not that I hated him any less for what he'd done just because he'd failed to wound me deeply enough to scar.

Finally, I stood, backing out of the room and heading in search of a bath to cleanse myself of the blood and grime coating me. I was exhausted, aching and bruised but even in my fatigued state, a smile found me.

I'd captured the Dragon. My task here was far from lost.

My dreams were filled with a silver wind which swept through immense tree trunks, whispering and calling out my name, laughing at me as I ran to try and catch it, but I always failed to keep up. And songs sung by children in haunting melodies which threatened to drag me from my sleep but never quite managed to rouse me entirely.

I woke in a cold sweat, my heart racing and instincts screaming at me to move.

I pushed out of the huge bed and crossed to the window where the pale light around the edges of the shutters announced the arrival of dawn once more.

It took me a few moments to unbolt and draw open the heavy shutters and I squinted into the dim light while my eyes adjusted. A frown furrowed my brow as I peered out over the top of the tangled rose garden into the depths of the forest beyond.

There was something in the trees out there.

My eyes skipped from trunk to trunk, hunting shadows and seeking answers. A flicker of something white had my pulse skipping over itself and I reached for the window latch so I could throw it open and gain a better look.

I cursed as the latch failed to move at my tug and gave it more of my attention, finding the thing half melted and fused to the window frame.

"What in the name of all the spirits…" I muttered, checking the next window and the next. Anger rose within me as I discovered every window in my room had been fused shut, making them impossible for me to open.

My gaze roamed over the forest again, hunting for any sign of what I'd thought I'd seen, but there was nothing there, only endless trees swaying in a slight breeze.

I turned and strode from the room, the large shirt I'd slept in billowing around my frame and tickling my thighs while my bare feet pounded a path along the carpeted floor.

I stormed down the stairs, heading for the drawing room where I'd left Hendrix recovering from his wounds and hurling the door open so hard that it crashed against the wall with a loud bang.

"You melted the window latches?" I demanded, striding into the room and throwing the curtains aside to reveal him cursing from within the blankets I'd given him.

"You kept trying to run off," he grunted as though his actions were logical and not at all insane.

"How did you manage to do that? Is your Fae Art fire?"

"I am well-endowed in many forms of power, little human. I'd have thought you'd have realised that by now."

I scowled at his less-than-forthcoming answer - though it was hard to see much of him in the gloom of the drawing room.

"I agreed to stay here, didn't I? We're working together now, aren't we?"

"Yes," he said, though the word was laced with amusement. "But I secured the castle before our deal was struck. If you've forgotten, I wasn't in much of a position to do anything last night."

I had no idea what this beast was or wasn't capable of. The wounds the Dragon had given him would have been more than enough to kill a human and truthfully, I'd believed they would have been enough to end him too. But he'd made it through the night, and his sharp tongue hadn't softened in the slightest despite his injuries.

"Is this the part where you thank me?" I asked.

"Thank you? For what? Helping haul my ass back here so that I could recuperate in peace rather than having to face the forest at night while bleeding all over the foliage? You brought me back here to serve your own ends and don't pretend there was any other reasoning to it. So tell me, have you managed to summon the Dragon yet?"

I pursed my lips, not wanting to answer that question because the truth was that I'd tried and failed. For hours I'd sat up in my bed, my fingers coiled around the Dragon amulet, the hum of its power buzzing in my veins as I tried to figure out how to call it forth, but nothing had worked.

"I haven't attempted it yet," I lied, and he smirked at me like he knew, and of course he knew. The bastard knew everything. He was utterly insufferable even while lying on the floor surrounded by bloodstained sheets. So yes, I had tried to summon the Dragon last night before I'd slept and no, it hadn't worked, but I'd planned on figuring out the rest of it today.

"How many years did you study Summoning before entering the Great Hunt?" he asked.

"It was my understanding that anyone could enter the Hunt?" I shot back. "I know that many Champions spend years training for battle and other matters but-"

"But you thought reading a few books and being determined was enough to see you through this forest and save you from the inevitable death awaiting you here? By the spirits, are all humans this wilfully stupid or is it a trait you alone cherish?"

"I'm not stupid," I growled, ire prickling at me at his dismissive tone. He knew nothing of me and my past, had no idea what my family had suffered through and why I'd had to come here or why I couldn't tell my parents that that was what I planned to do. "I trained in my own way and what I read on the subject of Summoning seemed more than sufficient to-"

"If it was sufficient then you would be able to call forth your Dragon, wouldn't you?"

That fucking smirk. If I could go back in time, I'd drag him out into the woods and leave him there to be devoured by the forest instead of having saved him from it.

"Then what are you suggesting?" I ground out, not wanting his help in anything but finding myself stuck seeking it time and again.

"Breakfast," he grunted. "I won't be back to my full strength for several days. So I suppose you're in luck, Ferris Creed, because I have time to kill and you need to learn how to Summon. So be a lamb and go fetch us a feast, then we can begin."

"You expect me to make you a meal while you just lie there and do nothing?" I demanded.

"I was planning on bathing to remove the blood from my skin. We can swap jobs if you prefer but I'm not certain I'll be able to keep the food dry if you insist on giving me a sponge bath while I prepare it."

I scowled at him but refused to dignify that with a response, turning away to find us some breakfast and leaving him to the impossible task of rinsing himself clean – he may have been able to remove the dirt from his skin but he would still be rotten to the core beneath it regardless.

HENDRIX

CHAPTER TWENTY

Fae may have healed faster than humans ever could, but this might have been one of the worst injuries I'd ever secured in all my six hundred and fifty-two years. I had never felt this incapable and the more I pushed through the pain, the dizzier I became.

Climbing the stairs had been the first task and doing so had threatened to see me back on my knees.

I'd managed to run a hot bath into the pale blue clawfoot tub and gritted my teeth through the agony as I stripped out of my clothes, but I hadn't yet made it in. Someone with the Art of water manipulation must have created the system here to pump water around this castle. It was something only the largest of the Fae households were privy to in Rivenspire - outside of those who possessed the Art themselves. I had been well-used to these luxuries in my old life, but the outcast existence held far less delights.

My fingers knotted around the side of the tub, the pain like wildfire in my flesh as I tried once again to enter the bath without passing out. I made it into the water but a roar of pure torment escaped me as it washed over my wounds. My eyelids drooped, too heavy to keep open against the cloying grip of darkness that was draped in my own agony.

Between the chaos of waking pain and unconscious nothingness, I found the past. The smiling faces of my family and the soft lull of my mother's laugh. I felt her fingers on my cheek, her kiss against my brow.

"Hendrix," she whispered. "*You cannot brave the world alone."*

"You're not dead, are you?" Ferris's voice called me back to the land of the living and I cracked my eyes open. The water had turned red with my blood, tainted with a murky swirl of dirt too.

"Not yet," I grunted, looking to the washcloth I'd left by the basin with a huff of frustration.

"It's just, there was an almighty scream and then you went all quiet."

"I didn't scream," I grunted.

"What was it then? A shriek?"

"I did not shriek, you insolent creature," I griped, then groaned as my muscles tensed and jarred my injuries.

"Great. Well, fuck you. And good luck with the bath." Her footsteps started padding away and I chewed my tongue, trying to fight back the word that was already forcing its way past my lips.

"Wait."

Silence. But no more footsteps.

"Human," I growled.

Nothing.

"Ferris," I tried, my tone softening the slightest amount.

"Hendrix?" she questioned dryly.

"I have left my washcloth by the basin. Be a lamb and-"

"Mehh," she baaed like a lamb, then her footsteps thumped away again.

I released a stream of curses, then gripped the sides of the bath, hauling myself to my feet with pain flaring across my chest. But all went black again and I crashed back down into the tub, sending water flying across the floor. I hit my head for good measure and dizziness settled over me thickly, making it hard to remain alert.

The door opened and light illuminated the hazy silhouette of Ferris as she entered the bathing chamber, the silvery cloud of her hair making her appear as some ethereal being. All I could do was stare, lost to a muted daze where she seemed to be the only thing in existence besides me. Those violet eyes held me hostage, choking away my ability to speak, but I managed to grumble an incoherent insult as she passed me by, retrieved the washcloth and tossed it at me. It slapped against my face and I peeled it off slowly, offering her a cold glare as my vision sharpened on her. The hardness in her gaze wasn't going to serve me any good. I felt helplessly weak in front of her and I despised the fact.

Her gaze dipped to my wounds as I propped myself up in the bath and dabbed the long slice beneath my collar bone, tensing from the contact.

"This is all wrong." Ferris shook her head at me. "You're going to get an infection washing yourself with that filthy water."

"Well, what do you suggest I do instead, lightwing? Hail down a healer?"

She strode forward and snatched the washcloth from me, rinsing it in the basin and wetting it with clean water. She returned, hesitating for a second and then kneeling beside the bath and dabbing lightly at my wounds. I stared at her face, rendered silent by the sudden contact, the closeness of her somehow making the pain more bearable. Her eyes never left my wounds as she worked, washing then rinsing and repeating, and my gaze never wavered from her in kind.

Her fingers grazed the uninjured skin beneath my right pec and a low growl rose in my throat, the sound both a warning and an invitation. She made no comment on it as her fingers continued to roam across my body, cleansing the shallower cuts. A fire started up in my skin that had everything to do with the way she touched me and there was no denying how enraptured I was by her.

"Who waits for you back home?" I asked, wondering if some forlorn human man was awaiting her return.

"Family," she muttered, not meeting my gaze.

"Children?"

"No."

"A husband?" I looked to the finger she might wear a ring on but it was empty.

"No."

"Betrothed then? I hear your kind wed young and breed early."

She slapped the wet cloth onto the slash across my ribs and I snarled in pain.

"Watch it," I warned.

Her eyes flew up to meet mine. "Watch your mouth and I'll watch my hand."

"It was a simple statement."

"No, it was rude." She pressed harder on my wound and I grabbed her arm, yanking her close so that her free hand slapped down on my stomach to stop herself from falling right into the tub with me. "If you want my help, then you'd better start speaking to me with respect," she hissed, unperturbed, though her pupils were wide as she stared at me, her words washing over my mouth so that I might taste the ire on them.

Light stirred within her silvery hair but I wasn't sure she noticed it, or the way the Dragon amulet glinted with promise. The spirit was close, but she didn't know how to wield it. Not unless I showed her. And I needed her on my side if I was going to use her to wield the Dragon for my own gain.

She pulled away from me, the air taut with tension and the imprint of her hand on my skin still burning hot.

"I meant no disrespect," I muttered, and she narrowed her eyes in suspicion.

"No, there's no intent to hurt my feelings behind your words because they're not aimed at me as an insult. They're a sign of your true beliefs about humans. And honestly, that's worse."

"Tell me about your people then. What am I getting so wrong?"

Her suspicion heightened but I gave her a patient look and hid a smile when she cracked and began to open up to me.

"We're strong. Stronger than you think and in ways you don't understand."

"I see."

"You don't see," she scoffed. "You're Fae. You walk this world with the air of a god, not a creature that breathes and feels and truly *lives*."

I frowned, seeing her belief in those words, and it made me crave something I couldn't even put a name to. "What am I missing then, lightwing? Explain it to me as best you can."

She slapped the cloth against my wounds again and I cursed, my fingers tightening on the edge of the tub. "There you go again with the patronising tone."

"Fine. Forgive me," I said through gritted teeth, and she went back to tending my wounds more gently.

"I don't think life has meaning without death," Ferris announced, and my throat tightened, her hammer striking the nail a little too close to my heart. "Immortality is too safe a game to play. Have you ever lost anyone, Hendrix? I mean *really* lost them? Before it was their time to go?" Her voice wavered, only a fraction, almost imperceptibly, but true pain lay there. A clue to her weakness. A thing I needed to dig out if I was going to learn the best way to control her. But there was more to it than that. I wanted to know, despite my better judgement. I was curious about this human, more so than I had been about anything in countless years. She confounded me, made me question things which I had long ago decided were fact, and I had to know what experiences had moulded the soul of this intriguing creature.

I thought on her question, my mind moving automatically to my past. Days of carefree joy with my family.

"No," I growled, harsh and firm, blocking out all thoughts of the history I held onto.

"Then there's no point in me trying to make you understand. Your life is void of all the injustices that ours isn't. We have to face the unfairness and find a way to move forward, to live for those who can't."

"You think I know nothing of unfairness?" I gritted out, knowing it wasn't the right response. Not when I was just trying to earn her trust. But I simply couldn't keep my mouth closed. "You think my life is a dream that never ends? Well think again, girl."

"What could possibly be so bad for a Fae? Even an outcast one. You have forever to right your wrongs. You have eternity to find peace again."

"Peace?" I scoffed. "Peace is for sinless souls, not those like mine cloaked in misdeeds. You are so very naïve, you cannot see what I am."

"What are you then?" she demanded, drawing the washcloth from my skin. "Because all I see is a privileged creature who has boundless time on his hands. He has no remorse, no conscience, just greed and power."

"Privileged?" I barked a callous laugh, all plans of winning her over currently abandoned as my anger took centre stage. "You wouldn't last a day in my shoes. If you walked one mile in my life, you would beg for your simple woes to be returned to you."

I felt well enough to stand, so stand I did, stepping from the tub and glaring down at her, dripping wet and stark naked.

Her cheeks flushed as she glanced at my cock, then leapt to her feet, grabbing a towel and hurling it at me. I caught it with a mocking laugh as she backed away, flustered yet trying to act as though she wasn't as she raised her chin defiantly. I held the towel in a fist so it hung down to cover me from navel to calf.

"You're a pig," she snapped, her hair shimmering with magic and her amulet gleaming against her chest.

The Dragon wanted to come and join the fight but that would do me no good. I had to keep it together so I could get her on my side.

I took a breath, calming my thoughts, wondering why this human got under my skin so deeply. I should have been able to manipulate her as easily as breathing, but instead she riled up a storm in my soul and shook the foundations of my plans practically before I'd laid them.

"Enough. Come now, a truce. There's no use in arguing over whose life is shittier."

"That's not the argument I was making," she growled, her gaze dipping to take in my dripping wet frame before her eyes shot back up to mine again, looking all the more furious.

I smirked, telling her I knew I'd distracted her, and her scowl deepened.

"The point is, life and loss go hand in hand. But between it all, there's hope. Hope for better days. Hope for things that were lost to be found again."

"What things?" I questioned, narrowing my eyes as I sensed she was hiding something from me still.

"Things that don't concern you," she said firmly, her jaw ticking, but she hadn't run away yet, she remained there to swap barbs with me and in doing so, it gave me the chance I needed to convince her to trust me.

"Oh but they do, pretty one. We're in this together now, you and I. So what is it that's making you shiver like that?"

She glanced at the goosebumps which had risen along her arms. "My reason for being here is none of your business, as your reason is none of mine."

"And what if I told you I'm here for the good of the world? Would you believe that?" I asked her.

"Not a chance."

I laughed darkly. "Good, because of course I'm not. My reasons are purely selfish. What boon do you seek, Ferris Creed? Perhaps our wants align? You spoke of the Necromancer before, the Hollows must bring on a riot of fear in your fellow humans."

"What does the Necromancer have to do with this?" She frowned.

"Perhaps I wish to stop him."

"Liar. You said you're here for selfish reasons."

"Maybe I want him and the Hollows gone for motives of my own."

"That's not why you're here," she accused. "And if you think I'm here to wish for that too, then you're dead wrong."

I tilted my head to one side, intrigued as usual. "I thought you might be here to save the world."

"Well I'm not," she breathed, a hint of guilt to those words, but mostly there was conviction. "I know what I want."

"Which is?"

She shook her head, eyes shining with her refusal to utter the truth.

I waited but she didn't break.

"I gave you my truth," I pushed.

"You're a liar."

I smiled, striding toward her but finding myself weak by the time I got there. She slinked into the doorway and I leaned against it, dipping my head toward her face, devouring her personal space and declaring it my own dominion.

"What've I got to do to earn your trust, lightwing?" My knees threatened to give out as stars burst before my eyes, highlighting her face like a beacon.

"I will never trust a Fae," she whispered coldly.

"I see," I growled, swaying forward as I leaned closer and throwing out my arm to catch myself on the doorframe behind her. I was consuming even more of her personal space, but she didn't run. Perhaps if I was in a less weak state she would have.

"Well do me a favour at least," I exhaled.

"What's that?" she hissed.

"Don't stare at my cock for too long when I hit the floor." The blackness swept in and I staggered out into the hall, slamming down onto my back, losing my grip on the towel as I went.

My skull rattled as I woke up, blinking at the fire in a nearby brazier as it came into focus. I was in bed and one look down showed that I was covered with a blanket and my wounds were dressed with strips of what I guessed had once been a white sheet.

Ferris was curled up in an armchair across the room, her nose buried in the diary. The darkness beyond the window told me it was night, so I'd been out of it for at least a few hours.

"How did you get me into this bed?" I muttered, still dazed.

Ferris didn't look up from her diary as she pointed to a rusted wheelbarrow across the room.

"How did you get me into that?"

She looked up reluctantly, a glimmer of amusement in her eyes. "You don't remember?"

I shook my head.

"I found the old thing in the kitchen store, so I brought it upstairs, and after trying to lift you into it for spirits only know how long, I gave up and prodded you in that gash by your neck instead."

I touched the wound with a frown, some vague recollection coming back to me now.

"Then you reared up with a cry like a dying goat and called me a 'ravishing silver unicorn' before you passed out again. When you fell, I shoved you into the wheelbarrow. I let you sleep in that for a while, and when you started moaning and mumbling about the Hollows, I steered you into your bed." She shrugged like it was nothing and went back to reading.

"What did I say about the Hollows?" I asked lightly, like the question didn't weigh a thousand tons.

"You kept saying 'they're waiting' but I don't know what for."

I grunted.

"What did you mean?" she pushed, and I shrugged.

"Fuck knows." But I did know.

Her eyes roamed over me, a slight frown pinching her brow as she assessed me all too keenly. I wasn't used to anybody looking at me the way she did and I certainly wasn't used to be surveyed in such a weakened state. I shifted in the sheets, waiting for her to call me out on my lies but even though I suspected she knew I'd been less than forthcoming with her, she didn't push.

"You need to rest," she stated finally, and I bristled at the assessment.

"Aw, have you been watching over me all curled up in your chair, pussycat?" I taunted.

Ferris snapped her diary shut and got out of her seat. "Just rest so we can get back to the task at hand," she said cooly.

"Yes, your highness," I mocked dryly.

She stalked from the room and kicked the door shut behind her, the space feeling altogether too empty in her absence, and I had to bite my tongue against the urge to call her back.

I was left with my own thoughts and a plate of food that had been provided for me to snack on. So snack I did. Because my little Dragon slayer needed me alive and kicking. And far be it from me to go dying on her. Not while I had a boon to claim.

It took another full day for me to feel strong enough to begin training Ferris in the ways of Summoning. But I was finally able to walk around freely without the assistance of my pet human and it was time to show her how to wield the Dragon.

We had spoken very little, so I'd had plenty of time to think on how I might sway her to work with me fully. Perhaps I was a little rusty on wooing others since I had been outcast for so many years. I didn't keep the company of strangers often but the old me had been likeable enough. At least for a time. Maybe there were still sufficient pieces of him left in me to gain Ferris's favour. She was only human after all, already easily glamoured by our kind. She may have hated us but she couldn't help but be enraptured by us too.

I found her in the lounge, poring over that damn diary again. I was pretty sure she must have had it committed to memory by now, yet she continued to study it tirelessly as if it might offer up another secret with each turn of the page. She took notes too, sometimes comparing the writings in the diary with those in her precious book on the spirits of the forest. She was plotting, scheming, planning…I just wasn't certain what precisely she thought a weak creature such as herself might achieve for all her efforts. Though the sting of her victory over the Dragon prickled against my attempts at dismissing her entirely. But that had been a fluke. I'd been the one to weaken it. The spirit should have been mine in truth.

I crept up behind her, noting the silken pink dress she wore. It hugged her figure and hung gracefully around her legs to caress her bare feet. Clearly she held no hostility towards the Fae-made items in this castle. Though I supposed she might have found amusement in stealing from those she despised so heartily. She didn't notice my approach and didn't stir at all until my shadow fell over her.

Ferris jerked around at the last moment, snapping the diary shut as if I might claim some of its secrets with a single glance, then she leapt from her seat.

"Well?" she prompted, glancing down to take in the fine linen shirt I had matched with trousers and shoes fit for a ball. She wasn't the only one of us who could play dress-up in this pretty castle.

"Well what?" I drawled.

"Are we getting started at last?"

"It seems we are." I offered her my hand and she glared at it like it was a viper about to strike. I moved it closer to her and she folded her arms in answer to my demand.

I fought the urge to snatch her hand and decided to play the part of someone more mannerly.

"I only wish to guide you in the skill of Summoning," I offered.

"Stop."

"Stop what?" I baulked.

She waved her hand at me. "This. This weird act. I know what you're doing."

"I'm not doing anything but repaying the woman who saved my life. But if you don't wish to learn to Summon, then so be it." I turned my back on her, meaning to stride from the room, and smiling when she called out to me. Just as I'd known she would.

"I want to learn," she insisted. "I'll do whatever it takes."

I turned to face her, offering her my hand again, a grin toying at the edge of my lips.

She reluctantly closed the distance between us and placed her smooth palm in mine. The discrepancy between our strength meant I could have crushed it like an autumn leaf, but instead, my fingers closed gently around hers and I drew her a step closer.

The scent of her skin was like oak on a summer breeze and I breathed her in despite myself, unable to deny the way my gaze trailed over the hard line of her lips and the musings about what it might take to thieve a smile from them.

"My father taught me how to summon," I revealed, thinking of him and his rogue grin. He'd had plenty of enemies in his life, but he had never shown his ruthless nature to us. He cared for my mother and his children like there was nothing more precious than us in this world. He'd killed for us. And I'd killed for him in the end.

"I can show you how. But you have to trust me, Ferris, if only for now. For this moment in time. Can you do that?"

"I'm not sure I can," she admitted, throat rising and falling. This dress wasn't good enough for her. It paled significantly in the face of her beauty.

"Try," I encouraged, catching her hand and twirling her under one arm and pulling her flush against my body, taking her other hand too. She stilled in my grasp but didn't move away and I found I liked the feel of her closeness all too much.

"It's a thought, nothing more," I said, lowering my head to speak in her ear. "But it takes courage and a will of pure power. I know you possess that. I've seen it in you. But I think you doubt yourself sometimes, Ferris Creed."

Her chest rose and fell, her answer coming in a soft exhale. "I'm working on that."

"Work harder." I called upon the Fox, its fiery nature keenly humming within the amulet. All I had to do was coax it free while keeping a leash on it with my mind, holding it back, making sure it listened to my command.

"It's important to maintain control of your spirit. The Dragon is yours to summon, lightwing, but it may be volatile. It may resist. But once you learn to force your will over it, it will do anything you ask."

"You mean it will do anything I demand."

"Same thing."

"It isn't," she hissed.

I bit back a retort, not wanting to fall into another argument right now.

"Just focus," I encouraged, inching even closer to her, the scent of her skin enveloping me, her warmth a beat of temptation away. At this proximity, she would surely feel the rush of the Fox's power as it raced from me, and perhaps knowing that feeling would be the key to unlocking it for herself. "See if you can feel it when I do it."

"What do you mean fee- *oh*," she gasped as I summoned the Fox.

I told the spirit to leave the amulet with a force of will, a command inside my head urging it to show itself. The rush of its magic moved closer, welling up within me like a vortex until my entire being crackled with the potency of its fire. It burst free, pouring from the amulet at my throat in a swirl of flames and landing in front of us, each flicker of fire collecting itself into its fur until the spirit sat beating its tail impatiently.

"Did you see how I did that?" I murmured, my lips brushing against the shell of her ear as the power of the Fox spirit shivered across my skin so close to hers. A river of energy was humming between us, bridging the gap from my soul to hers, allowing her to feel the very heartbeats in my chest. I could feel hers in kind, thrumming so powerfully, it wasn't like any heart I had heard before. Certainly no human's should beat like that, as if it was dictating life instead of the other way around.

"You must keep them collared," I urged, lashing the energy spiralling out of the amulet around the Fox with a will of possessive power. "Now you try."

"Alright," Ferris breathed, squeezing my hands. She could have let go. I didn't need to keep hold of her while she did this, but I didn't release her either, only gripping tighter.

Her hair began to shine, shimmering teal appearing between the strands, alive with the power of the beast she'd claimed dominion over. The energy in the atmosphere buzzed with a potent power that spoke of the Dragon. I wanted to see it. I needed to look into its eyes and declare it mine. Ferris may have been its wielder, but I'd be hers soon enough.

Her concentration cracked and I felt the connection between her and the amulet splinter. She whirled away from me, throwing a hand to her face as if she didn't want me to read the emotion on her face.

"What's wrong?" I demanded.

"Nothing," she gasped, but she dropped her hand and her eyes turned to the window, desperation sparking in her gaze.

"What is it?" I looked that way to where the sunlight gilded the forest canopy. But there was nothing there.

"I can't fuck this up," she said under her breath. "Everything depends on it."

"You'd better try again then," I instructed firmly, and she tore her gaze from the window, nodding and striding back toward me, thrusting her hands into mine.

She really didn't need to do that. But as she moved closer, I didn't let the words of protest pass my lips. I drew my little human into the cage of my arms and devoured the warmth she offered, not daring to let myself wonder why I didn't ever want to let go.

Ferris

CHAPTER TWENTY ONE

The wind howled against the windows, the trees thrashing wildly as if dancing to the beat of a song I couldn't hear. It was strange to stand within the cocoon of the conservatory while a storm blustered beyond it, the plants entirely unaffected by the raging maelstrom outside.

Six days had come and gone, my frustration waxing and waning like the moon in the sky far above us. I fought to summon the Dragon throughout every waking hour, falling exhausted and defeated into bed once darkness descended and rising with the sun to start again.

Hendrix wasn't helping, despite his claims that he could, and my aggravation at myself over never having sought guidance in Summoning before coming here was building with every passing hour. Of course I'd considered it, but I hadn't wanted any chance of my parents discovering my plans because I'd known that they would have moved heaven and earth to halt them before I'd begun. Besides, it wasn't as if the lessons were offered out freely or even openly. Those few humans who had made it their life's work to seek out and capture the small spirits which lingered in our lands didn't want to share their skills with anyone. Only the Champions were granted such tuition and even then, I knew they paid highly for the honour.

I had read several accounts of the Great Hunt which surmised that the two things weren't entirely similar and that learning to summon tiny spirits such as river runners and wind racers that had no real power beyond riding the paths of the elements they were linked to wasn't in any way the same as calling upon a ruling spirit such as the ones which were tied to the cursed forest.

I'd been led to believe that once an amulet of the forest had been won, calling forth the spirit within it would be somewhat intuitive and wouldn't require instruction. But it was apparent that it had been a foolish notion to believe in and one which I'd given faith to based on what was easiest rather than what would ensure I was best prepared for this undertaking.

I cursed myself for that choice hourly. It wasn't like me to take chances with the research I did, and I could admit to the fact that I'd made a serious mistake in believing that this would come naturally to me. But I wouldn't give up.

Inhaling deeply, I ran my thumb over the Dragon which had been carved into the face of the amulet I'd claimed and let my eyes fall closed as I tried to follow the instructions Hendrix had given me.

I pictured the Dragon in my mind, seeking out the tendrils of its power. I could feel it. That part was no problem. The storm raging outside the windows had nothing on the tempest that lingered just out of reach within me. But it was as though the Dragon and its magic were beyond a veil far thicker than any glass. Like all sounds were muffled and feelings deadened.

"Come on," I urged it beneath my breath, trying to be forceful in my command the way Hendrix had taught me, but the Dragon only twisted around the edges of my consciousness and withdrew in reply.

I gritted my teeth and tried again, my command firm and unrelenting, my determination making my muscles lock as I fisted my hands and pressed my boots against the ground more firmly. But again the Dragon denied me.

"You're still doing it wrong," Hendrix taunted, his voice a low rumble which sent a shiver down my spine.

I sighed.

"When someone goes out of their way to avoid you, it's good manners to take the hint," I muttered, resisting the urge to look back over my shoulder in the direction his voice had come from.

I could feel him prowling closer all the same. His presence was like a weight in the air which made my skin prickle and senses heighten. Perhaps it was my instincts warning of a predator at my back, but it was impossible for me to not know when he had entered a room.

"You must command the spirit to your will," he insisted, drawing ever nearer.

"I am," I hissed, anger flaring within me. His instruction had caused nothing but irritation the past few days. He was always standing too close, his aura too big, his words too goading. I couldn't think with him seizing so much oxygen around me. "I came here to focus."

"Are you calling me a distraction?" he teased, inching closer, his steps silent but presence pressing.

"Yes."

He released a low chuckle and irritation prickled my skin.

"Try again. Let me see where you're going wrong."

I bit down on my tongue to keep any sharp words from spilling free of it. Arguing with Hendrix was like screaming into the wind. It got me nowhere and only left me festering in my own vexation.

Still he closed in on me and still I refused to turn and look at him. I knew he wanted to rattle me, knew he enjoyed the game of tormenting me and wanting to gain a reaction. I wouldn't give him the satisfaction of earning one.

I closed my eyes and inhaled slowly, working to calm my

thrashing heart, reaching for the well of the Dragon's power which I could feel dancing around the edges of my soul.

My mind roamed over the instructions Hendrix had given me. Commanding, firm, unrelenting. I had to order the Dragon to submit to my will and force its compliance under my authority.

Hendrix inched closer until he stood at my back, not quite touching me, but I could feel his shadow wrapping around me, the atmosphere quaking with his proximity.

I exhaled, pointedly ignoring the Fae despite his determination to take my attention.

I touched my fingers to the amulet over my heart, gritted my teeth and commanded the Dragon to break free of it with every ounce of tenacity I possessed.

Power roiled and churned inside me, my skin buzzing with sparks of electricity, the storm beyond the windows howling with more ferocity as the strength of the Dragon buzzed in the air and triumph surged in my veins.

I reached for it, my entire soul leaning into the maelstrom of power that hissed and buzzed at the edge of my mind. With all the strength of will I possessed, I commanded it to reveal itself and emerge from the confines of the amulet.

Electricity burst through my veins, a cry spilling from my lips as the power of the Dragon burned through me, my silver hair flying back in an explosion of wind as an echoing roar erupted around me in a resounding denial which sent me flying forwards as though the force of it had struck me from behind.

My hands flew out, my eyes scrunching closed as the ground lurched for me but before I could strike it, strong hands caught me by the waist and heaved me upright again.

The wind dropped as my back struck Hendrix's chest, my hair falling around my shoulders as my breaths came in jagged, uneven pants.

Hendrix cursed as I slumped back against him, his hands shifting against my skin, one moving to splay across my stomach as he held me upright against him, the other shifting to clasp my jaw and tilt my head back to face the sky above.

"Open your eyes, lightwing," he growled, and I was too fragile in the wake of the Dragon's power to refuse him.

I blinked my eyes open and found Hendrix peering down at me, my head tipped so far that he was all I could see. His green eyes blazed with churning vitality, the truth of all he was laid bare in that endless green gaze of his.

My skin burned where our bodies were pressed so tightly together, my chest rising and falling heavily while the solid thump of his heartbeat struck against my spine.

"All those pretty vows and look at you now," he said, his grip on my jaw tightening, his thumb pressing against the pounding of my pulse. "Don't tell me this is you giving up?"

"Never," I panted, though my limbs were so weak I was certain the only reason I still stood was this beast's grip on me.

Hendrix's eyes tracked the word as my lips formed it, the edge of his own mouth lifting with amusement and raising the pure indignation I felt all too often in his company.

"You don't think I can do it," I accused, and his expression turned wholly grim once more.

"If you can't, then we're all fucked, aren't we, pretty human?"

"Stop calling me that," I griped.

"If you didn't like it, your pupils wouldn't dilate the way they do each time I bring it up."

"That's contempt," I hissed.

"Oh? So you feel no surge of heat within your veins when I tell you how very captivating I find those violet eyes of yours to be?" he murmured, staring right into my soul as he said the words, my skin prickling in reply to them despite myself.

"Captivating or not, they look at you with nothing but loathing."

"Your lips say one thing while aching for another," he said, his gaze shifting to my mouth, and for the briefest of moments, my eyes fell to his lips too, my throat bobbing against his hand where he still held me locked against him.

He was too close, his skin too hot against mine, my breaths too tangled with his own.

"Let me go." I managed to force the words out despite the weight of his proximity surrounding me.

"If I release you, you'll fall," he pointed out.

My legs still felt shaky from my attempt at forging dominance over the Dragon, but I refused to admit to needing the help of this Fae bastard.

"I'd sooner fall alone than stand with the aid of a Fae," I said.

Hendrix's fingers flexed against my jaw, the rough scrape of his callouses against my throat making goosebumps break out across my skin.

"Our webs are weaved together, lightwing. Like it or not, we're stuck helping one another until this curse shatters. And we need your Dragon to break it. So try again."

He was holding me firmly but not so tightly that I couldn't break free if I really wanted to, and I shifted as if I might push him away. But his assessment wasn't wrong. My legs were trembling, my breaths ragged, and the Dragon's aura still whipped around the edges of my mind as if I stood in the heart of a hurricane, one step in either direction enough to sweep me away into the abyss.

Or perhaps this right here was the abyss, in the depths of the eyes of the male I'd been born to hate and been cursed to entangle myself with.

"Again," Hendrix ordered, and I gave in, not because I was willing to follow his commands but because I needed to claim dominion over the Dragon for myself, my people and most of all, for Rissa.

His gaze held mine captive and I stared up at him for longer than I should have, the vibrant green of his eyes their own kind of puzzle in need of an answer.

My fingers shifted to the amulet at my throat, and I took a shuddering breath as I prepared to command the Dragon to follow my will once more.

My eyes fell closed and I exhaled slowly.

Please. The word swirled through my thoughts, reaching out to the spirit which had deigned to offer its amulet up to me and the power that had been lingering at the edges of my awareness exploded into sharp and violent focus all at once.

I remembered Hendrix's instructions a beat late, rallying my strength of will and ordering the Dragon loose with a bark of command that lashed from me towards the spirit until it finally burst free of the amulet.

Wind howled around us, my hair whipping out to tangle with Hendrix's dark locks as he released his hold on my chin and we both stared at the raging spirit which had exploded from its place of confine at my throat.

I staggered backwards at the force of its arrival, Hendrix's powerful body the only reason I wasn't knocked from my feet altogether.

The Dragon bellowed a roar filled with spite, and the glass windows of the conservatory all shattered in reply.

I screamed, ducking low, powerful arms banding around me as Hendrix drew me into the shelter of his body and crouched over me, shielding me from the falling glass which rained down alongside the fury of the storm which had been held at bay beyond it.

The world was a rush of noise, of horror, of violence.

The Dragon bellowed again, the bright silver of its pelt rushing over us, the feathers at the tip of its tail lashing the ground barely a foot away and sending mud flying into our faces.

Hendrix cursed and I recoiled into the shelter of his body while the rain crashed down on us. Drops of blood mixed with the water that ran over his arms and body, and I turned to look up at him in alarm.

"You're hurt."

"I'm fine," he grunted.

"Don't be an ass. Just let me see if-"

A huge crash boomed in time with a blast of thunder overhead and I cried out again while Hendrix's hold on me tightened, his body curling around me, more of his blood dripping down onto my arms.

I gasped as I peered out from beneath his bicep to the castle wall which the Dragon had just blasted a hole through. Debris rained down in a scattered arc, fire blooming as lightning struck the building, the storm turning to answer the call of the spirit I'd unleashed.

"No creature shall command me by force."

I flinched at the words that rattled through my skull, the power of them making the inside of my head hurt.

Another blast sounded as the Dragon continued deeper into the castle, tearing it apart in a furious rage.

Hendrix hauled me upright and I clung to his arm as I stared at the beautiful castle with fire blossoming from its windows and debris spilling into the air from endless puncture wounds to its carcass.

"We have to get out of here," Hendrix barked, hauling me away from the castle which looked set to topple at any moment, bricks and rooftiles cascading down its crumbling walls in an avalanche that was quickly gathering momentum.

I let him tug me along, my thoughts numb in the face of such wanton destruction, but as my boot scrambled over the crushed glass which had once been the conservatory roof, I fell still.

"What is it?" Hendrix demanded as I tugged my arm from his grip.

I broke into a run, ignoring the continued destruction the Dragon was wreaking and the bellowed commands of the Fae bastard to return to his side.

I vaulted over crushed and shredded plants, broken glass

crunching beneath every footfall, my gaze set firmly on the little wooden canopy I had made into my sanctuary.

Hendrix caught up to me as I ducked beneath the miraculously intact roof, his fingers locking around my wrist just as I snatched my pack from the soft chair I'd asserted as my own.

"What could be important enough to risk your life on, lightwing?!" he boomed.

"My books," I replied defiantly, hugging the pack to my chest with one arm as if he might try and haul it out of my grasp given the chance.

"You're a fool," he snapped just as a blast of thunder rent the air in two and the castle groaned in agony.

I didn't deny it, only started running with him as he yanked me away.

I glanced back as we raced through the storm for the forest beyond, my eyes widening as I took in the ruined castle, ablaze and collapsing. A tremendous roar burst from the building, and I gasped as the Dragon exploded from it, lightning blasting from its open jaws, rage written into every line of its body and the castle breaking apart beneath the might of its wrath.

"Never presume to control me again, Ferris, or your fate will follow that of this wretched building."

"Hendrix!" I yelled in horror as the Dragon tore through the air towards us, and the Fae warrior whirled at my shout, drawing his sword and readying for a fight I knew we'd lose.

But before the Dragon could reach us, its form dissolved, spilling away into silver smoke which rushed for me at speed.

The smoke struck the amulet with such force that I was thrown from my feet, my back hitting the dirt hard enough to knock the breath from my lungs.

A howling, haunting note of song ripped through my mind as the darkness came rushing in on me, and all I knew in that brief second before my destruction could claim me, was terror.

HENDRIX

CHAPTER TWENTY TWO

I'd thought my human would wake sooner than this, but she was still unconscious. After an hour of walking with her in my arms – and fighting the forest no-handed to forge a path – my patience shattered and I tore a couple of vines from a tree and tethered her to my back. Her head rested on my shoulder, her breaths brushing my neck, assuring me she hadn't passed from this world.

I'd pulled out the broken glass that had struck me in the back when the conservatory had been destroyed, but they would heal soon enough. The pain of her body pressing to the lacerations was far preferable to battling the forest without a blade. So with my sword in hand and her pack in the other, I made quicker work of putting distance between us and the castle. The Dragon had made such a commotion that anyone nearby would have immediately come to investigate, and I'd decided the best course of action was to disappear hastily. I preferred to remain anonymous a while longer and the knowledge that Ferris had the Dragon was not going to pass to anyone else while I could help it.

A root caught my ankle and I went stumbling forward with a

curse. I could have sworn the forest was full of wrath today, making my journey far more difficult than it should have been. My arms were covered in scratches while Ferris was somehow entirely untouched by the brambles I was carving my way through.

I had seen the way the forest bowed to her, and now the Dragon itself had marked her with silver hair. I was no fool. There was more to this human than there appeared to be. I'd seen it in her eyes when I'd first met her, and the forest had only offered more evidence since. It made me all the more curious as to why she had come here at all. What could a creature such as her desire between these cursed boughs? What was worth risking her fragile life for?

To add to the discomfort of my journey, the storm hadn't relented since leaving the castle and the rain was only growing heavier. I could barely see my hand before my face as I took a muddy animal track down a steep bank, nearly tripping straight into a rocky chasm. I leapt over it instead, scrabbling up the hill beyond it through waterlogged dirt and a thick mass of thorn bushes. The forest was laughing, striking at me with all it had while I gritted my teeth and never gave in.

At the top of the hill, I found mercy in the shape of a cave and hurried into it, pushing my sodden hair out of my eyes with a growl of frustration.

The forest would be able to claim us here if we stayed the night, of that I was damn sure. But the day was wearing thin and I couldn't keep moving endlessly without a plan. It was getting us nowhere.

Ferris murmured a wordless sound in my ear and I released a breath of relief. My human was waking up.

I untethered her from my back and she stumbled into me as her feet hit the floor, my hands moving to her waist to steady her. Her palm pressed to my chest as she looked up at me, confusion marring her brow.

"What happened?"

"What *didn't* happen?" I grunted.

"*Hendrix*," she insisted, touching her temple as if pain thumped there. My mood turned even more sour.

"Your summoning skills need some work," I gritted out, taking hold of the back of her neck and tilting her head back further so I could examine her. The irises of her violet eyes were full-blown and she looked far too pale. "Can you see straight?"

"Tell me what happened after the Dragon destroyed the castle," she insisted.

"Any nausea?"

"Hendrix," she bit at me again, and I sighed, releasing her. She was clearly well enough.

"Your Dragon collided with you and you've been passed out ever since. And as our little refuge is now shattered into a thousand pieces, I've been searching for another one."

She looked around at the tiny cave we were standing in and wrinkled her nose in assessment of it. "And this is what you found?"

I glared at her in answer to that. "Obviously we will not be able to sleep here."

"How late is it?" she asked, disconcerted.

I gestured to the pouring rain which veiled all glimmers of sunlight. "You tell me."

"Haven't you been keeping track of time?"

"Forgive me, princess, I was too busy hauling your ass through the forest – a forest which did not want me taking you anywhere it seemed."

"Well which direction have we journeyed in?"

"Southeast," I offered, knowing that much.

She glanced at the thorny marks lining my arms, then huffed a sigh, taking her pack from me and dropping down to sit on the floor and rifle through it.

"You're going to consult a book, aren't you?" I guessed dryly just as she produced the diary she'd found in the castle. "Wonderful."

"It led us to the Dragon. Who are you to question it?" She arched a brow at me, and I was forced to admit that she had me there.

I dropped down beside her and waited while she began reading, the only sound between us the thundering rain. She began to shiver, goosebumps marking her arms and her silver hair sticking to her shoulders. I shifted closer, offering her the warmth of my body, and she didn't move away when my arm slid around her and clamped tight. But she did glance up at me with those big eyes, the shimmer of them pushing a lump into my throat before she went back to reading.

A lock of her silver hair brushed my shoulder and I lifted it to examine it, noting the pearlescent quality of the silken strands and wondering what it meant. She tugged it out of my grip, gave me a hard look, then went back to her diary again. I couldn't win with her. She always seemed halfway between despising me and liking me, oscillating from one to the other as unpredictably as the wind.

Despite the glare she'd given me, she leaned even closer, and I was surprised at how eagerly she took the heat my body offered. It had been a long time since I'd been touched like this. She no longer recoiled from me like she once had, and I couldn't deny how familiar I was becoming with her company. Or how much I enjoyed it.

But how quickly this familiarity would shatter once she discovered the truth. So I had a mind to keep it for as long as possible, for her ignorance was my gift.

"She mentions a mill a few times," Ferris murmured at last, and I glanced over at her, nose close to the page and concentration pinching her brow. "From comparing the description to the map she's drawn…I think it must be to the south. If we can find a narrow stream and follow it downhill, it should take us right to it."

I listened for a stream, but there was no whisper of it beyond the torrential rain.

"Lead the way then, trail-finder," I taunted, gesturing to the stormy forest, and Ferris cut me a look for my dry tone.

"Scared of a little rain?" She got to her feet, tucking the diary into her pack and shouldering it.

I didn't get up. "The rain dampens our senses. We can no longer hear an enemy approach, nor smell a fire on the wind, nor see very far beyond the veil of water – this is especially true for you, human. It is the perfect way for the forest to disorientate us so I, for one, am staying here until it passes."

"Then you'll be here when night falls. Besides, you possess the spirit of the Bear, so maybe it can lead us to the stream. It might even deal with this rain for us." Her eyes glinted with the idea as it struck her.

Damn. That was too smart of a thought for me to have a sharp comeback to it. I wanted to refute it, but she was right. Why hadn't I come up with it myself?

"Of course. I thought of that already," I lied in an offhanded drawl, feeling her gaze burning against my face as I turned to glare out at the forest.

"Bullshit."

"I still believe it's not worth the risk of travelling in a thunderstorm of the forest's creation. It is likely a trap."

"Better a trap we can work to avoid than remaining here to die at dusk," she quipped. "Release the Bear and let's at least attempt to survive. I'm not planning on dying today. I don't have nearly as many years under my belt as you do, grandpa."

I rose to my feet, anger raking through my veins. "Who do you think you're giving orders to?"

She didn't back down under my scrutiny but I noticed her shoulders tensing beneath the weight of my stare. I could so easily make her fear me. I could make her eyes light up with terror with one simple truth from my lips, and it was so fucking tempting to share it at last. But I took a breath instead, forcing myself to focus on what was really important right now. I had to put my pride aside. But it was a weighty task.

I said nothing as I summoned the Bear, calling it from the amulet in a swirl of water. It landed beyond the cave, the rain splashing against its liquid form and becoming one with the spirit. What a thing to behold this spirit was. Water embodied in animal form, yet its teeth looked razor sharp, and its might was beyond words.

"Lead us to the nearest stream," I commanded.

"Can you part this storm for us too?" Ferris added, and the Bear looked to her with intrigue.

"It will not obey anyone except-" The words fell dead on my lips as the rain parted like curtains, creating a dry passage between two raging downpours. The Bear turned and began leading us onward and Ferris took the lead with a smile dancing on her lips.

I scowled at her back as I followed, irritation flashing through me at her smugness. How did this mortal creature wield so much power in this forest? It bent to her will in ways I could not begin to fathom.

Her manner of being right about things was starting to get deep under my skin too. That, combined with her unfounded confidence, her tireless persistence, and her inner strength was, well…infuriating. It captivated my mind when she was around and perhaps even more so when she was not. I chewed over it when I tried to sleep and it only caused me more wakefulness. She was quickly becoming the scourge of my thoughts, and I desperately wished to make her kneel to me.

I was an outcast prince for a reason, a Fae who had struck fear in the hearts of my own people. But this girl, this *human,* walked through this forest with the air of a being far more powerful than she could ever hope to be alone. But with that Dragon…well, if she learned of its gifts and worked it to her will then I'd be hard-pressed to stop her. It was clearly resisting her command though, the way it had destroyed the castle in an attempt to kill us was proof enough of that.

I was playing a risky game by encouraging her to learn how to wield it, because there was no guarantee she wouldn't turn on me once she did.

If the boon was to be mine, I had to try harder with her and truly win her onto my side. The truth was, I needed her. For more reasons than just the Dragon - though the spirit's aid would make it all the more likely that we would survive this cursed place and make it to the Great Elm.

From that diary to the bowing of the forest at her feet, Ferris Creed was a gift between these trees that had been granted to me and I could not squander it. Why a beast such as I had been offered her was beyond my understanding but far be it from me to deny it.

For a moment, screams echoed in mind and the past brushed by all too close, death crooning in my ears like a songbird. There had been so much blood the day I'd been outcast from Rivenspire. Every day since had been walked with the taint of it upon my skin and I'd come to embody it after so many years.

After I'd parted from my home, I'd fed on the harvest of my bad deeds. I'd become the monster they named me. And I planned to hunt down every last one of the Coterie for what they had caused, carve them out of their gilded towers and force them to face me Fae to Fae in the end. If Islasees really was here in the forest, then he would be the next to die for all he had done. And with a Dragon on my side along with the spirits I had already earned myself, how could I lose?

Perhaps Ferris really was the answer to all my woes.

"Your hair rather suits you like that," I commented, the brightness of it catching my gaze again. "Your beauty was obvious before, but that strength you possess wasn't. I see it more clearly now. The glimmer of magic upon you was all it took to unveil it."

She cast a withering look at me over her shoulder and I regretted voicing my thoughts.

"Don't play nice guy with me, Hendrix. I know the truth of you."

My jaw flexed. "You don't know the half of it," I muttered grimly.

She turned to face the path again, deciding not to answer me, and I swiftly moved to her side, my arm brushing hers.

"If you want to talk, then tell me more about this supposed key to the labyrinth," she demanded.

Feisty thing. If only she knew how lethal the fire she played with truly was.

"Ah, the key," I mused. "Well if I told you too much, you wouldn't need me anymore and I expect you'd run away with your pretty Dragon. I can't be having that, lightwing. I'm growing far too fond of keeping you."

"It's *me* that's keeping *you* now, Hendrix." She offered me a rogue smile and my mood simmered into something roiling and dark.

"I am no one's prisoner," I growled, thinking of the past. The clinking of chains, the ripe scent of blood in the air. There were ways a Fae could be tortured that no human could survive. I had known the taste of many torments. I didn't plan on ever returning to the feast.

"You've been someone's before." Her eyes narrowed, reading the truth in my expression.

"Yes. I was tortured once…years after I was outcast. I was taken by a Fae who held a long-lasting grudge against me – a male who had caused me all manner of torment in the past. And I believe that male is here in this forest. Islasees Bellatorn." The trees shivered around me as if they feared that name - and so they should.

"Who is he?"

"He's the Lord Protector. Leader of Queen Sorshana's army and King Arthrun's before her. His soldiers are broken in like horses to obey his every command. They're ruthless, mindless Fae that are brutally efficient in every sense. One word spoken against the queen and you will find yourself at their mercy – she is a fierce creature who took the throne and refused to relinquish it after Arthrun's death. Islasees has always been the royals' loyal hunting dog, willing to do their dirty work without ever questioning orders. He revels in it too. He's never happier than when he's making someone scream."

"Sounds like a delight." Ferris wrapped her arms around herself as if she could feel the chill of him in the air. "So, he captured you? You must have really angered the royals. What did you do?"

"What *didn't* I do?" I said with dry humour, but she didn't smile. She stepped away from me, warier than ever. That was no surprise, but I *was* surprised by how much I didn't like her parting from me. I couldn't remember how many years it had been since I'd kept a companion who didn't know the depths of my depravity.

She remained silent and I figured I had to give her something of the truth.

"I rebelled, I suppose. Some knowledge came to light about the royals and their lap dogs that I didn't care for."

"What knowledge? What did you do?"

There was that question again. What did I do…well, that was a twisted tale if ever one was told. She didn't need to know the whole truth. But perhaps I could share a part of it. She hated the Fae after all. We weren't so different in that respect. And some broken piece of me wanted her to know me better. The real me.

"I stood up to them. I punished them, at first in small ways. Acts of anger, you might call it. But that anger didn't lessen as time went on. It festered. The more I learned, the more riddled with hate I became. You see…there are a group of Fae in our realm who have been around so long that they established the foundations of Fae society. And there is one thing which Fae that old have in common, Ferris."

She met my gaze at her name, hanging on my next words.

"They are bored. I know this, because I am one of them. Or at least, I was. Time eats you from the inside out until you're left…"

"Empty."

I smiled grimly, nodding in confirmation. "People like them, like me I suppose, we do things. Bad things. Because when all the good wears thin, there is only bad left to explore."

"What kind of bad things?" Her voice was a whisper now, like she feared the answer I would give. And so she should.

I crept closer to her on the path and her feet slowed to a halt, the Bear ahead of us stopping too and waiting for us to follow again. She backed up against the sheet of rain behind her as I prowled closer.

"A lot of them got a taste for killing. Humans, at first."

She cringed.

"Then Fae," I continued. "A long time ago, they marked themselves as other. Called themselves the Coterie – an inner circle of Fae who command power. The requirements to be accepted into the fold is to be born into one of the seven great families and to reach the ripe age of two hundred and fifty. Most of their blood is royal – 'superior' as they call it." I sneered. "The rest of the Fae bowed to their power. And slowly, piece by piece, the Coterie took more and more from them. Riches, land, rights."

"I thought Rivenspire was a haven."

"That's a lie," I bit out, heat bursting through my veins.

"Says the outcast," she retorted, raising her chin.

"I was cast out for turning on them, for taking a stand against their heinous acts."

"Are you sure? Because it sounds like you broke the law too many times and they got rid of you for it."

I bared my teeth at her. "You have no idea what they're really like."

"Oh, I can guess. Trust me, I'm not sticking up for them. I may not have met many Fae but the ones I have are arrogant creatures who think nothing of those they see as beneath them. It's no surprise you all turned on each other. But if you think I'm going to feel sorry for you because your kingdom of monsters cast you out, then think again."

I shook my head at her. "I don't want your pity."

"Then what do you want? Because your sob story isn't flying with me. You allude to their terrible crimes, but what of yours? We all choose our path. You're an outcast because you're no better than them. It sounds like you might be worse."

A serpent coiled around the inside of my throat, no words able to get past it. Because what could I say to that? She was right. There was no hiding it even when I tried to paint a picture of the merciless Fae kingdom I had turned on, she saw me for what I was. I was no rebellious hero. I'd done things that would make her skin crawl. And sooner or later, she would discover that truth and I would lose her once and for all.

FERRIS

CHAPTER TWENTY THREE

We found shelter a few hours from dusk, an old mill with a broken wheel which lay on its side in an over-grown stream. Once again, my diary had proved itself a useful ally, and I couldn't help the smug grin that found me as I pointed out the shelter we were in such desperate need of to Hendrix.

The squat tower which the wheel had once been bolted to had partially collapsed. Piled rubble now left an opening which made that portion of the building untenable for shelter, but the grain store was sturdier.

"Human built," Hendrix grumbled, taking the lead as he stalked towards the dilapidated building.

"Sorry my people aren't offered the Art of preservation the way some of yours are," I muttered, my boots sloshing through deep puddles, more mud caking to their sides.

I was cold, wet and miserable. The Bear may have created a passage through the storm for us to traverse but water still dripped from every tree, every vine, every bramble and the forest floor was awash with what could arguably be named a shallow lake.

"The Fae are the blessed favourites of the spirits," he replied, earning a sneer of contempt from me.

"The Fae are soft and pampered by the lives of privilege the spirits offered you. You know nothing of hard labour and perseverance."

"Ah, how prettily you mutter your jealous words," he taunted. "I might feel inclined to pity you, did I not know your people to be both tenacious and vicious enough to thrive despite your…misfortunes."

Hendrix began to push the old, wooden door which blocked the entrance to the grain store, and I bit my tongue to halt the wandering of my fingers towards my slingshot. One sharp clip to his ear would remind him of just how vicious humans could be…

The door groaned and creaked, then finally buckled beneath his battering-ram of a body, swinging wide to knock against the inner wall. A cloud of dust departed the building and engulfed him, drawing a snort of amusement from me while he cursed.

"Oh dear, your pretty hair seems to have turned beige," I told him while he swiped the layer of dust from his face and turned a half-assed glare my way.

"The grain has spoiled. This place stinks worse than a human brothel."

"You must have frequented the wrong ones," I replied dismissively, brushing past him as I ventured into the grain store to take a look at our new shelter. "The brothel in my town only ever smelled of sweetness and sin."

Hendrix narrowed his eyes at me. "And how might you know that?"

"Same way as you do, I suppose."

I squinted in the dim light, sighing at what I found. The store had been filled to the brim when the forest had seen fit to snatch it. Sacks of grain were piled fifteen high from floor to rafter around every wall. It was a damn shame so much food had been lost and left to waste this way. Only a narrow space remained free in the centre of the store, hardly large enough to accommodate one of us throughout the night, let alone two.

"Can you lift some of those out of here?" I asked, glancing back at Hendrix whose long hair was still coated in a layer of dust and whose scowl could have cut a lesser woman to ribbons.

"Do I look like a pack mule?"

I tilted my head, considering him. "Your nose is a little too long to be a mule's but you do have that vacant kind of look in your eyes that they get at the end of a hard day's work, so I'd say you'll pass for one."

Hendrix barked a laugh, surprising me once more. He was so mercurial it was impossible to know whether he might turn to rage or mirth at any given moment - though I had to admit I found the latter preferable, even if it was more disconcerting.

He stepped around me, his arm brushing mine, my skin prickling at the contact. He was so big he took up altogether too much space, not just physically, but his aura seemed to expand to fill every inch surrounding me until I felt as though I was left with no choice but to breathe him in.

"What happened back there?" Hendrix asked as he hauled three huge bags of grain from the stack as if they weighed nothing and hurled them outside.

Mud splattered up in all directions and I leapt back, knocking into him in the process and causing him to drop his hand to the base of my spine to steady me.

"Back where?" I asked, glancing up into his green eyes before taking a measured step away from both him and the place he'd chosen to dump the bags of grain.

"The castle. With the Dragon. You summoned it but then it… well it lost its shit, didn't it?"

I flushed, wishing I could banish the embarrassment which was clawing its way into my cheeks and stepping further away from him so I could inspect the broken waterwheel.

"I don't know," I said with a shrug.

"Bullshit. What happened?" He tossed three more bags out and splattered several more trees with mud for good measure.

The Bear watched everything with tired eyes, a low grumble escaping it as it turned its gaze onto me.

I blinked, the weight of its stare summoning the truth to my lips despite my desire to hide any and all forms of weakness from this Fae brute who insisted on keeping my company.

"I...did what you said. But it felt all wrong somehow."

"You weren't forceful enough," Hendrix commented, and I scowled.

"Force is not your strength."

I gasped, whirling around and snatching the slingshot from my belt, loading it with a stone from my pocket in the next breath and staring out into the trees in alarm as I hunted for my target.

"What is it?" Hendrix was at my side already, sword drawn, brow low as he hunted the trees with me, his powerful body poised for attack.

The protection the Bear was offering us from the storm only extended ten feet or so, and beyond it a curtain of blustering rain and swirling leaves veiled our view of the trees.

"It came from over there," I said, bobbing my chin towards the dense woodland to the south, though truthfully, I wasn't certain of that.

"What did?"

"That voice," I said, sparing a frown for Hendrix whose gaze was now pinned on me alone.

"There was no voice," he replied, no uncertainty in his words, the Fae arrogance solidly in place.

My lips parted on a protest but the voice came again.

"You were not selected for this bond for your brute strength, spirit singer. Do not think to force me beneath your heel now."

I sucked in a breath, stumbling back a step at the rumbling voice which echoed within the confines of my own soul.

"The Dragon..." I mumbled, almost tripping on a root as I tried to back away from something which was impossible to hide from.

"Speak plainly, lightwing," Hendrix growled, catching my arm to halt my retreat.

My eyes flicked up to his, the panic which was rising in my chest stilling at the solid weight I found in his expression.

"I can hear the Dragon's voice in my mind," I told him, and his brows lowered over those stoic eyes.

"The spirit speaks to you?"

"Yes…no…I mean, I hear a voice which can't be any other." I shrugged uselessly but he didn't release me.

"What is it saying?"

"Nothing now. But the Dragon told me it didn't pick me for brute strength – I don't think it liked it when I tried to force it to fall to my command."

Hendrix scoffed, releasing me and giving the forest a lingering look before moving back to removing sacks of grain from our shelter.

"That was apparent when it tore the castle down around us. You'll have to be firmer with it the next time you attempt to call it forth. And I'd suggest waiting until we aren't approaching the night with only one chance of shelter to be found."

I frowned at his back, not agreeing with his assessment of what I needed to do to win the Dragon to my favour but not wanting to fall into an argument with him either.

I tried reaching out to the Dragon again, calling to it in the darkness of my mind, but I only found sullen silence as a reply.

My attention moved to the Bear who cocked its head at me, water spilling from its snout and ears with the movement.

"Can you talk too?" I asked it curiously.

"No," Hendrix answered for it. "My spirits remain dormant and silent while awaiting my command. They do not whisper words of madness in my ears, and you'd do well to ignore anything the Dragon attempts to hiss your way too."

I pursed my lips, not agreeing with him at all, but that was nothing new.

"Hello?" I felt like a fool as I tried to speak to the Bear within my own mind, but the spirit blinked as if perhaps-

A violent crash of thunder rattled the sky overhead and I flinched, having almost forgotten the storm which raged beyond the confines of the Bear's magic.

"The other sacks will tear if I try to haul them out. This is the best I can do, unless you wish to sleep on heaps of rotting grain?" Hendrix called, and I turned to our shelter for the night.

"It will do," I said, not looking at him as I took in just how small the space within the grain store was and just how closely we'd be spending the night with one another. "Thank you."

"I'm sorry, did the wild little human just deign to offer thanks to the brutish Fae?" Hendrix taunted.

"Don't get used to it."

I headed inside, taking my pack from my shoulders and moving into the sparce, though thankfully dry room.

Hendrix paused on the threshold, turning back to look at the Bear as he banished it. I watched as the spirit slipped out of its physical form, returning to the amulet Hendrix wore at his throat. Jealousy sparked within me at both how easily he wielded his spirit and the unfading sting over the Bear's ownership.

The rain slammed down into the clearing the Bear had created for us in a rush that exploded with sound, and I cringed away from the cold and wet while Hendrix stepped fully inside and slammed the door to block it out.

Night wasn't far from us and with the door closed, there was little to no illumination left in the grain store.

I sank down to my knees to the back of the cramped space, a shiver rolling through me at the weight of my saturated clothes. This would not be a night of comfort like those which had preceded it.

Hendrix sighed as he sat too, his knee knocking against my thigh in the darkness, my skin heating at the contact.

"Any chance you had a store of food in that bag you almost died for?" he asked in a low voice which broke over the crashing of the rain on the tiled roof above our heads.

"I gathered some berries while we were walking," I admitted, my hand moving to the bulge in my pocket to draw out some of the succulent fruit. "But I wanted to inspect them properly before eating them. Just in case I collected the wrong thing in my haste with the rain beating down."

Hendrix snorted. "Clever little thing, aren't you? Always planning your next move, always ready for the worst."

"Perhaps you lived too long in comfort," I said. "But where I grew up, the worst tended to come looking for you if you weren't expecting it."

Hendrix fell silent and I was unable to see more than the deeper shadow which marked his outline, so it was impossible for me to tell if he was considering my words with scorn or compassion, though of course I assumed the former. No doubt that insufferable smirk was tilting up the corner of his lips, those deep green eyes of his sparking with malice and amusement at the pathetic woes of the human he disdained so very much.

"What are you waiting for then?" he asked when the silence stretched and only the pounding of the rain sounded between us.

"Waiting?"

"The berries," he prompted.

"I told you, I need to inspect them before risking-"

"Go ahead then."

"In the dark?"

There was a moment's pause before Hendrix's dry laughter rolled through the room, the sound catching me off guard and making my heart leap in alarm.

"What?" I hissed, tensing as he aimed his mirth my way, embarrassment raising its head in the pit of my stomach - though I had no idea why he was laughing at me.

"You cannot see?" he taunted, his arm waving across the space between us, the movement making me flinch minutely as its shadow passed too close for my liking.

"I am not blind," I bit out. "I can see enough to know where you are and where the door is, but no, I cannot see well enough to be able to spot a blueberry from a black nightshade berry."

"One is blue while the other is black," Hendrix scoffed.

"I am well aware of that. Just as I am aware that I picked them in a hurry while the rain pounded down on a forest which is well known to enjoy playing tricks on desperate Champions. I have no intention of eating any of them without getting a clear look at what I am putting in my mouth. But by all means – you try them."

I took a handful of the berries from my haul and held them out into the space between us, my eyes slowly adjusting to the darkness of our shelter. I could see a little of his expression now, though mostly it was just a slight gleam to his eyes.

Hendrix hummed in thought, making no move to take the berries from me.

"Scared?" I taunted.

He snorted in dismissal, reaching out to snatch the handful from my grasp, his fingers grazing against my palm as he took my meagre offering and pressed the lot of them between his lips.

I sucked in a breath as surprise and alarm mingled within me and I lurched forward an inch as if I might strike him to knock the fruit from his mouth.

"Are you insane?" I gasped, but he only held out a hand to ward me off as I attempted to reach for him.

I watched the shadow of his jaw as it worked while he chewed, saying nothing, though traitorous thoughts arose within me. If he died from eating nightshade berries, then I'd be free to claim his amulets. My fingers curled into a fist in my lap, the stain from the berry juices sticky against my palm. My heart leapt and pounded at the thought – of course I should be hoping for that outcome but instead I only felt horror at the idea of it coming to pass.

I couldn't see him well enough to be certain of it, but I felt his gaze boring into mine while I watched him chew and chew and-

"Spit them out," I demanded, pushing forward and taking hold of his chin as if I might force his mouth open were he to refuse.

Hendrix's hand curled around my wrist and he tugged my hand from his jaw, his stubble raking across my skin as he relocated my grip to his throat. I could feel it bob as he swallowed in defiance of my command.

"Worried about me, lightwing?" he mocked, his other hand moving to brush a strand of hair away from my face in a touch so gentle it had me scowling.

"Why did you do that?" I hissed.

"Silly me," he said, not seeming the least bit chastised. "Looks like I trust your judgement even more than you trust your own. You're no fool, Ferris Creed. You wouldn't pick nightshade berries by mistake. It's not in you to be that ignorant even if you tried."

"I told you, I-"

Hendrix leaned forward until I could practically taste the sweetness of the berries on his lips, my hand still curled around his throat, our bodies all too close to one another.

"Tell me, pretty human, are you afraid of the dark?" he asked, his voice a low rumble which broke over me with a deeper tenor than the thunder which crashed in the heavens beyond our hiding place.

I swallowed, feeling his eyes on me, though I still couldn't see nearly enough of him to be able to glean what game he was playing with me.

"I don't like the dark," I admitted finally, my voice an exhale

that seemed to expel the fears which swum within my heart. "Not because I know to fear it. But because it's too full of memories. The kind I wish I could banish but know I never will."

"Tell me," he pushed, and for some reason I found I wanted to give him that answer. I hadn't spoken about her openly in so long. Everyone in our town knew what had happened and the gaping hole in my family spoke of her every day, but I never said her name, never spoke of it, never revealed this truth in me as if it were some secret. But it wasn't a secret. It was a tragedy. One which had led me into the darkness of this forest. One which had brought me to this place with a Fae male who I had every reason to distrust, but still I found myself wanting him to know about her because she was important. She was everything. And here we were, halfway through our time here, hiding from the dark outside, as close as I had ever come to fulfilling the promises I'd made to her so long ago, so why shouldn't I speak her name?

"Eight years ago, the forest took my sister, Rissa, as its sacrifice."

Hendrix stilled, his grip on my wrist tightening, his other hand falling against the base of my spine, pressing against me as though he might draw me closer to him, or at the very least, stop me from running away.

"She was taken to be a child of the forest?" he confirmed.

That old wound tore open in my chest, memories of that night flooding through me, of waking up to find her missing from her bed, our mother's screams of anguish, our father's silent despair. I'd run from our home in nothing but my nightgown while the rain poured down not dissimilarly to the way it was doing right now beyond the walls of the grain store. My bare feet had carved fissures in the mud as I followed the trail of her footprints from our home towards these cursed trees, my throat had been ripped raw with my calls of her name. But it hadn't just been her footsteps I'd followed. Alongside Rissa's bare prints had been a set carved with boots far finer than any worn by a human.

"She wasn't simply stolen by the trees," I hissed, trying to pull away from him, this beast who shared heritage with the one who had stolen her from me.

Hendrix fell entirely still as realisation dawned on him, but his hold on me didn't waver, he refused to let me retreat.

"The Fae offered her up?" he asked, his voice rough with the words.

"Yes," I bit out. "One of your people broke into our home while my family slept and stole her away from us on the blood moon to give her up as that year's Offering. One of the Fae deemed – not for the first time – that the sacrifice made should be human so that their kind – *your* kind – wouldn't have to face the burden of the payment. After all, what value does a human life hold when compared to that of the great and immortal Fae?"

"I fought against that notion," he said, his voice brittle, his fingers hard against my spine. "When I was still welcome at court and the curse of the forest was a distant but constant threat to our peoples, it was well known that the trees were luring children to them in sacrifice. I stood against those who wanted to ensure the humans always paid the price."

I shook my head, trying to escape him, and he let me scramble backwards, but he followed, prowling after me on all fours as my spine hit the sacks of grain and I was left with nowhere to retreat to.

"Hear me, Ferris. I fought against it with blood and steel. I fought."

"Why?" I rasped, tears burning the backs of my eyes. "Why would you fight for humans? Every year the forest demands a child in sacrifice and if one isn't offered up by either the Fae or the humans, then it lures one from their bed to claim instead. I have hunted the records. I've scoured every book on the subject. I've been to the shrine which stands at the southern shore and watched as Rissa's name was carved into the great, stone elm tree there along with so many others that there is barely a branch or bough left unscarred by their monikers. Each name is labelled with the year they were taken, and I counted every fucking one of them. And in the six hundred and fifty years since the curse began, there was barely a single year missed. I only found three unaccounted for following the first decade. Three Fae children taken. While *hundreds* of humans were forced to pay the price. Not because the forest ached for only human sacrifice but because each year, when the blood moon rose in demand for payment, the Fae would come hunting and select one of us to settle the debt and give the forest the Offering it demanded."

"I fought it," he insisted, though I had no idea why he was so adamant to make me believe him. "I tried to-"

"Whatever it was you tried to do, you failed," I spat, because even if he'd fought tooth and nail against the plotting of his people, it hadn't been enough and I'd lost my sister in the end.

"*That* is the story of my life," he conceded, finally pulling back, allowing me my own air to breathe, my own space to think without him filling every thought. Yet as he retreated, I found I didn't want him to leave.

I caught his hand and he stilled.

It was too dark for me to see much of his features and it was only getting darker as night fell outside, but I could just make out the twisting edges of the tattoo which marked his face, the ink so dark it seemed to drink any scrap of light that reached it.

I lifted my free hand and brushed my fingers over it without thinking.

Hendrix fell preternaturally still, his breath catching in his throat as I traced the line of the tangled mark, memory guiding me over the lines of it more than sight.

"No one has ever done that," he growled, a low warning to his voice which sent a shiver down my spine.

I hesitated, my eyes on his in the darkness, the raw truth I'd just shared with him making me bold for some reason I didn't understand.

"I'm not just anyone," I told him, my fingertips curving around the turn in his tattoo as I dared him to stop me.

"I'm beginning to see that," he admitted, his own hand coming up to knot in my hair, his fingers twisting into the wet, silver strands.

The space around us was shrinking, the grain store so small, I wasn't certain how we fit in it at all. My heart was pounding faster with every moment, my pulse racing to a beat which might have truly been a song.

"Can you feel that?" I asked on an exhale, because there was something stirring in the air around us, something buzzing against my skin.

"Death haunts my footsteps," he whispered, his fingers moving from my hair to skirt the side of my face. "But this feels more like her master than her."

"Providence?" I breathed, and the pulsing in the air grew thicker at the name of the spirit which had gone unseen in so long that he had been reduced to myth.

"Perhaps," Hendrix conceded. "Though the last time I felt him this close, I got that mark upon my face."

"Tell me," I demanded.

Hendrix paused, his fingers skimming over my jaw and raking down the side of my neck. My spine arched just a little, my skin prickling in a way which was altogether unacceptable. He was Fae. I hated him. Not just for that but for what he'd stolen from me too, the spirits which should have been mine.

"I...did something my people could not forgive," he said slowly, his fingers following the line of my collar bone, pushing the sodden neckline of my shirt lower, just a fraction, but it was enough to send goosebumps skittering across my flesh.

"Tell me."

My heart was pounding so hard that I knew he could feel it where he was touching me, my human body so bad at hiding its reactions to every move he made.

He leaned in, not speaking a word in answer to my demand, his lips so close to mine that for a moment, all other thoughts departed me.

"Stop," I breathed, but some other part of me, some foolish, wanton, insane part was screaming the opposite.

"Stop what?" His mouth brushed mine and whatever I'd been about to say dissolved into nothing.

"I can't stop staring at your mouth," he said in a low growl which had every thought in my mind scattering. "All the damn time. When you curse me, when you spit at me, even when you drive me utterly insane with your constant cleverness. It's infuriating."

I blinked at him, my eyelashes flickering as my brows pressed together, but I didn't draw back like I should have. It was as though some force was holding me there, a breath away from a kiss I shouldn't have wanted, a beat away from a mistake I wouldn't be able to take back.

"You shouldn't say things like that to me," I said.

"I know. But I find my tongue loosens around you in the most maddening of ways. You're a splinter which keeps working its way deeper and deeper beneath my flesh. I'm struggling to figure out a way to remove you – and finding I keep forgetting that I'm supposed to want to do so."

He was so close, his body so much bigger than mine, his presence so powerful I thought I might suffocate beneath the weight of it. But instead of drowning on each inhale I took of him, I was finding myself intoxicated by that same madness he claimed to be suffering in my presence because I still hadn't withdrawn, and now I was thinking about his mouth too.

It would be nothing at all for me to lean in and taste the poison of his tongue, nothing to let the dark consume me and give in to what it seemed to want.

It would be a secret we could leave hidden in this place come morning. One neither of us would ever have to speak of again…

"You're cold," he said.

I was shivering so I could hardly deny it, but I shook my head. "I don't care. But I do care what manner of beast I'm hiding in the dark with. Tell me precisely why you were given this mark."

Something shifted in the air between us, the heat which had been building struck through with ice. I knew he didn't want to tell me anything of his past. I fully expected him to say no, but again he paused, like his instincts were pulling him in two directions and he couldn't decide which of them to follow.

"Lie down."

"What?"

He gave me no choice but to comply, taking hold of me so suddenly that I found myself on my back beneath him in little more than a second. Hendrix placed his hands to the hard floor either side of my head and peered down at me, his long hair spilling over his shoulders to shroud us within it. Now I could see nothing at all.

"Do you have any clothes in your pack?" he asked.

I blinked.

"Yes," I said, a beat too late to cover my confusion.

"Then you need to get changed." His hand moved to the button at the top of my tunic, but I caught it before he could tug it free.

"What about you?" I demanded, fighting to ignore the flush in my cheeks. It wasn't desire. I hated him. I didn't care what he looked like, I didn't care about how powerful his body was or how the green in his eyes was so deep that sometimes I felt like I might drown in it…

"Did you pack clothes for me too?" he asked sceptically.

"No," I said, because of course I hadn't. I kept that bag packed and close at hand so I'd be ready to run from him at any given moment. "Only a fool would forget to keep their provisions nearby while lingering in this forest," I said. "Did *you* pack yourself any spare clothes?"

"I must be the fool of which you speak," he conceded. "But I have no problem sleeping naked so that my clothes can dry."

"What?" I squeaked, hating myself for the way my composure shattered so easily but unable to take it back.

Hendrix chuckled in amusement, then summoned the Fox abruptly, practically blinding me with its appearance.

I cursed, stamping my eyes closed while the warmth of the Fox rushed over me.

"You could have done that the moment we entered this damn shelter," I snapped, realisation dawning on me while Hendrix began tugging the buttons of my tunic open.

"I could do many things at any given moment, lightwing. You only have to ask me nicely and any one of your dreams might come true."

I slapped his hand away from my buttons and pushed myself upright, my skin flaming despite the cold which had sunk into my bones.

I squinted at the Fox as it leapt up onto one of the heaped sacks of grain. The warmth its flaming body provided was nothing short of sinful, and the magic it was created of made sure nothing surrounding it caught light either.

"Get changed before you catch hypothermia," Hendrix said, shoving my pack towards me. "And eat your berries. The last thing I need is you getting cranky because your belly is lacking in food."

"I do not get cranky," I snapped.

"She said crankily."

An honest to the spirits growl escaped me as I turned my back to him and obeyed his command to change because despite my desire to defy him at all turns, doing so in this instance would only hurt me.

I hated him. I told myself that over and over and over again while in the back of my mind, I could have sworn I heard something chuckling.

I shrugged out of my jacket and tunic, glancing over my shoulder at Hendrix, then jerking back towards the wall as I found him stripping off too, his shirt already discarded, the ink across his back drawing altogether too much of my attention.

Unlike me, Hendrix was keeping his eyes on the wall as if he were some kind of gentleman, so I quickly shuffled out of my pants and undergarments before pulling on the clean clothes I kept in my bag.

A ripping sound made me jump and I coughed as dust rose in the air, the ripe scent of mouldering grain pungent in my nostrils.

"What are you doing?" I asked, though I had learned my lesson and didn't chance a look around again.

"I assume you wouldn't be able to control yourself were I to remain naked before you, so I'm working with what we've got."

"What does that mean?" I asked, keeping my eyes on the wall where the Fox's flames created dancing shadows and revealed Hendrix's presence at my back as I was dwarfed in the darkness his figure created.

"You can turn around now." He sounded amused and that only made me more on edge, but I turned to face him, a laugh bursting from my lips the moment I laid eyes on what he'd done.

Hendrix stood shirtless, his sodden hair dripping and leaving runs of moisture down his chest, but despite all the ways in which that should have been distracting, I couldn't help but focus on the torn sack which he had tied around his waist as a method to cover his cock.

"I can take it off if you'd prefer?" he offered, eyes glinting with danger, and I shook my head quickly, knowing I'd just been all too tempted into considering that mistake while refusing to admit it to myself.

I didn't want him.

I hated him.

He was vile, repugnant, arrogant and…and…

My gaze moved to the sculpted muscles of his chest, my thoughts fragmenting once more while again that deep and rolling laughter sounded in the back of my mind.

"Do you think you can swerve from fate, spirit singer?" A deep and ancient voice sounded in my head and I flinched. I knew now that

it was the Dragon, but I had no idea how it managed to communicate with me in such a way and I found it more than a little disconcerting.

"Eat your berries," Hendrix reminded me.

I was glad of the distraction, so I did as he'd commanded, the light from the Fox's fire making it easy for me to ascertain that they were indeed safe to consume. I split my haul in half and offered some out to Hendrix, who accepted them with a thanks which only contained a little mockery.

"Lie down," he said when I'd finished and again, I complied. Not because I was suddenly inclined to follow his commands but because there was little else for us to do now other than sleep or talk, and after what our conversation had almost led to already, I figured sleep was preferable.

I took my thin bedroll from my pack and laid it in the small space before moving to lie on it and shifting over to the very edge on my side, my back to Hendrix who still stood with his arms folded, leaning against the sacks of grain.

"There's room for you too," I said, not looking at him.

He said nothing and I ignored the urge to look at him while making a pillow of my arm beneath my head.

The light of the Fox dimmed, though its heat remained, and I wondered if he'd commanded it to do that, wishing I could have even half that control when it came to the Dragon.

"Control is the issue."

"What's that supposed to mean?" I shot back into the darkness of my mind, but once again, the Dragon seemed to find nothing but amusement in me and didn't offer up anything more.

I stilled as Hendrix dropped down onto the thin bedroll at my back, my body tensing as he shifted closer to me, a grunt of irritation escaping his lips.

"What? I asked despite having decided against any further conversation with him.

"Most of me does not fit on your tiny scrap of a bed, especially while you take up so much of it."

"You should have packed better then."

"You should have thought twice before destroying our castle."

"You were the one who told me to summon the-"

I cried out in alarm as his arm coiled around me and he half lifted me off the ground before his other arm moved beneath my head and his chest pressed firmly to my back.

"What the fuck are you doing?" I hissed.

"This is the only way either of us will have enough room to sleep," he said, his voice a rough rumble against my spine, his stubble grazing my neck as he rested his head all too close to mine.

"I was perfectly fine before you manhandled me into this position."

"You don't appear to by trying to scramble away though," he pointed out, and I quickly shoved his arm in an attempt to make him release me.

"Stop."

"No."

"You're cold. I'll keep you warm."

"The Fox is doing that just fine," I insisted, my pulse coming rapidly once more as I found myself trapped in the cage of his arms and despite my protests, I couldn't deny just how well I fit there.

"Fine, I'll barter you for it," he sighed dramatically, his breath making my hair tickle my neck and a shiver run down my spine.

"For what?"

"For you to allow me to lay like this so that I have some hope of actually sleeping tonight and not waking in the morning to find every muscle in my body has cramped up."

"Seriously?" I griped, though I couldn't deny the delicious warmth of his powerful body where it was draped around mine.

"Yes. I'll give you something – whatever you want."

"Those spirits you stole from me," I said instantly, and he broke a laugh.

"Be reasonable," Hendrix chastised.

"One spirit then," I conceded, and he laughed again, his breath hot against my neck, my skin heating in reply to it.

I squirmed in his hold and he shifted his hand to my hip, forcing me still.

"Do that again and this sleepover will take a very different turn. It isn't only your mouth which has my mind wandering, lightwing," he warned in a low growl, and I fell utterly still.

Some mad part of me wanted to squirm back into him again, to call his bluff, to make him act on that threat and-

Nothing. Because I hated him and I wanted nothing at all from him - and why was the fucking Dragon laughing at me again? I wasn't even safe with my own damn thoughts anymore.

"The truth then," I said quickly. "About your banishment."

Hendrix stilled and said nothing for a long time.

"If you won't give me that much, then you can just-"

"Some of the truth," he said finally. "Because there are parts of it which even I cannot bear to recall and parts of it which would make you run screaming from me despite the night awaiting you beyond these walls."

I hesitated on accepting his offer because his words were laced with the truth of his warning. There were parts of his past I was better off not knowing. But I couldn't deny my curiosity when it came to the rest of it.

"Okay," I said finally. "If that's all you're offering, I'll take it."

Hendrix fell silent again but I knew he'd accepted my terms. His truth was on the tip of his tongue, and I was all too eager to learn it.

HENDRIX

CHAPTER TWENTY FOUR

"Have you changed your mind?" Ferris asked, a touch of disappointment in her voice.

"No," I grunted.

I'd fallen quiet, lost to thoughts of the past as I tried to piece it into a story I could tell her without unveiling the whole truth. But I didn't want to lie either. No one had asked this story of me in all these years. She wanted to hear it to understand me better and I found I wanted to share it. At least enough so that she could see the root of my malice.

"As I've told you, my time among the Coterie led me to truths I'd never intended to discover. Truths of their evildoings. And the fact is, things escalated to a point where I killed one of them for their misdeeds. It was a bloody fight, a wicked death, the type that stains the soul red."

Ferris remained silent but she didn't tense or pull away from me, choosing to remain in the cage of my arms despite how many times I'd warned her of the dangers that came attached to me.

"I ran from the carnage I'd reaped but I didn't make it far. I was caught with blood on my hands and placed in a cold cell for a long winter night while my fate was decided. Our kind deliver punishments equal to the sinners' crimes, and I had no doubt that death awaited me at dawn."

Ferris drew in a sharp breath, her fingers tightening on my arm. "How did you escape?"

I swallowed the hardening lump in my throat, knowing I would have to evade the details but wanting to give her what I could.

"When sunrise came, I was taken to the stone courtyard in the heart of Mithelnore. All executions are carried out there in front of any civilian who wishes to come watch. My name was a curse on their lips as I was tethered to a wooden pole at the heart of the square and branded with the mark of an outcast – a statement that I was not welcome among our people even in the afterworld. I can so easily recall the way my knees pressed to the unforgiving stone, how the wind was blowing in from the north, carrying the scent of ice from the frozen sea. I can relive that day any time I close my eyes as if it's branded there for me to suffer through time and again."

"What did they do to you?" she breathed, sensing the weight in my voice at what was to come.

"Not to me," I said darkly. "They could have stripped the flesh from my bones and I would have gladly offered the payment. But it wasn't me that bore the price in the end."

"Then who?"

"My family. My mother, father, my younger brother and sister. They dragged them out like rabid dogs, hands fisted around the backs of their necks as they shoved them down in front of me. They didn't cry or beg. They were strong, my kin. They were warriors with hearts forged of iron, and the only pain I found in them was when they looked at me."

"Hendrix, tell me they didn't hurt them," Ferris breathed, her nails digging into my arm.

"I cannot, lightwing." I took a weighted breath. "They killed my father first. They beat and battered him while my mother yelled his name. She was next, a swift slice to her throat that quieted her and caused a riot of agony among the last of us. They took Amelda slower." I squeezed my eyes shut, the horror of losing my little sister scoring a passage of pain through my chest. "My brother Kashton was the last, hauled in front of me, eye to eye, his words the crush of an anvil against my heart. 'I'll see you wherever our love guides us in the afterworld, brother.'"

I stopped talking, my throat clogged with the pain of those goodbyes.

Ferris rolled over in the cage of my arms, her fingers finding my cheek in the dark. "I'm so sorry."

I grunted in acknowledgment, unable to force out more as she curled into me, embracing me, her face settling against my neck. I pulled her tight to my chest, allowing my heart to split open and bleed with her there. As it had never done with anyone else.

"How did you escape?" she asked against my skin, and heat rippled through me at the touch of her lips to my collarbone.

"I lost myself to the rage of my grief, broke free of my bonds. I fought, I killed, I ran. It is a blur of death and savagery. Somehow, I made it out of Rivenspire." I knew precisely how. It was so much more than these words painted it out to be. And she might question how I could have done any such thing alone. But she nodded instead, perhaps keeping more questions to herself, or believing I might just be capable of such an escape given what she knew of my strength. I didn't offer any more information either way.

"We should sleep now," I muttered, drawing her nearer, my fingers gliding down the length of her spine. Her closeness helped to banish my demons again, and I was grateful when she nestled against me instead of rolling to face away from me once more.

"It must have broken you," she exhaled, her fingers skimming down my arm. "I know what that's like."

"Then we are alike for reasons I would rather we weren't."

She glanced up at me from the crook of my neck, her eyes bright with emotion as her pain surfaced to meet mine. I tucked a lock of silver behind her ear and drank in that grief, knowing it all too well.

"Is that why you're here? To try and bring them back from death?" Ferris asked, a tightness to her throat.

"No," I said truthfully, my voice dripping in darkness.

"Then why?"

"Goodnight, lightwing," I said firmly, and her eyes shuttered as she withdrew from me, her lips tightening at the edges.

"Goodnight, Hendrix." She rolled away but let me keep her against my body, not knowing that she was wrapped in the arms of not just a killer, but the most wicked monster on Rathian.

"We have to move on from this quarry," I growled, folding my arms as Ferris marched up and down the boggy area of forest where the diary had guided us to the potential location of the Boar. "It's not here."

Ferris sighed, turning to me with pursed lips. "We don't know that."

"We are wasting time. We've been searching for days and there has been neither hide nor hair of it. It has likely been caught already."

Ferris's throat bobbed, her eyes roaming the trees around us once more as if she might find the spirit if she looked hard enough. I walked up to her and took her arm, her eyes lifting to meet mine and a ripple of tension passing between us.

"Ferris," I urged in a low voice. "We cannot waste any more time."

She sighed, conceding. "Fine. Then where next?" She drew her pack from her shoulder, taking out the diary and flicking through it.

I left her to decide, knowing she had likely already planned three different options, listed them out, weighed the odds, methods and madness in her schemes, and wouldn't be swayed in the slightest by my opinion on the choice she came to. Not to mention the fact that I'd come to the realisation that acting against her plans was nothing short of foolish. My pretty little human had a mind for this forest, a knack for it too, seeming to understand it far better than I could ever hope to.

I moved to a nearby stream and crouched down to cup water and take a drink. As I did so, the thump of boots and crack of twigs made my head snap up.

I listened, counting five sets footfalls, moving fast, at a run.

I whirled around, sprinting back to Ferris and whipping her off her feet, clapping my hand to her mouth in the same movement to silence her gasp of surprise. Then I pelted straight for a large mass of ferns and slipped between them, dropping down and laying Ferris beneath me as we hid in the mass of foliage, allowing myself time to assess the threat coming our way.

I released my hand from Ferris's mouth as we shifted to lie next to each other, pressing a finger to my lips, and she nodded seriously, peering out beyond the ferns.

Two humans raced into the clearing, sweat beading on their brows, one sporting a bloody gash on his arm and the other with an arrow sticking through her shoulder.

The woman had a pinched sort of face and her slender body was lined with muscle, while the man was strong-looking with dark eyebrows that contrasted with his fair hair.

The two of them raced through the stream and the woman screamed as another arrow whistled through the air and caught her in the back. She landed heavily on the ground and Ferris shifted beside me as if planning some reckless move to help them. I clamped my hand down on her shoulder, giving her a firm look that told her in no uncertain terms that I would not be allowing that.

"I know them. That's Esther and Brian. They entered the forest with me," she hissed, shoving my hand off of her and scrambling to get up, but I caught hold of her wrist, tugging her back down sharply and wrestling her beneath me. Ferris cursed me, aiming a knee between my thighs which I only stopped by pressing my weight down onto her and slapping a hand over her mouth.

I raised my head again in time to see the man trying to help the woman to her feet, but he gave up when three Fae broke through the forest behind them.

My muscles tensed, pure hatred seeping into my blood at the sight of the ringleader.

Islasees Bellatorn wore a cape of darkest blue, his red hair swept smoothly back over the crown of his head and the sharp lines of his face as ruthless as they were handsome. He held no weapon in hand, but the two Fae either side of him did, the male holding a bow aloft and the female wielding a double-headed axe. I knew them both well; Benson Rawk with his jet-black curls and Jadina Calehive with her aquamarine eyes and short blonde locks. They were two of Islasees favoured warriors, fit for the dirtiest kind of work. They had been the ones to walk me to the stone courtyard upon the morning of my family's execution, they had taken part in their deaths, and they had somehow escaped the carnage I'd reaped that day.

Ferris thrashed beneath me as bitterness coated my tongue, my mind clouded by bloodlust. I wanted all three of their deaths so keenly that it burned me from the inside out.

I gritted my teeth, considering my options as I glared at Islasees. I ached to run him through with my sword and watch him die so very slowly at my hand. But Islasees could name me before I secured his death and unmask me to Ferris, revealing the rotten truth of who I was.

I couldn't bear to lose her. Not yet. And worse than all that, what if I failed in my plight entirely and left her exposed to their wrath? There were three of them after all, and Islasees Bellatorn was the most fearsome, battle-hardened Fae in all of Rivenspire. As much as I believed I could defeat him, there was a chance I would fail. And without me protecting her, Ferris might not make it away from him. I could not risk her death for anything.

So despite all my instincts telling me to do the opposite, I stayed in place and ground my teeth, warring with the urge to seek vengeance here and now. I would get another chance after all. The Great Hunt was not over yet.

The human she'd called Brian made a run for the trees, but Benson released another arrow that cut through his neck and sent him slamming to the floor, skidding through a mass of dead leaves. Benson ran to him, finishing off the twitching man with a short blade and rolling him over to check his throat.

Ferris made a noise of agonised grief against the palm of my hand, tears pricking the corners of her eyes at the deaths of the humans. But I knew what she didn't – Death had come calling for them before they'd even stepped out into that clearing. There had been no saving them from her call. I kept the company of that spirit often enough to know that once her mind was made up, there was no swaying the course of fate. But the glare Ferris gave me through the haze of her furious tears told me she wouldn't understand that even if I explained it to her.

"No amulets," Benson called to Islasees in disappointment.

"What about this one?" Islasees jerked his chin at the woman in the stream who was crawling up the bank, trying to gain her feet in the slippery mud.

Ferris struggled beneath me, but still I kept her pinned in the dirt, my hand tight over her lips. I could feel the weight of her hatred for me simmering in her stare, whatever else I'd begun kidding myself into thinking she might have begun to see in me burning away with the sting of it. But I didn't let her rise. Still I made no move to help the woman who was clawing her way up the bank with death stalking her last moments. It was already done. Death watched on in the shadows, nodding her head to me from within the folds of her heavy cowl.

"I'll find out what she has for you, my lord." Jadina bowed her head loyally to Islasees, then stalked over to the human with light-footed movements that didn't marry with the brutal swing of her axe. Ferris jolted beneath me as she watched Esther die, and Jadina leaned down, ripping her collar open to check for amulets.

"She has one!" Jadina whooped.

Islasees stalked over to the woman, his mouth turned down at the corners as usual, the humans' deaths stirring no emotion from him as he leaned down and ripped the amulet from her throat.

"That was hardly fair, Jadina," Benson drawled, sauntering back over to the others. "I'd marked her with my arrows. The kill belonged to me."

"That's not how it works, Benson." Jadina cut him a hard look and Benson muttered something incoherent.

Islasees only had attention to spare for the amulet, fastening it around his neck and releasing a sigh as the spirit became his.

"Which is it, my lord?" Benson asked curiously.

"The Rat," Islasees answered, tucking the amulet beneath his collar and revealing the glimmer of another amulet there.

My jaw ticked at the sight. He had two fucking amulets and he was clearly using his warriors to cut down other Champions to seize them for his own, working around the rules on stealing them with bloodshed. I should have expected nothing less from the brutal, warmongering Lord Protector. He always had been an underhanded bastard, using the shadows, trickery and deception to gain his wants more often than not.

"Where next, my lord?" Jadina asked, wiping her axe off on a row of ferns.

"The woman they were with headed south when she split apart from them a mile back, so south we will go," Islasees said darkly. "Once we've cut down the last of their worthless kind and taken whatever amulets they may have gathered, we can turn our gaze to mightier opponents."

"Even Princess Drava?" Benson hissed uncertainly, and my ears pricked up at that. So I'd been right, my aunt had come. But surely the Lord Protector wouldn't turn on a royal.

"If we need an amulet from her, then we will convince her to relinquish it," Islasees said firmly. "Queen Sorshana demanded we break the curse and seize the boon in her name. So it shall be done."

"Yes, my lord," Benson and Jadina replied.

Drava had been favoured as the next queen the last I'd heard, making her an opponent of Queen Sorshana in the court, and no doubt that was why she'd entered this foul place. If she were to end the curse of the forest, it would win her much favour with the Fae. Perhaps Drava was thinking to oust our queen from her position. It was a bold move. The kind I might have made myself once…

Islasees took off across the clearing, marching south with his two lap dogs in tow, and I waited several moments before finally taking my hand from Ferris's lips and climbing off of her.

"How could you?" she spat, scrambling to her feet and backing away from me, her hand moving to the slingshot she carried in her pocket - though clearly she wasn't entirely departed from her senses because she didn't draw it.

I sighed, not liking the fury in her expression one bit and wishing I could have chosen a different path for us to take so that we hadn't had to bear witness to that savagery. All it had done was serve as a reminder to Ferris of all the reasons she had to hate my kind, and I had been so enjoying the moments when she allowed herself to forget that with me.

"Death hung watching in the shadows, lightwing. She had already chosen this for their moment. I could not have stopped it any more than you could have. And though I greatly wish to see that male's body separated from his thick head, I could not take on both him and the others and keep you safe. All three of them are seasoned warriors and enough of a challenge for me that I would have needed more than a moment in which to rid them from this world. And that timescale could easily have been at the cost of your demise. So no, I did not jump in to avenge two strangers whose fates had already been sealed, but I refuse to risk you for anything, least of all a pointless cause."

Ferris blanched at my assessment of what we'd just witnessed, those angry tears still glimmering in her eyes, the violet blazing with more intensity and enchantment than I had ever seen. The Dragon's amulet at her throat lifted from her chest, glowing a faint teal colour as her silver hair stirred in a wind I couldn't feel.

I held my breath, expecting the beast to burst from her at any given moment, knowing that if it did, then Islasees and his cohort would quickly return to this place. And perhaps if they did, they'd find their deaths in the jaws of her Dragon after all.

But just as fast as the moment had come, it faded. The tears slipped past her hold, spilling down her cheeks as she crumpled with the weight of the truth I'd offered her, clearly accepting it and hating it at the same time.

I stepped forward, lifting my hands to cradle her face between them, swiping the tears from her cheeks, wanting to banish that hurt and pain in her tumultuous gaze.

She slapped my hands away from her with a sharp shake of her head, backing up and swiping the tears away for herself as she forced them to still.

"Come," I said, stepping from the ferns and reaching out to take Ferris's hand in mine.

I might come to blows with Islasees yet, but I would have more amulets to my name when I did. His death was written, but not this day. Not with her here and me unable to guarantee her safety. I'd already lost too many important people to the ruthless wrath of that male. I wouldn't risk her becoming the next.

"He has the Tiger amulet," Ferris hissed, tugging her hand free of my hold. "I saw the emblem."

"We cannot let him gain any more," I announced in a growl,

turning for the trees in the opposite direction to the one Islasees had taken, but Ferris caught my wrist.

I looked back at her, finding a crease between her eyes. "That Fae, you know him, don't you?"

I nodded stiffly. "I told you of him. Islasees Bellatorn, Lord Protector of the Queen."

She sucked in a sharp breath, her gaze darkening with that knowledge.

"You wish him dead," she stated.

"More than anything," I growled. "But our fates will intertwine again beneath these boughs. You will know when it's time for me to strike at him." I turned away from her, but she stepped into my path.

"That's a purposefully cryptic thing to say," she accused.

I tilted my head down, lifting her hand and pressing my mouth to her knuckles, watching as her eyes widened at the touch. "I never wanted to wrap you up in my past, lightwing. But I fear it is catching up to me. And once it stands in the starkness of day with us, you will no longer wish to keep my company."

She gently pulled her hand from mine, her eyes narrowed and full of burning questions. But she didn't voice them. Perhaps because she knew I wouldn't answer them. At least a little of that fury had retreated again, a little of that hatred for the Fae she cherished so forcefully - while forgetting she should have included me in its wrath. I supposed the enemy of my enemy truly might be my friend. Or maybe something far more significant than that.

"Whatever it is you're hiding from me, I can handle it," she said firmly.

"Then how about this - I promise the truth will come to light. But for now, let me remain in the dark with you a while longer while we hunt together. An alliance built of who we are in this forest, not of who we are outside it."

She hesitated, then slowly nodded. "For now."

"That is more than enough." I smiled ruefully, then gestured for her to lead the way. But she didn't, not at first. She moved to the bodies of the humans who had found their deaths in this place and carefully moved them so that they lay on their backs at the base of a large cherry tree beside one another.

She broke off the arrows which had taken down the woman and moved to the small stream where she took time selecting stones, plucking several from the water and tossing them aside again until she was satisfied with the four she had chosen.

I watched in silence as she placed them upon the eyes of the dead, using mud from the riverbank to paint an X and an O on them.

I wasn't entirely familiar with human death rites but there was a stoic reverence to her movements as she completed them. Though I knew it was foolish to linger here a moment longer than necessary, I couldn't find it in me to stop her from completing the task.

She gathered small sprigs of flowers from the brambles between the roots of the trees, and I reached up to pluck a few sprigs of elder flowers from a high bough to offer her too.

Ferris blinked at me in surprise but wordlessly accepted my offering, my small token of apology. Finally, she placed the bundled flowers in the fingers of the dead along with their weapons.

All the while, Death lingered in the shadows between the trees, watching her, assessing her. The spirit had long become a constant in my life, and though I could hardly claim to have a relationship with her, I did believe I knew enough to sense when she was pleased. And right now, Death was eyeing Ferris like she was something to behold, something to covet, something to desire…

I didn't like that one bit.

A growl slid up the back of my throat and a breath of laughter spun around me in the breeze before Death took my meaning and scurried away to offer her focus elsewhere.

Good. It would not do for that spirit to take too much of a liking to my lightwing.

When Ferris was finally satisfied, she muttered something which I didn't catch all the words of but I guessed was a promise to see this curse broken from what fragments I did hear. Then she turned to me at last.

Her violet eyes met mine and I stilled beneath their scrutiny.

"Where to now?" I asked.

Predictably she moved to take a book from her pack, handing the bag to me so that I might carry it for her, and I smirked as I accepted the small burden of it. Then, with her diary in hand, we made a path west while the forest parted for Ferris Creed, its roots and branches sweeping aside, a path appearing at her feet through a magic which was solely devoted to her even if she seemed blind to it at times. And I followed in her wake, wondering if I might just like to keep on following this creature for a long time yet.

FERRIS

CHAPTER TWENTY FIVE

Day seventeen.

Dusk creeps up on me each day with reckless cunning. I'm certain the trees are working together to try and lure me out into the night. When I sleep, I'm haunted by the songs of the Lost Children. I wasn't certain what it was at first, but as I sat by the window of the tower I took shelter in tonight, the truth struck me.

Out there, roaming the woods beneath the cover of darkness, is a legion of children who wish for me to join them in the dark. I've come to believe that the children who were stolen by the cursed forest during the blood moon Offerings are those same creatures who now steal between the trees in the dark. But I'm not convinced they are still those same, innocent beings they once were.

This place is rife with corruption. My heart breaks as I

listen to the cries of those who were stolen from their parents and brought to this cursed place, but I cannot do anything to help them, no matter how much I might wish to.

Their songs lull me towards sleep as I write this. I only hope I don't find myself walking the woods in the dark when I wake.

"Again with the diary?" Hendrix drawled.

I pursed my lips, closing it as I looked at him. We'd had little to show for the days we'd spent hunting the Boar and his mood had darkened with each passing day, leaving him prickly and searching for a fight.

I wasn't planning on giving him one.

"Go to sleep," I told him.

We were still taking shelter in the tiny grain store, his huge body sprawled across my bedroll while I sat propped against stacks of grain, reading by the light of the Fox's fire.

We'd dined on berries, nuts and a thin soup made from nettles and mushrooms. It hadn't been nearly enough to sate my rumbling stomach, so I imagined he was faring far worse.

"If I try to sleep now, you will only disturb me when you come clambering into my bed at some unspiritual hour. I need you to join me now if I'm to have any hope of actual rest."

"You're forgetting something," I said.

"What's that?"

"That you're the one who has come clambering into *my* bed. I'm the only one of us who had the foresight to keep my pack close at hand at all times and-"

"Excuse me for not expecting you to topple an entire castle with your atrocious attempts at Summoning," he taunted, and I almost gave in, almost bit back, almost rose to the bait.

"The Fae is a brute with no finesse or true understanding of what

we are," the Dragon spoke in my mind, and I jumped in surprise.

I'd tried reaching out to the spirit countless times over the last few days, running my fingers across the carved amulet at my throat. I'd willed it to speak with me, to offer me some guidance in Summoning or even in what we needed to be focusing on now, but until this moment, the spirit had been stoic in its ignoring of me.

I hadn't dared try to call it forth again, and even Hendrix had agreed it was better I didn't until we found somewhere more secure to base ourselves at night.

"What does that mean?" I breathed.

"In what way was I unclear?" Hendrix scoffed. "If everyone was as bad at Summon-"

"Shh." I pushed forward on my knees and pressed my palm over Hendrix's mouth to shut him up.

The Dragon laughed in the corners of my mind. *"Perhaps you should toss him out into the dark and see if the forest likes the taste of him?"*

"I would, but I fear I can't haul his dead weight through the door."

"You could always ask for help."

A laugh fell from my lips just as Hendrix knocked my hand from his mouth with a growl.

"Have you lost your mind, lightwing?" he asked.

"I wasn't talking to you."

"I suppose your imaginary friends are more interesting than me then, are they?" he scoffed.

"I was conversing with my Dragon, if you must know."

"Your Dragon?" Hendrix gave me a flat look which did nothing to disguise his scepticism.

"The Bear and Fox still don't talk to you?" I asked.

"They're animals. Of course they don't."

"They're spirits," I corrected. "So why would it be the least bit surprising that they can talk?"

Hendrix huffed irritably. "Nevertheless, I do not converse with the spirits I have captured, and if you wish to gain true control over the beast at your command, perhaps you shouldn't waste time on idle chatter with it either. Tomorrow we will find an open spot for you to practice Summoning it once more."

"You think that's wise?" I questioned, unable to banish the memories of the Dragon destroying our castle all too easily.

"I think it's necessary," Hendrix replied. "As is sleep." He indicated the spot beside him, and I tried not to look bothered by the idea of curling up in his arms once more as I gave in and moved into it.

Hendrix watched me the entire time, but I busied myself with getting comfortable and refused to return his stare.

Once I'd settled into the space to the right of the bed roll on my side, Hendrix lowered himself down beside me, draping his muscular arm around my middle and hauling me into the curve of his body.

I stilled.

He'd done the same thing each night, pulling me so close that our breaths fell into sync with one another, offering me his bicep as a pillow, his own head nestled against mine, his mouth a breath away from my neck. Each of his exhales roused gooseflesh across my skin.

But this night, his hand did not hang loose and still around my middle. This night, his fingers brushed against the skin at the top of my waistband.

I swallowed, shifting against him and receiving a low growl for the movement.

"I've warned you not to squirm," he said.

A defiant, insane, utterly foreign piece of my soul ached to test him on that threat. What would the warrior Fae do to the human woman who dared to press her body back against his? What would he do if she were to arch her spine or tilt her head so that his lips met with the skin of her neck instead of simply teasing her with the possibility that they might do so?

His fingers brushed across the top of my waistband again, his skin rough in the best possible way.

Truly, I hated him. Even more so for getting so close, for making a traitor of my flesh. One moment I felt like he was toying with me, but the next it seemed more like he was torturing himself, holding his body in check, keeping himself restrained.

What would he be like if he allowed himself to unleash fully?

"Hendrix…" I began, uncertain of my question, only that I wanted to ask it.

"Ferris," he replied, my name a rough demand, or perhaps a ragged plea.

I counted to ten, meaning to use that time to talk myself out of this madness but when I reached zero at last, my hand came down over his and I turned my face so that I could meet his eyes.

His pupils were wide and hungry as he drank me in, his dark hair casting a shadow around his features in the dim glow of the Fox's fire.

I flattened his fingers against my stomach, stopping their motion along my waistband.

He arched a brow, his arm tensing as he made to withdraw it, but I held him tightly and instead, shifted it lower. My fingers guided his beneath the edge of my trousers, my gaze never moving from the solid green of his as our combined hands made it to the top of my undergarments.

"I could destroy you so easily," he breathed, and I wasn't sure if it was meant as a warning or a promise, but my eyes fell to the movement of his lips as he uttered the words.

"You're wrong," I replied, because it wasn't destruction I found in his gaze, it was freedom, a wild and furious kind of freedom which would likely tear me apart should I dare to steal a taste of it. But I wanted to all the same.

His eyes spilled from mine to his hand, his fingers flexing beneath mine, the fabric of my trousers tightening around them, bunching against my core.

I gasped at the friction, heat blossoming between my thighs.

He was all the things I shouldn't want, but the only thing I could think of was how desperately I needed him to move his damn hand lower.

Still he hesitated, so I took him up on his promise. I arched my spine, my ass pressing back against his cock and a groan of pure need escaping me as I felt how hard he was.

Hendrix cursed, tugging me against him firmly, his fingers slipping beneath the very top of my undergarments, the full, huge length of his cock driving against my ass.

I almost begged him for more, almost pushed his hand lower just to relieve the ache between my thighs, to sate the need which was making my breath catch and entire body thrum with want.

Hendrix bit down on his lip, his eyes on my mouth, his muscles corded with tension as he fought to hold back. But he was going to shatter. I could see it in his eyes and despite everything that hung between us, the salt in so many wounds, the chasm of hatred between our people, I wanted him to break.

His head dipped at last and I tipped my chin up, unable to deny how the words he'd spoken about needing to taste me had lingered in my mind, running circles through my thoughts. I wanted to know the taste of him too. And here in the dark, I didn't want to deny it.

A loud bang on the door made us flinch apart, the hammering strike of a fist on wood coming in quick succession.

"Who-" I began, but Hendrix pressed his hand to my mouth to silence me, his eyes dark with warning.

"Ferris?" a voice called from beyond the door. A voice I knew better than my own name.

My eyes widened and I tried to lurch upright, but Hendrix still had hold of me and he yanked me back into his arms.

I shoved his hand away from my mouth.

"That's Rissa," I hissed, my pulse thundering wildly as my sister called for me again from beyond the door.

"That's not your sister," Hendrix growled, fighting to keep hold of me as I struggled to stand. "That's a lost child – even if it used to be her, the magic of this place has made her into something else. You've heard them calling before. You know they wish to lure us out into the dark."

Footsteps raced away from the door, soft laughter fading as Rissa ran from us and tears pricked the backs of my eyes.

Hendrix didn't release me until I sagged in his hold, defeat weighing me down against the bedroll, all other thoughts or schemes of insanity long since fled.

In the trees beyond our hiding place, a song started up, the sweet call of children playing in the forest, their words lost in the lilting melody.

She was out there. I'd already come to realise that the only chance I had of finding her in this place was by venturing into the dark. The only hints I'd gotten of her came at night.

"Afraid of the dark, human?" the Dragon rumbled in the back of my mind.

Hendrix was eyeing me suspiciously, still waiting for my answer. I knew he was right. I knew I should have been doing all I could to put the Lost Children and Rissa out of my mind, but I couldn't deny the ache in my heart which had risen at the sound of her voice calling my name.

"Okay," I said, wanting to placate Hendrix, needing him to stop looking at me like that.

Someone started banging on the wall at the back of the building, first one fist, then another and another until there were so many children knocking on the walls that dust shivered from the beams overhead and the whole building trembled beneath them.

Hendrix pushed to his feet. "Be gone!" he bellowed.

There was a beat of silence, then laughter rang out all around us, the joyful, unfiltered laughter of children.

Hendrix yelled at them again, moving towards the back wall and thumping his fist against it in reply to their calls.

I had less than the blink of an eye to decide on what to do but something more than my sister was calling for me out there. It was as though the forest was singing my name, begging me to come out, promising me all the answers I sought and more if I were only brave enough to seek them.

And perhaps it *was* brave to scramble to my feet and wrench aside the sack of grain which was barring the door. Or perhaps it was utterly stupid.

"Ferris!" Hendrix roared in warning, but I'd already yanked the door wide and hurled myself through it.

I slammed the door at my back in some vain attempt to protect him from what was out here because I knew in my soul that it wasn't meant for him. It was meant for me.

The Lost Children whooped and hollered out in the darkness of the trees, and I whirled around, finding their small and tear-stained faces peering back at me from all around the grain store, its roof and even the surrounding branches.

Their eyes glimmered with silvery light, something entirely unhuman about them as they watched me.

"Come, Ferris!" Rissa called, and I whipped back to face the forest once more, catching a glimpse of her white gown flitting away between the trees.

"Wait!" I cried as I took chase, the pounding of Hendrix's feet right behind me as he threw the door wide and roared my name.

But I was already gone, running into the trees with reckless abandon, racing after my sister while root, branch and bramble all twisted out of my way to accommodate me before tangling at my back to halt him.

"Rissa!" I cried, pleading with her to wait, to turn back. But all I caught were glimpses of her white dress and auburn hair flicking between the trees far ahead of me.

I ran until my legs burned with fatigue, my breaths coming in sharp and jagged pants which seared their way into my lungs.

Hendrix cried out behind me and I stumbled, almost turning around for him. But it was as though the magic of the forest had taken hold of my soul, lashing a cord to it and tugging me ever onward. I couldn't stop, I couldn't turn back. I could only race to catch up to the girl who I had come here to find.

I yelled her name again, entire trees uprooting themselves and moving out of my way as I ran after her faster and faster until finally I spotted her standing entirely still in the heart of a moonlit glade.

Rissa looked just how she had when I'd last seen her at twelve years old, her silver eyes sparking with secrets, her freckle-spattered nose straight at the centre of her heart-shaped face. But she'd grown too. She wasn't small like the other Lost Children I'd spied between the trees but had aged in the last eight years.

I'd lost a girl and now a woman stood waiting for me in her place.

I launched myself at her, meaning to hurl my arms around her neck, but a massive serpent launched itself from the trees to my right before I could, its hard body built of stone with rivers of glinting minerals and metals running through it, its bright eyes keen with knowledge.

The snake wrapped itself around my middle and held me there while I still reached for my sister, my fingertips almost grazing her hand.

Rissa smiled at me and my heart broke for all the lost years which weighed between us.

I opened my mouth to speak, so dazzled by the sight of her that I could hardly spare a thought for the enormous spirit which had me caged in its grasp.

"How are you here?" I demanded.

"Later, sister," she said. "There is something you must see first."

My lips parted on a reply, a protest, I wasn't even certain what, but she stepped aside before I could so much as utter a word.

Behind her was a towering horse chestnut tree, its roots a tangled web which extended into the clearing, trailing towards me where I scrambled in the hold of the Serpent.

Within the cage of those roots was a woman, one of the Cursed Ones I'd so often avoided.

Her hair was dark and shrouded her face, but she murmured something I had to strain to hear.

"Again and again and again," she muttered. "Each time we fail and the clock is reset. Again and again and again…"

"Rissa, what is this?" I demanded, but before I could get any form of reply, the Cursed One looked up sharply, her violet eyes meeting with mine in a fierce demand.

"Make it stop," she spat at me in a voice which was my own, with a mouth that mirrored mine. "End it on this cycle, Ferris. We've all suffered the failure too often."

Her words barely registered with me at all because I wasn't staring at some unknown Cursed One trapped forever and suffering in the grips of the forest. I was staring into my own face at a death which was mine and yet wasn't. Because the Cursed One wasn't an unknown human. She was me and I was her.

And my screams carried away into the night.

Hendrix

CHAPTER TWENTY SIX

"Ferris!" I roared into the malevolent forest.

The trees were groaning around me, vines twisting together as I slashed at them with my sword, trying to tear a path after her. But for every vine I cut, another two grew in its place, the passage forward impossible to forge.

But I would not give up.

The dark seeped from every corner of the wood, like it was a creature between the boughs, creeping from the roots to drench the trees in black.

I panted as I came close to exhaustion, my sword having swung so many times that my arm ached from the force. Countless strikes and I'd barely moved a foot in the direction she had followed those damned children.

Laughter tinkled behind me and I twisted around, sweat beading on my brow as I raised my sword and bared my teeth.

"Come at me, cursed beasts, and I'll cut you apart," I warned.

More laughter called in answer and the glint of eyes gazed out at me from between the branches above. I could just make out the shadowy figures of the Lost Children creeping closer, undeterred by my threat.

"Where is she?" I spat. "Return her to me or I'll rip this forest apart to find her."

"We know you," a boy's voice called out. "We know what you are."

"Does she know the truth?" a girl asked somewhere to my right, and I whirled that way only to find more laughter carrying off into the dark.

"King of Death and Ruin," voices whispered around me, then one of them started up an eerie song, letting it pour from branch to bough until it was all I could hear.

"You're heading to the deep places of the ground,

There you will lay in the earth without a sound.

Let them drag, let them rip, let them tear until its done.

They long for you, you, you, dear one."

Small hands gripped my wrist from behind and I jerked around again, swinging my sword with a yell. The Lost Children scattered, barefoot and racing into the dark again with echoing laughter in their wake, leaving ice in my bones.

"Get away!" I bellowed as more fingers brushed my arms from behind and I swung my sword in that direction instead, trying to slay these monsters with the faces of children. They were a lie. There was no possibility that any of them could truly be alive after all these years in the forest. They were a mirage of the Great Elm's design, put here to torture us in their own twisted way.

The song grew to a crescendo as light footsteps pattered around me between the trees, the flash of a ragged skirt, or a small hand brushing the bark of a wide trunk the only sign of their movements.

I could feel them closing in on all sides, above and around me. Their song was thrumming through my ears, burrowing into my chest. It was all I could hear, and somehow their voices sounded like knives against a chalkboard now, making me wince against the raking noise which grew ever louder.

"The forest seeks what has been stole,
And she'll break and crack your worthless soul,
'til you answer to the restless trees
And beg for mercy upon your knees."

"Enough! Where is she?!" I roared, slashing blindly with my sword as tiny hands pulled at me again. But my blade never struck a single monster.

A flash of movement beside me made me lurch around, but my head spun and the song droned in my skull, making me feel weak. I staggered toward a blur of children as laugher cascaded around me, trying to strike at them but finding my knees hitting the forest floor instead.

The song built inside my bones, echoing through me and driving me mad with some magic I couldn't unravel.

My mind was caught in the threads of their song as it wove insanity through my thoughts. Nothing I did could fight it away. I swung the sword again, but it slipped from my fingers and my hands hit the mossy ground to brace myself.

My muscles strained against the power of the song as it echoed fuzzily in and out of my head, mixing with the childish laughter of so many soulless creations.

"Ferris," I rasped, trying to get up with every ounce of strength I had.

But I could not. Part of me needed to answer to the call of the music, to give in and lie down and let the forest feast upon my bones. The more I tried to fight free of the Lost Children's allure, the deeper I fell into it.

"Get back inside," I commanded Ferris, knowing she was out here somewhere, but the dark had come and it was claiming her beyond my reach. I could do nothing but sink into the lull of the song and fall prey to the thundering dread that resounded through each note. Because every word that found me now sounded like that of monster whispering in my ear, not a softly spoken child. And as it lured me away from my plight to find Ferris, the final line imbued me with a sense of horror for what I might be about to lose forever.

"No soul escapes the bloodthirsty nights."

FERRIS

CHAPTER TWENTY SEVEN

"What is this?" I demanded, stumbling away from the tree where a woman who looked all too like me was reaching out a vine-coated arm and hissing warnings at the trees.

I turned to my sister, the girl I'd spent so much of my life determined to rescue, hunting for answers in her silver eyes but instead finding nothing where she'd been stood.

"Rissa?" I called as the snake's huge body coiled around my own, its rough scales glimmering in the shards of moonlight which punctured the canopy of the trees overhead.

"Don't fight the path that calls you," the Cursed One hissed, and I recoiled, pushing against the snake's twisting form, my own voice echoing in my ears.

How could she be me? How could she have my face? The tree surrounding her had consumed nearly all of her body, bark growing over her throat and jaw, moss tangled into her hair. She must have been there for years, left to suffer endlessly, caught in death but not fully departed.

"You're not me," I told the Cursed One, and the Serpent released a low hiss which sounded like laughter while the boughs and branches of every tree around us leaned closer as if they wanted to listen too.

The Serpent's grip on me tightened, crushing the breath from my lungs, and panic clawed its way deeper into my soul. I didn't understand what was happening, what I was seeing, why there was a Cursed One wearing my face. How could that be? Could I be looking at a glimpse of my own destiny? Or had I finally lost my mind in this damned and bewildering place?

Panic threatened to overwhelm me as I fought to push myself free of the Serpent's hold, but there was a single truth I could cling to, one which had led me to this place, one which would never be denied.

I'd come here for my sister. I *needed* my sister.

I craned my neck, hunting the trees for Rissa, calling her name once more, but she was gone.

I dug my fingers into the Serpent's body, the reality of what was happening to me settling in fast. But before I could be consumed by fear, the spirit released me. It unravelled itself from my chest so quickly that I stumbled and fell on my ass in the dirt.

I scrambled backwards in the mud, my eyes wide as I stared at the enormous Serpent, its body a thousand shades of metallic stone, a rough grinding sound accompanying its movements.

The Serpent's duty to the forest had been to the rocks and minerals but it was also said to be a warrior, the creature destined to protect the forest from outside harm. It was ferocious in its responsibilities and single-minded in its task. And that had been before the curse had taken hold of the forest and the spirits had all lost their minds. Who knew what it might be capable of now?

A rough cry made my head snap around, a jolt of lightning searing through my chest which burned its way down my body and left the pungent taste of panic on my tongue.

"Hendrix?!" I called, scrambling to my feet.

The Serpent loomed over me, raising up on its coiled body and peering down at me from a height which made its rocky head brush the lower branches of the canopy above.

It bared its fangs which glistened silver in the moonlight, its long tongue snapping out to taste the air and my fear right alongside it.

I backed up, all of the awful things in this clearing making my limbs tremble and heart pound to a frantic and terrified pace.

"Too many times death has claimed us before we captured our destiny!" the Cursed One yelled, and I cringed away from the woman with my face, hating her and hating myself for the cowardice the sight of her brought on in me. Was she a warning from the spirits? A fate yet to pass? Or was there something darker at work beneath these trees?

The Serpent hissed at me again but made no move to strike, and as another cry came from the depths of the woods, I turned and fled.

My pulse thundered in my ears as I ran, more footsteps hounding my own, Hendrix's cries all I could allow myself to focus on as I raced for him.

The forest was more terrifying than ever in the darkness, every piece of it more alive than in the day. Roots slithered out of my path, trees bent and bowed around me, leaves lifting, vines parting. The forest was helping me. Or perhaps it only wished to lead me to the same fate as the Fae warrior who had chased me into the night.

Something was tracking my steps, a hundred eyes boring into my back as I ran, but when I threw a wild look over my shoulder, there was nothing but that endless dark between the trees.

Orange light sparked up ahead, the blaze of a fire searing the backs of my eyes, and I threw up a hand to shield my vision.

Hendrix cried out again and I cursed beneath my breath as I ran on, knowing it was my fault that he was out here, hating that I even cared about the Fae bastard and understanding that I was going to do everything in my power to help him regardless.

A glade opened up before me, Hendrix laying in the middle of it, Lost Children rushing around him, his limbs bound in vines as they dragged him towards a yawning hole at the base of a gnarled yew tree. I was so filled with shock that I couldn't find thoughts for how terrifying it was and acted entirely on instinct.

I reached for my slingshot only to find it missing, my pulse racing with fits and bursts, pounding against my ears so hard I was deafened by the unsteady crescendo. Of course I hadn't had it with me. I'd been about to sleep before Rissa's voice had lured me into the forest and now I was without even my meagre weapon to aid me in this foul place.

Hendrix needed me. I didn't know how I was supposed to help him unarmed and alone, but I knew nothing would keep me from trying despite the foolishness that implied.

I pushed forward, meaning to rush out into the clearing, only to be yanked back by a cold hand which snared my upper arm and pulled me behind an enormous oak tree.

I swung a fist, my aim poor but fury potent.

Before I could land my blow, Rissa knocked my arm aside with a swipe of her own hand.

My sister smiled at me and my heart cleaved in two.

"Riss?" I breathed, tears blurring my eyes.

"I knew you'd come find me," she said. "I've waited a long time in the trees for you, Ferris."

I wanted to hurl my arms around her, drag her into my embrace and promise her everything would be okay while begging her forgiveness for how long this rescue had taken. But without a single word escaping my lips, her hand clapped down over my mouth and she pushed me back against the rough bark of the tree with surprising strength.

"Listen," she breathed in my ear. "There's no time to waste. The moon has bought you a moment of clarity before the madness of the dark can pierce you through the heart."

I tried to pry her hand from my mouth but she only frowned at me, her face so familiar and yet so changed. She'd grown, her features sharpening into those of a woman in place of a child, her auburn hair all wild curls tangled with moss and leaves, those silver eyes weighed down with more knowledge than any child could have born.

"I grew up," she stated, as if reading my thoughts the way she so often seemed to when we were young. Her eyes slid beyond me to the glade where the Lost Children were still hauling Hendrix towards that yawning hole which led to spirits knew where, his muffled grunts and cries cutting into me with each passing moment. He was thrashing and kicking, even champing his teeth at them, but they only laughed and dodged his blows, dragging him on again.

I made to go to him but my sister held me tightly, forcing my focus to remain on her.

"The other children…they're not like me," Rissa sighed, loosening her grip on my mouth to allow me to speak at last.

"Why not?" I asked, my gaze roaming over her, drinking her in. The relief at finding her here after so many years of hoping and wishing on what I knew to be nothing more than a slip of a chance were all compacting around me until I felt utterly overwhelmed in her presence. I wanted to cry, scream, laugh, beg, gush, pray, and everything in between.

"The forest keeps the Lost Children in its grasp, gifting them immortality, but with every passing year, they lose a little more of what they once were to the wildness of this place. Some still mourn the families they were torn from in small ways, clinging to trinkets from past lives, others don't recall ever being anything other than creatures of the wood."

"But you grew up," I said, echoing the words she'd offered me.

A sad smile tainted her lips.

"I did. Because I'm not born of the human realm nor the Fae realm either. Not truly."

I scoffed, shaking my head at her. "You claim the madness of this place hasn't infected you and yet you speak of not being human?"

"I am and I'm not," she replied, reaching out to brush a tear from my cheek and letting it hang from her fingertip. "Just as you are and you aren't too."

Rissa's eyes flared with a molten brightness and I recoiled from her, the teardrop on her fingertip illuminating in that same silvery hue before she flicked it at me.

I flinched, my eyes scrunching shut as the tiny drop of water splashed against my cheek and suddenly I was no longer standing with her on the edge of a glade but peering out from within the depths of the cursed forest at a woman who sobbed on its border. A woman who looked wholly familiar, though several decades younger than I now knew her to be.

"Mother?" I breathed, trying to take a step closer and finding I couldn't move.

"I beg you, great spirits," our mother sobbed, her fingers digging into the bark of the trees before her while her knees pressed into the dirt. "I beg you to bless us with a child."

A rush of wind blasted through the trees, a trilling song on its back which knocked our mother onto her haunches as it ripped her hair away from her face and she gasped in startled alarm.

I stumbled forward as that same wind knocked me from the vision, Rissa's hold on my shoulder the only thing which prevented me from falling to my knees.

"You were born of her womb, sister," Rissa said. "But you arrived there by magic. Just as you did so many times before to so many other mothers who came to beg the gift of a child from the Great Elm."

"I don't understand," I said, shaking my head while she cocked hers at mine.

"Don't you?"

I shook my head, my brain torn between putting all of the pieces of this puzzle together and the danger which surrounded us. I needed to get her out of here, I needed to get Hendrix free too.

"Come on, Rissa," I begged, taking hold of her hand and tugging, emotion thickening my throat because I'd come so far to find her and now she was really here before me, staring back at me with those eyes I'd dreamed of night after night, alive and whole despite the odds. "Come with me. I'll get us out of here. Just help me with Hendrix and-"

The Lost Children broke into a chorus of wild laughter, the sound so loud it was like a thunderclap, and I flinched away from it, trying to tug Rissa with me, but she didn't move.

"You know we can't leave this place," Rissa said sadly. "The forest closed its walls and the only chance at freedom is to break the curse. My fate is tied to it, Ferris. Even if I ran with you, there isn't anywhere to go. And if by some miracle we found a way out of the trees, my life is tied to the curse now. It has to be broken if I am to have any hope of being free of it."

I shook my head, pointless tears blurring my vision, a frustrated growl escaping my throat as the injustice of it all overwhelmed me. It wasn't fair. I'd defied all the odds in getting this far, and despite everything, I somehow stood before the girl I'd sacrificed so much to find. She was right here. But she wasn't free of this place and neither was I. Neither was anyone in the whole of Rathian while the forest's curse endured. So now the fate of all of us had become the burden placed upon me.

"I have the Dragon," I told her. "And Hendrix has the Bear and the Fox, plus I know another Fae has two more. Maybe we stand a chance of uniting them all and then you can leave with me-"

"I still won't be free," Rissa said sadly, her fingers brushing my cheek and sadness swimming in her silver gaze. "The Offerings were made in full, each of the Lost Children were *given* to the forest. That includes me, Ferris. I can't ever leave the Great Elm."

"Then what about the boon?" I asked, because that had been my plan all along. "Would the boon free you if I used it to ask for such a thing? Could it free all of you?" I glanced up into the trees where the Lost Children clambered and leapt between the branches with haunting grace.

The leaves around us rustled and shivered, words seeming to pass between them in a whisper I couldn't understand. But Rissa tilted her head to listen, and her eyes brightened at what they said.

"The others aren't all like me," she said slowly. "You could free them, but some have been here for hundreds of years and they wouldn't have anywhere else to go. But…those of us who still had homes and families to return to might be able to reclaim what we lost. The Great Elm says that the boon could be used to give us that choice. She would let us decide to stay or go. To live on eternally here or reclaim the mortality we traded when the trees took us into their domain."

"Truly?" I gasped, gripping her fingers so tightly it had to hurt, and her smile stole the breath from my lungs as she nodded.

A choked sob escaped me and I hurled my arms around her neck, crushing her in my embrace and finally succumbing to the surge of emotions which were threatening to overwhelm me. I'd been forcing myself to hold off on hope but she'd finally handed it back to me.

"Then I'll earn the boon," I said fiercely as if it wasn't a practically unattainable task. Yes, I had claimed one amulet, but I would have to seize more than any other Champion. With Hendrix already ahead of me and that other, murderous brute on a mission to murder his way to find the rest, it would be near impossible to achieve. But I'd do it. Somehow.

The Dragon made a sound like a low purr in the back of my mind, and I took strength in its encouragement as I straightened.

"The Serpent," I said, my eyes moving to the trees as I hunted for the spirit which my sister had been keeping the company of.

A low and sinister hiss came from directly above me and I flinched in alarm, whirling around and knocking into Rissa who steadied me with a laugh that was bright and clear and utterly at odds with the threat coming from above us.

"Not now," she warned, and the way the Serpent's eyes gleamed made it clear that it agreed with her. "But I'll bring it when the time calls and you will have its amulet."

"Truly?" I breathed, my heart lightening at the thought. If she could deliver me the Serpent, then I was so much closer to achieving my goal of freeing her from this place.

Hendrix cried out from the clearing beyond us and I turned to see the Lost Children hauling him into the mouth of that darkened hole.

"What are they doing to him?" I hissed, taking a step towards him, but Rissa caught my arm and jerked me to a halt.

"You care for the fate of a Fae?" she breathed in my ear, anger coating her words. "After what they did to me?"

"It's…complicated," I breathed. "But he helped me to get this far despite everything-"

"Despite the fact that they took me, hauled me from my bed and threw me to this fate without a care?" The trees groaned and rustled in reply to her rage, the Serpent hissing spitefully as it descended from the trees and started towards the Fae who I had begun to see as so much more than my enemy.

"I know, I do. But Rissa, he's…different." I wasn't even sure that was true and as she looked to me, I knew we both heard the uncertainty in my claim. But as the Lost Children hauled Hendrix closer and closer to the oblivion of that dark pit, I found panic rising in my chest, my pulse racing with fear and the desperate need to save him warring in my limbs.

"Fine," she hissed darkly, releasing me so suddenly that I stumbled a few steps. The Serpent coiled around us, its scales grinding together like rocks sliding over one another as it circled me, the threat in its posture clear. "But if you're wrong about him, then don't say I didn't warn you."

I tried to back up, Hendrix's groans pulling at my attention, but Rissa caught my chin and urged my gaze back to hers.

"This isn't our moment, sister," she told me, a sadness to her tone. "But know that this is not the first time you have walked this forest. However, it will be the last. You can't fail again."

"Again?" I repeated hollowly, trying not to think of the Cursed One with my face, trying not to remember how familiar the words in that diary had seemed to me.

"This time will be different," Rissa promised. "Because this time, the Great Elm created *me* to help you. When the moment comes, we can break the curse together. The forest wants you to succeed, don't you see?"

"I don't see," I protested. "I don't know what you-"

Hendrix cried out in pain and I whipped around.

"He matters in this too," Rissa said from behind me, her eyes gleaming with urgency as she forced my focus back to her, a bitterness to her tone as she admitted the fact - though I didn't understand what she meant by it. "You should really get him out of the dark."

The ground trembled beneath my feet, a low rumbling making me jerk around again to find Rissa rising up on the back of the Serpent, her face stoic as she looked down at me.

"The clock can't wait for you any longer, Ferris. When it strikes the hour this time, the curse *will* prevail. You're out of chances to change that fate. So make it count."

"Wait!" I cried as the Serpent turned and dove into the trees with Rissa riding upon its back, the forest swallowing them whole before I could even try to chase them.

I took a step in their direction, then turned again as Hendrix cried out in the heart of the glade. I needed more answers. But first, I needed to save him.

Hendrix

CHAPTER TWENTY EIGHT

The pit gaped ahead of me, the roots of the thirsty oak snaring my ankles and starting to draw me into that vile hole. I would lay there rotting, perhaps alive, perhaps dead, I didn't know. I might become one of those Cursed Ones who lingered on eternally, one with the forest, always yearning for escape but never finding it beneath the damp earth.

Between the delirium the Lost Children's song was driving me to, the yawning desire of the oak, and the clawing breaths heaving from my lungs, I found *her* voice calling to me.

The trees reared up on all sides while the Lost Children surrounded me, binding me every time I broke through one of their tethers and dragging me toward the open roots of a hungry oak. There she was, near-ethereal as the trees parted for her, shrinking away like shadows from the light.

Ferris's hair swept around her, the bright silver almost aglow as she ran for me with my name pouring from her lips once more.

"No!" I roared back. "Stay away!" But the song flooded over her and she staggered to a halt, enraptured by it, blinking to try and fight through the lunacy it caused.

"Dance the dance of the deadly night,
Come to us and we'll take you right,
To the heart of the ground where starved roots wait.
They'll feast on your bones and seal your fate."

The Lost Children laughed as they caught hold of their new prey, small hands fisting in Ferris's clothes and pulling her to the ground to lay at my side. My thoughts were heavy again, the song making me confused, the words pressing in on my mind and luring me toward insanity.

I smiled as Ferris looked to me, my human in all her gentle beauty. Those violet eyes met mine and fear flared in them as she began to thrash against the tethers the Lost Children were banding around her, rope and vine alike holding my lightwing in place and causing the madness to fracture inside my head.

With a will of my mind, I fought my way through the power of the song and commanded my spirits to free themselves of their amulets, willing them to attack the Lost Children. But the Bear and the Fox only pranced off into the trees with light merriment without any intention of harming them, as if some greater force held them from doing so.

I lurched upwards in anger, muscles bulging against my restraints and breaking enough of them to get an arm free. I caught one of the Lost Children by the hair, hurling him away from Ferris, but he only laughed and spun on his heel, his voice rising above the others' to trap me with the song once more.

"Rest, rest upon the silken floor,
Let us guide you to the thirsty door.
The oak, she waits, she'll be your home,
She'll bury you and drain your bones."

The towering oak beside us groaned as its roots shifted, reaching for me with unnerving hunger. The Lost Children howled like feral beasts as they dragged us closer to the monstrous tree, and I saw Death peering out at me between the trees. Her falcon's face was angled my way, a knowing look in her fateful eyes as she pulled her cowl closer around her head.

The song quieted me once more, my arm falling willingly to my side again as a croaky laughter left my throat to join that of the Lost Children's around us.

Perhaps tonight was as good a time to die as ever.

The lunacy stole me away again and I looked to Ferris, finding her on her feet, fighting the Lost Children, shoving them away and screaming at them to stop. But oh how they sang so prettily. And perhaps it would not be so bad to meet Death alongside her, between the arms of these hungry trees.

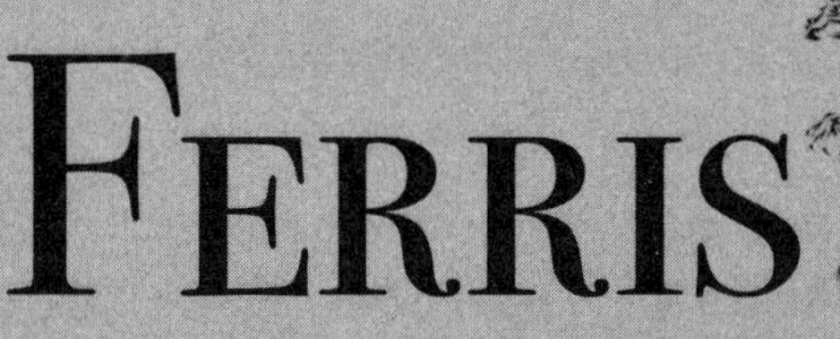

Ferris

CHAPTER TWENTY NINE

The taste of dirt on my tongue made me gag, pain burning my limbs as the Lost Children pinned me down again and dragged my arms so far behind my back that I was certain they'd tear them from their sockets at any moment.

Hendrix looked lost to the song once again, a throaty laugh leaving him as he called to someone in the forest. "I know you've longed to take my hand," he croaked to no one.

"Hendrix!" I cried, and his eyes met mine. They widened, clarity finding him between the woeful lyrics.

He bellowed my name, his muscles straining as he fought to free himself in a sudden bid of effort, blood running down his chest where his shirt had been torn from his body. The wild look on his face suggested he was still partly lost to the madness of the forest, but he could see me within it now too, every piece of him fighting to get free, not for himself, but for me.

The Bear and Fox were racing through the trees around us, their bodies little more than a blur of flames and water, their bellows echoing in the dark spaces, but they seemed unable to do anything to help.

I didn't know if Hendrix had lost control of them entirely or if it was the song of the Lost Children which had summoned them from his grasp.

I could feel the Dragon stirring beneath my skin, the beast agitated and furious but still refusing to reply to my commands as I bellowed at it to do as I bid from within the confines of my mind.

Hendrix roared in pain as the Lost Children looped more tethers around his body, so many of them clambering on top of him that I almost lost sight of him altogether beneath their tangled limbs.

They were going to haul him into that dark abyss at the base of the oak any moment and I wasn't certain I'd be able to reclaim him once they did.

The echoing beat of his pulse seemed to call out to me in the small space which divided us, each thump sounding like the strike of a clock nearing midnight. I didn't know if I was imagining it, but I could feel the weight of his death looming like a stranger in the room, stalking closer with each moment. And I found I couldn't bear the thought of him meeting with his end.

"Please," I begged, my voice ragged over the rawness of my throat. "Save him."

A rush of potent energy filled me with such raw abandon that I was blinded by the force of it as it burst from a place deep within my chest.

Silver light exploded from the pendant at my throat, shot through with bolts of teal lightning which blasted the Lost Children away from us, flinging them into the surrounding trees.

The Dragon bellowed powerfully, and the leaves were torn from the branches overhead, the trunks bowing back like stalks of wheat blasted in a storm as the might of its power swept through the moonlit glade.

I choked out Hendrix's name, crawling through the dirt to him as wind whipped my hair around my shoulders and lightning sparked against my skin. But it didn't hurt me. If anything, it filled me with more energy, aiding me as I scrambled to the male who I held such knotted emotions for within my heart.

The Fae warrior groaned as I caught hold of his hand, his green eyes lifting to pierce my own, his fingers fisting over mine.

"I've got you," he growled, as if he'd been the one to make it to me instead of the other way around, and a manic, fevered laugh burst from my lips.

Movement all around us had the sound dying as fast as it had come, the Lost Children racing back at us from the trees, though there was no sign of Rissa nor the Serpent among them.

Hendrix pushed himself up so that he could cradle me in his arms, the bulk of his body curving around mine as if that might be all it would take to save me from the death racing our way.

I cringed against him, the thump of his heart a wild beat against my ear as I pressed it to his chest.

"Please," I begged again, tipping my head back to look up at the Dragon which had made it into the heart of the heavens overhead.

"I see you finally found your manners, fated one," it replied.

Clouds swirled all around the spirit as it twisted in the sky, its serpentine body undulating, shards of teal electricity spearing in every direction as it dove towards us at a furious pace.

I threw up a hand to shield us as thunder ripped the sky apart and lightning blasted down into the glade, raising screams and curses from the Lost Children as it struck them.

I was blinded by the blazing light, Hendrix's arms tightening around me as we were lost to the rush of the Dragon's magic. Then suddenly we were flying, the spirit capturing us in its talons and heaving us from the ground in a rush of motion.

The Dragon flew into the darkness between the trees, the forest rushing to bend and twist out of its way, leaves slapping against my skin as we swung back and forth in its clutches.

Two blurs of red and blue light chased after us as Hendrix's spirits followed, the weight of their combined magic making the air buzz around us.

I lost all sense of direction, all notion of where we were within the Taking Trees, but I didn't care. The heat of Hendrix's arms around me were all I needed, the solid thump of his heart the balm my aching soul required.

The Dragon turned sharply, then dropped us to the dirt where we were sent tumbling across leaves and mud before skidding to a halt before the door to a house dressed in moss and tangled ivy.

I practically sobbed as the three spirits all twisted out of their corporal forms, returning to their amulets and leaving us on the threshold of salvation.

Hendrix muttered something about making sure it was safe as he stumbled through the door to the house and it was all I could do to stagger in at his back and bolt the heavy wood behind us, barring out the night at last.

Someone had closed shutters over the window and the two of us sagged against the door, slumping down to the floor as one.

Hendrix banded his arm around my shoulders and I leaned into him, my head finding its place against his chest as though his body had been carved just for me to rest it there.

"You're a fucking nightmare, lightwing," he growled, his lips against the top of my head, stubble tugging at strands of my hair, his grip on me so tight I had to think he might never let me go again.

I opened my mouth to protest but he only drew me further into his embrace.

"But you're *my* nightmare now."

Perhaps we should have risen from our place at the door. Perhaps we should have spoken of all the horrors we'd just endured and survived against the odds. Perhaps I should have told him of all the things Rissa had divulged.

But as I sat curled in his arms with the night pressing close beyond our small refuge, I found I had no energy to do any of those things. So instead I pressed myself more tightly against the brute I claimed to hate so dearly and wondered how I would have been able to go on without him had he met with death in those trees.

HENDRIX

CHAPTER THIRTY

Ferris filled me in on everything her sister had told her while I reclined in a mouldering chair and she paced back and forth in front of me, getting herself riled up into a storm.

"I've been here so many times before, Hendrix, born to die and be reborn over and over again, coming to this forest to end the curse. What does it mean? Am I some pawn in the Great Hunt? Does the forest own me?" She turned her blazing eyes on me and I shoved to my feet, capturing both of her wrists in my hands to make her focus.

"You are no one's pawn, lightwing," I growled, a river of turmoil winding through me at the hypocrisy of my words. Because hadn't that been exactly what I'd been planning to use her as from the start? But now… now everything had changed and my attachment to her had grown to a thread spun from iron, and I didn't know how I would ever let her go. But that didn't make her my possession, just as the forest had no claim on her.

The information she had fed me had rattled my mind at first, but it was becoming clearer now. I'd refuted the words of a Lost Child of the forest, but there was no denying what I saw in front of me when

I looked at Ferris. I had seen it all along. That touch of magic, that glimmer of power. It ran deeper than I'd ever known.

Her soul was born from the forest itself. She was no human, not in any natural way at least. Not fully. She may have worn the flesh of a mortal but her soul was built of magic itself. It was why the forest moved for her, why she didn't struggle to walk its treacherous paths. And it must have been the reason for so many other things.

"The forest may be in your blood but you get to choose what you do with that power, lightwing. Not the Great Elm or any spirit between these trees. You. Do you understand?" I demanded, but she shook her head, uncertainty spiralling through her eyes.

"Doesn't it mean the opposite? Aren't I made for something, Hendrix? If I've been here time and again, then there has to be a reason. Rissa said I'd failed every other time. This is my last chance to get it right, but I don't even know what I did wrong previously. This is the thirteenth Great Hunt. I've failed at whatever I'm meant to do twelve times, and we all know there won't be any more chances."

My throat tightened, the acknowledgement that she might just be the answer to the curse that gripped Rathian. But if she was destined for such a path, then the boon could never be mine. And I couldn't grapple with that possibility without agony splintering through me. Because I needed that gift more than she could ever understand.

"Ferris," I sighed. "We don't know anything yet. We need more information. This girl, Rissa-"

"She's not any *girl*, she's my sister," she said fiercely, her love for her sibling burning in her gaze. I knew that love for family as deeply as she did. There was no force greater than it in this world.

"Are you sure she wasn't some trickster wearing her face?" I voiced my own doubts.

"I'm certain."

"You have to be," I pushed.

"I am. And it doesn't matter anyway because what she said is undeniable." She pressed a hand to her heart. "I felt the truth of her words. I saw a Cursed One who had my face. It makes so much sense. Why I've been drawn to the forest all my life, it's why from the moment I got here, the forest has offered me paths and practically guided my feet through it."

"It's why you were marked by the Dragon," I agreed roughly, lifting a hand to take hold of a lock of her hair. "And why it speaks to you."

She nodded, her throat bobbing and eyes gleaming with all the knowledge she had gained. A wild protectiveness rose in me as I thought of Islasees hunting humans and all the other dangers that lurked in this forest. If she had been here before many times, then that meant she had perished here many times too. And I could not let that happen again.

"I always knew there was something special about you," I admitted.

"It doesn't make me anything more than I already was. I'm human, Hendrix. I'm not better than them. Don't you dare go seeing me as more than they are, because you should be seeing all of us for what we are."

I frowned, unsure if I was wholly convinced by her claim to humanity, but I knew one truth that couldn't be denied. "If they are anything like you, then they are fine creatures indeed."

"Thank you," she said, emotion burning in her voice, and I realised some part of her had just forgiven me for what my people had done to hers.

"We are not all monsters," I said in a low voice, knowing my reality would paint me to be the worst kind of beast. I was not among the Fae who should be offered Ferris Creed's forgiveness.

She said nothing and I stepped closer to her, the draw I felt to her only seeming to have intensified with this revelation, like I should have known it all along. And like it somehow was my secret to unveil too.

"I should be thanking you," I said, brushing my fingers under her chin and tilting her head back so that those endless eyes met mine. "Without you, the Children of the Forest would have claimed me."

"Without the Dragon you mean," she laughed hollowly.

"No," I growled. "You are its master."

"It doesn't like when you say that." She shifted from one foot to the other, and I guessed the Dragon had spoken to her again.

"Well, Dragon, if you are listening." I leaned down to speak in Ferris's ear, brushing her hair back from her shoulder as I did so. "You would do well to heed her demands, for she is the purest thing in this forest. There is no better master here for you than her."

I drew away and Ferris's brows lifted at whatever the Dragon said in reply.

"Have I angered it?" I mused.

"Yes. It called you a devious fiend."

"Did it now?" I gritted out irritably. "Listen, lightwing, I think we should work together from here on out."

"Isn't that what we've been doing all along?" she accused.

"Yes, but under the guise of me capturing you. I believe those chains have fallen to the wayside now, don't you?"

She thought on that, stepping away and gazing at the fireplace where we'd managed to build a decent fire.

"I pledge to protect you," I vowed. "I'll guide you to the Great Elm."

"And then what?" She glanced back over her shoulder at me.

I shrugged. "May the best of us win the boon. I'll fight fair if you do."

A smile broke across her face. "Alright then. Yes. We'll make it there together."

I offered her my hand to shake, but she knocked it aside as she came at me, looping her arms around my shoulders and drawing me into an embrace. I crushed her to me, scenting oak on her skin and breathing her in for too many breaths.

"I need to understand my place in this forest and what fate it has planned for me here," she whispered. "Will you help me, Hendrix?"

"I will," I swore, unable to deny this request from her lips. "Come fire or fury, I will."

CHAPTER THIRTY ONE

We'd taken a day and a night to recover from our encounter with the Lost Children. The morning after meeting with them in the dark, I'd woken to find my pack and all the possessions we'd left at the mill waiting for me on the doorstep. I could only assume that Rissa had been responsible for returning our things to us but there had been no sign of her among the trees.

The time that had passed had felt like we were holding our breaths, pretending the forest and the curse and everything beyond this house weren't there at all. I hadn't read the diary - which I now suspected had been written by some past version of myself – I hadn't ventured out into the trees to seek the Cursed One who still had my face either.

But as the sun rose on the second day, I knew I couldn't continue to ignore the questions which had arisen over my past, my future, and everything in between.

If I'd been born time and again, come to this forest over and over, then there had to be a reason for that. I had to be here for more than just Rissa.

The thought alone stung. I'd dedicated years of my life to this task, my only goal being her. But if I really allowed myself to think about it, I had been drawn to the forest before she'd been taken by it. We both had.

We'd snuck down the trail through the meadows behind our house as children, creeping as close to the cursed trees as we dared before running, shrieking, back to the safety of our parents. We used to play make-believe as Champions, pretending to sneak through the woods and capture the spirits.

I'd been humming the songs of the Lost Children to myself since I was too young to recall, and in all truth, I'd never found their call as chilling as all of my peers had claimed.

And now everything about that made sense. Right down to the way I'd never felt like I fully belonged in my village. Because I wasn't like the rest of them. The truth had been looking me in the face every time I'd peered into a mirror at my unnaturally violet eyes.

There was something *other* about me. Rissa too. It was why I'd been so utterly lost without her. Not just because I pined for and mourned the loss of my sister. But because she had been the only one to ever truly understand me. The only person I'd never felt slightly out of step with.

I loved my mother and father dearly, but I wasn't like them. I didn't yearn for a simple life away from the threat of the wandering trees and the fear of the Hollows. I'd always imagined up adventures for myself, always sought out the tiny spirits of the land and obsessed over their larger, more powerful brethren who had been all but a myth until I'd finally set foot in this place.

But if I was born from the forest, even if it was only in part, then what did that make me? Was I human? Or was I something…else?

"You are something which has never been before and will never be again," the Dragon rumbled inside my own head, and I flinched at the invasion to my thoughts.

"What does that mean? If I've lived twelve times before this, then isn't that the opposite of what I am?" I asked the spirit, drawing Hendrix's attention as he ate his breakfast.

His eyes bore into me where I sat by the window, but instead of turning to meet his curious gaze, I looked out into the depths of the trees and focused on the words of the spirit that came in answer.

"You are so literal," it scoffed. *"But aside from the chances you have had at this life before, there will never be another such as you. Each incarnation has been you, Ferris. No other. You have one foot in each plane. The spirit world and the mortal one. Human, yes. But also, not entirely so."*

"Is that why you chose me?"

The Dragon chuckled, its presence shifting around my thoughts and then receding.

"Perhaps."

I knew it was gone without needing to ask another question which would go unanswered and I sighed.

"What did the monster have to say to you?" Hendrix asked as the silence stretched and I finally turned to look at him.

The hatred I knew I should still harbour wasn't there as my eyes roamed over his features, snagging on the ink which curved around his eye before settling on the depths of his green gaze. We'd been through too much in this place for me to be able to claim the animosity which had once come so very easily.

I knew it made me a fool, but I wanted to trust him. Wanted to put my faith in this male who had risked his life for mine in the darkness of this place.

"We should head back out today," I said firmly, ignoring his question. "It's been twenty-seven days, and we have less than a fortnight left to break the curse of this forest or become doomed to perish in its hold."

"Says the woman who has lived countless lives," he noted, and I stiffened at the accusation.

"I have no memory of ever having lived before now," I told him plainly, though he knew this already. "And I consider losing all memories of who I am and what I love to be the same as death, even if this flesh might return in some form. Besides, if the forest has given me a chance to succeed here during each Great Hunt, then I don't believe I have any more chances left to me. The forest has encroached across all lands and chased both humanity, the Fae and even the Necromancer to the very edges of Rathian. This is the thirteenth Great Hunt and it will be the last, one way or another. We don't have fifty years after this. The forest will consume the land in that time and everyone still clinging to life at that point will either be devoured by it or be forced to leap into the sea, which is just as certain of a death."

"Then what is it you suggest?"

"That we head out," I said firmly, as though I hadn't been mulling over all those things and had always been making this plan. "There are still spirits unaccounted for. The map says the closest one to us is the Stag, so I say we go hunt for it."

Hendrix gave me a smirk which made my stomach knot, then stood fluidly. "Then by all means, lead the way."

I made to grab my cloak, then paused, a frown pinching my brow as I looked to the enormous Fae warrior once more.

"So we're really working together now then?" I asked slowly. "Truly, I mean. As a…team?"

"Is that what I am to you, little lightwing? A teammate?" he asked, his tone low and making my skin prickle.

"I don't think there's a name for what you are to me," I muttered, tugging my eyes from his before I became snared in them.

We were running out of time to break this curse, and whatever pull I may have felt towards Hendrix, I refused to let it distract me from what I'd come here to do. I may have found Rissa, but she was still trapped in this forest, still locked in the magic of its curse. I needed the boon to free her from it. I needed the curse to end to free the whole of Rathian from its poison so that we might live to enjoy her freedom too. Anything else, *everything* else, would have to wait.

I led the way outside, eyeing the paths between the trees with suspicion, though not with the same fear I'd had when first entering this place of curses and chaos.

Perhaps that made me a fool, but I had come to think of this forest as more of a lost soul than a vicious one. The Great Elm was in pain, she needed her children back, and I knew well the ache of yearning for a reunion with lost loved ones.

It was several hours of trekking through the undergrowth to get to the predicted position for the Stag on the map and I steeled myself for the day ahead. We would have to keep an eye out for another form of shelter or make certain to leave ourselves enough time to return to this little secluded house if we didn't find one.

Hendrix moved to my side, not taking the lead for once but instead walking with me as we strode out into the trees.

"Something wrong?" I asked.

His hand brushed against mine, my fingers flexing automatically as if to snare his, before I forced them still again. Hendrix peered down at me with that infuriating smirk of his as if he knew precisely how my body reacted every time he got close to me the way he was now.

"I'm well aware the forest favours you, lightwing. The trees bow as you pass, the brambles twist out of the way of your boots. So why make my own path through this desolate place any harder than it needs to be? If I stick at your side the trees will make a road for me too."

I rolled my eyes at his assessment, certain that he was placing far more importance upon my presence in this place than the trees themselves did, but I couldn't deny the ring of truth his words held.

The forest did move for me at times, especially when I asked it to.

My steps faltered as I considered that, and Hendrix took a few more paces before realising I'd fallen behind and turning to face me.

"What is it?" he questioned but my focus was on the wood, not him.

I glanced from trunk to branch, vine to leaf, then I took a deep breath and raised my chin as I put my theory to the test.

"I wish to travel to a glade several miles to the west of here, where I believe the Stag may linger in the shade of twin chestnut trees. Would you make the path a little easier for me…please?"

Hendrix scoffed, looking at me like I was insane. "You can't seriously think that the forest will…"

His words trailed off as a gust of wind swept around us, setting the leaves in the trees rustling with that hissed laughter which made my arm hairs stand on end.

Before Hendrix could mock me any more for asking a favour of the woods, the trees in front of us quaked, leaning back and shifting aside. Brambles and bracken slithered across the dirt, disappearing to the sides, taking small stones and leaf litter with them until an unnaturally perfect pathway lay there between the ancient trees.

"You were saying?" I mocked, my grin big and beyond hope of reining in.

The Dragon rumbled a laugh in the back of my head and I strode forward with a spring in my step as Hendrix muttered curses and jogged to catch up to me while the trees shifted back into place behind us.

Despite the forest making our journey much easier, it was still a long and tiresome trek to reach the glade where we suspected the Stag might have been lurking.

As we walked, I toyed with the amulet at my throat, rolling my thumb over the carved Dragon there.

"Of course you just ask nicely and the forest jumps to attention," Hendrix muttered, almost to himself.

He'd been making a fair few of those comments ever since realising that the path the forest had gifted me refused to remain clear for him alone. He couldn't wander ahead of me nor trail behind without roots tripping him and trees shifting into his path.

Better yet, he couldn't get the forest to grant him the same favour as it had done me. I'd greatly enjoyed watching him suck up his pride and say 'please' to the trees when asking them to create a pathway he could follow to a private spot where he might take a piss, only for them to do the opposite and plant more obstacles in his path instead.

I was definitely smug about it. And why not? As a Fae, he had been granted every advantage in this place from the moment the Champions had entered the forest. He was faster, stronger, more powerful, older, supposedly wiser – though I drew the line at admitting to that – but he wasn't favoured by the forest. And it was driving him mad to endure it.

I reached out to the Dragon as we walked, asking it nicely if it would like to leave the amulet. It obliged me instantly, swirling around us in a rush of wind before darting up towards the sky where it set the clouds roiling overhead.

Hendrix huffed.

"What?" I taunted.

"It's just ridiculous. And you know it," he grunted. "The spirits I captured are well in hand. What's to say your Dragon will be of any help when you need it to be? If you are asking in place of demanding, then you're open to the very real possibility that the answer you get will be 'no' when the time comes that you need it to be a 'yes' the most."

"Green may be your colour, Hendrix, but jealousy doesn't suit you," I teased.

He looked ready to argue his case, but a flash of movement caught our attention further up the path, the kick of hooved feet a brief visage before they sank away into the trees.

"The Stag," I gasped, breaking into a run, but Hendrix was faster, bounding ahead of me easily, drawing his sword from its sheath as he went.

I cursed him, my mind not going to my weapon but instead to all I knew of the Stag and what I might need to do to lure it to me.

The Stag's domain was the moss, lichen, fungi and soil, all things which cloaked the forest floor and provided nutrients to the air and earth. The spirit itself was said to be taller than two men, its antlers hung with draping moss, their span so wide the trees had to shift aside to allow it passage between them.

It valued nourishment and longevity, its job to maintain all plant life here and be certain that the trees thrived under its care.

I dropped to my knees, hauling my pack from my shoulders and scrambling to open the strap securing it.

Hendrix's footsteps pounded away from me until they were lost in the depths of the forest, his pursuit of the Stag taking him from the path we'd been traversing. I could only hope he wouldn't chase my spirit so far that it was unable to smell the gift I'd brought it.

I dumped the contents of my pack onto the ground, shoving clothes, books and food aside until I found the jar of brown sludge which I'd kept wrapped in the heart of my belongings.

I twisted the lid, the ripe scent from its contents filling my nostrils as I opened it at last and held it out before me as I stood.

The concoction was a mixture of seaweed, leaves and eggshells, my own personal recipe for some highly nutritious tree food which I'd sourced and fermented as part of my preparations for coming to the forest. It was basically a tree feast all wrapped up in a jar, and hopefully it was exactly the bribe I needed to woo the Stag.

"Come on," I muttered, turning on the spot, my ears straining for any sound of the Stag as I hunted the spaces between the trees for a sign of my quarry.

My hope began to dwindle as I took off in the direction Hendrix had taken, but before I could leave the path the trees had created for me, there was a great crash of hooves and the huge Stag leapt between the trees.

I gasped as the beast almost trampled me, my jar spinning from my fingers and thumping down in the dirt.

The Stag snorted, lowering its antlers at me as it pawed the ground with its hoof, and my heart sank.

Though this creature was beautiful, it was no spirit. Its coat was a tawny brown, dappled along its flank and its horns, though impressive, were nothing more than the horns of a wild deer just like those which had stolen a taste of my mother's roses whenever they got the chance.

Hendrix's pounding footsteps rang out in pursuit of what he believed to be the spirit and the creature bolted, turning towards the path and fleeing on thundering hooves.

The Fae burst onto the trail a beat later, almost colliding with me and making me curse as he kicked my carefully prepared offering.

I scrambled to retrieve it, scooping the nutritious mix back inside where it had spilled and securing the lid with a sigh.

Hendrix made to take chase again but I caught his arm to halt him. "That's no spirit," I said.

"I see that," he growled, irritation coating his words as he dropped his arm in frustration and we were left watching the stag as it raced away into the distance.

HENDRIX

CHAPTER THIRTY TWO

We'd given up on the Stag after four more days of tireless hunting, walking in circles hour after hour in case we came across it. Eventually we'd had to agree that either some other Champion had found the spirit or that we were not looking in the right place for it.

I could feel time slipping by in this forest like water down a hill, and I still only had two amulets to my name.

It wasn't enough.

I needed more if I was going to get a chance at earning the boon. And despite my alliance with Ferris, there was no part of me that would turn from that goal. But she would no sooner turn from hers either, leaving us at a stalemate. And the truth was, I really did care about her losing out on the boon if I stole the chance from her.

The forest had called to me so many times, and yet this was the first Great Hunt I'd chosen to attend. It was no coincidence that I'd found Ferris here. We were meant to cross paths, I had no doubt, because ever since I'd set eyes on her, I had been drawn to her inexplicably. And now all I wished to do was protect her, but if we managed to get a chance at the boon, then I would be forced to break her heart and seize it from her. How could I make any other choice? How could I turn from my chance to claim the next spirit we came across when so much was riding on me collecting more amulets?

The wind stirred around my shoulders and dread rooted itself in my soul.

Death felt closer again today, her hand brushing mine, reminding me all too starkly of why I had come here, and the weighted oppression of her company was taking a toll on me.

"It can't be far now," Ferris muttered to herself, checking the map in the diary once more.

We were hunting for the Wolf now, our failure with the Stag hanging over us like a dark cloud, only adding to the sombre mood that had gotten its claws into me.

"These boulders are mentioned in one of the diary entries." Ferris gestured to the giant rocks around us that were caked in jade moss, and I grunted in affirmation.

The rain was setting in again, growing to a persistent downpour. The droplets were collecting in Ferris's hair, and as a shiver tracked through her, I silently commanded the Bear from the amulet and ordered it to part the downpour for us.

A sunlit path opened up, relieving us of one blight at least.

"Come on, this way," Ferris urged, walking side by side with my Bear and even offering it a stroke on the flank as if it was some pet to be coddled.

I shook my head, but my eyes trailed over her and I found myself drawn into the gentle aura around her. She was never going to gain full control over the Dragon if she continued to treat the spirits like sweet animals, yet there was something to the assured way she urged my Bear along that was clearly effective. It had me looking at her too long, my eyes travelling over the sheen in her hair, the curve of her lips as she smiled at the spirit beside her, and I found it all too hard to look away.

My footsteps felt leaden as they tracked Ferris's, thoughts of the past rolling in on me like an unstoppable tide and drowning the lightness of her presence in darkness. I heard too many terrors spinning through my mind; my sister Amelda's gasped cry just before her death; my mother's silenced scream when that blade had slit her throat; the roar of desperation that had left my father as he fought for freedom, and as always, my brother's final words to me. Words I could never escape. *'I'll see you wherever our love guides us in the afterworld, brother.'"*

They were waiting for me to join them one day soon. Death would take my hand as it had taken theirs. Perhaps all this inner turmoil over my wants and Ferris's wouldn't matter in the end, but right now, it was all I could think of between the haunting ghosts of my past.

"You're very quiet today," Ferris commented, and I grunted.

She glanced back at me with a frown. "What is it?"

"The past, the present, the future. All of it," I muttered darkly, lifting a hand to rub the mark which had been inked along my temple.

"We just have to keep going," Ferris urged. "Don't dwell on what's done, dwell on what's possible."

I nodded mutely, trying to drag my mind from the dark place it had descended to, but the depression had its grip on me. Countless days I'd spent in the bleakness of these torturous feelings, caught in the reality of what my life had become. I knew what had to be done now, but sometimes it was so hard not to occupy the land of regret or fester in the guilt over what would happen if I took away Ferris's chance at the boon.

Where I stepped, the moss began to wither, darkness spreading up from the roots to devour it, and I gritted my teeth, trying to stop the power that was spilling from me. It would unmask me to Ferris if she looked too closely, if she saw how the lush undergrowth was starting to wilt around me. This was what I was, a plague on the land,

and I so often lost control of it. If only she knew. Perhaps it might be best if she saw it now, but that thought made me recoil inside.

"Hendrix?" Ferris questioned softly, and I met her gaze, a crease between her brows and true concern in her eyes. The way she said my name broke the spell of horrors rolling through me and the darkness lifted a little from my soul. So few things had ever cracked through the bleak cloud that hung over me. There were sometimes weeks that slipped by in a haze of gloom, but if she had been there, perhaps I would never have fallen into it at all. Ferris walked this world with passion and desires blooming from her like daises awakening to the sun. And I was started to crave the way the world bloomed around her. Or perhaps I was just starting to crave her.

"I'm fine," I assured her. "I'm focused."

She opened her mouth to say more but a piercing howl carried our attention to the path.

"The Wolf," Ferris gasped, then she broke into a run.

I chased after her, urging the Bear to lead the way on with a bark of a command, my hope awakening once more, latching onto the first sign of a spirit we'd had in days.

Ferris sprinted ahead of me, asking the forest to part for us and making our journey easier. The Bear led the way in front of her, the sheeting rain flanking us on either side as we tore along in its stead.

Darkness shifted between the trees ahead of us, the swish of a black tail and another piercing howl. The Wolf was close but it was a creature of shadow, so we would easily lose sight of it if it escaped to the darkest regions of the forest.

"Cut it off!" I bellowed at the Bear, and the beastly spirit of water veered to the left while I charged off the dry path and into the pouring rain, unsheathing my sword.

The Bear drove the Wolf back my way, the spirit turning to run, a patch of deepest darkness enveloping its form. But I was there waiting.

The gloom was thick, but there it was among it, its beautiful pelt a thing of pure shadow. The Wolf brought shade to the forest floor, kept it cool and damp and offered shelter from the beating sun. It was a creature of purest darkness, its fur a swirling mass of ebony tendrils. And it would soon be mine.

I swung for its head, my sword cutting through the air, but the rain abruptly stopped and the Wolf was bathed in sunlight instead. It flinched away from the brightness, diving for the shadows and avoiding the swing of my sword.

Ferris was there, leading my fucking spirit, *my* Bear right after her, guiding the sunlit path through the rain to direct the Wolf away from me.

"Ferris!" I roared as she drove the creature into a small cave, my footfalls chasing my human's.

Ferris was ahead of me, running into the cave, the rain parting either side of it so there was nowhere for the Wolf to run unless it wanted to step into the light – and it clearly feared such a thing.

Ferris closed in on it, lowering down and offering her hand to the spirit hiding in the shadows. Two bright blue eyes peered from the gloom and the Wolf's nose met with Ferris's hand.

I stalled, watching her with enraptured fascination while battling with the chaotic need to seize the spirit for myself. But several seconds passed and all I did was stare because Ferris looked so utterly fitting before the spirit, a curtain of silver hair around her shoulders, her eyes glinting at the Wolf in offering.

A resounding clash of warring emotions tore through my chest. Because for one eternal moment, I was considering giving up my chance at the spirit. To step back and let her take it. She'd made better moves than I had in this plight. She deserved it true enough.

But as I considered the loss of the boon and the promise I'd made to my family being shattered into a thousand fragments, my soul was forced to harden against those thoughts. I couldn't let them down. I had to fulfil my vow to them.

"Pin her down," I barked at the Bear, and my spirit obeyed, slamming into Ferris and weighing its mighty paws on her chest.

"No!" Ferris screamed in horror at what I'd done. "Don't hurt it!"

I didn't listen, running past her into the cave and swinging my sword through the dark. The Wolf tried to run and Ferris's screams cleaved the air in two, making a riot of twisted emotions rip through my chest. But I couldn't betray my family. I owed them my complete commitment to capturing it.

Ferris cried my name, a tone of anguished betrayal making me despise myself for the act. But she had no idea what I had at stake. If she'd waited hundreds of years for an answer to her desperation, she would understand.

The Wolf released a yelp that told of my victory and it swirled away in a whoosh of twirling darkness, a final mournful howl echoing out into the forest, marking its submission to me. An amulet lay shining on the cave floor in its wake, the gleaming mark of the Wolf engraved upon its surface.

I stared at it mutely, a weight of guilt pressing in as Ferris's cold stare burned into me.

"I had to," I breathed, though I wasn't sure she heard me.

I picked up my prize, fixing it around my neck and jerking my chin at the Bear to command its retreat. Ferris glared up at me, soaking wet, with all the wrath of the spirits in her eyes.

"It's nearly dusk," I said, offering her my hand.

"Fuck you." She kicked dirt at me, then shoved to her feet. "I'm done with your bullshit."

"I need the boon," I offered in a low voice, hating the way she was looking at me. She saw me as a cheat. And honestly, I was one. I knew what I'd done. I knew what it meant to her.

"And I need it too," she said, her voice cracking with desperation, her hand going to her heart to show how deeply it hurt her. And it fucking hurt me too to know I'd caused it.

"You'd take them from me, given the chance," I shot back at her, falling on anger to hide the turmoil I felt over what I'd done.

"That's a lie. All of them should have been mine and you know it – you're the one who's playing this game dirty. But I've got the message at last, you bastard, and I'll be ready for your bullshit next time." She stalked away into the trees.

I followed quietly at her back, my skin prickling at her ire. I tried to smother the guilt I felt and pushed it deep down inside me. Because I may have vowed to protect Ferris, but I had still come here to succeed in one task and one task alone. I despised being this way with her, but it was my only choice. I couldn't let anything turn me from my path. Not even the human girl who had her claws in my heart.

FERRIS

CHAPTER THIRTY THREE

Two days of squatting in ramshackle buildings which barely offered shelter had done little to dampen my fury at Hendrix. Again he'd used me to gain a spirit which never would have been his otherwise. It rankled something deep within me, rage tearing at the piece of me which was wholly human and had suffered the cruelty and abuse of the Fae for far too long.

He'd spoken of Fae who hunted my kind for sport as if that were simply something that happened and there was nothing to be done for it. But I wouldn't let the wounds of the past go unanswered, and I refused to keep playing this hunt for his gain. We might have made a truce to get to the end together, but he clearly wasn't going to fight fair like he'd promised, so I didn't plan on doing so either.

The past few nights had been filled with the horrors of the forest, vines creeping through cracks in broken walls and screams of unknown origin rattling the ceilings.

Hendrix was unbearable in his smugness, and my anger at what he'd now stolen from me three times was clawing at the insides of my skin almost as keenly as the Dragon was.

"He forgets himself in this place," the Dragon growled in the confines of my mind while I scowled at the back of the Fae who had claimed to want to work with me. But it was clear now what should have been apparent the whole time – every Champion in these woods was out for themselves. Hendrix more than any other.

Perhaps he really had meant the things he'd said to me, really did appreciate my ideas and see my worth, but all that really amounted to was that he now thought of those merits as things at his own disposal.

I was more than tempted to part with him, to turn and run off into the trees and never again find myself swallowed in his shadow.

"Spit it out," Hendrix demanded, stopping suddenly in a small glade at the edge of a little pond swamped in green weed.

I pursed my lips and made to turn away, but he caught hold of my chin and forced my eyes to meet with his.

"Let go of me," I said coldly, but his grip only tightened.

"Not until you say the words which I can see spinning behind those enrapturing eyes of yours, lightwing."

I wanted to refuse, to turn away just to spite him, but why should I? Why shouldn't he face the vitriol which had been burning its way up the back of my throat ever since he'd used me to take yet another spirit from me?

"The Wolf should have been mine," I hissed, stepping closer to him instead of backing away, my gaze simmering as it locked with his. "And the Fox and the Bear too for that matter."

"Then why is it that their amulets sit firmly around my neck? Besides, I thought we were a team?" Hendrix teased, a smile at the edge of his mouth like this was all some big game to him, but it was the farthest thing from that to me.

"Don't smirk at me like it doesn't matter which of us claims the amulets. You know as well as I do that the one to return the most spirits to the Great Elm will be the one she bestows her boon upon. I need that favour – *Rissa* needs to be free of this place. If you know anything about me at all, then surely you can understand that?"

I jerked my chin out of his hold as tears flared in the corners of my eyes, my heart pounding at the truth of the words which were eating at me. It wasn't just that he'd stolen them out from under me, it was that in doing so, I'd failed in what I'd promised my sister. I'd sworn to free her from this infernal place and I was running out of time to make good on that oath.

"You're not the only one who needs the boon," Hendrix said in a low voice, his words making a chill seep through my veins. There was pain in that admission, a truth he hadn't shared with me. At least not in full.

"Why?" I demanded, forcing myself to turn back to him. "Tell me what it is you seek to gain which will not be achieved by the fracturing of the forest's curse? You told me that you aren't planning to ask for it to return your family from death to you and truthfully, I don't believe even the Great Elm would be capable of that anyway. So what is it?"

Hendrix worked his jaw, his gaze slipping from mine, a slight shake of his head making it clear he didn't intend to elaborate.

"There are many things that I would wish to fix in this wretched world," he said, still not answering my question in full.

"Things more valuable than my sister's life?"

"I didn't say that." He reached for me, but I backed away.

"Your actions said it plainly enough. I might have forgiven you for the Bear and even the Fox because I hadn't shared my truth with you when you seized them. But the Wolf?" I shook my head, backing away, but he wasn't going to allow me to escape so easily. His long strides made quick work of catching me, his hand snaring the back of my neck, his green eyes blazing with a wild determination as he drew me closer.

"I'm sorry, Ferris," he said, his voice rough, his skin hot. "Is that what you need to hear from me? That I fucked up? That I always fuck up? Isn't the mark on my face a clear enough indication of that? Didn't I tell you plainly when we met that no living being wants any piece of me? I am all the things you thought me to be when we met and many worse horrors besides."

"That's not the male I saw when the Lost Children came for me," I breathed, a single, traitorous tear tracking down my cheek. "The person you were that night wasn't selfish and cruel but brave and self-sacrificing. He risked everything to come after me-"

"Rescuing you is nothing short of selfish," he barked, dragging me closer, his words a slash against my lips, a curse I had no choice but to inhale. "Because I found you here in these woods, my lightwing. I found you and marked you as mine. You're my luck, my prize, maybe even my salvation, but there is nothing about that which betrays goodness or heroics because I did not risk my life to save yours. I offered it up freely rather than allow you to be anything other than mine."

"That's madness," I breathed, my eyes falling to his lips which hovered so close to my own, my body aching for a kiss which would be so much more than a sin. "I'm human, I'm nothing to you. My lifetime passes by in little more than a blink to your kind-"

"Yet it doesn't, does it, Ferris? Not for you. Again and again you've been reborn. Thirteen times you've heeded the call of the cursed forest while thirteen times, I've fought to ignore the pull of it. Except that pull never faded when I stepped into these trees. It never lessened one bit. Not until you stumbled across my path. Not until I captured you."

"What are you saying?"

"I'm saying that I don't think the forest was ever what awaited me here. I'm saying that all those years I spent denying the call of the trees, I think I was really denying the call of you. My lightwing. My elusive spirit." He brushed his fingers down the side of my face, his green eyes studying the violet in mine while I fought to remember to breathe, fought to remember that I was supposed to hate him, that I was furious with him. That he had used and betrayed me no matter the pretty words he spun which had my heart pounding wildly the way it was now.

"They weren't me," I said feebly. "Those other women who wore my face. I don't remember them. I don't know who they loved or what they dreamed."

"I never knew them either. And I think there's good reason for that. Because you are the one I was destined to find. You are the one who I truly came here to claim."

His lips brushed mine with that final word and a knot tightened in my gut, a flush of heat racing through my limbs, a surge of want exploding in every piece of me, and all the reasons I had to deny his words, to deny *him* just faded away to nothing.

My eyes fell closed, my lips parted, chin tilted and-

A Raven's cry cut the air to ribbons as a swathe of darkness far deeper than any shadow cast by nature cut through the trees and swept over our heads.

We ducked and I threw a hand up to protect my face, the silken feathers of the spirit brushing across my arm as it passed.

"That way!" a man yelled, and Hendrix hauled me back to my feet as a pair of Fae warriors burst into our clearing in pursuit of the spirit.

The dark-haired one spotted us and fired off an arrow which shot for my face so fast I could do nothing but scream.

Hendrix threw himself in front of me, the arrow piercing his bicep, and a snarl of feral fury tore from his lips.

"The Raven is ours!" the fair-haired Fae warrior yelled, drawing his sword and aiming it at us in a clear threat. "Leave it to us and you'll find we have no quarrel with you."

Hendrix bared his teeth, ripping the arrow from his arm and tossing it towards them, placing himself between me and the newcomers in a protective stance.

"Your arrow says differently," he snarled.

"I shot for the movement," the dark-haired Fae said, raising a hand in apology. "I expected the Raven, not…who exactly are you, anyway?"

"And what is that mark on your face?" the fair-haired warrior added, his eyes narrowing as he took a closer look at Hendrix.

Hendrix stilled in that unnatural way of his, cutting a look my way which spoke of a thousand warnings.

"It's none of your concern," he growled, all simmering violence as he took a step closer to them, placing himself between me and the threat they posed.

I glanced between them, the sound of the Raven's wingbeats drawing further away with each wasted moment. I couldn't miss my chance at it for a second time. I had to capture it. For Rissa.

"Forest, lend me a path," I pleaded beneath my breath, then turned and sprinted away into the trees.

Cries rang out behind me and I ducked on instinct a beat before an arrow slammed into a tree right where my head had been, the branches shifting to shield me at my back.

Hendrix bellowed in fury, his roar sending birds racing from the canopy overhead as I sped away from him and the clash of swords sounded behind me, marking the fight he'd fallen into.

I cast a fearful look over my shoulder, but already the sight of the Fae was lost to me. Hendrix was a formidable warrior though. I had to believe he could look after himself.

The Raven had a good start on me, but the forest seemed to know what I was looking for, a pathway opening on my right, then twisting sharply left and spearing through the trees. I was running so fast that the tips of the branches and their leaves skimmed my arms and face as they pulled aside for me.

A patch of silken darkness up ahead urged me on faster and faster, my own heart a pounding rhythm my boots fought to keep up with.

The Raven was the guardian of the night in the forest. It wouldn't be wooed the way I had hoped to do so with the Stag, and it wouldn't be tempted into action as the Fox had been with the fire. Nor did it fear the day as the Wolf had done because the light was its twin in so many ways. I had no plan in place to lure it to me, but I was still determined to capture it at last. I wouldn't let it get away a second time.

Shouts and the crash of swords echoed behind me. I threw another glance over my shoulder, hoping Hendrix and the Fae would keep each other distracted long enough for me to do what I needed.

My boots splashed into a stream, water sloshing over the tops of them and chilling my ankles but I ignored it, hunting the treetops for a patch of darker shadow.

Birds swooped between the branches overhead, squirrels and other rodents racing back and forth too, the motion drawing my focus but only distracting me from my target.

"Come on," I muttered, hunting the space between the greenery with growing desperation.

A cry came, pain haunting it as it spun through the trees at my back, and my heart leapt in panic before I recognised Hendrix's bellow of challenge a moment later. He wasn't the one in pain.

Then I spotted it. A patch of deepest midnight lurking near the top of a wide pine tree to my right.

I broke into a run, leaping for the lowest branch, my fingernails biting into the bark as I caught it and hauled myself skyward.

The Raven was watching me, I could feel the weight of its gaze on my movements as I climbed, and I began to fear it would take flight the moment I made it up to its perch.

"The world is hurting," I said in a low and soothing voice. "The Great Elm is hurting. She needs us to bring you all back to her."

In the depths of that midnight shadow, the Raven cocked its head, its metallic beak catching a shard of light and allowing me to make out the shape of its head. It could rip into my flesh with that beak all too easily, but it wasn't animosity I read in its expression. The Raven was listening to me.

"That's why I'm here. Maybe you've seen a girl with my face in these woods before? Maybe she spoke to you as I am now, or maybe she got it all wrong and that's why this curse is still spreading? Either way, I'm here now. I want to help. I want to return the forest to what it once was. Can you remember the way it used to be? When you would guide the blanket of night over the trees and watch them in the darkness so that all here could slumber in peace?"

The Raven released a low caw, the sound pierced with magic that struck a chord deep inside my chest and brought a tear to my eye. I didn't think the spirit could fully remember the days I was describing in its maddened state, but it grieved them, it held an emptiness in its soul which would only ever be fixed by the ending of this curse.

I heaved myself up onto the branch it had chosen for its perch, adrenaline coursing through my veins and a healthy dose of fear accompanying me into the treetops. If it swooped at me, I could easily be knocked right out of the trees and break my neck on the forest floor so far below. But I didn't think it wanted to hurt me.

The Raven hopped closer, its weight making the branch bounce wildly, its size dwarfing mine where I crouched before it and my stomach swooping at the motion.

"That's it," I urged, reaching out with trembling fingers, my balance all too precarious. "I'll do all I can to end this torment. I only need you to help me, to join me and-"

A rush of motion below us made me look down, the Raven cawing in alarm as Hendrix pursued the fair-haired Fae out into the stream with a furious cry.

My lips parted in horror as Hendrix hunted the male down and swung his sword for his neck with a brutal efficiency which saw blood flying in a great arc, death filling the space all around us as the Fae's head fell into the stream a beat before his body followed.

My eyes met the wild rage in Hendrix's expression, terror consuming me as I found myself looking right at the monster he had so often warned me he was. He'd chased that male down and executed him without hesitation. It was brutal and violent and horrifying and for what?

Hendrix heaved in great breaths as he stared up at me, a moment of full understanding passing between us as he was revealed at his very worst and I was forced to face it head on.

Then his eyes moved to the Raven at my side, my hand outstretched and so close to touching it that barely a breeze could slip through the divide.

He drew a dagger and hauled his arm back to throw it.

"No," I gasped, lunging for the Raven, betrayal slicing through me even faster than the blade slit the air in two.

My hand pressed to the Raven's metal beak and a pulse of magic struck me in the chest like a gong clanging to announce the hour of midnight.

Darkness enveloped me, and I would have screamed had there been any air in my lungs to do so. Instead I was lifted from the branch, my arms flying wide as silken wings draped around me, encompassing me and constricting tightly before bursting apart into a layer of night itself.

The midnight air enveloped me right down to the marrow of my bones and then slipped beneath the surface of my skin, a thump sounding as an amulet fell onto the branch before me.

I lurched for it as my vision returned, fingers knotting around the metal chain before I had even realised that those same fingers were now coated in runes so beautiful and haunting that I could have sobbed to look upon them.

I was so caught up staring at the new markings on the fingers of my right hand that I almost didn't notice the dagger lodged in the trunk of the tree right where the Raven had been.

My gaze snapped back to Hendrix as I dropped the Raven's amulet around my neck, and I hated how much that betrayal felt like a punch to the gut. He may as well have spat in my face as he looked at me with the burning intensity he now offered.

"You swore to me that you would not do that again," I hissed, ire and treachery sour on my tongue, every moment I'd allowed myself to consider him something more than a self-serving brute coming to haunt and mock me as I stared into his endlessly green eyes.

"It was going to attack you," he growled. "And I nearly lost you to those bastards a moment ago. You can't seriously have expected me to just stand here and-"

"You lied to me," I spat, refusing to let him ply me with excuses and bullshit. "You broke any fragile trust I'd been building in you and for what? Tell me why you think you deserve the boon so much more than I do. Tell me what it is that you value so much more than the life which was stolen from my sister!"

"It wasn't about the boon or the spirits or the fucking amulet!" he yelled, but all I could see was the blood coating his hands, the body of the male he had hunted like a beast and cut down while he ran for his life.

"You told me you were a monster," I said, reaching inside myself for the Dragon which always lurked just beyond my grasp, awaiting my call. "I should have listened before now."

The Dragon answered me at once, spilling from the amulet and coiling around me so that I could leap from the branch onto its back.

"You will not leave me, Ferris Creed!" Hendrix roared as he realised what I was doing, but through the burn of my tears and the solid weight of his betrayal in my gut, I refused to listen to the desperation of his cry. And without allowing myself so much as a single look back, I sped away from him on my Dragon and left him to rot in the grip of the trees.

HENDRIX

CHAPTER THIRTY FOUR

"Ferris!" I roared after her into the storm the Dragon had left in their wake, rain crashing down over me and I broke into a run, my only thought to find her, make her listen to me.

She'd seen but a glimpse of my depravity and run as far from me as she could get thanks to it. The sting was a barb in my chest that buried deeper than I could bear. I'd known this was coming, but this was nothing. Nothing at all in the face of my truth. So why not unveil it now? What use was it to hide any longer?

It was inescapable, this tarred soul of mine. I was the shadow of death upon Rathian and Ferris had feared me long before she had known me. She just hadn't realised that yet. And now she was gone. My spark in the darkness that I'd foolishly convinced myself I could keep for my own, snuffed out just like that.

"Ferris!" I bellowed again, but no answer came as I chased her fruitlessly through the trees, the forest barring my path at every step. The roots raised and the branches groaned in protest to the swipe of my sword against them, while I fought to cut a trail to the one thing in this forest worth having.

"Let me explain," I rasped, my chest heaving as I fell still, giving in to the trees as brush and vine bound together in front of me, refusing my passage while she flew with ease ever further away from me.

She could be a mile from here already in any direction, and if she didn't want to be found, she only need ask the forest to keep me from her. That thought alone carved a fresh wound through my tainted heart.

I eyed the blood on my hands as fat rain drops splashed down to wash them clean, the bright red hue the stain of death upon each finger. I had killed that male, the Fae who'd come here with reckless abandon and who had cast an arrow at my lightwing. That had been the reason for his end. The fact that he had dared to threaten *her.*

I did not regret it. But that was the point, wasn't it?

I ripped the arrow out of my arm, tossing it aside as blood ran down to my hand and dripped from my fingers. It would heal soon enough. I didn't care about the wound, I cared that this arrow had been intended for Ferris, not me.

In the quiet that followed Ferris's departure, a chasm tore apart in my chest. She was gone. That truth was crushing me and fracturing something in my mind. I hadn't even intended to take the Raven from her, but her trust in me had been shattered the day I'd stolen the Wolf. Perhaps that was when I'd really lost her. That knowledge was an anvil to my heart. She who had enraptured me from the moment I'd found her in the forest. She who had drawn me to her more viscerally than all else between these trees. I'd spent years denying the forest's call, but perhaps it had been *her* call instead. Because there was nowhere on Rathian that felt more like I belonged than at her side.

The roots around my feet were creeping closer, slithering like vipers as if sensing prey within their midst.

I dropped to my knees, hands hitting the soft earth and blood dripping from the wound on my arm to taint the soil as despair unravelled within me. And then I felt it. The darkness unlocking, spilling through me like mist upon a dark sea.

I saw the face of my family in my mind and Ferris joined them there.

Gone. All fucking gone.

But Ferris, she still lived. She was here in this forest, not lost to the grip of death. Which meant I could find her, capture my light in the dark once again. The idea brought on a river of ruin which flowed through my soul as the plague inside me answered the call of my most desperate desire.

The blight inside me spread like a disease, spilling into the earth, unable to be called back. I couldn't control it now that it had its grip on me, this roiling power which had once been a part of the Art I'd been gifted with. It had been twisted by some vile magic in the moment of my family's deaths and turned me into this bringer of ruin.

"Do you see now?" I growled, a lilt of manic laughter rising in my throat as I turned my gaze up to the canopy. "Do you see what I am?!" I boomed, and a crack of thunder punctuated the words, the heavens still rioting in the wake of the Dragon's storm.

My desperation to return Ferris to my side sent a fissure cracking down the centre of my soul. I could feel the darkness rising in answer to it, the lull of it a wicked song that hummed through my being.

I couldn't stand to be lost in these trees without her, I couldn't bear to think of her roaming the forest without me at her side. My need for her had burned its way into me far deeper than I had ever admitted to myself, but now that I found her missing, I could no longer deny it. Ferris Creed had awoken a deep desire in my soul and without her there would be no filling the wound her absence revealed. I had to find her, had to bring her back to me, had to do whatever it took to return her to my arms.

Death spilled from me into the roots of the trees and the earth blackened where I knelt, every piece of life withering beneath my power. Petals turned black, then crumbled to ash while the roots dried out and the trees - *oh* how the trees began to scream.

Black veins crawled along my skin, marking me as *him*. The bane on this land. The Necromancer the Fae and humans feared more than perhaps the Taking Trees themselves. I was the only beast in Rathian that could make the forest shudder so.

It tried to retreat from me, branch and bough bending to escape my wrath, but even I did not know how to stop it now. My power was a plague that drank its fill of death until it was sated, and I couldn't predict when that would be.

I rose to my feet, baring my teeth at the perishing trees around me, their bark turning black, cracking and splitting up their trunks.

"You will answer to me," I called out to the forest. "You will bend apart and offer her up to me. Because she is *mine!"*

The forest howled in agony as the taint of death spread from me and I found my passage no longer barred.

With Ferris firmly in mind and darkness weighing heavily on my wretched soul, I started after her, hellbent on tracking her down. She may have turned from me, but I was not done with her yet. I would show her everything. Let her see what I was so that I could watch the truth dawn upon her violet eyes.

A twisted part of me wanted to witness it when she learned of the name I had been gifted when I'd fled from Rivenspire. Because at least I could watch as she truly saw me, even if all it caused her was terror. She would perceive all that I was and there would be no more veils between us. She would be mine once again, and there would be no escaping this time. Not once she knew my full name. Not once she knew why she should have run from me the very moment I laid eyes on her. Because that was when my obsession had begun and it had its talons in me now, guiding me to her, and I'd gladly let it take me.

Gaunt faces peered at me between the trees as they were summoned to me by the darkness of my power, and I nodded grimly to the dead ones. The Hollows had come, drawn to the seed of death I was reaping as they sought out their callous king. Among them was the fair-haired Fae I'd killed, stirring back to this half-life he was now trapped in and seeing me through the lens of knowledge.

"The Necromancer," he rasped, his eyes bloodshot and dark.

"Bow to me," I growled, and he did so, a murmur of terror leaving his pale lips. He would struggle with this new form, one foot here and one foot in the afterworld, never quite himself and always yearning for an end to his torment. He would only be gifted it if his heart was destroyed or head severed from his shoulders.

"Come then," I growled as more of them stepped between the trees, all those whose bodies had been wasted by death here in the forest. The glint of magic in their eyes told of the merciless power that still bound their unfortunate souls to this world. "Let us follow her into the deep dark wood and show her the king of death. For she will be my queen."

FERRIS

CHAPTER THIRTY FIVE

The Dragon had taken me right across the forest when I'd fled Hendrix's company, and I couldn't deny the way the northern parts of the woods felt different. The birds sang more softly here, the wind was more of a breeze, and even the leaves on the trees seemed more golden in tone than that deep green.

The silence kept me company in place of the brooding Fae I'd grown used to having at my back. And though I refused to admit I'd made any kind of mistake in running from him when I had, I could admit that it was a much lonelier place here without him.

I'd spent two days hunting for the Phoenix, searching an old stone tower which smelled of ash and was coated in narrow creepers thick with violet flowers, but there had been no sign of the spirit. The Phoenix was the opposite to the Raven in that it coveted sunlight and had once made certain that every tree, plant and shrub within the forest got to feel the rays of the sun on their leaves so they could flourish to their fullest potential. The two spirits were said to be in love with one another, creating balance as they flew over the trees, adoring what the other could bring and endlessly admiring the changes their magic brought to the forest.

I had no way to tempt such a spirit out but after hunting and searching, turning over every loose leaf and stone, I had finally come to the conclusion that another Champion must have claimed the beast I sought. I'd found evidence of a campfire not far from the tower and boot prints in the mud by a burbling brook. Between that and the haunting emptiness of this place, I had concluded that any further searching of this place was futile.

"What now?" I sighed, sinking down on the crumbling stone steps before the tower and taking the diary from my pack.

A little chill rolled down my spine as I turned the pages, the ghost of its previous owner seeming all the closer now that I understood she had been me in some form.

I'd spent many hours wondering over the lives I'd lived before, searching through my memories for a glimmer of something beyond what I had experienced in my own twenty-two years, but there was nothing there. I didn't believe the versions of me which had come before had truly been me. They might have had my face, my body, even some form of my spirit, but this life I was living now was the only one I would ever know or accept as my own.

I supposed in a way the other versions of myself were like ancestors. They may have contributed to my make up in some small part, but they hadn't influenced it directly. They weren't me and I wasn't them. Which I had decided to believe was for the best – they'd failed in this task after all. And they hadn't had Rissa either.

I'd stepped out into the night twice now in hopes of meeting with my sister again, calling her name into the dark before fleeing behind closed doors once more.

I didn't seem to need to fear the Lost Children the way the other Champions did but that didn't mean there weren't other things which lurked in the darkness that might take a bite of me if I lingered there too long.

Even the forest seemed less hospitable once the sun had fallen from the sky. The trees were more hostile, more wild, as if the sun were the only thing reminding them not to become as malevolent as the curse demanded.

I wasn't sure if there was truth in those assumptions but neither the Dragon nor the Raven had denied them.

"Where should we hunt next?" I asked, summoning both of my spirits and watching as they materialised before me.

The Raven cawed in greeting, hopping up to perch on the step at my side, swathing me in darkness so deep that I had to lean forward to hold the map out of its reach to be able to see it at all.

The spirit released an amused chirrup and nuzzled against me. I'd been surprised to find out how affectionate the spirit could be the first time it had done such a thing, but I'd soon grown used to its exuberant greetings. The Raven didn't speak as often as the Dragon did in my mind - though it always listened intently when I was the one talking.

The Dragon was more austere, moving through the clearing at the base of the tower, its long, serpentine body coiling between the trees before it laid itself down facing me, its regal head resting atop crossed front paws.

"We could head west and hunt for the Carp," I mused, tracing the lines of the map, though in truth, there were notes in the diary about the Carp's location which made it clear that it was very much a guess on the part of the woman who had drawn it. "Or…east in hopes of finding the Unicorn."

I glanced at the Raven who simply cawed again, its silken wing draping around my shoulders, no answer clear in either gesture. The Dragon huffed wearily like it was tired of my shit. Crotchety thing that it was.

I hmmed, considering the options. The Carp was an interesting spirit to say the least. My book on the spirits wasn't exactly complimentary about it when describing its powers or the responsibilities it had once held.

I tugged the book free of my pack and read over the now-familiar words once more, my eyes drawn to the white and orange Carp which glimmered in the illustrations beneath the chapter heading.

The Carp is a curious spirit indeed. Some theorise that its creation was something of a jest by the Great Elm, or perhaps a mistake altogether. Though large and beautiful in its own way, the Carp's dominion was over puddles – a most peculiar endeavour.

It is said that the Carp liked to flick its fins and throw water around the forest to create these puddles, though their use to the trees and the creatures within them is questionable. Of course it was the Bear who ensured all of the forest was kept watered and even made certain to care for the streams, brooks, rivers, ponds and lakes within the forest's bounds which kept the trees and animals sustained for their thirst.

Why then was there a need for puddles?

It is always hard to divulge the purpose behind the actions of the spirits, but in this case, there seems to be no answer which makes any kind of sense beyond perhaps boredom or a desire for amusement.

The Carp is no fighter, nor is it particularly fast even in the water. It would likely be the easiest of the spirits to capture, especially as it so often leapt from its pools and ended up flapping around on the forest floor until such a time as one of the other spirits took pity upon it and returned it to its domain.

"Easy does sound nice," I commented, though I had to wonder that after this long, if the Carp was so easy to capture, wouldn't one of the other Champions have already done so by now?

I knew of course that the Dragon, Raven, Bear, Fox and Wolf were accounted for already. It seemed the Stag, Boar and Phoenix had been found too, if my fruitless searching was proof of anything. The Rat and the Tiger had been taken by Islasees. So all that might now remain were the Unicorn, Carp, and Serpent. The Serpent which Rissa had been riding through the trees…

I frowned as I thought on that. Rissa wasn't a Champion, and to my understanding, couldn't claim a spirit for herself, nor had she been wearing an amulet. So how had she bonded with it? Would she really be able to convince it to join with me? If so, then I could count myself as having three amulets already. One more would surely mean I had the most in that case. And if not and someone else had gained four too, then I needed to have the more powerful set. The Carp wouldn't help much with that.

I flipped to the part about the Unicorn.

The image on the page made my heart ache as I took it in. The Unicorn was a stunning white mare with a golden starburst on its brow where its horn stood proud, shimmering with ethereal light. Its mane and tail were a carpet of pale blossoms in every shade and style, roses, peonies, tulips, daisies and many more besides, all draping down around it to brush along the floor.

> *The Unicorn was the bringer of life to the forest, spreading blossom and blooms wherever its hooves fell. Often agreed to be among the most powerful of the spirits of the forest, the Unicorn is shy and elusive by nature but can be brutal and unrelenting when provoked, using its horn to maim and even kill if it feels the life of the forest is being threatened.*

I drummed my fingers against the pages of the book, looking between the two spirits I'd already won. My confidence in this task had grown immensely since gaining the Raven for my own. Yes, claiming the Dragon had been colossal, but until I had tempted the Raven into joining with me too, I had feared that my method of trying to prove myself worthy to the spirits might have been a fluke.

Now I felt far more confident that it would work again.

The Fox had come for my flames, the Wolf had been herded by the light I'd steered, and I truly believed that my idea for securing the Unicorn might just work too.

"Let's go after the Unicorn," I decided, as my spiritual companions clearly had no intention of giving me their opinion.

The Dragon raised its head, then released a heavy breath which made the feathers around its jaw ruffle.

I made quick work of repacking my bag, then slung it onto my back and strode down the tower steps to the enormous spirit.

It still took my breath away to look at the beast of legend, still made my heart pound faster to approach it.

"Would you mind flying me across the forest to this spot?" I asked, holding out the map for the Dragon to look at and pointing to the little Unicorn drawn in a place several miles to the east.

"Climb on then, spirit singer," the Dragon spoke in my mind, staying low on its haunches so that I could climb up onto its back. I had wondered whether the Raven might also be able to carry me while flying. It was far smaller than the Dragon but still much larger than I was, so I imagined it could. And of course it would be far more subtle too, but I got the feeling the Dragon would not take it well were I to ask for the other spirit to take on the task.

I climbed up the Dragon's smooth body, marvelling at the shining scales and little sparks of teal electricity which zipped across them. They didn't hurt when they made contact with my skin but buzzed vibrantly, awakening something deep inside of my soul which resonated with them on a base level.

"Ready?" the Dragon purred in my mind, amusement clear in its tone.

I moved to wrap my arms around its neck, the soft feathers of its ruff tickling the side of my face as a little burst of adrenaline surged through my limbs. "Ready."

The Dragon leapt into the air in a rush of motion, racing for the sky above the tower and shooting across the treetops so fast that tears were torn from my eyes at the motion.

The Raven cawed as it took chase, a swathe of night scoring across the sky behind us.

Thunder rumbled overhead as the Dragon's passage stirred the clouds and my hair streamed out around me in a wild tangle.

A grin found its way onto my lips, the rush of our passage through the sky leaving me utterly elated as it stripped away my fears, my regrets and my doubts. Nothing which had led me to this moment could have been wrong. Nothing about the decisions I'd made could have been different. I had to believe that. Even though there was an ache in my heart which asked if I'd been right to run from Hendrix. He had betrayed me, but he'd protected me too after all. He was bad, just as he'd always told me, but he hadn't tried to conceal the fact from me. I'd just been too stubborn to see the whole truth of it.

And despite it all, he'd never done anything to hurt *me.*

Regardless of those nagging thoughts, Hendrix was long behind me now. Perhaps our paths would cross when we made for the Great Elm. Perhaps by then I'd have three spirits of my own and he would be forced to truly treat me as an equal.

That thought stirred me, banishing my doubts once more as the Dragon dove from the sky and plummeted into the grasp of the trees once more.

We stopped so suddenly, I was almost hurled from the back of the spirit and only managed to stay in place by gripping the feathers around its ruff so tightly that they were in danger of tugging loose.

We'd landed in a dale where shards of sunlight punctured the canopy of the trees overhead and illuminated patches of wildflowers in their own personal spotlights. The scent of the blooms was enchanting, something about this place so serene that I found myself relaxing just a little despite our intent.

"Go that way," I said, pointing to a space between the trees where daisies, buttercups and forget-me-nots carpeted the forest floor like a beautiful tapestry.

"I thought you'd learned not to bark commands at me like I'm some common mule," the Dragon griped, its anger lashing against the inside of my skull and making me cringe.

"I'm sorry," I said quickly. "I'm only keen to-"

"Perhaps you will learn from this folly if you are forced to recall what traversing the forest is like without my help."

The Dragon shook like a dog leaping out of a river, and I yelled in alarm as I was tossed from its back less than gracefully, falling on my ass in a mound of white and blue flowers.

The spirit's clawed feet hit the ground either side of me as it growled in my face, and I cringed away from it as sparks of electricity slashed against my skin.

"Heed my warning, spirit singer, for I won't do you the courtesy of offering up many more."

In a flash of silver and teal light, the Dragon's body broke apart, swirling into the amulet at my throat with such speed that the force of it flattened me on my back in the flowers.

I blinked at the Raven as it hopped closer, offering me a soft caw which sounded a little pitying and a little judgy, like it thought I should have really seen that coming, and before I could even think to ask it for its help in place of the Dragon's, it slipped back into its amulet too.

Clearly I had a lot to learn about conversing with spirits. I had to say, the spirits were certainly far touchier than I'd have expected. Grumpier too.

I huffed in irritation, brushing some flowers out of my windswept hair as I stood.

This was fine. I could find the Unicorn on my own and capture it alone too.

I ignored the lingering doubts and got to my feet, looking around at the stunning flowers, certain from them alone that I was in the right place.

I moved quietly, creeping along the path carpeted in daisies and other small blooms, the scent of the flowers settling some old ache within me as I moved deeper into their embrace.

This place was like something from a painting. Great swathes of wisteria in shades from deep to pale purple, pink and even white all hung over my head. Insects buzzed drunkenly between the blossoms, so overwhelmed with choice that it was a veritable feast for them.

I rounded a huge cherry tree, its branches thick with pink blossom, the petals slowly tumbling down around me and brushing against my cheeks on their way to the ground.

The Unicorn raised its head as I stepped into its clearing. The spirit was far larger than any horse I'd ever laid eyes on before, its limbs slender and ethereal, its mane of flowers draping down its side and parting for the glimmering golden horn on its brow.

The spirit regarded me warily, pawing at the earth and lowering its head in threat. This was not a creature that would run from a fight, and as I looked more closely at the trees which surrounded its dale, I found the faces of at least six Cursed Ones watching me with intrigue.

Had they met with their fates while trying to capture this beast? It seemed the most likely reason for so many of them to be in this place and my gut knotted with the urge to flee.

I bit my lip, my plans for luring this spirit to me falling apart. I had thought to pick some of the flowers it so cherished and lay them out in a trail for it to follow. That seemed like the thoughts of a fool now that I stood looking into the eyes of my quarry. Enraging the Unicorn would not go well for me.

So instead, I gave into a thought which likely was nothing but lunacy.

The Unicorn snorted in warning, its horn pointed right at me as it pawed the ground again, the soil turning over beneath its hoof and flowers bursting to life there in the next breath.

I opened my arms wide to show it I held no weapon, then very slowly, sank down to sit among the wildflowers at the base of the cherry tree.

"I came here in hopes that you might agree to help me," I said in a soft voice.

The Unicorn whinnied, the sound carrying that hint of magic to it which shook something in the heart of me, shattering my humanity and wrapping me in the wildness of its power.

I sucked in a breath and the spirit charged.

There was no way I could escape, no hope for me to get out of its path, so I threw up my arms and called my sister's name. I wasn't sure if it was meant as an apology or farewell, but before I could figure it out, the Unicorn leapt over my head and galloped a full circle of the cherry tree.

I shrieked in fright, recoiling against the bark, then lurching away as one of the Cursed Ones caught a knot of my silvery hair in its fist.

I stumbled out into the heart of the dale, my scalp tender from the hair which had been ripped free of it, and the Unicorn trotted closer, its golden horn glowing brighter the nearer it came.

"Please?" I begged, my throat thick with a mixture of fear and hope. If the Unicorn denied my request, then I could already tell I wasn't going to be capable of capturing it by force. This spirit was both fierce and powerful. A stone wouldn't fell it and I had no other weapon, not that I wanted to cause it pain even if I had.

"You know, you really don't need to be looking at me like I'm some kind of threat," I said in a rush, unsure on exactly what my plan was at this point but hoping it might at least pause in its murderous intent to hear me out. "I wouldn't even hurt a fly. I mean that. One time, there was this moth trapped in my room, and it kept flying around and around by the rafters while I was trying to sleep. And I know what you're thinking – a moth couldn't possibly be that loud, but truly this thing was flipping and flapping and bumping off of everything, even after I doused my lantern. And of course even back home we knew better than to ever open a window at night in case the spirits came to… well not that I think all spirits like to lure unsuspecting humans to their deaths or anything like that because you don't seem at all the type to do such a thing. But there are the Hollows to consider too, and the lure of the night and well…anyway my point is that I let the moth have my room for the night and had to curl up on the hearth downstairs because I couldn't bring myself to hurt it."

I cringed back as the Unicorn lowered its head before me, the spirit's wide eyes meeting with mine and capturing me in that place, a breath stalling in my lungs, fear coiling all around me.

With a snort that sounded almost bored, the Unicorn stepped forward and touched the tip of its horn to my brow.

Its power enveloped me, stealing the breath from my lungs as it surged through my limbs and almost knocked me from my feet.

I stumbled backwards, leaning against a tree as the rush of magic faded and a wild laugh tumbled from my lips. The Unicorn's amulet sat on the ground before me and the weight of it settling around my neck was like a balm to my soul.

Three spirits. I'd captured *three* spirits! The chances of anyone besides Hendrix having matched that number were seriously low. Would Rissa be able to help me with the Serpent? If so, then I was almost certain that I would be the one to seize the boon. I'd be able to rescue my sister from this nightmare, break the curse and return us to the lives that had been stolen all those years ago.

A flash of warmth caught my attention, and I looked down at the intricate floral pattern which now coiled across the back of my right hand, like a knotted bouquet of every kind of flower the forest had to offer. The Unicorn had marked me just as the others had done. And I was finally living up to the promise I'd made eight years ago.

HENDRIX

CHAPTER THIRTY SIX

I'd taken shelter in houses and an old tavern, never staying more than one night so that I could keep moving. I was hunting her more than the spirits now. Death was dripping from me like a plague of locusts come to feast upon the earth, every tree, bush and flower I had passed wilting in the wake of me. And all the while, I was consumed by thoughts of Ferris almost as deeply as the darkness shrouding my mind.

The Hollows remained close, waiting in the shadows, hounding my footsteps, more and more joining their ranks. I despised their presence, their ever-watching eyes. They never spoke to me. Not these. Not like some. And I preferred it that way. These were not freshly dead, they were the starved husks of former humans and Fae alike, following the eternal power that always drew them back to my side. The longer it had been since their demise, the less their souls remained intact, but I only needed to grasp a whisp of it to root on this side of death. That was all I required to add them to my army.

I had found no sign of Ferris apart from a single feather that had been heading north, confirming she had kept to that path. So north I walked, every day, as far as I could from the moment dawn came to the very cusp of sundown while the forest surrounding me withered and the trees groaned their demise.

I never stopped moving unless I had to.

My frustration only deepened at the knowledge that I could move far swifter than this in the world beyond the cursed forest. When Death was close, I could take hold of her cloak and she could pull me through the crevice between this life and the afterworld, transporting me to wherever I wished to go on Rathian in the blink of an eye. But here, between these damned trees, The Great Elm refused my passage whenever I tried.

So now that night had forced me to take shelter once more, I waited for dawn to come, wide awake and staring at the door of the old tavern I'd slept in, snared in haunting visions of the past.

I tried to remember something good, only to be called back to a day when I had taken Amelda down to a graveyard on the edge of a winding stream on the border of Mithelnore. She'd been so young. Still a child and so curious about life. She'd been so very happy in her youngest days. A girl who always smiled, always looked for reasons to laugh. She'd been so fearless too when she'd watched me use the Art of speaking with the dead to catch whispers from our fallen ancestors among the gravestones. There weren't many graves in the whole of Rivenspire, but we were a family of warriors, and so death had found more of our family than most. Perhaps that was why the spirits had blessed me with such an Art.

Our great, great grandfather had asked if we could pay a visit to a friend who had stolen his favourite hat and return it to him, and Amelda had promised she would do so and leave a cat's turd on his doorstep as punishment. I'd nearly pushed her in the stream for being such a rogue. But she had been *my* rogue. Wild as the wind and as impatient as a sea storm.

My brother Kashton was different, more brooding in his ways, but family had always brought smiles to his lips like no other thing had. He took after Father where Amelda had always been more like Mother with her recklessness. Together we'd found a balance that had created a haven in Rivenspire. The Coterie hadn't drawn our attention much beyond the odd comment made by Father because of his required attendance to the monthly gatherings. Once I became old enough to join, I'd quickly realised the mirage we'd painted for ourselves, blinded by ignorance. For the Coterie were a taint who had willingly spread evil into our lands without my notice. But once I had seen it, there was no unseeing it. I wished to protect Amelda and Kashton from the fate of a world ruled by them and a corrupt king whose reign never ceased. I hadn't meant for the cards to fall how they did. Father had hated them too of course, but he'd tried more peaceful methods of changing the ways of the Coterie. He had not wished for a violent answer but there had been no choice in my opinion.

My gaze fell to one of the Hollows as she stepped up to the window outside, pressing a palm to the glass and watching, always fucking watching. Her mouth was parted, revealing rotten teeth and those unblinking eyes were shot through with dark veins. She was a stark reminder of my curse, and I could have sworn those eyes were full of blame.

I grabbed an old oil lamp from the table beside my seat and hurled it at the window, the thing slamming into it and sending a crack splintering out across the glass. The Hollow blinked but didn't move.

"Be gone," I barked, but she remained.

I carved a hand down my face, shutting my eyes to hide from her condemnation, needing to think. Where might Ferris go? Which spirit would she seek next?

No matter how hard I tried, I couldn't remember the images on that map. Was the Unicorn to the north or was it the west? Had she sought any others? Had she succeeded?

I missed her bitterly. That was the crux of it. I wanted to hate her as she hated me, it would make this all the easier, but I knew what awaited me when we found each other. Nothing but ire would ever be offered from her to me now, and that was such a bitter fucking pill to swallow.

Spirits be, I had come here as a lone creature hellbent on seeking the boon. I did not mean to find a distraction such as her. No male as cursed as I would ever suspect a gift like that. Punishments were my expectation of the world. I was responsible for the deaths of so many, for every Hollow that walked upon Rathian. I could not control them in full, only will them here and there, and even that power was not ironclad. But I was still their king. They answered to me, and the violence they delivered was very much my sin to bear. Once upon a time, death had been but a gift I could wield in small doses. I could catch whispers from the beyond, but when I'd watched my family die, that magic had festered into a ruinous calamity in my veins.

I shuddered at the memory, dropping my hand and blinking out at the door, forcing it from my mind. No, I could not go there again. Too many times had I replayed that day. Now was a time for the present, not the past.

I pushed out of my seat as the light of dawn haloed the Hollow at the window and knew it was time to move once more. She was calling to me again, as perhaps she had been calling to me all along, drawing me to this forest. And now that I'd found her, I refused to let her go.

"I'm coming for you, Ferris," I whispered to no one but myself, stepping outside to find the mass of Hollows had grown in the night. Thirty or more lingered here, the dead standing like statues between the trees, waiting for me. Every tree around them stood dead, their leaves pooling on the ground and their bark as dry as ash.

"Follow me then," I commanded them. "We will be death in plain sight, a walking nightmare for all who scurry between these trees. Let them find us. Let them try their hand at killing the king of death, then let them join you among your bloodied ranks and fall in line for good. Every one of you will assist me in my task. We march until we find her!"

FERRIS

CHAPTER THIRTY SEVEN

My pride over gaining the Unicorn was fast souring. The Dragon remained angry at me despite the amount of times I'd apologised, and it had also banned both the Raven and the Unicorn from assisting me while it enacted its punishment.

I had no idea how long it planned on maintaining this treatment, but I found myself walking endlessly through the trees in hunt of a place to spend the night while dusk descended all around me.

To make it worse, I was becoming more and more certain that I was being followed.

Not for the first time, I was doubting my decision to run from Hendrix. Yes, he had been an ass and yes, I was angry with him, but at least at his side I hadn't had to fear the other Champions or whatever foul things lurked within these trees. And…in my solitude, I could admit to myself that I missed him. I missed the weight of his stare when I was reading, I missed the dark humour he produced with wry cunning. I missed the protection he offered me of course, but if I was being truly honest with myself, then I could admit that I missed the heat of his body against mine in the dead of night. I missed the low rumble of his voice when he called me lightwing or spoke my name. I even missed the way he got my blood boiling with fury, riling me up in a way no other had before. And I missed all the unspoken wants between us, the way he sometimes looked at me like he might devour me whole and the way I had begun to think I'd let him if he tried.

I expelled a rough breath, forcing the Fae from my thoughts and from my fantasies alike. He was a sin I never should have been tempted by. A lie I never should have listened to. And a want I'd spend the rest of my days denying I'd ever felt. So I would banish him from my mind and force myself to remain focused on my task.

I'd grown complacent in the favourable treatment the forest offered me and for the last few days, I'd tried to convince myself that there was nothing to fear within the depths of the cursed forest.

That had been nothing but a pretty lie. Perhaps the trees themselves weren't intent on my demise but that didn't mean there weren't other things within this place that were.

And despite the Lost Children having let me pass before, I didn't trust them to do so a second time. For Rissa's sake, they'd allowed me safe passage once – and only while she'd been in my company. My sister was both one of them and not. She had continued to age since finding herself within the snare of the forest. She was born of the same spirit magic which had gone towards my own creation. I didn't know what that made her, but I didn't believe it gave her any kind of real or lasting control over this place or the beasts which ruled it.

I was also growing fearful over how long it had been since I'd seen her. I'd heard the Lost Children singing in the trees at night but never her voice. There had been nothing to suggest she'd come close to me since the return of my pack after our meeting in the dark, and I feared the reasons for her absence.

I so wanted to believe that ending this curse might be the answer to freeing her too, but I knew it wasn't. She'd told me that her fate was bound to this place now. When she was selected as an Offering, she'd been given to the Great Elm. So she was trapped here, curse or not. I couldn't just rely on hope.

Even claiming ownership of the three spirits wasn't enough. I needed to be certain that I had done all I could to ensure my victory over the other Champions. So I'd set a trail in hunt of the Carp.

If the Dragon had been willing to offer me its help, then I could have traversed the trees in a matter of hours. As it was, I still had around a day's travel ahead of me before I would reach the pond where the Carp had been rumoured to linger.

The spirit I really wanted to try and find was the Serpent. I had hopes that my sister remained with it, but I had no clues as to its location. After seeing the way it moved through the trees with Rissa, I had to think it wouldn't be found lurking in its territory the way the others seemed to. So I'd have to rely on her being able to bring it to the Great Elm when it mattered. I didn't like leaving any part of my plans to chance like that, but I trusted my sister and it was going to have to be enough.

I wasn't sure, but I had the feeling Rissa had managed to lure some of the madness out of the Serpent. Had helped the spirit remember more of what it once had been and the purpose it had been created for. As that included rooting out enemies of the forest and destroying them, I had to fear what that remembrance might mean for any Champions it stumbled across.

Gloom pressed in beneath the trees. I likely still had an hour before night fell, but once the sun dipped towards the horizon, the shadows stretched out like long and grasping fingers, snatching far more of the light from this place than I would have liked.

A branch snapped somewhere behind me and I turned, my hand falling to the slingshot in my pocket.

I swallowed a lump in my throat. That wasn't the first time I'd heard a noise in the trees behind me.

I scoured the shadows for a sign of movement and stumbled back a few steps as something shifted in the dark.

"Now would be a really great time for you to forgive me," I muttered to the Dragon whose only response was a low scoff in the back of my skull. "If I die out here then there won't be any way for me to save the forest."

"Perhaps you will hold that thought in mind the next time you think to order me about like a dog, spirit singer."

"Is that all you have to say?" I hissed as another branch broke, this time from a spot further to the left. There was more than one something trailing me through the trees.

"No."

"Then you'll help me?" I pleaded.

"I didn't say that."

"Then what?" I hissed.

"I was only going to make a suggestion." The Dragon's words coiled through my mind, faint teal light shimmering along the edges of its amulet.

"What's that?" I took my slingshot from my pocket as fear trickled into me.

"Run."

The Dragon's warning was entirely unnecessary as it was punctuated by two figures stepping out of the trees, their faces gaunt, their eyes hungry and feral.

I cursed, placing a stone in my slingshot and aiming at the Hollow which was closest to me but as it broke into a run my shot went wide and I was left with no option but to launch myself into the trees and run for my life.

I tripped on roots hidden in the shadows and cried out as my fingers tore on a thorn bush.

The Hollows shrieked in delight as they took chase, more than just two sets of footsteps pounding after me in the dark.

In all the horrors and wonders of this place I had almost forgotten the Hollows. Fucking fool that I was, I hadn't even been looking out for them.

Since I'd found the Dragon I'd seen nothing of the dead which rose at the Necromancer's command and had put them out of my mind, hoping that the few who had ended Colton had been here by mistake, some fluke of luck meaning they'd crossed into the forest when it had opened itself for the beginning of the Great Hunt.

If I hadn't learned anything else in this place then I should have at least known better than to give in to hope. That had been something which had been more than elusive to me for most of my life and certainly hadn't been anything I was fool enough to depend on. I made my own destiny. Or I meant to. And the only way to achieve that was by facing all the horrors of this world head on and planning my way around them.

I'd let myself become caught up in the curse and the spirits and the amulets, and I'd admit it to myself – I'd gotten caught up in Hendrix Draven too. I'd let his strength infect me with the belief that I was safe, I'd let his words torment me and raise what could only be madness within my mind because I'd let myself linger not only in his company but in a fantasy which never could have been more than a fleeting moment of pure insanity. And where was my Fae warrior now when I needed him most? Certainly not keeping me safe. All because I'd decided running meant giving myself and Rissa a better chance at the boon. But what use was the boon to my corpse when the Hollows caught up to me and ripped me apart?

I had nowhere to run to, no safe haven awaiting me. I pleaded with the Dragon to help me but it refused, only making my fear deepen.

I called out to the forest to help instead and it opened a pathway for me between the trees. But as I ran towards it three more Hollows burst from the undergrowth ahead, forcing me to swerve aside and throw myself through a tangle of nettles and brambles which bit at every exposed patch of skin they could find.

My pack was weighing me down but I gripped the straps tightly in my fists and ran on, refusing to consider dropping it.

More and more Hollows burst from the trees, forcing me to lurch aside and change direction over and over again. Their breath was rancid on the air, their empty eyes pinned wholly on me while they raced after me on rotting limbs in dishevelled clothes.

A tear pricked the corner of my eye as I tried to turn and once more found one of the heinous creatures blocking my path. The ground began to slope upwards but every time I tried change direction and find an easier route, the Hollows swept in to block me off and force me higher up the hill.

My breaths were a ragged saw in my chest, sweat coursing down my spine where my clothes were trapped beneath my pack. My hair was tangled and sticking to my cheeks as a choked sob fell from me.

I didn't try to aim my slingshot again, knowing only too well that it would do me no good. Even if I could fell one of the monstrous beings, there had to be fifty of them chasing me through the trees.

They were going to catch me, they would rip me apart with tooth and nail and all I had done, all I had thought to do, would come to nothing.

"Ferris!" Hendrix's voice boomed through the dark up ahead and a spear of that one, most dangerous emotion struck me directly in the heart. Hope.

I almost wept with relief as I called his name in reply.

The rising moon was casting silvery pools of light between the trees as I raced father up the hill and I caught sight of him standing right at the top, a familiar tower at his back. Both saviour and sanctuary in one place.

Was it fate that had led me to him in my moment of greatest need or had the forest been working to aid me in my path once again? Either way, it was a stroke of luck which had me near to sobbing with relief. I'd missed him when I'd run from him. Almost enough to have made me turn back and seek him out had I known where to begin my search. I'd been so stupid to flee from him. I'd been angry and hurt and fearful of what would come at the end of this hunt if I couldn't win more spirits for my own but I had wanted to turn back and find him again despite it all. And it seemed the forest or fate or maybe a twist of both wanted us reunited too.

I found some small measure of resolve still lurking in my limbs and pushed myself to run faster, refusing to look back. I could feel the Hollows mere inches behind me, their grasping fingers surely about to take hold of me at any moment.

Hendrix waited for me at the top of the hill and as I burst into the clearing surrounding the tower he swept past me, sword swinging, blood flying, Hollows falling.

"Enough!" he bellowed, swinging his sword as he dove at the beasts which grasped for my heels.

I scrambled further from the sounds of fighting before I got to my feet once more, my pack falling in the dirt at last while heaving breaths tore from my lungs.

I was no warrior, but Hendrix? Watching him cut through the Hollows was like watching a dance of well-practiced and beautiful steps.

He cut the Hollows down so simply I might have questioned why I'd been so filled with terror while I ran from them. But as they fought to get past him, feral, hungry gazes locked on me, I knew my death had only just passed me by.

Hendrix cut the last of them down and turned to me, blood dripping from his sword, face cast in shadow, his eyes burning with a relentless, furious power which I could feel wrapping around me like the arms of a storm.

He dropped his sword and strode for me, gripping my face between his hands and staring down at me with a ravenous devotion that set my heart racing even faster than fleeing from the Hollows had done.

Madness struck me as I stared up at him. The kind of madness which wars were fought over, which songs were sung for, which folk wept and killed for. The most dangerous type of madness in this world or any other. Because in the arms of this brute, this infuriating, maddening male, I suddenly felt as if I was exactly where I was supposed to be.

Shadows mapped lines across his skin, darkness clinging to his features in a way that set my entire being on edge but I was lost in the fact that he was here, that he had found me, and that I never should have run from him at all.

I took hold of his wrists where he clung to me and I pressed up onto my toes as I captured his mouth with my own.

Hendrix stilled for all of a heartbeat as a pulse of raw energy raged between us and then he dragged me closer, his mouth captivating mine, his tongue sinking between my lips and my body melting into his.

I'd been kissed before. Kisses were something and nothing at all. But not this kiss. This kiss was like a breath of frozen air on a balmy summer's night, stealing all of my attention and devouring me whole.

Hendrix didn't kiss me like any man had ever kissed me. He possessed me with that kiss, destroyed me and consumed me and worshipped me.

I was lost in him, all the things I'd been trying to deny about the way he made me feel and the things he made me want just spilling away to nothing as he kissed me like I was all he'd ever wanted in this life or any other.

A stillness fell over the world as I lost myself in his kiss, the taste of him awakening every piece of my soul as I fell for the trap I'd been fighting to avoid since the moment I'd first laid eyes on him.

But the stillness wasn't just that of this connection. It was the entire world falling silent like in the moment before a predator might leap from the trees.

My eyes fluttered open, my gaze meeting the wild tempest in Hendrix's, the green I'd come to grow so familiar with seeming so much darker in the moonlight.

Black shadows crept from his eyes, painting lines across his skin, dark magic leaking from him and making me step back suddenly, a spell shattering as if a bucket of cold water had been hurled over us.

Fear captured my heart before I even realised why.

In the trees surrounding us, beyond the corpses of the Hollows Hendrix had cut down, figures stood like statues, their hungry eyes consuming me. There must have been at least thirty of them stood frozen, their desperate wants held at bay by some power I was only just starting to realise was resonating from the Fae before me.

"You," I breathed, stepping back but he didn't relinquish his hold on me, his voice a low growl as he replied.

"Do you see the truth of me at last, lightwing? Do you understand the horrors I warned you about now?"

My heart was a bird thrashing against the bars of a cage which was coiling tighter and tighter around it. I could see the shadows on his skin all the clearer now, see them for the darkness they were, feel the wretched weight of their poisonous magic as it clawed its way through his veins. The bony hands of death which were painted around his throat seemed to be gripping him more tightly, those tattoos flexing as if they were made of so much more than ink. A collar for a beast worse than any other.

In the spaces between the trees Hollows stared at us with feral hunger in their eyes, their lust for life and death kept in check, their bodies taut with tension, their wants suppressed by their master.

Their master who stood before me, whose kiss still stained my lips, whose truth had been right there for me to see long before this moment but which I had so determinedly fought against admitting to. Because allowing myself to see it meant admitting to myself that the male I'd been captivated by since the moment we first met, the one I'd desired and dreamed of, had ached for and pined for against my better judgement, had been a monster all along. The monster who had haunted my nightmares in every quiet moment, the one they all whispered of in the dark.

His name wasn't Hendrix Draven. It was one which was renowned and feared across the realms of human and Fae alike.

"You're Bane Crownthief," I exhaled, terror holding me captive as thoroughly as his hold on me did. "The prince who was cursed for stealing a crown he wasn't worthy of. The Fae whose twisted magic allowed him to raise the dead. You're the Necromancer."

HENDRIX

CHAPTER THIRTY EIGHT

Ferris retreated from me, one step after the other marking each crushing moment of reality as it sank into her. The truth. There, written in the dark for her to see at last.

Her kiss still lingered on my mouth, the touch of sweetness I'd stolen already souring by what was to come. But I had made my decision. I'd hounded her here, wielded the Hollows to trap her and now that she was in my cage, I had no intention of letting her go.

The sunlight was draining quickly from the sky and as she turned to run – though there was nowhere for her to go – I caught her by the hand and marched her for the tower's door.

"Let go of me," she snarled, trying to twist out of my grip but my fingers only tightened on hers as I pushed her ahead of me into our sanctuary for the night.

"And let you run off in the forest to play with the Lost Children?" I growled, kicking the door shut behind us and releasing her hand. "The trees might favour you, Ferris Creed, but I will not risk your life for anything."

She staggered away as if I'd burned her, turning to face me and backing up against a stone wall at the base of the spiral stairway awaiting us.

"You lied about everything," she spat, betrayal written across her face.

"I never lied," I growled, stalking closer and she snatched her slingshot from her pocket, aiming a rock at my forehead in warning.

"Stay. Back," she commanded forcefully, though the tremor in her shoulders told of the fear rioting through her flesh.

"Are you going to kill me, lightwing?" I whispered, taking another step toward her, wondering if she might just loose that stone against my brow. Oh to die by her hand. That was far too sweet a death for me to be offered.

"I will," she hissed between her teeth. "Don't come any closer."

I lunged and her rock whistled past my ear, crashing against the back wall before I grabbed her wrist, whirling her around holding her tight to my body with her back to my front, locking her arms to her sides with one of mine.

"I have a story to tell you," I growled in her ear and she slammed her heel down on my foot, but she didn't hold the strength she needed to fight me off. "We're stuck here together tonight one way or the other, lightwing, so you may as well hear it."

"I want nothing from you," she spat. "Let go of me."

I did so, snatching her slingshot and pocketing it for good measure. She seethed at me, taking hold of the Dragon amulet at her throat and my brows arched as I spotted the Unicorn nestled there beside the Raven.

"Dragon," she called. "Please help me."

I glanced warily around, her desperation to escape me leading her to a maddened plan. Was she going to risk a night in the forest just to evade me?

The Dragon didn't come and the tension ran from my shoulders as a twisted smile found its way to my lips instead. No, she had not yet gotten control over it. So tonight at least, she was mine.

"Well, it looks like it's just you and me then, lightwing," I said with a taunting smile.

Ferris turned and sprinted up the stairs, fleeing deeper into the tower.

I followed with lazy steps, catching up to her when I made it to a large circular room with a wooden floor and a broken staircase that led to the next level. There were no more doors in here, no place to escape to and Ferris realised that as she twisted to face me once more, her face paling of colour.

"If I wanted you dead I'd have done it ten times over by now," I said darkly and her throat bobbed as she absorbed those words. I wanted to calm the riot in her flesh, despising how she glared at me, how firmly her walls had come up, but there was no stopping the path we were on.

"What *do* you want then?" she demanded, her hand going to her amulets and gripping them protectively. But she knew I couldn't kill her and take them for my own. Even if I could, there was no chance of that now. Ferris Creed had become far too precious to me in ways I doubted she would ever believe.

"I want to offer you the truth. All of it," I said earnestly.

"I don't care what you have to say. You're a monster," she hissed and I tilted my head down, darkness rolling from me in a tide I couldn't control at that assessment. I didn't care for the way Rathian looked at me, but her? I couldn't bear that judgement in her eyes.

Death seeped from me into the floorboards in an uncontrollable wave and they groaned and cracked as they felt its touch. Then it crawled up the walls and made the moss there shiver and wilt, the bricks drying out, the mortar crumbling.

"What are you doing?" Ferris breathed in horror.

I scrunched my eyes closed, trying to reign in the death pouring from me, retreating from my human as it crawled out towards her.

"Get back!" I barked and she heeded my command, pressing herself to the wall on the other side of the room. Fuck, I had not meant to put her in danger. I was meant to protect her. But this power in me was wild as ever.

"Stop," she gasped as the roof groaned above us and the tower shuddered while death seeped into every crevice it could find between the bricks.

"I'm trying," I gritted out through my teeth, desperate to get a hold on it. It couldn't take her from me. Not *her*. "The dark is so very fucking deep right now."

The walls shivered as if they might buckle and Ferris yelled out in panic, "Stop it, please. I'll listen to whatever you have to say, just stop!"

Something about the fear in her words managed to gutter out the death spilling from me. I took a heavy breath as the weight of destruction settled back inside me and my gaze fell to her violet eyes in relief.

"Speak then," she said icily. "Though it will change nothing. The moment dawn comes, I will run from you and never look back."

The hatred in her gaze clawed at a ragged wound in my chest. I'd known this day would come, but I hadn't known I would be so attached to this woman when it did. I couldn't have predicted how viscerally her hatred would cut through me. How much it would scar my heart.

Perhaps she was right. These words were futile. But I felt, in a way, I owed them to her. No living soul had heard this story before, not from my lips. And perhaps none ever would again. But if there was to be one who listened, let it be her. Even if it changed nothing in the end.

"I never lied," I repeated. "Omitted truths? Yes."

"Your name isn't Hendrix Draven," she hissed. "There is lie number one."

"Ah, but that name does belong to me. I was born Hendrix Bane, but my mother was a Draven before she wed my father."

Ferris glared at me. "So you twisted the truth, that is equal to a lie in my eyes."

"Alright," I conceded. "And…well, I supposed I lied another time too now that I think on it."

She blew out a breath through her nose. "In case you hadn't realised, this little speech isn't going well for you, Necromancer."

The coldness in her tone was nearly as crushing as the terror in her gaze. But all I could do in answer to it was offer my story and let her judgement fall how it would. I side-stepped, moving a little closer but she mirrored me, moving the other way, evading me like we were opposing magnets. But surely she knew were the opposite. We'd been drawn to each other these past weeks. It was undeniable. I'd lived long enough to know desire in a woman when I found it aimed at me. And never had I felt such want as I had from her. It matched my own in its volatility, its rawness.

"My second lie was about this." I tapped the mark on my temple, a roiling tempest rising inside me as I recalled the moment I was given it. "I told you that there were hundreds of Fae outcast from Rivenspire. That was not true. It is rare."

"I should have known," she muttered, emotion burning through her features that spoke of betrayal once again. "Your kind can never be trusted."

"I think you might be right about that," I agreed in a dark tone, stepping left again and she did the same to keep space between us.

"You betrayed your own people," she accused.

"For reasons you might understand if you would only listen," I urged and her jaw flexed.

"How can I believe a word that leaves your rotten mouth? You manipulated me. You used me. You told me things to make me feel sorry for you. That bullshit about your family-"

"Do not dare speak a word about my family!" I bellowed, the floorboards shuddering under the tenor of my voice as I lost control at her dismissal of their brutal executions. "I did not speak a single word of a lie about their deaths. The Coterie executed them for my crime. They were killed before my eyes, their dying screams still haunt me to this fucking day. Every time I close my eyes I see it. Every time I try to sleep, I dream of it. That was no lie. Don't you ever suggest it to be so again."

Ferris nodded mutely, her cheeks as white as ice and her eyes unblinking. "So let me guess the rest of your story," she said, her soft voice growing harder as she spoke. "You somehow raised an army of the dead and let it sweep through Rathian. You let innocents die violent deaths as an answer to the wrongs done against you. You have let hundreds die. You have unleashed a plague upon our already cursed land and you expect me to what? Forgive you for it?" Her brow creased and tears blazed in her eyes but she didn't let them fall.

She didn't want to see any other reality than the one that everyone else believed. It was futile to answer her but I did. Because the path I was walking was one that would lead me into the waiting arms of Death anyway. She was the last person who might ever listen to my story. And though she didn't want to hear it, for my own selfish gain, I was going to make her listen. Let my tale be told so that I might go into the ground all the more restfully knowing that at least one living creature had known the truth. Whether she believed it or not.

"No, I don't want your forgiveness," I said hollowly, giving up on trying to close the distance between us and instead turning to face the glass window that looked out over the forest. I could just make out the shadow of the Great Elm in the distance, but the night was pressing in thickly, like a blanket of black silk had been laid over the canopy.

"It is partly true what they say about me. I killed King Arthrun, but I did not covet the crown. I only wished for a new reign to come. Arthrun had been seated on the throne for hundreds of years – far longer than any other ruler before him but Providence had never come to select a new monarch. There was something gravely wrong about that. Everyone whispered of it. My mother was sure there was more to it than what he told the kingdom. He declared himself the Last King; the one Providence had promised to select one day for an eternal reign of peace. But Arthrun was greedy and cruel. And once I found myself old enough to join the Coterie and was welcomed into the fold, I saw what my mother had whispered to me of. Arthrun liked his blood sports. He had humans taken from their beds, stolen away in the night to partake in his twisted games."

Ferris looked revulsed at that and I nodded gravely. "He did the same to any 'lesser' Fae he took a disliking to. It was ritualistic sadism, all carried out in the name of the spirits. Arthrun would have the Coterie pray to them and declare his bloodshed an offering to their supremacy. And all the while, I saw the sick and bitter truth beneath his lies. All I know of the spirits is purity, they are not creatures who demand torture for their own gain. Not even Death herself covets such things. No, that is the desire of sick bastards like Arthrun. Fae with too much power and too much time on their hands."

I took a heavy breath to calm my wrath, waiting to see if Ferris might comment on what I'd said but she remained silent. So I continued.

"Years went by where I was forced to keep the company of the most cruel Fae among the Coterie. My parents shuddered at what they saw, but neither said a word. For to speak out against the king was to find yourself placed into the execution pit yourself. But the more time passed, the more I could not stand what I witnessed. I could no longer stay my hand and pretend to go along with it, pretend to be one of them. Something had to be done."

"So you killed him," Ferris whispered at last and I sensed that she was closer to me than she had been before. But I didn't look around.

"Yes," I growled. "And I do not regret it. Not for a second. That monster needed to be dealt with. Providence would not have chosen him as the Last King and even if he had, I would rather deal with his wrath over the heinous creature he had placed on the throne.

So I trained in secret for the task. I studied the king's palace meticulously – it's a hallowed place, built on the bones of an ancient monster that was slain by the very first Fae royal to be selected by Providence. I studied every door of that palace, every window, every avenue I could take in my plot to assassinate him. And when the night came, I snuck into his quarters and attempted to kill him in his sleep. But he woke before I could strike him and we fell into a bloody battle before I managed to drive a dagger into his heart. In that moment I saw something. Something I still do not understand to this day..."

"What was it?" Ferris pressed, like she was hanging on every word I spoke now.

"Providence," I said thickly. "Just for a moment, a glimmer of him in the living quarters beyond the king's bed chamber. All I saw was a strange grey haze around the spirit then a blaze of violet ignited in his gaze, those bright cat's eyes I'd heard all the songs about gleaming from his feline face. He was there, then gone into that grey mist. And to this day, I do not understand why."

I fell quiet and so did Ferris, the silence passing between us broken only by the howling wind that whipped around the tower.

"I took his crown," I said eventually, shattering the quiet like my fist through glass. "I took it and ran – that crown holds a fierce power and I did not want one of the Coterie to claim it. But when I found my way out of the palace, I accidently alerted a guard as I made it to the outer wall. The cries were already going up in the palace. The king had been found. Blood soaked my chest, my hands and the guard who saw me put two and two together. I felled him with a heavy punch to the head, but I should have killed him even though he was an innocent. Had I done so, I may never have been caught. My family may never have been executed. That guard's death might have stopped the axe of fate from falling how it did. But..." I trailed off. I'd gone over that night in my mind so many times, seeing all the ways I might have prevented what had come next. But there was no undoing the past. The coins had settled where they had fallen, meeting heavily with the hand of fate and binding themselves to it.

"I hid the crown," I muttered. "It still lays in that place to this day. Buried somewhere in the trees that spread away from the palace walls, though the exact location is a blur. I suppose it doesn't matter now anyway."

"No," Ferris agreed quietly. "So…you were caught?"

"Yes. And you know the rest. But what you don't know is what happened *after* my family were killed while I knelt there in that stone courtyard with all the world ripped away from me. The Art of speaking to the dead had been my gift from the spirits, but it twisted that day. I called out for Death to assist me, begging her to answer my plea. And she came. Death herself took my hand and spoke in my ear, words that crossed from the afterworld to this plane of the living. '*You are death and death is thee.*' I felt her power pour into my heart, awakening a terrible force that rattled through my flesh and burrowed into my bones.

The spirit of Death's power latched itself to my Art, mutilating and warping it into some new, deeper, darker magic. And these marks appeared upon my neck, inked there by the shadow of Death herself." I gestured to the bony hands that were tattooed around my throat. "Then…the dead around me began to wake. I wielded this new strength and dragged my family back from death, somehow tearing their souls from the grip of the afterworld and lashing them back to their bodies. In terrified, delighted wonder I watched as they rose to their feet while the Fae who had come to witness their executions screamed in bloody horror. But they were not as they had once been. They were ravenous in their wrath, my mother, father, sister and brother racing out to kill all those who stood close, tearing at their enemies with nothing but their hands. Any who met with death joined their army, bowing to the destructive revenge I had so desperately wanted to reap. They answered to the call of my ragged heart that day, every kill another solider turned to my will. And the death they harvested was great.

"I still recall how Islasees Bellatorn turned and fled from the tide of Hollows I'd sent after him, the very man who had wielded the knife that had silenced my mother's screams. The one who had watched in dark glee as his soldiers beat my father into a silent grave, who had commanded that my sister and brother followed them into death. He who had placed the outcast mark upon my flesh. I bellowed a vow to the spirit of Death, promising I would hand Islasees's wretched soul to her myself. But then the power she had offered me began to wane, I lost my grip on it and could not guide it like I had at first. It still spilled from me in a tide, flowing in every direction and I couldn't stop it. Like it was chasing every drop of life around it, determined to snuff it out.

"My family came to me, surrounding me with bloodshot eyes and ice-white features and as they drew me to my feet and my mother whispered, 'you must flee.'"

My hands fisted on the narrow windowsill as I let all the pain of that day pour out.

"What happened next?" Ferris asked, her voice a raspy plea to know the end.

"Islasees gathered his ranks. His army met with that of my Hollow creations and a brutal war was fought between them. But Islasees only had eyes for me. He chased us, me and my family, hounding us towards the edge of Rivenspire until we were forced to abandon the only home we had ever known. Since that day, I have had little control over the Hollows at all. Sometimes I can will them here and there when the power gets it claws in me but..." I shrugged. "Death comes and goes like the tide. It leaks from me unbidden and creates more Hollows who sew more death wherever they may go."

A heaviness hung in the air at my words, shaking the foundations of everything we had built our shaky alliance upon. This was my olive branch, the only one I had to extend. And she might refuse here and now.

"What happened to your family?" Ferris asked. She was closer again, drawn to me by some madness and I was tempted to turn to her and pull her near – but she would only cringe away now that she knew what I was.

"They wait for me in the Blight," I said thickly. "They have remained at my side ever since that day, caught in the grip of death yet unable to leave this world. At first, I thought they were truly back from death, but over time I saw that they were not. Part of them is here and part of them is in the afterworld. They've lost their spark, their desire to live but still they linger here in some half form that is not enough to sate them. They cannot even perish as the other Hollows are able to. I have pleaded with Death herself to return them to me fully or to allow them to pass into death at last. But there is only one way to release them from my curse."

"The boon," Ferris breathed and she laid a hand on my back.

I stilled, confused by her touch, how she reached for me when I was baring my deplorable soul to her.

"It is my only hope to free them," I admitted.

"It's my only hope to free Rissa too," Ferris answered and my chest hollowed out.

I turned to her as her hand fell to her side and my heart sank at the broken look on her face.

"Only one of us can have their wish fulfilled, lightwing," I said darkly, reaching for the amulets at her throat and brushing my fingers over the spirits she'd won for herself.

She took my hand, gripping it as if making some deal with me and I ached to draw her into the cage of my arms, but I remained rigid, uncertain how we would move forward from here, or if we would do so at all.

"Our trust is shattered," she admitted and my throat thickened. "But…"

Everything hung on that word, every fragment of my being waiting to hear the next words to pass her lips.

"Some foolish part of me is telling me I am right where I'm supposed to be."

"Then stay," I gritted out, aching for her to do so down to the roots of my very being.

Her hand tightened on mine, a firmness to her fingers telling me she was in charge in that moment. "If I choose to leave, will you stop me?"

"Yes," I said roughly, knowing it was so, casting all lies aside and giving her the ugly reality of what I was.

She nodded slowly, her fingers falling from mine and a roiling storm of tension rising between us. "Then I guess I'm staying."

At that declaration, the dark power of death receded inside me, somehow dispelled by it. But I couldn't fathom how such a little thing could hold sway over the tumult of death that had been pouring from me.

"Tonight or forever?" I smirked, relieved to feel the oppressive aura lifting from my soul at last.

"I'm not sure," she answered, her throat rising and falling as I stepped deeper into her personal space.

I released her hand and trailed my fingers over her throat, a growl of want rising at her touch. "Let's focus on tonight for now."

"Alright," she agreed, stepping closer to me, desire rising between us as tension corded the air, threading it with unspoken words.

I'd never felt drawn to anyone like this before. And something about the way the air was shifting and how her eyes were trained on mine told me everything was about to change for us. It was as certain as the sun rising upon the dawn.

FERRIS

CHAPTER THIRTY NINE

Hendrix grasped my face between his hands and kissed me so forcefully that my entire world narrowed down to that point of contact between us. My fingers curled around his wrists, holding him right there in that place, dragging him to me in case there were any lingering doubts that this was what I wanted.

Because despite me knowing the full truth to the darkness in him, despite me realising the entire breadth of who and what he was, my want for him hadn't lessened at all.

If this was insanity then I would gladly be carted away for it, locked in some dark space to forever dwell on the feeling of his mouth against mine, his aura surrounding me like a blanket of shadow and heartache, my own reaching out to combine with his and join in its pain.

And this *was* pain. This connection between us burned with so many hurts and wounds which we'd both suffered, so much injustice and despair, the agony in our hearts so sharp it cut us open to bleed into one another. Yet his pain was somehow a balm to my own, the hurt and want and loneliness he had endured in it a mirror to the aches of my own soul. And as our kiss deepened and his dark power roamed wild around us, I only found myself needing more of it.

Hendrix's fingers pushed into the silver strands of my hair, electric energy spilling in spikes of teal that cast light through the darkness of his lethal power and somehow held it at bay.

"All those times I was drawn to the forest and denied it," he cursed against my lips. "Only to find that it was *you* I was aching for all along. I should have come here sooner."

"No," I said roughly, my gaze rising to meet with his, the shadows in the room making his eyes appear the darkest I'd ever seen them but there was a vibrancy to them too, a spark of life which I hadn't even realised he'd been missing until I found its focus pinned on me. "I wasn't me in all those past lives. The woman who lived twelve times before failed in every single attempt to come here and face this destiny. I'm not like them. I won't fail. And no other version of myself would have been the one who is standing here with you now."

"Then I am glad to have waited six-hundred years to come seeking you, lightwing, for no other creature has ever captivated me the way you have and I am wholly convinced that you were worth the wait."

"I think it's time we both stopped waiting then." I stepped away, breaking from him and he hounded after me, backing me up towards the wall while I unfastened the buttons of my tunic, his gaze devouring the movements as I tugged, one, two, three of them free-

Hendrix grabbed hold of me, driving me back so that my spine collided with the rough stone of the wall and taking my wrists into his grasp before pinning them above my head.

I gasped and his mouth collided with mine as he devoured the sound, his free hand gripping my jaw so that he could tilt my head back to meet with his. I pushed up onto my tiptoes, aching to close the distance between our bodies, his huge frame consuming me in its shadow, his powerful body pinning me against the hard stone.

The full length of his cock drove against me in urgent want, straining at his fly, his want for me so visceral I could taste it on the air I gasped down between his ravenous kisses.

His tongue sank between my lips and I moaned, my spine arching so that I could press myself more firmly to him, feeling every hard plain of his body and wanting to explore each inch of it at leisure.

Hendrix's hand slipped from my jaw down my throat and to the neck of my tunic. He groaned into my mouth as he slowly began to unfasten the rest of my buttons, his fingertips rough against my skin as they brushed my flesh.

He kept going at that torturously slow pace, his body coiled with tension and his power thick in the air as if he was working hard to restrain himself but I didn't want him holding back with me. I wanted every rough edge, every piece of his strength.

He tugged my tunic off of my left shoulder, releasing my breast and I moaned loudly as his hand finally found the rounded flesh, his fingers tugging on my hardened nipple and sending a jolt of heat directly to my core.

But he was still holding himself back, his touch more of a caress than a claim.

I broke our kiss, my teeth tugging at his bottom lip and drawing a growl from the back of his throat as I stared up at him, panting with want and a determined need.

"I won't break," I said roughly. "So don't treat me like I will."

"I'm Fae, lightwing," he growled, his chest heaving, that restraint so close to snapping in his gaze. "Your kind and mine are not built the same. I can't bear it if I hurt you. I can't be the cause of your pain-"

"Then stop holding back," I demanded, flexing against his hold on me, tugging at my wrists and forcing him to tighten his grip to keep me in place beneath him. "I want you, Hendrix Bane," I said roughly. "I want you in all of your darkness and corruption, I want you in the depths of your strength. I have lived thirteen times over and have been waiting for you in every one of those lifetimes. I don't have to remember them to know that's true because I can feel it. Can't you?"

"Yes, lightwing. I feel it," he said, his mouth inching closer to mine, the fragile control he was maintaining on himself threatening to shatter. And oh, how I wanted it to shatter.

"Then don't make me wait any longer," I demanded and at last, he broke for me.

Hendrix kissed me so hard that there was no space for even a breath of air between us, his tongue invading my mouth, his body crushing me to the wall while his grip on my wrists tightened to the point of pain.

I moaned loudly, the need in my flesh all consuming, my breasts aching for his touch, my cunt so slick and wanting that I grew desperate for him to sate that haunting want. I'd been thinking of this moment from the second I'd laid eyes on him, devouring the sight of him, drinking in fantasy after fantasy and never once allowing myself to admit such a thing, even within the confines of my own mind. But we'd stripped ourselves bare in this place, set aside all lingering lies, given up our most harrowing truths. The only thing left wanting was this. Him and me. The biggest lie we'd both been guilty of, the one I was most eager to shatter.

Hendrix dropped his hold on my wrists, hauling me into his arms where I knotted my legs around his waist and arched my back against the wall so that I could feel the hard ridge of his cock riding over my clit.

I almost fell apart at that single, wicked point of friction, wanting to give in to the building pleasure which my body already knew he would be wringing from every piece of me this night.

He gripped the sides of my tunic and ripped it down my arms, baring my breasts entirely and dropping his mouth to capture one of my nipples between his teeth.

I cried out as he bit me, a sinful jolt of pleasure spearing from the point of pain to my core just as I ground myself against his cock again, tension coiling in my flesh so tightly I could hardly draw breath.

Hendrix cursed at the sound which spilled from my lips, gripping my ass in his hands and rocking my hips again, the rough fabric of my trousers where it was caught between my clit and his cock creating a beautiful friction which had me moaning even louder.

"Oh lightwing," he groaned, rocking my hips again. "You're making this too fucking easy for me."

My hands landed on his shoulders as he leaned back, my fingers knotting in the fabric of his tunic and tugging as I tried to haul it off of him. But as I made to drag it upwards, he rocked my hips again, the friction between us almost too much to bear.

"Wait," I gasped, trying to tug his tunic off of him but he only repeated the movement, faster, harder, the length of his cock providing the perfect pressure against my clit. It was happening too fast, too easily. I'd been wanting this for so long, while I'd been denying myself the pleasure of even satisfying those needs myself, refusing to admit what I'd been wanting from him and knowing that if I gave in to pleasuring myself to relieve this ache it would have only been this infuriating male on my mind while I did so.

So I'd buried this want, this *need*, for weeks. And now he was going to unburden me all too easily.

Hendrix leaned back further, rocking my hips so that my clit ground against his cock over and over again, gaining speed with each thrust, his gaze fixed on my breasts as they bounced at the motion. My hands fell to squeeze them and his eyes lit with a feral need as I tugged and teased at my nipples, relieving some of the ache in them while he only built me up higher and higher and-

A cry burst from my lips as I came for him, pleasure exploding through my body and burning its way across every inch of my flesh.

Sparks of teal electricity glistened in my hair, my cry echoing in

the hollow tower and his groan of need punctuating the heat which burned brightly throughout my soul.

Hendrix kissed me hard, keeping hold of me as he moved us away from the wall and instead lay me out on the floor beneath him.

My body felt boneless in the wake of the bliss he'd delivered but still I reached out, my fingers tugging at the hem of his tunic until he gave in with a dark laugh which promised me we were nowhere close to done.

I sucked in a breath as he threw the tunic aside, his dark hair falling over his shoulders, the skeletal hands which were inked around his throat seeming to inch lower and tighten on his skin as he swallowed thickly while drinking me in.

I lay panting beneath him, biting down on my bottom lip while surrounded by a swathe of silver hair and he took my ankle into his grip before deftly unlacing my boot.

The swirling vortex in his gaze told of his need to have me, the feral want in his expression filling me with a bravery I'd never fully felt while in a position such as this with any other. His gaze was a worship upon my flesh, his hunger a need to which I was the only thing that might sate him. I was the only thing in the world beneath his scrutiny, the only thing that mattered at all in the heat of his stare. And I knew that I was looking at him in exactly the same way.

My eyes drank in the powerful build of his body, the cut of his muscles nothing short of sinful where they carved across his abs and then dipped over his hipbones to delve beneath his trousers.

His cock was a rigid outline against the thin material which was straining and threatening to burst beneath the stress of his want for me. The size of it had my pulse racing, wetness pooling in my core, my flesh already desperate for more of the vicious delights I knew he was about to deliver to it.

"Stop stalling," I panted, my hands roaming down my body, teasing at my aching nipples again while he took far too long in tugging my other boot free.

"Just enjoying the view," he replied, his voice dark and wanting, his eyes pinned on my movements just as mine were pinned on his.

I cursed him and slid my hands down my body so that I could tug at the ties of my trousers, pushing a hand inside them the moment they were free and moaning loudly as my fingers dragged over my throbbing clit. Then lower, a ragged exhale escaping me as I arched my spine and pushed my fingers inside my cunt, soaking them with my wetness and offering up a hint of the pleasure I was so aching for.

Hendrix growled in an utterly animalistic sound, falling too still, in a way that was all Fae and not human at all. I met his gaze as I drove my fingers in deeper, a challenge bright in my eyes as I gave my body a taste of what it wanted, sighing loudly and arching my spine into the movement, though I knew I wouldn't come close to satisfaction until it was him in my place.

"You should not have done that," he warned and I gasped as he caught the ends of my trousers and tugged them so hard that I was yanked almost into his lap by the movement, my ass hitting his knees where they pressed to the floor.

My hand was still buried in my undergarments, my fingers driven deeper inside me by the jerk of motion. I whimpered beneath him before drawing them out and circling my clit with them instead, my wetness making the sensation all the better.

Hendrix caught my wrist and tugged my hand free, lifting it to his mouth and capturing those same fingers between his lips. He sucked on them hard, his tongue driving between them and licking firmly, his eyes on mine with nothing but promise in them.

I cursed, my heart fluttering like a butterfly's wings in my chest at the warning in his gaze.

I tried to push up onto my elbows, reaching for him, wanting to touch him, explore his scars, paint the lines of his tattoos with my fingertips. But in the same moment he released my fingers from his mouth and took hold of my hips, flipping me over so that my knees struck the wooden floorboards, my silver hair falling like a shroud around my face.

"Hendrix," I begged, bracing on my forearms in anticipation of his cock, but in place of it he gripped the backs of my thighs and widened them before dropping his mouth to my core. Hendrix gave me a kiss which was enough to break my world apart into so many shattered pieces that I knew it would never fit back together in the same way again.

I cried out as he buried his face against me, his tongue dragging over my clit before roaming backwards and sinking inside of me. No one had ever done such a thing to me before but I knew with that single action that even if a hundred men had attempted it before him, none would have come close to doing what he did with that wicked mouth of his.

I fell forward, my chest striking the wood, hands grasping either side of me and fingernails biting into the floorboards as his grip held my ass up and he drove his tongue even deeper inside me.

The noises I made were worse than sinful, they were depraved, delighted and utterly immoral. And if I died right there in that moment with my nipples grazing the rotting floorboards of a tower in the heart of the cursed forest and my cunt being devoured by a male known to be the worst Fae that had ever lived, then I would go willingly into death without a single regret. Because I was tasting pleasure which surely wasn't meant for the living, I was committing a sin which couldn't possibly have deserved such bliss as its reward.

Hendrix groaned against my clit, lapping it hungrily while I fought to remember to breathe between the waves of ecstasy that were consuming me entirely.

He tilted my ass higher, sucking my clit between his lips and *tugging*.

I came with a cry which should have felled the tower around us, my elbows biting into the wooden floor as I arched back and threw my head to the sky in a veritable howl. My body was an explosion of pleasure, my head spinning, vision darkening but he hadn't stopped.

"Hendrix," I begged, my nails ripping into the wooden floorboards as I tried to haul myself out of his grasp because I couldn't take any more. My body was wrung out, my breaths were ragged and choked in my throat and my body was humming with a bliss so pure I knew it couldn't get better than this.

"Ferris," he replied in a rough grow, his mouth still pressed to my clit, nothing but a warning to my name.

He released his hold on one of my thighs and for a moment I thought he would let me slump to the floor in a puddle, give me a second to breathe, to think, to-

I swore as he drove two fingers inside me and sucked my clit between his teeth in the same movement.

My body was already spent, my flesh nothing but an instrument which played to his tune no matter how certain I was that I couldn't take any more of it. And as he fucked me with his hand and kept my clit clasped in the cage of his teeth I came again, harder and rougher than before, my cry more of a scream, my cunt gripping his fingers tight as if caging them inside me. But still he moved them, curling them and driving them deeper until the pleasure he was feasting on devoured me again.

Tears burned the corners of my eyes as I gave in to the intensity of his power over me, my body a willing prisoner to his delicious torture.

He withdrew his fingers, lapping at my wetness while pulling back and finally releasing his hold on my thigh so that I could slump fully to the floor beneath him.

Hendrix chuckled darkly as he rolled me onto my back and I lay there beneath him, utterly destroyed before he'd even begun to take his own pleasure.

"Give me…a moment," I panted, making him laugh harder and the sound unlocked something deep within my soul, making it sing

in the echoes of my climax. When had he last known a moment of happiness like this? When had he last felt the touch of another?

I wanted to ask but I could hardly make the thoughts fall into line in the wake of all he'd done to me and instead I watched as he stood and finally started to remove the rest of his clothes.

I fought back a curse as he removed his boots and socks first, still making me wait until finally, all too slowly, he unfastened his trousers and pushed them off too.

My mouth dried out as I took in the sight of his cock which sprung free with eager rigidity. If I'd thought it was big when appreciating its outline through his clothes then I'd known nothing of its truth.

A bead of moisture glistened at its tip, veins standing out along the heady length of his shaft and as he closed his fist around its girth and gave it a luxurious stroke, I almost begged him to let me take his place.

I whimpered as I watched him, knowing he was torturing me just as I'd done to him. My mouth watered as I drank in his movements and I couldn't help but wonder what he might taste like if I took him to the back of my throat.

"Up," Hendrix commanded and I was so deeply intoxicated in the spell of him that I didn't even have a disparaging retort for the demand.

I forced my leaden limbs to obey, wondering if I could truly take any more of this decadent pleasure, while knowing I needed to feel the fullness of him inside me just as certainly as I needed air to breathe.

Hendrix gave me that fucking smirk as he pointed me towards a table which sat against the far wall, his eyes alight with that heavy restraint once more as he stared at the movements of my naked body. He was going to break. And when he did I wasn't wholly sure I'd survive it. But there was no part of me that would even consider backing out now.

I obeyed him, knowing I'd live to regret it but unable to care about dominance or his alpha bullshit because if the look on his face was anything to go by then I would be nothing but rewarded for my compliance.

My ass hit the table and I gripped the edges of it as I pushed myself up to sit on it, my thighs pressed together and chest still heaving with exertion - though I was fairly certain all I'd done was fall prey to his possession.

He remained in place by the wall, his eyes devouring me as I lifted my gaze to meet his and I forced myself to raise my chin with a confidence I wasn't certain I felt.

"Well?" I asked, tilting my head so my silver hair fell over my shoulder and concealed one breast from view. "Is that all you've got?"

Hendrix was on me in a heartbeat, his hands closing around my waist as he drove me further back onto the table, his lips colliding with mine as a rough and commanding growl slid between us.

Every difference between the Fae and humans was clear in him. He was so powerful, so strong, his power flaring around us and crawling up the wall at his back, making the stone quake and wood groan as the rush of emotions made it spill from him. But not one drop of his death magic touched me.

He kissed me hard, fingers knotting in my hair as he bore down on me, the taste of my own pleasure on his lips making my heart riot in my chest because I had never known anything like this male before. He was a force of nature, a magnet drawing me in, my opposite and my equal. Everything in my body was screaming at me to lay my claim on him and never give it up no matter how little sense we might make in the world beyond this moment.

Any pretence at restraint fell away as he kissed me, any attempt to be gentle forgotten as he lost himself in the heat between us as certainly as I'd been lost from the moment his mouth had met with mine.

Hendrix gripped my thighs and shoved them apart before tugging me to the edge of the table, his mouth roaming from my lips to my throat.

The tip of his cock butted against my entrance and I bit down on my bottom lip as my body throbbed with a want so consuming I could think of nothing else.

I wound my arms around him, one hand fisting in his long hair while his teeth sank into a spot just beneath my ear and the other roaming up the wide plain of his back, his muscles flexing beneath my touch.

My nipples grazed the bare skin of his chest as we crushed ourselves together and then his hips were driving forward, his cock breaching my entrance and a desperate plea spilling from my lips.

"More," I begged as he sank in to me, inch after inch stretching me open and finally finding his place at my core.

"So fucking wet," he groaned into my neck, his fingers bruising where they drove into my thighs. "So fucking tight."

I garbled some noise in reply but the feel of his cock pushing into me was taking up every beat of my heart, every breath in my lungs, every thought in my mind. He was so big. It should have hurt for him to be stretching me the way he was, but he was right in praising my wetness. My cunt was utterly soaked in anticipation of him and every inch that he conquered inside my body was nothing short of bewitching because it was casting me under a spell I never wished to wake from.

Deeper and deeper he pressed into me, his muscles bunched with tension as he forced himself to take me slowly, languishing in the feeling of my cunt welcoming him home.

When he was finally sheathed to the hilt, I released a heady exhale and he lifted his gaze to meet with mine.

"If you thought there was ever a chance of me letting you go before this, then know now that I never will," he panted, drinking me in, holding me tight, his cock so deep inside me that I couldn't summon words even if I'd been able to think of any. "You're mine, lightwing. And I'm going to show you how I plan on worshipping you from this moment until my last."

A cry broke from me as he drew back then slammed into me again, the fullness within me sharpening with the thrust and everything inside me zeroing in on that contact between our bodies.

Hendrix cursed as he started to fuck me harder, the table beneath us thumping the wall and groaning beneath the force of his passion.

I clung to him, crying out with every thrust, my heels digging into his ass, my fingernails carving into his back.

Deeper and deeper he pushed, dust spilling from the walls as the mortar was knocked loose from the strikes of the table against it. He was frantic, feral and all-consuming in his lust for me, his mouth worshipping mine with a passion so intense it was bruising.

He drove forward again, knocking me onto my back and looming over me, his hands tangling in my hair, kneading my breasts, squeezing my ass and I was exploring his body just as desperately.

His cock drove into me so deeply that it forced the air from my lungs with each strike and I arched my spine up, gripping his ass to steal more and more of that divine pleasure.

"Bane," I gasped between kisses and he pulled back, his pupils dilating at my use of that name, the one people hissed in curses all over Rathian, the one which had become a title more than a name. But I claimed it as I was claiming him. He was my bane after all. And one I so willingly clung to.

"Fucking hell," he groaned, taking my leg and pushing it over his arm so that the shaft of his cock rode over my clit as he drove it into me again. "You really will be the ruin of me, lightwing."

I had no words for him because a few more thrusts in that position had me coming apart at the seams, my cunt so full that I could hardly bear the sensation of it tightening around him in climax, stars bursting before my eyes as I fell into the chokehold of the pleasure he demanded from me so thoroughly.

I cried out and he groaned, fucking me harder, faster, chasing my climax and forcing it to go on and on, ecstasy spiralling through my body and bursting from me in another explosion as he finally bellowed a roar and spilled himself deep inside me.

The table gave way with an almighty bang and Hendrix somehow managed to roll as we fell so that I landed on top of him, boneless and destroyed, his cock still buried inside me.

I collapsed onto his chest, our amulets tinkling as they tangled with each other, my cunt still pulsing around him, the echoes of that pleasure sinking into my bones where I suspected they'd linger on eternally.

Our ragged breaths filled the silence as his fingers painted intricate circles against my spine and as my eyes began to flutter shut, I noticed the way his magic was creeping up the walls all around us, making the tower groan and complain - though the structure still held its ground.

I wondered if it might all come crashing down on our heads while we slept. And I wondered if I should fear that dark power coming for me while I lingered in his arms.

But I didn't.

In the cage of his hold, I found myself at peace despite all I knew of who and what he was. And as the exhaustion in my bones called me towards slumber, I didn't resist it. Because Hendrix Bane may have been a monster to all of Rathian and beyond. But here in the dark, where we were alone, barring the amulets knotted at our throats, I found I didn't fear his claim on me at all.

I woke to the sound of Hendrix's deep breaths, his presence in my space so very apparent as always. I shouldn't have found comfort in the knowledge that he was close, shouldn't have been nursing an ache in my chest over the truth he'd shared with me or an ache in my body from the voracity of the possession he'd taken over my flesh but…

I lifted my head to watch him where he slept beneath me, neither of us having moved from the position we'd collapsed into after our fervid union.

I supposed he might have kept me close to make sure I'd be safe in the night – and that I couldn't run again without his knowledge. But I found myself believing he'd kept me there in his arms without motive. Simply not wanting to relinquish the distraction we'd stolen with one another in the dark.

But now daylight was shining through the gaps in the shutters and reality had reared its head to peer at us once more.

I supposed I was his captive. But I wasn't planning on running regardless.

I should have. Of course I should have. He was every foul and evil thing I'd feared for my entire life. He was horrors and hatred and power no being should ever hold sway over. But he was also the male who had saved me more times than I wished to admit. The male who had held me in the dark to keep me from freezing. The one who had hunted me through the trees when he should have been focused on the spirits. The one who had ravaged my body with such heated desire that I knew I'd never find pleasure in the company of some mere human man again. Not that I believed the way he'd unravelled my body had simply been because he was Fae. It was because he was Hendrix Bane and I'd become his creature now, one way or another.

I was a fool for finding something redeemable in him but maybe that was just how it was. I could accept such an assessment of myself, especially after having spent so many days in this forest. Of course he might have lied in the tale he'd told me but I found I didn't doubt a word of it. The raw emotion he'd expressed wasn't something that could be faked and the truth was that he had good reason to covet the boon. But so did I. And that was the one true divide left between us.

But whatever I may or may not be, and whatever we were to one another, the time had come for us to end the hunt. We had four days left to unite the amulets at the heart of the forest and we could only hope that all of them had been won by one Champion or another because we were out of time to seek more ourselves.

I bit my lip as a gnawing fear started up in the back of my mind – Hendrix had won three amulets just as I had. I was counting on Rissa delivering the Serpent more than ever at this point and I still feared there was a chance that another Champion could have found more spirits than either of us.

Islasees was out there, hunting Champions and spirits alike with the aid of his heinous brethren. It was such a Fae thing to do. So underhanded and conniving. Rage ate at me as I considered the possibility of a bastard like him stealing the boon out from under me at the final moment.

I had to fight to regain my composure, reminding myself that there was a good chance he hadn't found any more spirits and that, with Rissa's help, I would have four to my name. It would be enough.

"Hopefully," the Dragon mused and it did not sound at all convinced.

I eased back a little so that I could study Hendrix while he slept… or perhaps I should have been calling him Bane now? I had to admit the moniker suited him better somehow. It was darker, harsher, truer. I found I rather liked the taste of it on my tongue.

He was achingly handsome to look upon. I'd known it from the moment he'd first removed his mask and revealed his features to me but it was freeing to admit it so openly to myself while studying his strong features. There was certainly no point denying it while the ache of his cock claiming me still lingered between my thighs along with the seed he'd spilled inside me while gasping my name in frantic pleasure.

The outcast mark by his left eye was beautiful too, though I knew he hated it. But it spoke of a time which mattered greatly in his life, a change which had taken place and marked him on the inside profoundly, so I found it right that it had made its mark on the outside too. I supposed it was like my spirit marks in that way.

I carefully pushed myself upright and Bane opened his eyes as if he'd never been sleeping at all.

Had he felt my gaze lingering on his features? Had he been able to trace the pattern my thoughts were turning in?

I didn't know. And that was terrifying in itself. I'd heard countless rumours of the terrible magic the Necromancer possessed and I was too afraid of the answers to ask him the truth of them.

Perhaps he could read my thoughts the moment they sprung into my mind. Or knew my fears more intimately than I understood them myself. Maybe he'd been conversing with the dead about me, finding out my secrets from those I'd loved and lost. Though thankfully I hadn't been touched by death itself all too often in my lifetime. At least it hadn't taken anyone from me who knew me well enough to be able to divulge anything of use to him.

I reached out to brush my fingers along the lines of the tattoo on his face and his brow pinched, though he allowed me to do so.

"Good morning," I said, colour staining my cheeks and the edge of his mouth hooked into a smirk.

"That is the truest thing I think you've ever said to me," he agreed, lifting his hand to caress the curve of my bare ass, a trail of heat following the path of his fingers.

I swallowed thickly. It was sorely tempting to take another taste of his flesh, to feel the power of his body owning mine once more… But if last night was anything to go by then doing so would be anything but swift and we were already more than short on time as it was.

"We should probably not follow that line of thought," I said, disappointment colouring my tone.

"What thought was that exactly?" Bane asked, his hand trailing over my shoulder and skimming down my chest towards my peaked nipple.

He was already hard beneath me, his cock digging into my stomach, the temptation so very difficult to resist.

"Last night," I said in a rush as I followed those thoughts through to their obvious conclusion and realised something which should have occurred to me sooner.

"Yes? I remember it well," he teased and I knew he was going to make me say it. Every fucking bit of it.

"You...climaxed inside of me," I said, my cheeks now scarlet though truthfully that was the least of all the things he had done to my body.

"I remember that part particularly well," he agreed and I gasped as his other hand shifted between us, his fingers brushing over my clit in an offering I was all too close to taking him up on, but I needed to finish what I was asking him.

"Well, usually, I would take a tea after such...exertions...you know...in case of..."

I arched my brows at him and he smirked wider still, clearly planning on making me speak every part of it. I might have punched him but he chose that moment to push two fingers inside of me and I cursed instead, clutching his chest in surprise.

"Bane," I gasped and he truly smiled then.

"Say that again. That's fast becoming my new favourite sound on your lips, lightwing, especially when you say it with such wanton pleading."

I tried to go on but he rolled us over, flipping me onto my back and sinking his fingers deeper inside me, his thumb taking command of my clit. I forgot my trail of thought as he explored me with his hand, rubbing and flicking and pumping his fingers until I panted his name in an exhale of pleasure and he stole the taste of it from my lips with a hard kiss.

"Don't worry, pretty lightwing," he breathed into my ear as I lay there panting beneath him. "My kind don't reproduce easily and never with humans. It can't happen. So you can enjoy the pleasures of my cock as often as you want it without having to fear ending up with a babe inside your womb for the trouble."

His words filled me with relief because truly I hadn't been able to stop thinking about the fact that I wouldn't find the necessary ingredients for the tea I required in these trees. And I knew I wasn't going to be much good at resisting the temptation of his body regardless of that concern.

Bane gave me a lingering look as I lay there beneath him, clearly seeing that I was no longer capable of denying him anything and instead forcing himself to move back with an irritable sigh.

"I would love nothing more than to spend the day buried to the hilt inside of you, lightwing, but I fear we need to focus our efforts on other *exertions* as you call them – at least until night falls again and we find ourselves trapped in the dark once more."

I nodded, seeing the sense to his words even though my body was very much in favour of ignoring it. But he was right. I needed to focus on finishing my task here.

Bane called the Bear from its amulet, commanding the sprit to provide us with water so that we could bathe and refresh ourselves. I was glad of how cold it was as I faced the wall to clean my body though the marks on my skin didn't fade regardless. I dressed quickly and was glad to find Bane had done so too, making it easier for me to concentrate on what we needed to do next.

Bane's eyes tracked my movements as I took hold of my pack and drew it closer, the corner of his lips quirking as I tugged my Fae book free of its place.

"Always seeking answers from crusty old pages," he commented.

"Not answers," I retorted. "But I will forever research the chaos before me in hopes of it making more sense when I'm faced with it."

"And what particular brand of chaos are you researching on this fine morning, lightwing?" he purred, his tone of voice making me swallow impulsively.

"The Great Elm," I said, trying not to show the moment of disquiet though he already knew how keenly he affected me.

I opened the page at the very back of the book, the final chapter in this tome on the cursed forest.

"The Great Elm is said to be in mourning," I read, my gaze devouring the words, my fingers caressing the beautifully inked pages. "For the curse stole the minds of her children and along with it, their love."

"I heard she was the one who spun the curse in the first place," Hendrix interrupted.

"Why would she do that?" I asked, frowning at him over the top of my book.

"Why do any of the spirits do any damn thing? Why did Death choose to mark me as her servant instead of taking me into her grasp? Why has Providence allowed the Fae crown to go without placement for hundreds of years? Why do they sing in the sky or dance in the rain? Why choose some for blessings and others for curses? They are and always have been without any true purpose that I can define. They seem not to care for what is good or right or just or fair, neither do they revel in what is cruel or vicious, hurtful or callous. They just are – and trying to understand their purpose is a fool's errand which I refuse to be drawn into."

"Fine." I snapped my book closed and stood. "You want to deal in facts? Then here are some which I have spent the night thinking on. We have taken ownership of six of the thirteen spirits between the two of us and I think it highly doubtful that any other Champion will have managed to claim so many which means we are the most likely candidates to qualify for the boon. I have hunted the haunts of both the Phoenix and the Stag – which you were present for - to no avail and so believe they have been won by others. We know that the Tiger and the Rat were taken by your Fae friend-"

"Do not even jest about me and that male having any form of

kinship," Bane growled, the sound making the hairs along the back of my neck raise in warning.

I squared my shoulders as if priming for a fight but forced a long exhale instead.

"Fine. I didn't mean to suggest you held any care for him and I know that your confrontation with him will be unpleasant but it also cannot be avoided any longer. We have four days left before the curse consumes us and we are lost to this place. It's time we head for the Great Elm and hope that all of the other spirits are on their way there too. If we find any to be missing then perhaps I will be able to hunt them out with the aid of the Dragon before our time lapses entirely."

A low grumble in the back of my head made it clear the Dragon was not on board with that plan and I fought a cringe. I didn't want Bane to know that I was currently unable to call on any of my spirits for help thanks to my mistake in enraging the Dragon and I only hoped that I would be able to convince it to work with me again before we made it to the labyrinth and whatever challenges awaited us there.

I frowned as I thought on the boon. Clearly Bane needed it as desperately as I did but my understanding of the forest's favour was that only one Champion could earn it. And as much as my heart hurt to think of all he and his family had suffered, he had gotten them back. Rissa hadn't even had her chance at a real life. She'd been a child when she'd been taken and no matter what I felt towards Bane, I wasn't going to change my mind on what I'd come here to do. Nothing was as important to me as that.

"Can we agree to work together at least until it becomes clear that only one of us is able to proceed?" Bane asked, seeming to read the way my thoughts had wandered and clearly not wanting to broach the issue of which one of us would win the boon in the end.

Neither of us could kill the other for our amulets but we could offer them up willingly. I would sooner die than do so and forgo my sister's freedom however, so there was no point in me getting into that discussion with him. No doubt he felt the same way about offering me the amulets he had won – even if they should have been mine in all fairness.

I felt that same bitterness rising in me again but I stamped it down. It would do me no good now anyway.

No, both of us would have to hope that we could convince whichever other Champions made it to the labyrinth to offer up their amulets to us. If I got lucky then there might be some humans still alive who had managed to find one or two of them. They would certainly favour giving them up to a human over a Fae. And the one Fae who I knew to be headed to the Great Elm held as much hatred in his heart for Bane as the Necromancer did for him. So I doubted he would give up his prizes despite them sharing heritage.

And then there was Rissa.

Rissa who had the Serpent working with her. Rissa who had promised to meet me at the heart of the forest when the time came.

So I was fairly confident I had four amulets to my name already. Surely the boon would be mine.

My heart pattered wildly in my chest as I allowed myself to believe in that for the first time.

I was a creature who thrived on facts and figures, on research and reasoning. And whatever way I looked at this, through some madness or miracle, it seemed like I really could be the one to claim the prize of the forest and if so, then I would finally be able to bring my sister home.

Bane met my eyes as I shouldered my pack, his gaze dark with plots and schemes of his own which made my hopeful confidence twist and sour in my gut. He didn't look fearful or even defeated.

No, Bane Crownthief appeared to be nothing short of eager to head to the heart of the forest and face the final challenges that awaited us there.

And that alone was enough to stoke a torrent of doubt in my soul.

HENDRIX

CHAPTER FORTY

It took us almost the entire day to journey to the labyrinth and in that time, fewer and fewer words passed between me and Ferris. When we'd left the tower, I'd half expected her to race for the trees even after the night we'd shared. I'd believed that the reality of what I was would sit fully with her in the cold light of day and she would no longer be able to bear it. But she seemed to have truly decided on remaining at my side. I had to admit I was overjoyed by that - especially since the roiling power of death had stopped spilling from me unbidden - but I didn't know what plot she might have in mind yet.

For now at least, she was staying with me despite what she knew about me. Every time I thought to ask why, I found the words stalling in my throat. I was cautious of learning her reasoning in case I despised the truth of it. She was a clever thing and perhaps her decision to stay with me wasn't solely based on our unusual connection. I had the key to the labyrinth after all and perhaps that was her main reason to stay with me now. Or had last night really changed things between us? Had she fallen into the pull of desire for her own pleasure? Or were there true feelings involved from her side?

I couldn't pluck answers from the air. All I really knew was that she'd withdrawn from me slowly as we approached the labyrinth. With each step we took closer to the Great Elm, the words she offered me became more and more focused on the task at hand. Perhaps it was solely because of the pressure she felt to break the curse or maybe it was because she knew just as I did that we were approaching the final moments before the boon would be seized. Did the sound of my footsteps at her back remind her of the lies I'd already told? Was she starting to remember the fear which haunted my presence once more? Was the name Bane Crownthief echoing in her mind alongside all the tales of my destruction?

My name was a tar across Rathian, a black seed sewn into the hearts of its people. She'd likely heard countless stories of my merciless violence and each were as good as fact to her. I couldn't even deny how true they were.

No, I certainly wasn't blameless. I had doled out my revenge to the Coterie every chance I'd gotten over the years since I'd left Rivenspire. I'd favoured a dramatic style when it came to their deaths, wanting to cast terror into the hearts of all those I hunted and make a statement about my desire for vengeance. I'd wished to kill every single Fae who had watched my family die and had cheered their demise. Any who had survived the wrath of the Hollows deserved a bloody conclusion at my hands. Ferris may have seen her fair share of brutality between these trees but she hadn't seen anything yet when it came to me.

Still, here she was. Knowing my name and letting me walk in her shadow regardless. Honestly? I was content to selfishly take whatever I could get from her even if I was just a pawn in her plans now.

The Hollows shifted around us in the woods, all kept at bay by a will of my mind, none of them ever showing their faces in Ferris's presence. But they were here, doggedly tracking my footsteps.

A haunting tune started up in the trees and I caught Ferris by the elbow, tugging her to a firm halt as my muscles tensed in preparation of an ambush.

The Lost Children peered down at us from the shadows between the branches, bare feet making a passage from one bough to the next while they sang. I hadn't even noticed their approach and the thought of that set me on edge. No creature was capable of creeping up on me.

"Brave the maze if you dare.
The Great Elm waits, the deal is fair.
Return her darlings to her door,
She'll tame her trees and take no more."

"It's still daylight," I muttered in confusion. "They shouldn't be here yet."

"They won't hurt us," Ferris whispered, her violet eyes trained on the Lost Children as she brushed her fingers over the amulets at her throat. "I think they've come to watch us succeed."

"Or fail," I said darkly and her gaze fell to meet mine.

I realised how long it had been since my eyes had met hers and I was gravitationally drawn closer to her as we locked sights, my fingers curling tighter around her arm.

"Ever the pessimist," she teased, though I could see the way her mind was turning over the facts, planning for the worst. She was afraid of what was coming. And so she should be. After all this time, I couldn't believe the end would be a simple affair.

"I think you know as well as I do that I'll fight tooth and nail to get you to the Great Elm, lightwing."

"Then prove it and let's finish this thing." She took a step away but my infatuation with her overwhelmed me. I grabbed her, pulling her to me, knowing what I had come here to do and that my last chance at a moment of pure sin with her was now or never again.

"Ferris Creed, you're my last everything. My last desire, my last want in all the world. So spare me one more moment of intoxication in your presence beneath these trees. Remember what we were here, not what we are beyond all of this."

There was a ragged plea to my voice, my need for her a tangible thing inside me that was invulnerable to all jeopardies.

"Why do you say it like that? Do you plan to die?" she asked, the crack of emotion in her voice telling me she didn't want that. And I was so fucking delighted to know it.

"We may yet survive this," I admitted in a rough tone. "But I have long had a taste for death upon the air and something tells me it is hounding our footsteps closer than ever before today." I glanced over my shoulder, not finding her Falcon's face gazing out at me, but I sensed her there all the same. And she was hungry.

The leaves stirred and the Lost Children's song halted as if they were listening to the omen in my words.

"We should go," Ferris said urgently, but I didn't release her.

"I ask of you one thing, lightwing…one more kiss. My last. If you have spent this day remembering all the worst things that I am then hate me while you offer it but give it willingly if there is still a part of me that you believe is worth more than the dirt we stand upon. Kiss me if you believe I hold any value at all in your eyes because I have come to realise that you are the only living creature I have met during a thousand lifetimes who I care to be worth something to."

Ferris's eyes widened at my words, drinking me into their bright, shimmering sea of violet. Then she tiptoed up and her lips met mine with a firm and hard passion that tasted like the nectar of my salvation.

I fisted a hand in her silver hair and kissed her like the sinner I had long ago been branded. And within that kiss, she melted. Her fears giving way to something so much purer, a want for me that crossed all boundaries that had been drawn between my kind and hers. We were not Fae and human while we stood beneath those whispering trees, we were our desires. Desires which wanted nothing more than for us to shed the skins that housed our souls and become one and the same creature.

Long before I was ready to part, she was gone, pulling away and turning to her path with no more words to offer me. But she had given me all I needed to walk this trail to the end. A taste of what could have been. And though what I'd had of her would never sate me, it was enough to settle the torment inside my soul upon this final hour and keep me walking toward the conclusion of our journey side by side.

Ferris reached the top of a rocky outcrop and the vines hanging in front of her parted like a curtain at her touch, revealing a path which led to a stone door with the emblem of the Great Elm carved into its surface. It was set into a rockface that towered up toward the sky and I had no doubt that the labyrinth lay within this hill.

We were not the first to arrive.

Princess Drava had come after all. She stood with her flowing ebony hair braided down her spine, a curved dagger in grip and a ferocious look on her striking face. Her full eyebrows were lowered over charcoal eyes and I noted the Phoenix and Stag amulets shining at her throat. She had no entourage in tow – or perhaps they had not survived if she'd had one to begin with. An axe was strapped to her back and her clothes were a fine, hardwearing navy fabric fit for the task of breaking the curse of the forest.

Two humans stood away from the door, casting wary looks at the Fae princess and talking in low voices.

Ferris lowered to a crouch, gesturing for me to join her and I did so, gazing down at the three Champions below. We were far enough away to remain undetected and with the shadows of the trees still shrouding us, I doubted we would be spotted easily.

"That's Devlan," Ferris whispered, pointing out the muscular human man with silvered hair who was sporting the Carp amulet around his neck. "And that's Helga." She pointed to the tough-looking human woman who had won the Boar spirit.

I made a mental count. Islasees possessed two of the other amulets, the Tiger and the Rat, leaving only the Serpent unaccounted for. That would become a problem if no one appeared with it. We would be forced to go searching for it and with only a few days left before the Great Hunt finished for good, we might be facing failure already. So I just had to hope someone would turn up with it soon.

I glanced at Ferris, eyeing her amulets as she looked at mine. We were at a tie for holding the most spirits, and perhaps that meant either one of us could demand the boon once we reached the Great Elm. We might end up racing to get there first and the thought left me uncomfortable. I needed this, but so did she. And the truth was, I was going to have to steal it from her even if it wrecked me to do so.

Princess Drava struck the stone door with her dagger, carving a line into it but it didn't budge.

"How in the spirits am I meant to gain access?" she hissed to herself, stalking back and forth in front of the door, ignoring the presence of the humans entirely.

"It seems you weren't lying about the key after all," Ferris muttered.

"A liar? Me?" I smirked but she didn't smile back, instead tutting under her breath and looking away. "Bitterness doesn't suit you, lightwing."

"You can't call me lightwing when you're being a smug dick."

"But you will always be my lightwing. My good luck charm. Even when I am a smug dick."

She cracked a grin at last. "Did it ever occur to you that I'm my own good luck charm and you just came along for the ride?"

"Yes, actually," I sniggered and her smile grew.

"Come then. Let me see this key." She arched a brow at me, holding out her hand.

"As if I would hand it over so willingly." I stood up lazily, pushing my shoulders back and sauntering down the path with little to no care of how the Champions were going to react to my arrival.

Drava turned, her body stiffening as she took me in and I offered her a nod of greeting, knowing it was a mockery of what we were to each other now.

Drava was not my immediate aunt. She was my great grandfather's sister. She hadn't been there the day my family died, but when I'd tried to reach out to her after escaping Rivenspire, she had not replied. She had cut us off in our hour of need and I held no warmth in my heart for her any longer.

"Bane Crownthief," Drava gasped, her throat bobbing as her eyes trailed over my face. She grew pale, mystified horror spreading across her features, her disbelief at my presence making her retreat one step, then two.

It was unusual to see a Fae of her strength unsettled in such a way and I rather liked watching her cower. She wasn't an active member among the Coterie, her attendance at their gatherings brief. Perhaps she even held a distaste for their activities. But her inaction was a statement of her true character.

"Crownthief?" Helga murmured, sharing a look with Devlan before both of them raised weapons between us. They seemed to be waiting for me to confirm the title offered to me and I held no qualms over keeping it a secret anymore.

"Hello, Aunt," I drawled, smiling at Drava coldly to unnerve her. "You need a key for that door." I gestured to it, hearing Ferris closing in on me from behind but I held the Hollows at bay among the trees, hidden out of sight and waiting for my summons.

"Is that the waif who followed us around for days?" Helga hissed, jerking her head at Ferris. "What the fuck happened to her hair?"

I rounded on the offending Helga who had cast those words against my lightwing, my gaze setting coldly upon her and making her raise her sword all the higher. "If you call Ferris Creed a waif again I shall summon my Hollows to crack and shatter your bones one by one."

"Stay away from me," Helga growled, grabbing the amulet at her throat as if she was considering setting the Boar on me.

"Who says you're even the Necromancer?" Devlan chimed in, his dagger pointed at me as if he planned to hurl it at my head.

"This could be a trick of the trees," Drava whispered, nodding hopefully and glancing up at the canopy as the wind stirred the leaves.

"You want proof?" I purred and they all shifted foot to foot, but Helga called out to demand it.

I drew upon my dark connection to death and the Hollows crept from the trees, just close enough to show their presence. My will over them was not absolute, but when they were this close it was always easier to direct them. Though the longer I wielded this dark power the closer I came to losing myself in its grip and already I could feel the dark veins crawling across my skin, mostly hidden beneath my clothes for now but soon they would be noticeable around them.

Devlan cursed, wheeling around to raise his sword to defend himself from the dead lurking among the trees.

"Monster," Helga spat at me, her eyes wild with fear as she turned her gaze on the approaching dead.

Ferris was watching me closely, a flicker of caution to her eyes like she thought I might turn this dangerous side of me on her at any moment. But surely she knew better.

"You should never have come here," Drava growled, backing up again. "You are not welcome."

"Ever arrogant, I see. You do not own this forest, Drava, though I am sure you believe that every scrap of earth within your sights could one day be yours. Providence is not coming to choose you." I gave her a mocking look then turned to the door as she started spewing curses at me.

Ferris moved to my side, waiting expectantly for me to produce a key. But instead I took a short knife from a sheath at my hip and slashed a shallow cut across my palm, making her inhale sharply in surprise.

The blood oozed as I pressed it to the stone door, speaking of the secret the Hag had offered me, loud enough for all to hear – for what was the point in hiding it now?

"I met with a Hag before I came to the cursed forest," I said. "She spoke to me of fate and of this very door too. And she told me how to open it."

"What did she say?" Ferris asked, a yearning need building in her voice for the answer.

"That the blood of the imperial shall unlock the labyrinth's door."

"Is that so?" a deep voice rent the air in two and a sneer pulled at my lips as I rounded on Islasees who was stepping out of the trees with Jadina and Benson either side of him.

The Hollows stirred around him as if sensing my desire for this male's death alongside those of his vile companions and vitriol spilled through my gut.

"And why would a Hag offer you such information, Bane Crownthief?" Islasees hissed, glancing around at my Hollows warily with tension lining his shoulders.

The use of that name made my ire rise and I pointed my bloodied knife at him as I answered. "I traded for knowledge of the Taking Trees and she gave it well. It seems royal blood will open this door. I paid her the gift of my flesh as the price. She took over my body, wearing it as her own for one full month and did the most heinous of things with me for that time. But the price was paid and she was true to her word."

"And yet the door remains closed," Islasees commented and I let my Hollows creep closer to him, making his two Fae cronies shift uncomfortably, but they didn't strike at them. Not while we assessed each other, predators eye to eye. They took stock of my amulets while I took stock of Islasees and readied for an attack.

I glanced back at the door, finding Ferris examining it and looking to me with an urgent frown.

"Why isn't it opening?" she hissed.

"Let us not do anything foolish," Drava stepped in, glancing at the Hollows then to Islasees and me. "We have all come to rid Rathian of the forest's curse. What were the words she used? 'Blood of the…"

"Imperial," I finished for her. "Imperial means royal. My blood should open it."

"But you're an outcast, aren't you? Perhaps that means you're no longer royal," Devlan piped up and I shot him a glare that made him tense.

"He has a point, Necromancer," Drava said, walking cautiously past me, her dagger gripped tightly in her hand but she didn't raise it at me. The rips in her clothes and stains of blood upon her told of what she had been through to get here. Not even meeting me between the trees was going to sway her from getting to the Great Elm. And time was waning. The sun was drifting out of sight and all colour was draining from the day.

Drava cut her arm with her dagger and smeared it across the stone door. We waited. Bated breaths were held around us and the song of the Lost Children started up in the trees once more. It was a faster tune this time, threaded with notes of terror that set a hum of dread through the remaining group of Champions.

"Pray for life.
Death is coming.
She is singing.
She is hungry.
She is ready to devour.
She will feast upon the hour."

"For the love of the spirits, it's not opening," Drava growled in anger, striking her fist against the door.

Islasees walked toward us, his gaze driving into mine, daring me to make a move against him as he brushed past me to examine the labyrinth's entrance for himself. Hatred bled through me, my need for his death rising like a winter storm and begging for retribution.

His back was to me. I could strike at him, drive my knife between his shoulder blades and sink it into his heart.

But then Ferris touched my hand, just enough to bring rationale back to the surface of my mind. If I killed Islasees I could not take his amulets and the boon would never be mine. But he might just set his bloodhounds on me to take my own.

I fixed my gaze on Benson and Jadina instead, noting how they had drawn a little closer, a tension to their shoulders telling me they were confident of taking down the Necromancer. But more fool them if they truly believed that.

"Try more blood," Islasees urged Drava and I glanced back to find her making a deeper cut on her other arm, letting it bleed onto the stone door where it dripped down to the rock at its base.

"Sweet Elm, how she cries,

How she's waiting for her prize.

She is ready, she is waiting,

-it's not good to keep her waiting!"

"Shut up!" Benson barked at the trees as the Lost Children gathered above us to watch, but their song only grew in volume.

"We're running out of time," Jadina said anxiously. "Can't we break through it? Or perhaps there's another way in."

"Bane," Ferris breathed and I looked down at her, seeing the desperation in her gaze. "It's not working."

"*More*," Islasees commanded, losing his patience and grabbing Drava's arm to drag it across the stone and squeeze more blood onto it.

"Run, run, run to the Great Elm beyond the door!

Run, run, run, she can wait for you no more!"

"You're hurting me, let go," Drava snarled, but Islasees only squeezed tighter, pushing Drava against the wall. "Stop!" She lifted her dagger but Islasees was quicker, a concealed blade in his hand sweeping out and slitting her throat in one deep slash.

Shock jarred through me.

Drava couldn't scream, only grasp at the gaping wound as blood poured from her neck and Islasees caught a fistful of her clothes and shoved her roughly against the door.

I snarled as I shoved Ferris behind me, lurching forward to break up this hysteria and swinging my knife for Islasees's back before he could turn his violence upon my lightwing. He wheeled around before I could land the blow, his sword drawn in a heartbeat, rising up to clash with my knife. The force he used sent my blade skittering across the ground but I threw my fist instead and it slammed into his face, sending him stumbling sideways.

In my periphery I saw Devlan run in and snatch the Phoenix and Stag amulets from Drava's slumped form, clasping them around his own neck and snatching a victory from her demise. Though there was still no sign of a Champion sporting the Serpent amulet so none of us were victorious yet.

"Bane, watch out!" Ferris warned.

Islasees's two lackeys ran at me together and I unsheathed my sword, parrying blows from both sides and calling upon the darkness within me. It answered my plea, the potent, wrathful magic crawling through me and promising death, puddling around my feet to wither the grass at my boots. The flood of blazing chaos filled me to the brim, my need to protect Ferris burning through me and spurring it on.

With a crash of thundering footfalls, the Hollows came rushing to my aid, one latching its arm around Benson's neck and two more throwing Jadina to the ground.

Islasees swung his sword for my head as he tried to push me toward his bloodthirsty comrades – but they were too distracted by the Hollows who had come to rip them limb from limb to be of any help to him now. We fought to get the upper hand with a desperate vehemence and among the havoc, I found a smile dancing upon my lips. Because it had been a long damn time since I'd fought with the fury of my kin humming in my veins. And if this day was about to be my last, then I may as well revel in the thrill of the fight.

FERRIS

CHAPTER FORTY ONE

"So typical of the Fae to think themselves the only creatures powerful enough to hold the key to a prophecy," the Dragon scoffed in the back of my mind while Bane and Islasees fought each other and the other Fae fought with the Hollows, cutting down the dead one after another.

I'd scrambled away from the fighting, not needing to risk my neck by getting in the way.

"What do you mean?" I hissed, looking around in alarm as Helga dove behind another tree with Devlan, the two of them seeming as content as I was to stay out of the Fae fight and hide from the Hollows.

"Why would the key be the royal blood of the Fae?" the Dragon muttered, its voice rough with disdain. *"What care does the Great Elm have for their crowns?"*

"But if she doesn't care for their crowns then what does it mean 'imperial blood?'" I asked, quoting the words Hendrix had spoken about the key, realisation sinking into me as my fingernails dug into the bark of the ash tree I'd hidden behind.

"What, pray tell, does the Great Elm value most dearly?"

I scoured my mind, the riddle to that question setting my thoughts scattering. We needed to figure it out. We had to get inside the labyrinth and return the amulets to the Great Elm itself. So what did she care about? The trees, yes. The Lost Children perhaps? I tipped my head up to search the branches, looking between the countless faces that watched us from above.

"How am I supposed to convince one of them to come down here?" I muttered, looking around for a place where I might be able to start climbing but the Dragon huffed loudly, its power spilling from the amulet in a gust of wind which spun my hair around my face.

"Yes, she loves her children, but they are not born of her magic," it harrumphed like this conversation was so very draining.

I opened my mouth to make another guess but cried out as a grey and rotting hand took hold of my wrist and hauled me out of my hiding place. The Hollow grinned, its skin sagging as it branded its yellowing teeth at me.

"Ferris!" Bane barked, lurching towards me, though Islasees swung his sword out to block him.

"Risking your life for a human, Crownthief?" Islasees sneered as he forced Bane to parry a savage blow and I was thrown to the ground beneath the Hollow. "I knew you were low but the reek of desperation on you has truly deepened if you're reduced to fucking the short-lived peasants now."

I kicked and fought beneath the impossibly strong corpse, its yellowed teeth closing in on my throat as it lunged for me.

My spirits were writhing through the corners of my mind, waiting for my call but with the Hollow's hands locked around my throat I was unable to make it.

Bane lunged for me but Islasees blocked his advance again and he roared a wordless command as he was forced to block his opponent's sword once more.

The Hollow jerked back as if a string had cinched tight around its neck and heaved it from me.

I gasped as I scrambled away from it, the ground turning to festering spoil at my boots as the dark power of the Necromancer bled from Bane. I didn't know what would happen to me if I touched it but with his focus on his fight with Islasees, I couldn't risk finding out.

"You'll hold your tongue if you value keeping it inside your skull," Bane growled, feinting to the right then swinging for Islasees's gut, cutting the fabric of his tunic and drawing a thin line of blood.

"Get out of the way," he barked, his eyes on me and I nodded as I scrambled aside, not needing to be told that twice. But Islasees watched our interaction with calculating savagery and a knot tightened in my gut as I ran for the closest trees.

"Grab that human!" Islasees bellowed at his pair of brutish followers though their attention was firmly fixed on the hoard of dead beings who were intent on their demise and they couldn't follow his command. Yet.

"Think, spirit singer, you're allowing yourself to get distracted," the Dragon chastised as I ducked behind a horse chestnut tree and hunted the shadows for signs of more danger.

"It's hard not to be distracted when most of the creatures in this glade would like nothing more than to see me dead," I hissed.

"Less griping, more thinking."

I bit back a retort and did as the spirit had commanded, running over all it had told me along with the Hag's words to Bane. Not a Fae royal. And it wouldn't be human either – not that any of our royalty were here if it had been. Not a Lost Child but something the Great Elm cared about, something born of her magic…

"Is it you? You and the other spirits?" I gasped, darting from my hiding place as the fight between Jadina and the Hollows she was fending off drew too close.

"We spirits don't bleed in the way of living beings," the Dragon dismissed.

No, they didn't bleed like a human. But…I did. I was human but I was born of the forest, I'd been born of the forest over and over again, always following the call of this place. I'd come here thirteen times and if I really was the key then that made sense because they would have needed me to open the door. That was why the Great Elm had given me to my mother. It was why the forest and the spirits favoured me too. They knew I was the one who was needed to open the door and allow them to return to their mother. It seemed impossible that such an enormous task could have been placed on my shoulders all along but it was the only truth that made sense.

"It's *my* blood?" I guessed, my heart thumping wildly at the thought, the Dragon's only reply that deep and mocking chuckle in the back of my mind.

But that was enough for me. The moon had risen into the sky overhead, the trees were all thrashing back and forth while the Lost Children sang their wild songs. Every amulet was here barring the Serpent and I had to have faith that my sister would deliver that last piece of the puzzle in time.

I could only believe that this was the first time any set of Champions had come so far and for every life I'd lived before in whatever form that may have been, I could well have been the key. So if that was the case then I was going to have to unlock the labyrinth.

"Please, help me," I begged of my spirits and at last the Dragon relinquished, allowing the Raven and Unicorn to join it as all three of them burst from their amulets at my throat.

The rush of power spilling away from me had me staggering, a gasp catching in my throat. The Dragon roared and the fighting taking place in the heart of the clearing before the entrance to the labyrinth stilled for a beat as the incredible beast tore past over their heads.

The Raven circled me, cawing in wild warning as I ran for the stone door, the image of the Great Elm carved upon its face seeming to writhe across its surface as if beckoning me closer.

Islasees released the Tiger from its amulet at his throat and the enormous beast leapt straight at Bane, slamming into him and sending them both tumbling away across the clearing.

The red-haired Fae turned my way with a sneer, lifting his sword as he levelled his focus on me but the Unicorn charged at him before he could get close, its horn lowered and flowers blooming everywhere its hooves struck the forest floor.

Islasees was forced to throw himself aside, the Rat leaping from its amulet as he ducked behind the trees. I stared in wonder at the spirit he'd sent after my Unicorn as the creature raced forward. It was the size of a large dog and where its fur might have been on a real rat, this creature was instead crawling with insects of every variety, its job to protect and ferry them around the forest.

The Unicorn turned to charge at Islasees again but the Rat raced into its path, squeaking shrilly and sending a flood of cockroaches spilling away from it across the ground to swarm my spirit and hold it back.

I shrieked in alarm as the carpet of insects hissed and chittered, climbing the Unicorn's legs and tail, sending it whinnying and rearing up in panic.

The Raven swept around me as I stumbled back, my path blocked by the Hollows behind me, the Rat and its hoard of insects ahead, and Islasees striding from the shadows on my right, his sword drawn.

"Benson!" Islasees barked. "End her!"

I whirled around as Benson shot an arrow for me, my death flying for me so fast I was only able to stare it in the eye as it came.

Bane bellowed from the trees beyond the clearing, the Tiger roaring in what sounded like pain. And then the Raven was there. My sweet Raven with wings made of midnight was diving into the space before me, the arrow which had been meant for me instead piercing its breast.

"No!" I cried, lurching for my spirit as it crashed out of the sky, tumbling across the dirt and knocking a swathe of cockroaches aside.

I threw myself down with it and it gave me a harrowing caw, its feathers silken soft beneath my fingers for a moment before it spilled away into tendrils of night and returned to the amulet at my neck.

"Sleep," it whispered in my mind before its presence faded away and I scrubbed tears from my cheeks as I stood, hoping against hope that it truly only needed rest now.

Islasees leapt from the trees and came for me again, Bane lurched into his path, his teeth bared in a feral challenge. His shirt was torn open with four bloody gashes showing through it where the claws of the tiger had cut into his side, but he wasn't slowed by the wounds and there was no sign of Islasees's spirit returning from their fight.

"You're alive," I breathed, the relief palpable in my tone and my beautiful Fae warrior turned a roguish grin my way that made my heart fall over itself.

"As if a little Tiger could make a dent in me," he crooned just as another tremendous roar came from the trees where he'd been and I caught sight of the Bear locked in combat with the Tiger, the two spirits fighting a battle of brawn and savagery.

Islasees bellowed in fury, launching himself at Bane and they fell back into a furious fight, their swords colliding so fast that it was impossible to trace the movements.

I was forced to back away from them, though as I turned to run for the door, I found my way barred by both the Hollows and Jadina and Benson whose focus was split between the dead they fought and following the commands of their leader to strike at me.

Jadina hacked the head off of a Hollow with her double-headed axe, opening up enough space for Benson to ready another arrow in his bow, aiming it straight at me. I threw out a hand, warding off the strike while crying out for help which came not from my Dragon as I'd expected but in a rush of grinding stone and a war cry from the lips of the girl I loved more dearly than my own life.

Rissa rode the Serpent from the trees in a charge, a wild laugh spilling from her as Benson released his arrow and it simply bounced off the spirit's rocky scales.

Relief rushed through me at the sight of her. She was here. She'd brought the Serpent. We had all thirteen spirits and the end to this nightmare was finally within reach.

The Dragon dove from the trees above me, plucking me into its grasp and hurtling across the clearing so fast that tears were ripped from my eyes by the rush of wind which assaulted me. It dropped me before the stone door and I tumbled across the dirt, landing in a heap by the trees closest to it.

A gasp drew my attention to Devlan and Helga who were lurking in the shadows, taking cover while the Fae fought one another.

"I never thought you'd make it this far," Devlan told me plainly, the look of stunned awe on his face enough to soften the blow of the insult.

"I'm used to being underestimated," I replied before shoving back to my feet and setting my gaze firmly on the door to the labyrinth.

"They'll kill you out there," Helga hissed but I barely glanced back at her.

"And you think they'll spare you hiding there? We need to get inside that labyrinth and return the spirits to the Great Elm. That's how this ends. Or did you forget that part?"

They exchanged a loaded look but I was already running from them, racing for the door, my gaze locked on my target and all of the fighting, the spirits, the Fae and the Hollows, just fell away because I had to get to the door.

The Serpent slunk through the canopy overhead, Jadina and Benson once again occupied by the Hollows and unable to fire at me.

Rissa called out in encouragement as I sprinted across the clearing, tearing a small dagger from my pocket.

The blade sliced into my hand a beat before I reached the door and I slapped my palm to its surface with a cry which met with the blast of power that resounded from the stone.

The image of the Great Elm emblazoned on the huge plate of rock sighed, its branches whipping back and forth as the doors began to part, my blood smeared across the runes which had kept it sealed for so long.

Magic rattled through my bones, a tether seeming to reach out from me to not only the spirits I'd claimed but to each of the thirteen magical beings in the clearing, forming between us for several heady seconds.

The fighting all fell to nothing as every spirit present felt the weight of that power awakening and we all watched in reverence as the door slowly opened.

Finally, the entrance to the labyrinth loomed like the yawning mouth of some great beast hoping to swallow us whole and I found myself standing before it, ready to dive in regardless.

Your task's near done, the end near come,
Thirteen spirits brought home as one.
But as your journey reaches its end,
The time has come to turn on friend.
Though you all have hunted well,
One alone, this curse shall fell.
So no more will the blood rule stand,
You may claim prize with swords in hand.
By death or cunning, by arrow or blade,
For this last task the price shall be paid.
So make your choice in this final hour,
Will you gift or steal their power?
For when the amulets return,
Only one Champion, the boon shall earn.

There was a pause in which the whole world held its breath as those words sank in, each of us turning them over within our minds and realising at once what they meant. There was no longer any rule in place to prevent the Champions from killing one another to steal the amulets. And if that was the case then this would turn from a fight to a massacre and I – alongside the remaining humans – knew that we would not be the last one standing when that happened.

I was no warrior but I was fast and I already held three amulets – four if I could count the Serpent as mine with Rissa's aid. There wasn't time to waste on puzzling out the rest of the Great Elm's song. Islasees and his cronies were already circling like vultures with their weapons ready.

I locked eyes with Bane whose green gaze sparked with panic as he took me in.

"Go," he commanded. And then the Dragon swept over my head and led the charge into the darkened passages, sparks of teal lightning guiding me after it with urgency as my doom rushed close at my back.

I broke into a run, the Raven bursting once more from its amulet and flying over my head, the Unicorn galloping at my heels as it shook off the cockroaches.

And every remaining Champion took chase too, their spirits bursting free of their amulets as we all chose different paths and plunged into the unknown.

HENDRIX

CHAPTER FORTY TWO

I sprinted after Ferris with her name spilling from my lips in a desperate bellow as Islasees raced after her with his Tiger on her heels. I knew what he was planning. Ferris held three of the most powerful amulets here and he planned on murdering her to claim them.

I took chase with my sword raised, tearing through the winding tunnel that cut through the roughened rock.

The hairs lifted on the back of my neck in warning and I whirled around, narrowly missing the shot of an arrow as it went whistling past my head. Benson had his bow aimed for my skull while Jadina ran at me with her double-headed axe held high and a look of murderous intent on her face. Hollows chased after them, but they stumbled over the dead that the two of them had cut down, slowed in their pursuit while my magic urged them on.

The strike of Jadina's axe met with the swing of my sword and she landed a hard kick to my chest that sent me stumbling into a tunnel away from the path Ferris had taken. I cursed in fury as she cut me off from my lightwing, leaving her to the mercy of their ruthless master.

Benson loosed another arrow and I lurched aside, swinging my sword in a deadly arc and drawing on the call of Death within my soul. I could feel her here, feeding on my sadistic desires. She knew what was coming. She had seen what became of my enemies when they came against me. She knew how quickly their blood would pour once they got close to the savage Necromancer.

A few of my Hollows joined us in the tunnel with shrieks of feral rage, engaging Benson and drawing his focus from placing an arrow in my head. Jadina came at me with savage intent, her eyes alight with the game as if she really thought she could win it, but she was so very wrong.

I could cut them down so prettily, but a more fitting end came to mind for these two who had had a hand in my family's deaths. They would face one of the most torturous ways to die. Ripped apart by a vicious beast.

A single command in my mind sent the Bear rushing into the fight, slamming into Jadina with tooth and claw, making her scream hellishly.

I released the Wolf next with a dark smile upon my lips and it joined the fray in a swirl of shade, landing on large paws and tearing past the Bear to meet with Benson. The male had only just cut through the last of the Hollows when my Wolf collided with him, sharp teeth and ragged claws slicing through his flesh and making him scream just as my family had once screamed. This was what they deserved. I wanted it to be slow. To be agonising.

Before the Bear could finish Jadina where it had her pinned to the cave floor, I caught her by the hair and made her look me in the eye, holding the Bear off with a will of my mind.

"You play with death, you pay the price. Look where your violent little games got you, Jadina. I saw what you liked to do among the Coterie, I saw the cruelty you dished out, and you remember well the day I watched you toy with my family before you helped kill them, don't you?"

"Please," she gasped, her face bloody from a nasty gash in her cheek, pain written into every corner of her face. "Have mercy."

"You had no mercy upon my family, wretch." I sneered. "I'll have no mercy in return."

I stepped back and let the Bear have her, the spirit making messy work of the kill while Benson's screams joined Jadina's in the dark.

Death watched on with keen excitement, whispering sweet promises in my ear of leading them to even greater torment beyond the doors of the afterworld.

I watched in dark glee as the Wolf tore one arm from Benson's body then ripped out his throat to silence the last of his screams.

Then all was quiet, death well dealt, but I would not let these two cretins rest. I let the dark pour from me, a tempest of malice seeping across the tunnel floor and encasing their bodies in the grip of my power. They began to rise, bloody and twisted as they gained their feet, their bloodshot eyes taking me in with horrified realisation of what they'd become.

"You will hunt down your Lord Protector and kill him," I ordered.

"No," Jadina rasped, touching her ragged wounds in terror. "What have you done to me?"

"You are Hollow." I smiled my most vicious smile. "And you are mine to wield."

Benson let out a gurgling groan, unable to speak since his voice box had been torn into by my spirit, but the torment in his eyes was clear.

"Hunt him down!" I bellowed and they turned, racing into the tunnel, forced to obey me.

I released the Fox to join its companions and urged it to lead the way with its blazing fire lighting the path.

We doubled back at a fierce pace, chasing after Ferris as panic consumed my thoughts over her safety. I would find her. I would protect her. No force in Rathian could keep me from that task. And when I had her, we would head for the Great Elm and figure out how to slot together the final pieces of this puzzle. Then I would seize the boon this very night. It was my right, my calling. Nothing could turn me from it so long as I could ensure Ferris was safe.

Though my spirits were silent, I felt their energy crashing around me like they were as determined to find Ferris as I was.

"Seek her out," I called to them and the new Hollows I'd awoken, locking my focus on her and vowing I would reach my lightwing before Islasees could lay a finger on her. "Protect her at all costs!"

FERRIS

CHAPTER FORTY THREE

The deafening roar of the Tiger made the deep dark of the tunnel rattle around me and I threw up my hands to shield my head as small stones fell loose from the roof above.

I almost ran straight into another dead-end, cursing as the Dragon bellowed in fury and flipped around, its feathers brushing against my cheeks as I ducked to let it turn then sprinted after it down a new path.

This place was endless. A maze with no heart and barely enough air to breathe.

The other Champions rushed through the passages, their boots echoing all around me making it impossible to tell which direction they were coming from, the cries of all of the spirits mixing into a tumult which had my skull ringing.

A figure burst from a tunnel ahead of me and I raised my slingshot before lowering it again as I recognised Devlan. The older Champion had the Phoenix he'd taken from Princess Drava's corpse racing along behind him, lighting the way with beams of sunlight which almost blinded me. The Stag clopped along at his back and the Carp was flopping feebly in his arms.

I backed up, uncertain of where we stood with one another now. We'd been allies of sorts in the start of this and we were both human. But we each had three spirits and if either of us killed the other then we'd have six. That was almost certainly all that would be needed to win the boon.

Devlan pointed a dagger at me awkwardly around the heavy body of the spirit of puddles then cursed as it was almost knocked from his hand by the Carp's flailing fin.

"Humans shouldn't be fighting against one another in this nightmarish place," he grunted, bobbing his chin towards a tunnel on my right. "I say we work together to end this fucking curse and see this thing done. I dare say the Fae will be happy to cut our throats either way and maybe we can give ourselves something of an advantage as one."

I hesitated for a heartbeat, the Unicorn pressing close behind me and peering over my shoulder at the man who I hadn't really gotten to know and could hardly say I trusted. But he was right. We were better off together and I was hardly in a position to fight him regardless. He was a warrior and I was not. But he was offering me an alliance.

"Okay," I agreed. "Lead on."

However I may have felt about an alliance with him, I wasn't fool enough to give him my back. Devlan grunted in agreement, eyeing the Dragon which gave him a menacing snarl before he took off down a new tunnel, still clutching the Carp to his chest.

I broke into a run again at once, not bothering to offer any opinion on the tunnels he chose as each appeared exactly like the last. I had tried asking my spirits for guidance too but none of them knew their way through this maze.

We raced down a long passage and almost crashed into the wall at the end of it, cursing and whirling back to run the other way.

A deep roar echoed through the darkness in that direction and I stumbled to a halt but we had no other choice, nowhere else to turn.

Devlan swore, hoisting the Carp higher in his arms and jogging down the passage despite the thundering footfalls which seemed to be closing in on us.

The Dragon coiled in the shadows behind me, the Unicorn nudging its nose to my back to keep me moving.

"Please check the way ahead," I breathed to the Raven and the bird swooped past us, darkness closing in around it so deeply that I could hardly see my own hand before my face.

I exchanged a glance with Devlan and we kept going, stepping into the shadows despite the fear which warned us not to.

A shriek from the Raven came a second before the Tiger leapt from the darkness, claws spread, teeth bared, a roar bellowing from its throat. The spirit's striped coat was alive with movement as small mammals and birds clung to its skin, its job that of protector to the beasts of the forest.

The Unicorn knocked me aside and it looked as though the Carp attempted to do the same for Devlan, its wet tail slapping him across the face as it bounced wildly in his hold, but it did him no good.

The Tiger's teeth closed over his skull with a crunch that ripped right into me as I screamed his name.

Islasees appeared from the gloom, swinging his sword at my Raven as it tried to claw at him and causing it to spill away into shadow to avoid the blow.

The Fae's eyes locked on me, the certainty that I was his next target paralysing me with fear.

But the Dragon had no intention of allowing my end to come so easily.

The great spirit bellowed as it threw itself at me, its talons wrapping around my body as it hoisted me from the ground and exploded into movement, knocking Islasees and his Tiger aside so that it could carry me to safety.

I craned my neck to look back, watching with a sense of sinking horror as Islasees stooped to snatch the amulets for the Carp, the Stag and the Phoenix from Devlan's decapitated body, stealing them for himself.

He had five amulets. And I still languished with three. My heart broke open at that truth. That murderous bastard had seized the advantage at the last moment and my only chance of seizing it from him was to try and kill him.

I'd come into this place knowing that I wouldn't ever win through battle or bloodshed, brawn or vigour. Taking those amulets from Devlan had been my last chance at winning this thing. And now I might never be able to rescue my sister from this ruinous place and everything I'd had risked in coming here would be for nothing.

HENDRIX

CHAPTER FORTY FOUR

Through some miracle, I made it out of the labyrinth before all others. I'd only met two dead ends before finding a shaft of light that led me outside to where the Great Elm loomed at the heart of a circular courtyard ringed with a high wall. The tree's bark was covered in rivers of beautiful markings and its branches fanned above me with leaves that gleamed beneath the rising moon. Dusk had given way to the dark blanket of night during the time it had taken us to reach this place, and I feared how long I had been parted from Ferris.

I could feel the Great Elm's power down to my bones, this spirit of the ancient wood. It was assessing me as I approached it with the Bear, the Wolf and the Fox around me, casting its judgement upon my worthiness. My spirits let out groans and whimpers of joy, like they were hopeful of what was to come at the culmination of the Great Hunt. Jadina wailed, clawing at her hair and looking around in anxious need. Because she had not yet done my will, but she was clearly in turmoil over it as Benson remained close to her in anguish.

The Great Elm's power crackled through the atmosphere,

drawing the hairs on my arms to stand on end and my lips to part in awe of it. It was so very fearsome, but majestic in its size and beauty too. Its strength hummed in the earth, buzzing in the air. This sacred being could offer me the boon. I was so close to capturing it, so close to all I had dreamed of for so, so long. It was an ache in my soul that demanded an answer tonight. But not just yet. Not until Ferris was safe.

I wrenched my gaze from the ancient spirit and all its power as I sought out a far more important being.

"Ferris!" I yelled, looking from one tunnel opening to the next, having no idea which one I might find her in. But as if in answer to my cry, her scream carried from one to the right and the Raven swept out of it in a whirl of shadow, followed by the coiling bulk of the silver Dragon.

"Ferris!" I shouted again in relief, running forward to meet her as she sprinted from the labyrinth in the Dragon's wake, the Unicorn right behind her. But beyond them was the Tiger with a snarl on its lips, its body coated in the creatures of the forest, small critters clinging to its shape, chattering and shrieking at me in warning.

The Tiger collided with the Unicorn, knocking it to the ground and making it whinny in alarm. But the Unicorn was a beast of its own, its hooves striking the Tiger in the chest, poison ivy blossoming beneath its strike, making the Tiger roar in agony and shrink back.

I met with Ferris and caught her hand, shoving her behind me as Islasees stepped from the tunnel with the Rat running at his heels. The dog-sized spirit was covered insects, its body a river of moving ants and shifting cockroaches, their wings flickering. With a squeak, the Rat ran to meet with swoop of the Raven and they collided in a clash of claws and talons.

The Bear, the Fox and the Wolf ran to assist Ferris's spirits, the collision of magic around us crackling through the atmosphere and setting the air alight.

At a will of my mind, Jadina and Benson ran at Islasees, caught in the grip of my potent power as they turned on their own master.

Islasees gasped in horror at what I'd done to them, a sneer curling his lip as he brought up his sword and beheaded Jadina with a barbaric swing of his blade.

"How dare you!" Islasees bellowed at me as her head thumped to the ground, lunging for Benson next and cutting him down the same way. Islasees gazed at his dead comrades with a look of rage then stalked toward me with his bloody sword lifted.

"Your wicked magic is a taint on Rathian," he spat.

"Stay back," I growled at Ferris, raising my own sword as Islasees slowed to a halt in front of me, glancing from me to my human with intrigue.

"You protect such a being as that?" he scoffed at me. "Why not take her head and have her amulets? Though I will defeat you regardless."

"Do not dare lay your eyes on her," I warned, raising my sword as our ancient hatred rose between us.

Islasees glowered at me with an icy despisal of everything I was. "Death has addled your mind, Crownthief. I recall how you sneered at the humans alongside so many of our people."

"*Your* people," I corrected, tapping my temple to point out the mark. "I'm an outcast remember?"

He stepped to the left and I mirrored his movements, glancing at Ferris as she backed away toward the Great Elm.

"Yes, so why have you abandoned your wasteland to join the Great Hunt? You want the boon I suppose. Do you believe the Great Elm can reinstate you into Fae society?"

"As if I would ever wish for a place among the filthy Coterie again."

"What then?" He stepped forward but didn't make a swing for me. He was testing me, trying to predict how I might move next. But I wasn't going to let him play his war games with me. "I don't think even the Great Elm can bring your family back from death." He said it with such gloating at their demise that I couldn't stop myself as I ran in and cast the first blow.

Islasees's sword whipped up to clash with mine and then we were dancing a violent dance, his years of brutal training making him a terrifyingly efficient warrior. I was not so well practised these days but I was larger than him in stature and I had been born of warriors. We were powerful in different ways but both of us were capable of cancelling out the other. I just had to make the right decisions in this fight. Because it wasn't just my life I was fighting for now, it was Ferris's too. And I would never forgive myself if I failed her.

The Wolf howled keenly as it collided with the Tiger beside us and the Dragon swooped down from above, a mighty strike of its tail knocking the Tiger on its back, allowing the Wolf to leap on top of it.

I didn't imagine these spirits could destroy one another but their fight meant they would not interfere with me and Islasees.

It was better this way because his death needed to come by my hand and mine alone. He needed to see the moment when I snatched away his victory from him and I'd watch as I crushed the life from him in payment for all he had done to my family.

FERRIS

CHAPTER FORTY FIVE

The weight of the Great Elm's power was crushing, its presence sending my senses ringing and mind scattering as I stumbled closer to it. I had never seen anything like its majestic beauty. Everything about it from the fluid patterns which were mapped across its trunk to the delicate leaves in every shade from emerald green to blood red, sunshine yellow, glimmering gold which rippled with movement as if each one of them were sentient.

I could feel the spirit's joy as it took us in, the Dragon, Raven and Unicorn all bristling in reaction, lifting their heads and inhaling huge breaths laced with memory and a sense of belonging which stole the air from my lungs. And then the Rat, Bear, Tiger, Wolf, Fox, Stag and Phoenix all paused too as if the call had reached them as well and for a moment which rang on into eternity, I was certain they remembered themselves.

I had so often referred to the Great Elm as a mother missing her children but of course those same children needed their mother just as keenly, if not even more so.

Tears spilled down my cheeks as I beheld her, the warring of the two Fae seeming so insignificant in her presence. But I couldn't allow myself to ignore them.

I tore my gaze from the magnificent tree whose branches seemed to brush the sky itself and forced myself to focus on the danger which was coming for me.

Islasees was hell bent on making it to the Great Elm first, fighting to get past Bane and even if I could beat him to the tremendous spirit, he had more amulets than me. My only hope was that Bane might cut him down and take them – but if that happened then the boon would be lost to me too.

The songs of the Lost Children were louder here and as I looked to the Great Elm, I found them all clambering through her branches, her leaves brushing against their hair, their cheeks, a welcome home which only encouraged their sweet lullaby.

Helga burst from the Labyrinth with a startled cry as she took in all that was happening and Islasees whirled towards her, sword swinging.

"Take it!" she shrieked, stumbling back and ripping the Boar's amulet from her throat. "I only want this curse ended. I don't want to die for the boon."

Islasees grinned, holding out his hand but Bane rushed him, forcing his attention back onto their fight, the world rocking beneath the power of their collision.

Helga didn't slow her movements though, her arm wheeling back then snapping out as she hurled the amulet away from her - not towards the Fae warrior - but to me.

I almost missed it in my shock at what she'd done, my arm shooting out at the last moment, fingers tangling with the Boar's amulet as I gaped at the woman who had just gifted it to me.

"A human should be the one to end this," Helga panted. "We are the ones who paid the highest price for the curse."

As the Lost Children continued to sing their eerie songs from the treetops, hundreds of voices coiling together in a song of loss and sacrifice, I knew that she was right about that. A rush of heavy power swum through my limbs as the Boar's magic met with my soul and I felt the slight burn of its mark appearing upon my right shoulder. And now I had four amulets. Perhaps all hope wasn't lost after all.

Islasees wailed in horror as he took in what had happened, hurling himself more viciously at Bane, a wild swipe of his sword cutting into the Necromancer's arm. Bane grew more feral at the wound, the blood only urging him on as their swords clashed and rang out against one another.

"Ferris!" Rissa's cry had me racing toward the edge of the glade before I even spotted her. She was riding the Serpent once more, its stony flesh scraping against the bark of the Great Elm as it slid down it, headed straight for me. "Claim it!"

I didn't know what she meant but the Dragon snarled from within the confines of my mind in agreement.

"This is a part of your destiny, spirit singer," it growled. *"Now prove to me that you are worthy of fulfilling it."*

I had no way of knowing what it wanted from me but it seemed like some piece of my soul was already perfectly attuned to what it needed.

The Serpent rushed ever nearer, its fangs bared menacingly and my sister clinging to its back, her eyes wide with want, with hope, with fear.

Any sane person would have leapt out of the spirit's path.

But I lifted my hand, met the giant snake's gaze and spoke to it in a clear and commanding voice.

"Join me," I said, my voice ringing with an ancient power that set my veins buzzing and limbs vibrating.

Its body hurtled closer, the rumbling of rock and ruin crashing down upon me and I bit back a scream before it slammed into me, not in solid form, but in a cloud of thick smoke.

The Serpent's amulet fell at my feet and I snatched it as the heavy, ancient roots of its power rocked me to my core. Another mark seared its way onto my right arm, curving along my bicep as I claimed yet another spirit.

Rissa was launched free of it, a joyous cry escaping her as she caught hold of one the Great Elm's branches and clambered into its canopy to join the other Lost Children in their haunting song.

Bane and Islasees still fought ferociously at the foot of the enormous tree. But now I had five spirits and they were five of the most powerful too. Surely more powerful than those Islasees had won.

The boon was mine. I only had to claim it.

At the base of the Great Elm its roots tangled together and formed a series of plinths, each with a spirit represented in its shape.

I set my gaze on those hallowed places and broke into a run.

Islasees saw what I was planning and threw himself at me, leaping into my way with his sword swinging. But Bane was there, ferociously beautiful as he blocked the blow and met my eyes for a second that resounded through me like a haunting cry to the depths of my soul.

I darted around the battling Fae, hurling myself aside as their swords clashed right where I would have been standing and then I raced on once more.

I could have wept with joy and relief as I made it to the foot of the tree and tore the amulets from my neck.

"No!" Islasees bellowed, a knife embedding itself in the root right beside my head before Hendrix's roar of fury stole his focus and their battle consumed them once more.

One by one I placed them where they belonged. Raven, Boar, Serpent, Unicorn and finally the Dragon itself.

A rush of magic swept around me, lifting my silver hair from my shoulders, almost plucking me free from the ground itself. I choked out a sob as I prepared to beg this most wondrous of spirits for the return of my sister at last.

But before I could make my request, an ethereal voice called to me within my mind, quelling that hope like a flood to a spark of flame.

"You must return all of them, spirit singer. All. Or the boon is void. And the curse shall not be broken."

HENDRIX

CHAPTER FORTY SIX

"Bane!" Ferris yelled as I got the upper hand in my fight with Islasees at last, wrapping one leg around his knees and felling him. He hit the ground hard as Ferris's voice rang through the air. "The Great Elm demands that one person must bring *all* the amulets to her. You have to give me yours!"

That news rattled through me and shattered everything I believed about how the end of the Hunt would go. I brought my sword down for Islasees's head, but the bastard rolled aside and kicked me hard in the shin, making me stagger back a step.

He gained his feet but instead of coming for me he turned and sprinted for Ferris with his weapon in hand.

"No – not lightwing!" I raced after him as she turned and fled, one bough of the Great Elm lowering down to allow her to climb onto it.

Islasees grabbed for her ankle but the Great Elm lifted her out of her harm's way and he snarled in anger, slashing his sword into the spirit's roots. The tree shuddered, the ground quaking with her utter rage at what he'd done and he fell onto his ass two steps ahead of me.

I leapt toward him with murder in my veins, sword raised and fury fuelling my limbs. I'd take his head for what he'd done. He would die this day; I would not miss this chance.

But Islasees gained his feet, scrambling upright and darting aside before I could land my blow. My sword scraped down his arm and he cursed as blood poured from the wound. It wasn't enough. But I had him on the back foot now, retreating and nearly falling time and again as the Great Elm's roots undulated, trying to knock him asunder for his strike against her.

"The forest is on my side it seems," I jeered him as the Lost Children sang louder in the trees and the spirits around us turned from the Great Elm and clashed together once more with escalating ferocity. "Death knows your name, Islasees Bellatorn. I have whispered it in her ear and she has whispered it in return."

Islasees's red hair was out of place and true panic ignited in his eyes, the sight a sweet one to behold. He swung at me wildly, trying to find his rhythm again but between the rippling roots and my oncoming advance, he was losing control.

"Bane! Please listen," Ferris's voice reached me from the branches above. "We can only end this if one of us returns *all* of the amulets to the Great Elm."

"Then hand me yours!" I shouted back to her, lunging for Islasees but the bastard ran, tearing away from the roots of the Great Elm before turning to face me among the ring of battling spirits.

I snarled in frustration, turning from the tree and racing to meet him once more, his sword meeting mine in a clash of steel that reverberated down my arms.

He was no longer losing this fight and the world was falling into chaos around us. All I could think of was how I *needed* to seize the boon and of what would happen when I claimed it. It was all I'd sought after for years. It had kept me hungry in a life that had long been empty of sustenance. And now the time had come, I would not turn from my path. Even if doing so was going to break Ferris forever and shatter my heart in the process. I despised myself for hurting her, but I couldn't break my promise to my family. I owed them this. I'd just never expected to bear the weight of so many doubts in my heart when it came to this moment.

FERRIS

CHAPTER FORTY SEVEN

I cursed Bane and Islasees as I ducked behind the shelter of the Great Elm's coiling branches where she sheltered me from their ferocious battle.

I had no hope of defeating either of them and claiming their amulets for my own. If Bane would offer his up then perhaps I'd have stood a chance but of course he wouldn't. And I couldn't even blame him. He ached for the boon just as I did. But what he desired was death when I wished only for a life which had been stolen. A life which should have been. And I couldn't give her up no matter how much I could see his pain nor feel empathy for his wants. I'd die first.

A scream almost strangled me at the hopelessness of it all, at how far I'd come and how much I'd achieved. And now at best I would be killed by the monster I knew, at worst by the one I'd watched cheat and murder his way to this place.

It wasn't fair. I knew that was a petty, pointless, childish sentiment to cling to but it was the truth.

Rissa had been a child when the Fae had thrown her to the forest. Her life was worth saving so much more than any immortal would ever be able to understand. But they were going to take her from me again.

Despair threatened to devour me but then a voice slunk into my ear as the Dragon swept down from the canopy above and placed itself on a branch between me and the Fae who would so gladly part my head from my shoulders.

"You really are far too human for your own good," it grumbled, feathered tail swishing from side to side like a vexed cat.

"What?" I breathed, blinking tears of frustration from my eyes.

"Haven't I given you the answer to this problem already?"

"What problem? Stop speaking in riddles, please. I have no mind for puzzling them out in this moment."

"Fine," the Dragon huffed. *"Then plain I shall be. Spirit singer I named you because that is what you are. Part human yes - much to my disquiet, but born of our kind too and able to speak our language well enough to coax us to your side."*

"What good does that do me with spirits which have already been claimed?" I begged, my eyes moving to the Tiger and Bear which were engaged in a furious battle at the will of their masters.

The Dragon scoffed in disgust. *"Claimed? By brute force and violence. Does that seem to you to be the best way to make a bond with our kind?"*

I stared at this creature of wonder and magic, everything I had done to get me to this place rushing through my mind in a blur. Everything I had attempted, everything that had failed and far more importantly, everything that had *worked.*

My gaze snapped to the Tiger and locked there, air filling my lungs as I sucked it in deep and pushed myself tall.

Madness. This was madness. But it felt more right than almost everything else that I'd ever done before. The Great Elm seemed to sense my need and the branch I was sheltering on swung down to the ground once more so that I could leap free of it.

"Join me," I called, though as I listened to my words I realised the Dragon was right, mixed in with the language I had spoken all my life was a tumultuous song. A song which couldn't be heard with ears or felt with any human sense. It was a song of magic. A song of the spirits. And as the Tiger heard my call, it released a roar and spilled away into a cloud of vibrant smoke.

An amulet dropped to the dirt at my feet and I gasped as I snatched it.

Power flooded through me, the Tiger's mark appearing on my skin, a twisting pattern on the back of my right hand, but I had no time to waste on admiring it.

Islasees cried out in horror as he realised what I'd done, the Phoenix circling around his head then shooting straight for me with flames erupting from its beak and talons of molten metal aimed straight for my heart.

With a single request spilling from my lips, the Phoenix burst into smoke too, its amulet dropping before me only to be joined by the Carp, Rat and Stag as I called them into my grasp as well.

The heady weight of so many connections joining to my soul struck me with wild brutality but somehow I managed to remain on my feet and endure it. All of their marks stitched themselves onto the flesh of my right arm, merging with the rest, painting my skin in an intricate pattern which I only wished I had time to study.

Magic rushed through my flesh and a scream of rage and anguish escaped the Fae warrior. Bane swung his sword, almost decapitating the male he hated so much but years of battling had Islasees ducking aside in the last breath, a slice opening across his side in place of cutting him two.

He turned and bolted for the labyrinth with a howl of fury and I was left staring at Bane as the truth of what I was and what I would do next settled between us.

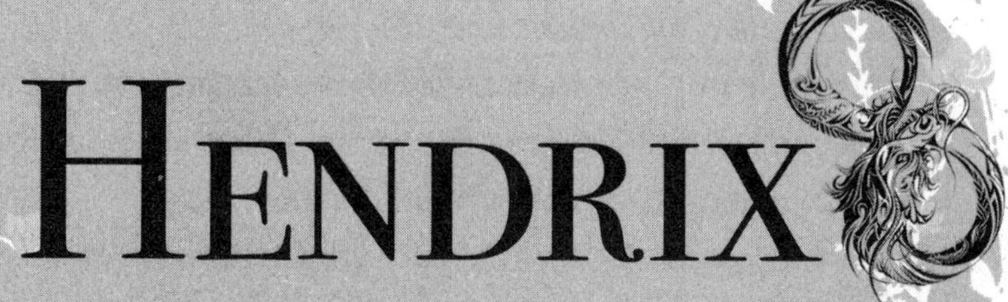

Hendrix

CHAPTER FORTY EIGHT

"Lightwing," I rasped as Islasees's amulets shone around her throat, shaking my head in refusal of what I was seeing. I stepped toward her, she and I the last of the Champions. Even the urge to hunt down Islasees couldn't turn me from the Great Elm now. It was over. The boon was ours. One of ours.

"Please," I whispered, despising how broken I sounded as the reality of our dilemma closed in on us.

Ferris was something other. A creature of the forest herself and I wasn't sure she even realised that the Lost Children were singing *to* her, *about* her.

Her hair glimmered like starlight and power rolled through her, commanding the attention of even the Great Elm at her back. All of my spirits ran to the tree, eager to be reunited with their mother, for the final deed to be done.

"Give me your amulets," I begged, already knowing her answer, the suffocating weight in my chest telling of what was coming next.

I lowered to my knees in front of Ferris, tossing my sword aside and showing her the rawest, most shattered version of who I was.

"I need this. For them," I croaked, the failure of my task pressing down on me and choking the very air from my lungs.

Ferris's eyes brimmed with tears, her pain becoming my own as nothing but the soft and haunting song of the Lost Children carried through the air.

"She has come, the task is done.

We've waited oh, so very long."

"Ferris please," Rissa breathed from the branches of the Great Elm and Ferris lifted her head to gaze up at her sister, a tear slipping from her eye and sailing smoothly down her cheek.

"I'm sorry, truly I am," Ferris whispered, a sob catching in her throat as she dropped her gaze to me. "But I came here for my sister. I won't leave without her. I *can't."* Her pain was clear on her face as she made her choice and magic stirred around me in the air, the amulets at my throat beginning to glow. I grabbed onto them, desperately trying to keep hold of them but they slipped through my fingers like a gust of wind. They were there one moment then gone the next, falling at her feet with a resounding clang that marked my loss.

"I'm so sorry, Bane," she repeated, tears rolling in an endless stream down her cheeks, the pain she felt at making this choice enough to rent another fissure in my heart. But she didn't relent, the magic of what she was summoning the spirits to her, calling them away from me. Runes appeared on her arm and she gasped as their power connected to her soul.

"No!" I cried, lunging to my feet, trying to snatch the amulets back but she picked them up and fixed them around her throat. My chance at the boon vanished just like that, crushing my heart to dust. The pain suffocated me to my roots, the weight of what I'd lost falling down on me like a thousand tons of molten rock.

"Bane," she stepped closer, reaching for me and using that name just to cut me all the deeper.

"Ferris, please," I rasped, reduced to nothing at her feet. "Listen to me. My family are living half a life, trapped here in this world, aching for death. They suffer through every day." My voice broke on those words but somehow I managed to go on. "They want peace, that's all. How can you take that from them? They've lived hundreds of years in agony. They cannot sleep, yet they are fatigued by living. They cannot eat yet they starve for nourishment. They begged me for freedom. My own baby sister, my younger brother, on their knees as I am before you now and they pleaded for a way out. And here you are, denying them that when it is all I have sought for year after year. My mother weeps for her family, my father has lost himself to the wildness of death. They are trapped, don't you see? I am trapping them in a cage designed of misery and they must face it eternally unless I can break their chains." My fingers dug into her ankle and Ferris lowered down to a crouch, her arms wrapping around me, her tears falling to wet my tunic.

"Oh Bane, I cannot even imagine how terrible that is."

"Then please, offer me this. Please do not take it from me. From them."

She fell silent, her arms tight around me, her face pressing to the crook of my neck. "I…"

The silence hung between us, my pain a living thing writhing from my body into hers. She was going to give it to me. I could feel her hesitation, her change of mind.

Hope blazed through me with all the promises of the world gliding alongside it.

"Please," I choked out one more time.

She leaned back, her violet eyes wrought with agony as she stroked my cheek. "I can't," she rasped, those words a dagger to my chest.

I recoiled from her, my teeth bared and heart shattering to jagged shards in my chest.

"Forgive me," she begged.

I shook my head, muted by my agony as she stood up and placed the amulets on their plinths, offering them to the spirit of the forest. Magic shivered along the ground, building with promise as the Lost Children sang a song of rising hope.

"Yes, Ferris!" Rissa cried to her sister, her eyes glittering with delight.

As Ferris placed the final amulet on its plinth, the Great Elm groaned with exuberant joy, the trees around us shuddering until a shockwave of pure energy exploded through the atmosphere, throwing us onto our backs side by side. The Lost Children clung to the Great Elm's branches, crying out their song to the sky, the power of their rapture tangling with the threads of my soul, trying to make me feel it too. But I refused to give in to the magic of their melody.

I shielded my eyes as the Great Elm began to glow like the sun, blazing brighter than any star in the sky as ripples of power echoed out from it all across the forest and beyond. The thirteen spirits gathered close around the tree, eyes bright and full of understanding as the madness lifted from their shimmering bodies. They raced out toward the Great Elm with howls and hoots of joy, remembering their roles among the woods, the Raven dancing beneath the moon and guiding the night deeper between the boughs, while the Tiger released the animals from its back and let them climb the trunks around them or burrow into the earth, and the other spirits rushed to fulfil their own tasks.

The Dragon roared as it raced around the trunk of the enormous spirit tree and the branches of the Great Elm shivered in reply, its leaves reaching out to brush across its scales before it found the rest of the spirits and welcomed them home too.

The song of the forest reverberated through the air, no longer weighted with maddening pain - though still an ache of loss lingered in its tone.

Red and white mushrooms sprouted across the bark at the base of the Great Elm as the Stag rubbed its horns against its trunk. Flowers pooled over its roots as the Unicorn cantered by. The Phoenix sung a lilting tune and landed in a high branch alongside the Raven, the two birds nuzzling each other in a long-awaited reunion.

The Boar rutted its tusks through the dirt, tiny shoots erupting in its wake and the Rat released the insects which crept across its back so that they too could hurry to greet their lost mother.

Their reunion was a brief balm to my pain, the rush of magic that swept around us stealing the breath from my lungs and hurling my dark hair around my face.

The Bear shook its coat and droplets of cool water coated me, their touch a kiss to my skin. The Fox bounded from branch to branch, yapping its greeting to the spirit who had given it life, the Serpent coiling over branches beneath its feet. Even the Carp seemed filled with joy as it flopped and flailed in a puddle formed in the crooked roots at the base of the enormous tree.

It wasn't just the cursed forest that was mending, Rathian was healing too, I could feel it in the earth itself, the oppressive weight of the forest's power finally lifting. The curse was broken. And in the wake of its power, Ferris stood up, moving closer to the Great Elm as if lured by some spell. Her head lifted as she met the gaze of her sister in the branches above and a tangible moment of relief passed between them.

"You did it," Rissa sighed, a choked sob racking through her chest. "The boon is yours."

"I can hardly believe this is happening," Ferris whispered as a single shoot grew at her feet, up and up, growing a hundred times the speed it should have, then the little vine coiled around her hand.

"Speak the boon you wish for," an ethereal voice shivered through the atmosphere and I realised it was the spirit of the Great Elm itself.

"Ask it," Rissa rasped, desperation pouring through her voice.

I shook my head in denial of what was happening, but Ferris spoke the words, asking the Great Elm what she'd come here for, what her heart most desired above all else. And if I hadn't lost my own chance at my wish being granted, I might have urged her on. But instead, only resentment coursed through my blood, a bitterness that wouldn't shift.

"Release the Lost Children. Let them return home to their families with my sister among them. Please release them so that they are no longer prisoners of the forest."

"It is done," the Great Elm answered and an enormous boom echoed through the ground, the roots of the Great Elm rippling in a wave that spread out in every direction. The Lost Children sang louder, their voices a river of glee as their skin shimmered with rivers of gold.

"You're free!" Ferris cried to Rissa as light glittered along the Lost Children's bodies, revealing chains that danced across their skin.

"It's really happening," Rissa gasped as the chains began to break, one after the other, making the Children squeal in utter joy.

Rissa cried out in pained delight as her own chains relinquished, and she leapt from branch to branch to descend from the tree. She dove from above, colliding with Ferris in a fierce embrace, the two sisters sobbing at their reunion and slumping to the ground as one.

Panic coiled inside my chest as the shoot encircling Ferris's hand recoiled and returned to the earth. I scrambled forward on hands and knees, trying to catch hold of it myself.

"Wait!" I begged, looking to the Great Elm as the spirits stilled around it's huge trunk in contented quiet.

"I'll do anything. I'll give *anything* for one more boon. I assisted her." I pointed to Ferris. "I helped bring her here. One gift is all I ask. My family are in the grip of death but on and on they linger, ever suffering, but unable to pass on to the afterworld no matter what I do to try and release them to it."

I felt Ferris watching me but I couldn't turn from the Great Elm, my desperation palpable.

"I wish for death, nothing more. Bring the spirit of my demise here. She stalks my every move regardless. Have me. Take me and my family into the grave. I want for nothing more. Release them and take me too."

"Bane," Ferris gasped, that final drop of truth falling upon her at last.

And there it was. I had never intended to live a day beyond the last of the Great Hunt.

I hungered for death as if it were nourishment, for there was nothing more for me in this wretched land. My family knew no peace and I only wanted to take them with me into the afterworld which we had all been denied for so long.

"You cannot die." Ferris lunged for me, tugging on my arm, trying to draw me to my feet but I didn't turn to face her as I spoke in a low growl.

"My death will end the plague of the Hollows. The last curse upon Rathian will be gone."

"But you will be gone too," Ferris said in anguish as if that possibility truly hurt her.

I looked at her then. This woman who had taken my last hope from me, and all I could feel was anger. She had snatched it from my grasp. Even though I'd known it might come to this, I couldn't fight how ruinously I hated her for it. It was a bitterness that cut through my bones and branded me her villain.

"Death will not have you yet, Crownthief," the Great Elm spoke to me through the tremors in the air and I felt her almighty power coursing through my veins, drawing my gaze from Ferris as she backed away from me with her sister.

I rose to my feet, snatching my sword, intending to cut through its damn trunk, but as I stepped forward, roots snared my ankles, binding around my calves and forcing me to a halt.

"Patience," the Great Elm purred. "You are not done with living yet. For there is much you must achieve."

"I will do nothing except seek my wish until I find a way to grant it," I spat.

"You and the spirit singer are destined for a greater path. You must seek Providence, my dear, lost spirit. I believe someone trapped him, whether human, spirit, Hag or Fae, I do not know, but I believe he is caged, unable to escape."

I swung my sword at the roots of the Great Elm, refusing to listen to her drivel. The tree groaned as I hacked through one of them, the spirits rearing up, howling and roaring at me. More roots entangled me and I cut at them viciously, fury lining my limbs. I'd lost everything, fucking *everything* and now this spirit dared ask more of me?

"You are fated. Born for this task. I have called you and she here time and again to meet with this moment. Your souls are destined to intertwine, bound together to return Providence to me."

"Never!" I cried, slashing more fiercely at the roots.

"Bane – stop!" Ferris yelled but I had no ear for her. Not now that she had stolen away my chance at freeing my family from the Hollow curse. She had no idea what it was to live year after endless year in servitude to Death. She had pined for her sister for a barely a moment while I had longed for my family's freedom for *centuries*.

"Find Providence and I will let you have your boon," the Great Elm spoke through the fabric of the air itself. "And until then let a lesson be learned of my power. You may have eternity to find my lost love, Crownthief, but your own beloved does not."

"What lunacy are you spewing now?" I demanded. "Haven't you done enough to Rathian? To me? To all of us!?"

A small tree grew at my feet in a miniature version of the Great Elm, its trunk gnarled as if it was as ancient as the spirit itself.

"This tree will blossom as if in spring, flourish as if in summer, turn gold as if in autumn, and wither as if in winter, your spirit singer will perish and your curse of Death shall drag you deeper than ever before, the dark will sink in until there is nothing left of you but rot."

"You cannot do this," I rasped as Ferris cried out in horror. If I had thought that this could not get worse, it had. The Great Elm was cursing me, layering onto my already miserable existence and branding me her pawn in a game I refused to play.

"The tree will not follow the seasons of your land but will move through seasons of its own. One by one, in a time that suits my own desires. So when its winter comes, you must have returned Providence to me, Crownthief, or your spirit singer will die and your Hollow curse will have you. I pray when we meet again that your arrogance has been tempered."

"Please don't do this," Ferris called to the tree, tears brimming in her eyes. "I did what you asked. I've done nothing to wrong you."

My throat thickened at the sight of her pain, despite what she'd taken from me, despite the hatred festering inside me, she did not deserve this fate.

"Take heart," the Great Elm spoke to her instead. "The fate you face may not come to pass if you wield the gifts you have been blessed with. Your soul is connected to mine, to my children's too. They will assist in your search for Providence so that you might have a chance at living. And while you search, you will come to discover what you were born for. The power in your veins is great indeed. Do not squander it, spirit singer."

As one the spirits swept from their plinths, moving on wing and paw and hoof to hurry over to Ferris. They ran to her, nuzzling and pawing at her before sweeping away into the trees as if celebrating all that had come to pass. Ferris shook her head at the Great Elm in refusal of what had been had asked of her, but no words parted her lips.

"No more amulets," the Great Elm sighed. "They are your allies. But you know this by now."

Ferris nodded silently, looking to me in fear, her own rage rising to meet with mine.

"Take the small one," the Great Elm commanded me and roots

snared me in their grip, forcing me to bow down and scoop the little tree from the earth and clutch it to my chest. The roots only released me when I held it for myself and I scowled at them for the prisoner they'd made me.

I locked my gaze on Ferris. Ferris with all her power, the gift of the thirteen spirits now running in her veins. Reality hit me like an anvil to my chest.

She was my answer. The Great Elm had told me itself.

If anyone could gift me death, it was her. So there was no chance of her leaving me now.

"You'll come with me," I said darkly and Ferris frowned, her throat bobbing as she backed away.

Rissa stayed close to her sister, a possessiveness in her expression that set my hackles rising. But I only had eyes for my lightwing.

"You caused this, so you'll damn well fix it," I snarled at her but she shook her head, her refusal clear in her eyes. "You will not leave my side until it is done!"

FERRIS

CHAPTER FORTY NINE

I backed away, the echoes of the Great Elm's weighted power resounding through the air, drawing my heartbeat in time with its melancholy rhythm.

The forest was healing, the spirits surging out through the trees, racing to accomplish the tasks they'd almost forgotten were theirs. But my connection to them remained, like thirteen ties to my soul, each of them tugging in different directions just enough to leave the link between us in place. I stumbled a step as I concentrated on that sensation, closing my eyes and envisioning thirteen golden cords trailing away from my heart and out into the world. I felt as though I could reach out and pluck any one to summon them back to me, our bond deepening without the amulets instead of fading away.

My right hand and arm were marked with the spirits' runes and still my hair hung in silver strands around my face. I'd been branded by this place and forced to acknowledge what I was within it. It seemed the truth of those changes in me weren't going to be taken away with the ending of the curse. 'Spirit singer' the Dragon had called me. I could feel the melody of their music in the chorus of my soul as though it had always been playing for me and I'd simply never looked in the right place for it before.

I took in a shuddering breath, fixing my eyes on my sister who was watching me with a new brightness to her silver gaze.

"Rissa?" I panted, reaching out to her, meaning to take her hand and lead her from this place which had stolen her childhood from us. But my sister didn't take my hand. Her eyes weren't fixed on me or the Great Elm or the spirits or even the Lost Children who had begun to creep from the trees, their songs now silenced, their gazes curious and cunning. No, Rissa had eyes only for one thing in the heart of the forest and that was the Fae I had so foolishly bared my soul to in this game of treachery and betrayal.

I didn't want to face him. My heart was raw with the truth of what I'd claimed alongside Rissa's freedom because I couldn't relinquish the ache in my chest now that I'd accomplished what I'd come here to do. I'd always known there would be a high price to pay if I were to stand a chance at winning the Great Hunt. But I'd never considered that *I* wouldn't be the one forced to pay it.

"Rissa," I insisted, urging her to come to me but instead her lip curled back from her teeth like a beast snarling at its prey.

"Do you feel the ache in the air?" she growled. "Can you still taste the taint on every inhale?"

I stepped closer to her, catching her arm and shaking it hard enough to force her eyes onto me.

"We need to go," I hissed.

But as I tried to draw Rissa towards the labyrinth, meaning to run from this place and the devastation I felt at leaving Bane here, the Necromancer let out a low, warning growl and I stilled.

"This isn't freedom," Rissa breathed, the air seeming to sigh in agreement at her words, the branches of the Great Elm rustling as if they too had been thinking the same thing. "Rathian's cage is simply harder to see now."

"What madness are you whispering to the wind, sister? This isn't the moment for it."

Silver eyes snapped to mine and something in Rissa's gaze made me step back, dropping her arm suddenly while my pulse spiked in alarm.

"Do you know what Rathian means in the old language?" Rissa asked me. "The language of the first spirits?"

I shook my head, caught between panic and terror as heavy footsteps prowled towards us at my back. Bane was closing in on me, I could feel the thick weight of his magic as it crept towards my heels, the ground withering beneath his footfalls, the trees wailing as they died in the grasp of his magic. The only living thing that seemed unaffected by his power was the small tree that had wound itself onto his arm, its branches locked tight.

The Great Elm bristled, her branches writhing across the sky as if battered by an oncoming storm.

"It means 'homeland'," Rissa went on, her fingers curling like talons at her sides, her body tensing like a cornered animal trapped against a wall. "Not *their* homeland, Ferris. Ours."

"Where do you think you're going now, butcher of souls?" Bane growled and I jerked around, placing myself between him and my sister, intending to shield her from him - though some small part of me wondered if I ought to be doing the opposite.

"I didn't want this at the cost of your family," I breathed as he stepped closer to me and I forced myself to meet his ruined gaze, fearing the hatred I knew I would find there in place of all else now.

Bane's eyes were dark with shadows and his foul power was spilling from him so potently that the ground the trees parted, inching away from his ruinous touch. The small bones of dead creatures rose from the dirt, collecting around him as they reformed, his terrible power calling them back towards the verges of life.

Fear came for me and I stepped away, trying to urge Rissa toward the entrance to the labyrinth. But she stood firm as I knocked against her, her chin landing on my shoulder as she peered past me to the Fae who had damned a thousand souls to wander everlasting in his army.

Bane lifted a hand in demand, his gaze hard and the festering power which rolled from him making my stomach knot with fear. His intention was clear, he meant for me to go with him now as the Great Elm had instructed. But I had no desire to become a pawn in another game of spirits and fates which were painted out before me regardless of my own desires.

"Let me take her home," I begged, my voice small. "At least allow me that much."

Would I go with him then? Once I'd seen her safely into the arms of our parents, would I let the master of death lead me away? Would I follow the wants of the Great Elm and hunt with him for Providence? It seemed impossible to even consider it but did I really have any choice in the matter?

"And what, pretty lightwing, did you allow me when I knelt before you and begged for your mercy?" he hissed, a sapling wilting as he knocked it aside, its leaves shrivelling and turning brown before tumbling to the dirt to be crushed beneath his boot.

The branches of the Great Elm rustled at Bane's back as he snarled at me, the spirit unnerved by his magic and lashing at the Necromancer with power of its own.

I shook my head, pushing against Rissa who only hissed like a snake in my ear.

"You see the contempt he holds for this sacred place?" she spat. "You see what he does in the garden of our mother?"

Her words clapped like thunder in my ears and I rounded on her in spite of the terrifying male who was closing in on me as though I were his prey to devour.

"Our mother is at home, broken and grieving over your loss - and mine too no doubt," I said, shock scarring my words, hurt at the way she so easily gave that term to a damn tree when it had been our mother who had carried us in her womb, who had nursed us as babes and loved us with all her heart.

"That human never tried to find me," Rissa exclaimed, hurt flashing through her bright eyes. "And you know what we are – I showed you the truth of it. We were never really a part of that woman. We're spirit-born, Ferris. We're like the ancient ones whose homeland this was long before the Fae and the humans and even the Hags roamed this place. We are among the creatures who are worthy of the bounty this land offers. They are nothing but usurpers who seek their own gains, bargaining and sacrificing to earn the favour of the spirits. And now one of them has gone further, they've taken Providence and twisted him to their own designs."

"You don't know that, not for sure."

The Great Elm cried out above us and I clapped my hands over my ears as the terrible sound of her rage washed over me, around me, through me.

When the echoes of her fury finally subsided, I found myself staring at Rissa and finally seeing what I'd been so wilfully blinded to until now.

The Lost Children, though freed from the shackles of the forest, were not running from this place in delight but instead were creeping closer to my sister, bounding around her with gazes full of admiration and devotion so emphatic that it unsettled the deepest parts of my soul. I'd freed them with thoughts of saving them but there they stood, surrounding Rissa as though she were their home and always had been.

My heart leapt in alarm as strong hands closed around my shoulders and Bane's rough growl sounded against my ear.

"If you try to run from me, you will regret it," he warned and a shiver of pure terror ran through my limbs as everything coating the ground beneath me withered and died, his power pulsing out in every direction, falling just short of consuming me. I was in his thrall, utterly at his mercy and the blazing fury in Rissa's eyes told me she'd realised it too.

"This is over, Bane," I breathed, my voice rough with a fear I wished hadn't betrayed me.

"Over?" he growled, his tone a spill of ice down my spine. "Oh no, my lightwing. This isn't even close to over. You took your chance to claim your boon. And now it appears that you're the only hope I have of claiming mine."

I turned my head to meet his gaze despite my better judgement, needing to see what I feared I'd find lurking in his green eyes.

Terror took hold of me as I found nothing but bitter resolution and rioting hatred in his expression and I jerked out of his hold so suddenly that he lost his grip on me.

Rissa tugged at my hand, hissing at me that we needed to leave while a blur of tears made it impossible for me to see anything at all.

And wasn't that all I'd wanted when I'd come to this place? Hadn't I achieved everything I'd ever dreamed of in releasing her from its grasp? I should have been overwhelmed with joy, not heartache and a creeping fear that nothing was as it had seemed.

I should have been glad to turn my back on all I'd done here, I should have been furious to find the Great Elm was working to bind me into another task, another impossible undertaking. But as I looked back to Bane, I only felt the sting of remorse and the greatest sense that I was missing something vital.

My eyes remained locked on Bane's, a thousand pointless words reaching the tip of my tongue and falling away again. I'd told him how sorry I was. But sorry didn't change this fate.

I gave up on any hope of reasoning with him as I took in the feral hatred that blazed in his green eyes and I knew what I had to do.

"Don't," he warned, seeing the decision in my expression.

But I did.

In a surge of desperation, I turned and ran, diving back into the labyrinth with Rissa at my side, my sister's hand clasped firmly in mine.

Bane's terrible power took chase as we fled, death and ruin dogging our footsteps as we ran as fast as we could, from what I'd done, from what I was, from *him.*

Echoes and haunting screams chased us into the darkness of the passages as the Lost Children ran after us too, keeping pace and filling my gut with dread. They seemed no less lost than they'd been before I'd freed them from their ties to this place. Something was wrong. I could feel it in the tightness of Rissa's grip on my hand and the bright gleam of her eyes in the dark. But still I ran because I didn't want to admit to my doubts, didn't want to notice any of the things I was beginning to see.

"Ferris!" Bane roared, sending a flood of cold fear rolling down my spine.

Rissa yanked on my arm to force me faster and I allowed myself to think of nothing but the warmth of her skin against mine because I had dreamed so long of this moment and I refused to let it go without a fight.

I only stayed on my feet by mere luck, the path somehow guiding us true and leading us straight back out into the forest without meeting any dead ends.

But it wasn't a path to salvation, or freedom, or home which awaited us there.

It was an army.

An army of Hollows whose souls were as empty as the brute who had chained them to this macabre pantomime of the lives they'd once known. And as they surged forward to take hold of us, meaning to make me a prisoner of Bane Crownthief once more, not one of them took notice of my screams.

"You see?" Rissa snarled as the Lost Children flooded from the labyrinth around us and fled among the Hollows for the trees, somehow darting between the arms of the army of the dead and clambering up into the branches where the Hollows couldn't chase them.

The Hollows were distracted by the Lost Children as they surged around them and my heart pounded in fear at how close they got to those monstrous creatures before darting aside and evading them time and again.

"He allies himself with the mistress of Death because it is she who gains the most while the other spirits are weakened," Rissa insisted urgently, drawing my focus back to her. "She lends him her ear and allows him this sacrilege while Providence is lost and the usurpers of power twist the other spirits to their will. Don't you see it, sister? Don't you see what we must do?"

I shook my head, trying to back away but Rissa grasped my arm, her fingers digging into my flesh and drawing a cry from my lips as a burn raked across my bicep and the runes there began to twist and writhe. I yanked on my arm but she held me tighter, a frown drawing her brows together as she moved so close to me our foreheads were almost touching.

"You don't perceive it yet, but you will," she breathed, her words lost to the searing pain in my arm. I cried out as I tried to wrench free of her grip again but she only tightened her grasp, her fingernails biting into my flesh, blood oozing from the small wounds.

I looked down at my arm, sucking in a sharp breath as I realised a set of coiled runes were crawling across my flesh and onto hers, my connection to one of the spirits pulling so tight I feared it would snap.

I reached out to that magical tether, calling for the spirit, begging for its help along the chord which connected us but all I heard in reply was a low hiss and the grinding of stone.

"Rissa, you're hurting me," I gasped, shoving her back and finally she relented, stumbling away from me with a deep frown on her face.

Something snapped like a branch in the heart of a silent forest and I doubled over as that sound echoed through my body with resounding force, my connection to the Serpent shattering, its departure carving a bloody wound into my soul.

A ragged sob escaped me as I fell to my knees, clutching at my arm as the pain fell away and I was left with a patch of bare skin where the Serpent's coiling mark had been.

I peered up between tangled strands of my silver hair, panting through the pain, my heart throbbing at the betrayal of what Rissa had done to me as I stared at those same runes which now stained the curve of her bicep instead of mine.

"When you come to your senses, seek me out," Rissa said sadly, the look she gave me one of pity and disappointment.

"Wait," I gasped as she started to back away, the realisation that she was leaving me sinking to the pit of my gut like a rock to the bed of a lake.

I scrambled to my feet but was forced back as a Hollow made it around the Lost Children and ran at me.

The Serpent burst from the trees, aiming straight for us, its enormous body carving a path through the Hollows whether they ran for it or not. But it didn't come for me. It surged toward my sister while I was left to sprint away into the forest, the Hollow racing after me, its rotting teeth bared in desperate want.

I sprinted between the trees, my battered heart too bruised for me to be able to do more than call out to the spirits which were still tied to me, pleading for their help.

Those glimmering chords which bound them to me began to hum within my soul, the trampling of feet and beat of wings racing after me as they answered my call. But it wasn't a spirit I crashed into in the darkness between the trees, nor a monster risen from death to destroy me. Yet it was a beast all the same.

Bane caught my chin in his grasp and forced my gaze up to meet with his, a darkness in his eyes which made me remember how much I didn't know about him, how much shadow stained his past.

"There is no escaping this, Ferris," he breathed, his hand slipping from my jaw and capturing my hand in its place. "If there is one thing my cursed life has taught me then it's that. Fate has a cruel sense of humour."

Movement in the trees behind me had me twisting around, my pulse a riot in my chest, my veins alive with adrenaline as panic threatened to overwhelm me.

Everything I'd come here for had fallen to ruin. Rissa wasn't the girl I'd lost all those years ago, she didn't want rescuing and now I feared what motivations she did cling to.

I hunted the trees, expecting to find Bane's Hollows there, the one who had been chasing me had been so close after all. But it wasn't the dead who lingered at my back but a figure cloaked in heavy shadow whose silhouette was enough to strike terror coursing through my bones.

I screamed as my gaze fell upon the falcon's head which peered out at me from beneath her cowl, the weight of her dense power coiling around me so tightly that it threatened to choke the life from me with a single inhale.

Death stood watching us with eyes bright and intent unknown. But as I tried to run from her, Bane tightened his grip on my hand and yanked me back again.

"Come, lightwing," he growled, all tenderness gone from that name he'd given me, scorn and mocking in its place now. "It seems destiny has a mind to toy with us a little longer. And I so wish to disappoint her."

He reached out towards that great and haunting spirit as though he had nothing at all to fear from Death. And I supposed that was true enough for the Necromancer.

My spirits were almost with me, I could feel them closing in, hear the Dragon's roar on the wind, but Bane acted before they could make it to me, clasping Death's cloak between calloused fingers.

We were ripped away into the fabric of the night before I could so much as scream.

Death enveloped us in the folds of her cloak, the screams of lost souls and stench of festering flesh suffocating me as it pressed so close I choked on it.

I was released as abruptly as I'd been captured. I slammed down onto my feet in a cold and barren place, a road of black stone hard beneath my boots, Bane's body solid as I stumbled into him.

Before us stood a castle carved out of nightmares, its twisting towers and oppressive walls darker than the night's sky at its back.

A cold wind whipped my silver hair across my face and I shivered at the sting of it against my cheeks. There wasn't a tree to be seen. The Taking Trees were far behind us, my spirits along with them, my sister lost too.

Bane released my hand and stalked toward the iron gates which blocked the road ahead of us, leading to that castle and whatever horrors it housed.

"Welcome home, lightwing," he growled, his voice raw with bitterness as he sneered at me. "It's time you met the ones you just betrayed. And don't expect a warm welcome; there'll be no mercy between these walls."

He left me trembling in his wake, the beady eyes of Death surveying me with intrigue. I cowered beneath her scrutiny, fear wrapping me in a tight embrace as the only living soul for miles around stalked away from me, his body rigid with a potent fury which wrapped me in the arms of despair.

I glanced down the barren road at my back but there was nothing to be seen in the endless planes which swept away behind me before being stolen by the blanket of night.

A cry went up in the dark, one which speared me with a fear so piercing I hardly dared to draw breath.

My only choice was to follow the Fae who delivered me to this monstrous place, despite no part of me wanting to take a single step within the walls of his cursed castle.

With the knowledge that I was certain to regret this, I found myself hurrying after him, the horror ahead preferable to those at my back. Because Necromancer or not, Bane Crownthief was my only chance of escaping this place and our destinies had been cast as one.

AUTHOR NOTE

Well, that was intense. For Ferris, for Hendrix, for you guys, and for us. Because this was a leap into a brand new world and that always feels something like taking a breath of crisp, fresh air right before leaping from the top of a mountain and hoping we might sprout wings before hitting the ground.

Not to be dramatic or anything.

So how did you fair in the deep, dark woods?

Growing up, our dad read us stories of magic and mayhem where we would both be enraptured and perhaps a little terrified of what might come next. I can remember being curled up beside him as we travelled into Mirkwood with Bilbo Baggins and wondering if we might ever make it out of those terrifying trees. And now here we are, wandering in our own magical forest, battling spirts in place of spiders and falling for the black-hearted Fae instead of being captured by wood elves. It's not the same, but I can't help but wonder if a piece of my imagination got lost between those trees when I was a little girl and never really wanted to escape them, even though I was terrified of what might happen if I didn't. It would explain a lot.

Perhaps that's what us readers and authors are, just lost children running between the pages of one book after another, being stalked by monsters or hounded by chaos, ever on the hunt for a happily ever after – only to dive into another perilous adventure the moment we find it.

Adrenaline junkies of the paper and ink variety.

There are certainly worse ways to pass the time.

So if you are a junkie of the binge them and banish them kind, the type who puts books in the freezer when they need a time out, the sort to hurl paper or electronic device at a wall and cry tears over characters whose lives are born and bled on the page alone, then welcome to the forest of our depraved machinations. Sorry for the pain, but we're not sorry too. You came here looking for anguish after all. You chose to step into the trees with us. And may you tread this path with us again and again and again.

Because we aren't done with you yet, dear reader. And this story has only just begun…

Dun, dun, duuuuun…

Ahem. Also thanks so much for reading our stuff and cheese. I've said it before and I will continue to scream it from every rooftop because we cannot thank every single one of you enough for having given our books a chance. If this is your first foray into our words, then welcome. If you are well-versed in our language of literary ruin then welcome back, you beautiful glutton for punishment. I hope you enjoyed this new chapter in our tomes of torture.

There is plenty more still to come.

Love, Susanne & Caroline

DARK FAE

Dark Fae is a dark why choose fantasy romance series with one vampire girl, four dark shifter men with secrets, and a murder that just doesn't add up. With all of the mysteries behind her brother's death finally coming together, Elise is about to find out if the darkness of her past will be enough to tear her and her Kings apart or if the five of them can find a way to come together against the odds.
This completed series is set in Solaria 5 years before the Zodiac Academy books and 10 years before the Darkmore series.

Scan the QR code below to start the series now:

ZODIAC ACADEMY

Zodiac Academy is a dark, enemies to lovers fantasy romance series which follows twins Tory and Darcy Vega who find out they're Fae and have to learn to harness their power while trying to defend their throne from the four Heirs who want to claim it in their place.
This series is set in Solaria 5 years after the Dark Fae books and 5 years before the Darkmore series.

Scan the QR code below to start the series now:

DARKMORE

Darkmore is a dark why choose fantasy romance series set in a prison for the most dangerous magical criminals in Solaria. It's full of black-hearted Fae who Rosalie is determined to conquer in her quest to break out her childhood sweetheart, Roary Night. It has enemies to lovers, rejected mates and second chance romance themes. This series is set in Solaria 5 years after the Zodiac Academy books and 10 years after the Dark Fae series.

Scan the QR code below to start the series now:

AGE OF VAMPIRES

In a war-ridden, post-apocalyptic world, shadows cling to the towering remnants of skyscrapers that once dominated the skylines, and rural landscapes only serve as a haunting reminder of the self-destruction of humanity. The emergence of vampires has plunged the world into a living nightmare and perpetual darkness has settled over much of the land, as the final fragments of humanity struggle to survive as livestock within realms ruled by the most powerful vampire lineage, the Belvederes. This is a fantasy romance series with a heart-pounding plot and a cast of morally grey characters you're bound to fall in love with.

Scan the QR code below to start the series now:

NEVER KEEP

This is an enemies to lovers fantasy romance series set in the same world as Zodiac Academy, but it's a dark and villainous tale of its own. You haven't met tainted souls like these before or enemies that hate each other as deeply as these characters do. Never Keep, will leave your heart raw and bloody. You'll be left gasping for breath and aching for more of the twisted Fae who lurk between the pages and they might just be irredeemable...

Scan the QR code below to start the series now:

DISCOVER MORE FROM CAROLINE PECKHAM

&

SUSANNE VALENTI

To find out more, grab yourself some freebies, merchandise, and special signed editions or to join their reader group, scan the QR code below.